Also by Joe Joyce

Fiction

Echoland

The Trigger Man

Off the Record

Non-Fiction

*The Guinnesses: The Untold Story of
Ireland's Most Successful Family*

Blind Justice (with Peter Murtagh)

The Boss: Charles J Haughey in Government
(with Peter Murtagh)

Plays

The Tower

www.joejoyce.ie

First published in 2014 by
Liberties Press
140 Terenure Road North | Terenure | Dublin 6W
T: +353 (1) 405 5701| www.libertiespress.com | E: info@libertiespress.com

Trade enquiries to Gill & Macmillan Distribution
Hume Avenue | Park West | Dublin 12
T: +353 (1) 500 9534 | F: +353 (1) 500 9595 | E: sales@gillmacmillan.ie

Distributed in the United Kingdom by
Turnaround Publisher Services
Unit 3 | Olympia Trading Estate | Coburg Road | London N22 6TZ
T: +44 (0) 20 8829 3000 | E: orders@turnaround-uk.com

Distributed in the United States by
International Publishers Marketing
22841 Quicksilver Dr | Dulles, VA 20166
T: +1 (703) 661-1586 | F: +1 (703) 661-1547 | E: ipmmail@presswarehouse.com

ISBN: 978-1-909718-57-9
2 4 6 8 10 9 7 5 3 1

A CIP record for this title is available from the British Library.

Cover design by Anna Morrison
Internal design by Liberties Press

ECHOBEAT

Joe Joyce

Prologue

London
Autumn 1940

The pounding on the door woke him. Even before he came to full consciousness he knew what was happening and was telling himself, No, no, it's not possible. The woman beside him sat up with a start and said something in Russian.

'No,' he said in the same language, more to himself than to her. 'It can't be.'

The pounding continued and he got out of bed, pulling on his pyjama bottoms, his anger rising. They had no right. He went into the hallway and saw that they weren't knocking: the wood around the lock was splintering. They were breaking down the door.

'Hey!' he roared with all the authority of his status. 'Stop that.'

There was a moment's silence. Then a voice shouted, 'Police. Open up.'

'You can't come in here.'

'Yes, we can. Open the door.'

'You have no right,' he shouted back.

The door shook and a crack in the jamb by the lock widened.

'Stop that!' he roared again and opened the door, thinking it was going to cost the government to repair the lock.

There was a huddle of men outside, all in plain clothes. The one in front was middle-aged, sour-faced. He held up a sheet of paper.

'Warrant for your arrest,' he said. 'Defence of the Realm Act.'

The young man shook his head, emphatic. 'You know who I am?' he demanded with an air of incredulity. 'I'm a diplomat. Diplomatic immunity.'

'Not anymore.' The policeman gave him a humourless grin, pushing forward.

'Stop,' the man ordered, putting his hands up to try and halt the wedge of heavy men coming at him. 'You hear what I said? You can't come in here.'

'Did you hear what I said?' the policeman shot back. 'Your diplomatic immunity's been waived. Ambassador Kennedy said to lock you up. Throw away the key.'

He stepped back, stunned, and they flowed past him into the flat. A younger detective, his own age, grabbed him by the bare arm and pushed him towards the bedroom. 'Get dressed,' he snapped.

In the bedroom, the woman had put on his pyjama top and she stared at them, her eyes round with horror. This was what happened under the Bolsheviks, not in England. The detective ignored her. The sour-faced policeman came in and started opening drawers, taking a sheaf of documents from one.

'Put those back,' the young man ordered. 'They're confidential. The property of the United States government.'

The detective who had brought him in laughed, enjoying the rare experience of seeing someone caught red-handed. 'You like to bring work home?'

'He can't stop working,' the sour-faced one smirked, heading for the door. 'Office day never long enough for him. Reading all these secrets.' He raised the documents in his hands like a farewell.

From the other rooms came the noise of doors opening and closing and furniture being moved. The young man dressed himself slowly, his face hot with indignation. He couldn't believe his own government would go this far, do this to him. All he had ever tried to do was tell the American people the truth.

An older man with a hooked nose came in carrying a leather-bound notebook. He held it upright in one hand as if it was a bible and he was about to ask the young man to swear an oath. He said nothing, just smiled.

The young man closed his eyes and bit his lip, his stomach suddenly hollow. They had trusted him with that. Given it to him for safe keeping. When they were being rounded up, one by one. It'll be safe with me, he had assured them. I've got diplomatic immunity.

When he opened his eyes the older man was gone. The detective who had brought him in took his arm again and said, 'Come on.' At the door, he turned back to the woman. 'You can get dressed now, Irina,' he said with dismissive familiarity. 'Go on home. We'll be looking at things here for a long time.'

The detective closed the door behind them and pulled the man downstairs, bumping against each other as the man resisted the pressure to move faster.

The street was empty of people though the dawn was late. The gritty light blended the yellows and browns of the old bricks and the acrid smell of burning from the night's bombings hung in the still air and tainted every breath.

The detective opened the back door of a black Rover at the kerb and pushed him in. He still couldn't believe it as he fell sideways onto the back seat. That they'd do this to him. That the ambassador would've allowed it. But he knew who was to blame. Rosenfeld and his Jew friends.

One

Paul Duggan pressed the bar and pulled down the window and had his hand on the outside door handle as the train slid into Dundalk station with glacial slowness. He glanced at his watch and cursed again under his breath. Fifty-five minutes late, which meant that he was more than forty minutes late for the meeting.

He turned the handle and the door swung out and he waited a moment for the moving platform to slow a little more before he jumped. He swerved around an elderly porter who said something he didn't catch about young fellas in a hurry and he ran up the ramp as the coal smoke settled on the station.

He ran across the bridge over the down line from Belfast and out into the cold, clear air and jogged into Anne Street, the mental map of where he was going clear in his mind. The town was in a mid-morning torpor, frost still in the gutters and on the footpath on the shaded side of the street. As he neared the town centre there were sprigs of holly in shop windows and Christmas trees in front parlours.

He counted off the side streets on Clanbrassil Street and swung around a muffled woman carrying a shopping bag and found the pub. He hesitated a moment at the door to catch his breath, hoping the contact hadn't left. He pushed the door open.

The front of the pub was a grocery shop. It was empty as he went past the counter and around a partition of brown wooden slats and into the bar. There was only one customer, a man sitting on a bench in the far corner, his features barely distinguishable in the gloom. He had a half-full pint of stout on the table before him.

'Mr Murphy?' Duggan asked.

The man moved his head to one side, neither confirming nor denying his identity. He was in his late thirties, strongly built, and his grey face was marked by lines of tiredness.

Duggan told him his name, dropping his voice although there seemed to be nobody else within earshot. 'Captain Anderson asked me to come and meet you. He's sick, couldn't get word to you in time.'

The man shifted on the bench and took a packet of Gold Flake from his overcoat pocket and placed it on the table.

'Sorry I'm late.' Duggan sat on a wooden stool across from him. 'The train stopped a long time in Drogheda.'

'You work with Liam?' Murphy took the last cigarette from the packet and slid it closed.

Duggan nodded, not bothering to explain that they normally worked in different sections of G2, the army intelligence unit. Anderson was on the British desk, he on the German desk. But things were very busy right now, especially for the British desk, and distinctions were sometimes blurred as they tried to keep up with the growing threats from both sides.

'Got a bad dose of flu,' Duggan said. 'He thought he'd be able to make it but he took a turn for the worse last night.'

Murphy nodded and straightened up on the bench, taking a drink from his pint as if he was now satisfied that Duggan was who he said he was. Duggan wondered idly what his real name was. Call him Murphy, Captain Anderson had told him, and he'll know I sent you.

'You want a drink?' Murphy asked, inclining his head to one side to indicate a side door off the bar. 'Knock on the door there.'

'No thanks, too early for me.'

'And too late for me.' Murphy sniffed and had another drink of stout.

'You're still on the night shift,' Duggan said, a statement. 'You must want to get to bed.'

'I don't have much for you,' Murphy took a deep breath of cigarette smoke and blew it out slowly. 'We're run off our feet, can't keep up with the repair work. Every convoy that arrives is in a terrible state. And that's only the ships that survived the crossing, the ones that weren't sunk. They're losing so many ships.' He shook his head. 'So many men.'

Duggan nodded, in sympathy and encouragement. All he knew about Murphy was that he was a welder, working in the Harland and Wolff shipyard in Belfast, and that he came home to Dundalk once a week.

'The latest convoy lost seven ships,' Murphy continued. 'Another half-dozen damaged, some barely afloat. They had no protection at all. Not a single warship.'

'None at all?'

'Not one. So they say. The few survivors from the ones that were sunk were in a terrible state.'

'You saw them?'

Murphy shook his head. 'Canteen talk. One of the lads saw some of them being brought ashore. Terrible burns.'

'Things are looking bad for them? For the British?'

'The U-boats are picking them off like fish in a barrel. They don't seem able to protect them at all.'

Murphy flicked his empty cigarette packet across the table with his index finger. 'The list of ships in dock at the moment for repairs.'

Duggan put the packet in his pocket.

'Some other bits of gossip,' Murphy stubbed out his cigarette in the tin ashtray. 'A new battalion has landed at Larne.'

'Oh?' That could be very significant, Duggan thought. 'Were they rotating? Replacing another one?'

'I didn't hear tell of any soldiers leaving.'

'Any idea which regiment?'

Murphy shook his head.

'Infantry?'

'I don't know.'

'Any idea of the insignia on their uniforms?'

Murphy gave him a hard look. 'The man I heard it from didn't say. And I couldn't very well ask him for a detailed description.'

'Sure,' Duggan backed off. 'I understand.'

'There's also a rumour about some Yanks turning up in Derry.'

'What kind of Yanks?' Duggan asked in surprise. The US was neutral too, though supplying Britain through the Atlantic convoys.

'Military types.'

'In uniform?'

'No. But they say you could tell anyway.'

'What are they doing there?'

'No idea.' Murphy finished off his stout. 'They were in the docks area. With some Brit naval officers. A couple of the fellows from Derry were codding each other about it, saying the Yanks are coming. You better lock up your wives and daughters.'

A thought struck Duggan. 'Could they be Canadians?'

'Canadians been there a while,' Murphy shook his head and hinted at a grin. 'The Yanks were in civvies. All very hush-hush. Which is why people were talking about them.'

'Any sign of them in Belfast?'

Murphy shook his head. 'That's it. Only tea-break gossip,' he stood up. 'I'm off to the bed.'

'Thanks,' Duggan said. 'And sorry for delaying you.'

'Tell Liam I hope he's better for the Christmas.' Murphy picked up a holdall from under the table and went out the side door he had said to knock on earlier.

Duggan stayed where he was and smoked a cigarette, listening to the creaks in the building and the ticking of a clock somewhere.

The Dublin train stopped with a grinding of metal and vented a cloud of steam across the platform. Duggan got up from the bench and waited as a couple of passengers got off and headed for the customs men behind their makeshift counter. He was just about to get on when he caught sight of a man hurrying through the dissipating steam and boarding the next carriage. Henning Thomsen. The first secretary at the German legation in Dublin and widely believed to be the Nazi party man there.

What's he doing in Dundalk? Duggan wondered. He climbed onto the train and walked down the corridor away from the carriage Thomsen had boarded. It was unlikely that Thomsen would recognise him but he didn't want to take any chances. Their paths had crossed only once before: Duggan had been in the back of a car watching the comings and goings at a party at the German Minister's residence, unofficially celebrating the fall of France. He had had a good look at Thomsen but it was unlikely that Thomsen had seen much of him. Still. He went down the corridor, looking into compartments for an empty seat. The train was full, mainly of groups of middle-aged women and a scattering of boisterous young men his own age. Soldiers, too, he thought, though they were all in civvies as well. And they had all come from across the border. Southerners in the British forces, on Christmas leave.

He spotted a spare seat in a compartment with five middle-aged women who gave him dirty looks as he entered, making it clear he wasn't welcome. The women resumed their chatter as the train finally began to move and pick up a little speed. Duggan ignored them, mentally putting together his report on Murphy's information, and keeping an eye on the corridor to see if Thomsen passed by.

The most significant thing, he thought, was the arrival of more British troops at Larne. Fears of a British invasion had increased ever since Churchill's threatening comments a month earlier about Ireland's continued neutrality. A most heavy and grievous burden, he had called it. The fact that the convoys from North America were suffering such losses increased the prospects of a British invasion to secure western Irish ports. If they were deploying more men in the North, that was an ominous sign. But, then again, they may only be rotating regiments, and the landings might mean nothing.

The door opened and a ticket collector checked their tickets. As soon as he was gone the women began to pull out brown paper parcels from under the seats. The woman beside him elbowed him hard in the ribs. 'Listen, son,' she said. 'You better get out of here or you might see something you shouldn't.' The woman opposite him cackled and they all began tearing open their parcels and pulling out a variety of clothes. One was already taking off her coat and cardigan and unbuttoning her blouse.

Duggan left and the blind on the door's window was pulled down behind him. He stood in the corridor and looked out at the passing fields. The sun was blinding, already low though it was only the middle of the afternoon, glaring across the half-frozen landscape and casting long shadows from the hedges. A handful of cattle gathered around a pile of hay, munching steadily, their breaths rising in the cold. The train thundered across the Boyne viaduct and he looked upriver, a pewter ribbon between its darkening banks. Might be another battle here, he thought, aware from overheard talk at headquarters that the river would be the defensive line for Dublin once again if the British came over the border.

He thought about going to the bar, to see if any of the British soldiers were there and try and pump them for information. Not a good idea, he decided. Anderson and his colleagues probably had lots of sources of information among them. Anyway, he was more intrigued by Thomsen's presence on the train. What could he have been doing in Dundalk? The same as myself. Meeting someone with information about what was going on across the border. That was most likely. He couldn't go into the North himself. Far too risky for him. So he must have a source or sources in Dundalk. Just like us. Which would hardly be surprising. There'd always been a strong IRA presence in Dundalk and they were very happy to help the Germans.

He moved along the corridor, towards the carriage Thomsen had boarded, and walked past all its compartments. Thomsen was in the third one, sitting by the window, reading a newspaper. Duggan glanced quickly at all the other occupants. A priest reading a book. Two women and two middle-aged men. They all appeared to be by themselves, each minding his and her own business. He passed by without pausing and meandered down to the back of the train and found another seat.

It was dark by the time the train reached Dublin. Duggan took his time alighting, wanting to make sure that Thomsen was ahead of him. He caught sight of him walking fast towards the exit on his own and began to follow quickly. The women whose compartment he had shared were being stopped by customs men behind the wooden tables half-blocking the platform. They all carried light shopping bags now and there were no signs of their parcels. But they were well wrapped up in bulky clothes.

'It's just a few sweets for the children from Santa Claus,' one of them said to a customs man, opening her shopping bag as wide as it would go as if it was an insult.

'Don't ye have anything better to be doing?' another sighed as the regular cat-and-mouse game played out. 'We were only up there for a day's outing.'

Duggan passed by quickly, keeping an eye on Thomsen's back. Beyond the ticket check Thomsen headed for the ramp leading down to street level. Whatever he'd been doing, he'd done it in Dundalk, Duggan decided, veering off to the stairs. He took them two at a time down to Amiens Street and unlocked the chain on his bicycle and walked it across the road.

The street lights were on but making less impression on the gloom than the glow from shop fronts. He cycled up Talbot Street, slotting into a convoy of other cyclists and weaving around the shoppers overflowing from the narrow footpath outside Guiney's clothes shop. Unplucked turkeys hung neck-down in the window of a butcher's and boxes of cigarettes in festive wrappers were lined up in a tobacconist's, topped with a pyramid of cigars. Passing faces were tense with the urgency of the fast-approaching Christmas deadline.

He turned into O'Connell Street at the Nelson Pillar, balancing the bike with brakes and pedals as a bus went by, its interior blue lights casting its passengers into spectral relief. A group of carol singers belted out 'Adeste Fidelis' outside Clerys and a tram clanged its way through the traffic on the other side of the central median, now an air-raid shelter, its grey concrete wall broken by posters for the Christmas Eve sweepstake to raise money for the Red Cross. The ads on the buildings around O'Connell Bridge were dark, no longer flashing their messages for Players cigarettes and Bendigo tobacco and, beyond, Bovril. He threaded his way across another line of cyclists and in front of a plodding dray into Bachelors Walk. He cycled fast down the quays by the darkening river, speeding up as the traffic eased and had worked up a slight sweat by the time he reached the Red House, the offices of G2, in army headquarters on Infirmary Road.

'Enjoy your mystery tour?' Captain Bill Sullivan greeted him as he came into their shared office and slumped into his chair.

'Long day for very little,' Duggan said, placing a carbon paper between two sheets of flimsy white paper and winding them into the typewriter.

'Boss wanted to see you when you got back.'

'Urgently?'

'Don't think so.'

'Anything happening?' Duggan opened the empty Gold Flake packet Murphy had given him and shook it upside down. A few strands of tobacco fell out.

'There's a war on,' Sullivan said.

'Still?' Duggan pulled at the silver paper in the packet and a small pad of folded paper came out with it.

'Your secret mission didn't end it after all.' Sullivan made no attempt to hide the hint of resentment at not having been told where Duggan had gone and what he'd been doing. He was in his mid-twenties, a couple of years older than Duggan, whom he believed was favoured by their immediate commander.

Duggan gave a short laugh and turned his attention to unfolding the pad of paper. Torn from a lined copybook, it had a handwritten list of ships' names in neat capital letters. He typed his report quickly, its structure already clear in his head, and added the vessels' names at the end. He read it through when finished and signed his initials at the bottom.

'By the way,' Sullivan said as Duggan got up. 'Are you coming to the New Year's Eve dinner dance in the Gresham?'

'Yeah,' Duggan said without enthusiasm. 'Sure.'

Sullivan held out his hand. 'One pound fifteen.'

'One pound fifteen?' Duggan stopped. 'That's very expensive.'

'It's New Year's Eve.'

'I haven't got anyone to bring.'

'Don't worry, we'll fix you up with someone. But I need the money by Thursday.'

'St Stephen's Day?' Duggan scratched his head, thinking he could maybe borrow a few quid from his father over Christmas.

'That's Thursday,' Sullivan said, as if Duggan was a little slow. 'You back on Thursday?'

Duggan nodded and left, dropping his report for Captain Anderson into the office that dealt with the British and went on to Commandant Charles McClure's office. There was a visible haze of cigarette smoke over McClure's desk as usual, stoked by a spiral of fresh smoke from a cigarette lying in an ashtray. Duggan gave him a quick run through of what Murphy had told him and of seeing Thomsen on the train.

McClure leaned back and picked up his cigarette without thinking. 'It's not good,' he sighed. He was in his mid-thirties, a narrow face with bright brown eyes. 'If they go on losing ships at this rate.'

Duggan nodded, knowing what he meant. It wasn't good for neutral Ireland. The British had to do something about the losses and one option was to blame the lack of port and other facilities on the west coast of Ireland for making it more difficult to defend the transatlantic convoys. Everyone in G2 was all too aware of the danger, especially now that Churchill had made it clear in his recent speech how impatient he was with the situation.

McClure and Duggan had talked it through afterwards.

'Invading us doesn't make much military sense,' McClure had suggested. 'But they've got to do something. And that just might be it. Seizing Berehaven and re-establishing their naval base down there.'

'That's as far away from the border as you can get,' Duggan had pointed out.

'Exactly. So they'd have to launch a full-scale invasion to get there. It'd be madness. A pointless diversion, causing needless havoc.'

'Surely their politicians aren't that mad,' Duggan had offered, more in hope than belief. He had a politician uncle and knew just how carried away they could get when they persuaded themselves of something.

McClure changed the subject now, switching to the new element in Murphy's information. 'Tell me again about the Americans in Derry.'

Duggan told him. 'It seemed very vague,' he concluded. 'Just gossip really. Maybe somebody jumping to conclusions.'

'It wouldn't surprise me if it was true.'

'But why would they be there?'

'Planning. Looking at setting up their own naval facilities in Lough Swilly.'

'But Roosevelt's promised not to get involved in the war,' Duggan said.

'The election's over,' McClure gave him a wry smile. 'Besides,' he raised one finger, 'he only promised not to involve American soldiers in foreign wars. He's been doing his best to provoke Germany into declaring war on America with all the help he's been giving the British and so on.'

'You think they will?'

'Been too smart to fall for it so far. But it's going to cause us a lot more trouble if the Americans get involved.'

'It could shorten the war, though.'

'And drag us into it. They'd be much more demanding than the British and even more impatient with our neutrality if they abandon theirs. Anyway,' McClure stubbed out his cigarette and began flicking through a pile of papers on the right of his desk, 'let's not get carried away with hypothetical situations. We've enough on our hands. External Affairs wants a briefing on our German friends.'

'Yeah?'

'We're going to see them on Thursday,' he came to the bottom of his pile of papers without finding what he was looking for and began again from the top, more slowly. 'Put together a report on all the suspected agents.'

'All of them?' Duggan asked, thinking of the work involved and the lack of time. He was due to take the train west to his parents' home the following day, Christmas Eve, and return on the first train the day after the holiday. On the other hand, he could do most of it off the top of his head. He didn't need to consult too many files.

McClure thought for a moment. 'No. Just the confirmed ones.'

'With Hermann Goertz at the top?'

'As usual,' McClure sighed. Goertz was an experienced German spy and had evaded capture since the previous summer when he parachuted into Ireland. He'd been in contact with the IRA and other pro-German groups and individuals, but always seemed to be one step ahead of the Irish authorities.

McClure found what he was looking for. He fished out a single sheet of paper from his pile and handed it across the desk to Duggan. There was a name and address handwritten along the top of the page – 'Gertie Maher, Iona Road, Drumcondra' – and 'Adelaide Agency', with an address in O'Connell Street, underneath.

'She could be the one we're looking for,' McClure said, changing the subject again. 'The person to work in Mrs Lynch's place.'

Mrs Lynch's café on Liffey Street was popular with German airmen and sailors who had been washed up in Ireland one way or another and interned in the Curragh military camp. They were allowed out on parole on day releases and tended to congregate in the café when they visited Dublin.

'Real name Gerda Meier,' McClure continued. 'Aged twenty. From Vienna. Jewish. Her father wisely got his family out in 1935, seeing the way the wind was blowing. Came to Cork and set up some kind of textile factory.'

'She speaks English?'

'With a Cork accent,' McClure smiled. 'It mightn't fool Corkmen but I doubt if our German friends will be able to detect the discrepancy. She's a shorthand typist or receptionist with that flat-renting agency in O'Connell Street and is willing to give up her Saturday afternoons to be a waitress in Mrs Lynch's and let us know what she hears.'

'And it's been cleared with Mrs Lynch?'

McClure nodded. 'But she won't pay her. And on condition that Gertie, Gerda, doesn't frighten the customers by talking politics.'

'So are we paying her?'

'She doesn't want money. She's happy to strike a blow at Herr Hitler any way she can. Go and meet her and see what you think. Make it clear to her that we only want her to keep her ears open. Listen to whatever they're chatting about. Not to engage in any chat with them. And, obviously, not to let them know she understands German.'

He was already stuck in Henry Street the next morning when he realised his mistake: he shouldn't have come this way on Christmas Eve. The street was crowded with shoppers who had taken over the roadway as well, reducing traffic to less than their own walking pace. He abandoned his attempt to cycle through them and walked with the bike up past the raucous shouts from Moore Street. He was almost at the side of the GPO when the crowds thinned enough and he threw his leg over the saddle and pedalled up to the Pillar and turned left.

The Adelaide Agency was close to the Carlton cinema, a shiny metal plate beside a narrow doorway leading straight onto stairs. He went up to the first floor where a sign on a door identified the agency and said to knock and enter. Inside there was a cramped reception area with two bentwood chairs and a small square table between them and a desk with a young woman behind it. She was talking on the phone, running through the details of flats to let in Rathgar.

Gertie Maher, he thought, Gerda Meier. She had black hair that curled up in a flounce just above her shoulders and dark brown eyes and was gesticulating with her right hand as she enumerated the advantages of the flat she was describing. He listened carefully to her accent. He doubted it would pass muster with any Corkman, probably not sing-song enough, but it was hard to place.

She paused to listen to something on the phone and then began to describe another flat. He picked up a typed list from the table and glanced down at it. The Adelaide Agency's market was immediately clear to him: larger flats in the better southern suburbs, suitable, as one said, 'for two ladies (Protestant)'. The prices looked expensive, £60 a year for a two-bed.

She finished on the phone and he turned to her, unsure which name to call her by.

'I'm Paul Duggan,' he said, showing her his identity card. She looked at it carefully and put her hand out and said, 'Pleased to meet you'.

'I understand you're willing—' he began but she put a finger to her lips.

'We must speak quietly,' she said, dropping her voice and pointing over her shoulder to the door behind her.

Duggan nodded and continued in a quieter tone, '—that you're willing to help us.'

'Yes,' she nodded. 'I will spy for you.'

'It's not exactly spying,' he said, taken aback by her directness. Then, realising what he had said, he added, 'I mean, not like that. It's not dangerous.'

She shrugged. 'I'll start on Saturday, after lunch. We're open here only for the morning and I'll go to the café at two o'clock.'

'Okay,' he said. 'That's great.'

The door behind her opened and a middle-aged man came out with his overcoat on and his hat in his hand. He glanced at Duggan and immediately dismissed him as a client.

'I'll be about an hour, Gertie,' he said to her, ignoring Duggan.

'Yes, sir,' she replied. And to Duggan, 'If you decide which area you prefer we'll identify the best places for you.'

Duggan looked after the man and dropped the list he realised he still had in his hand, on the desk. 'Your boss?' he asked.

'Mr Montague,' she said.

'Does he know your real name?'

'My real name is Gertie,' she gave him a defiant look. 'Gertie Maher.'

'I mean, where you come from?'

'*Sprechen sie Deutsch?*'

He nodded.

'He doesn't know anything,' she continued in German. 'We don't have conversations.'

Duggan nodded. 'You know the arrangement with Frau Lynch?' he asked in German.

'Yes.'

'And you know what we want?'

'Yes. I'm to listen to what they talk about and see who they meet and report to you. I'm not to talk to them about politics or the war. They must not know I understand German.' She rattled it off like a lesson she had been taught.

'Good. That's what we want. Nothing dangerous.'

'Can I flirt with them?'

Duggan laughed and then wondered if he had understood her German correctly. 'Only in English,' he said, in English.

She nodded, as if she was merely accepting another instruction.

'I'm sorry they won't pay you,' Duggan continued, not specifying who 'they' were. 'Since you're giving up your Saturday afternoons.'

'It's nothing. Maybe I'll get some tips,' she gave a hint of a wintry smile. 'Take some money back off the Nazis.'

'I hope the work won't be too hard.'

'I don't think so,' she shrugged. What was there to serving tea and coffee and pastries? 'Are you the spymaster?'

'Me?' Duggan laughed in disbelief at the idea. 'No. Do I look like a spymaster?'

'Who do I report to?'

'Oh,' he realised what she meant. 'To me.'

'I will see you there?'

'No, I won't go there. I will call here on Monday.' He took a fountain pen from the desk and wrote his phone number on a sheet of paper and added his first name only. 'If there's anything urgent you can call me at that number. If I am not there and it is really urgent ask for him.' He leaned down and added Commandant McClure's name under the number.

'You can't come here every time.' She took the sheet of paper and folded it over and over until it was as small as she could make it.

'No,' he agreed. 'Just this Monday. Then we'll make another arrangement.'

'Okay,' she stood up and held out her hand. She was about five feet ten, a couple of inches shorter than him. 'I will see you then.'

'And thank you very much for doing this,' he repeated as he shook her hand. 'We really appreciate your help.'

As he went down the stairs, Duggan felt slightly uneasy. She insisted she was Gertie Maher, not Gerda Meier, but she seemed keen to speak German. Would she do what they wanted? Or did she just want an opportunity to hurl abuse at some Germans?

Two

'Good Christmas?' Commandant McClure asked as Duggan drove along the northern quays. It was getting dark and the streets were empty, in the last hours of their holiday torpor before public social life began again.

'The usual,' Duggan passed a couple of cyclists. 'At my uncle's for Christmas Day.'

'How is he?'

Duggan glanced at him, unsure whether that was just a polite inquiry or something more. His uncle was Timmy Monaghan, a Fianna Fáil backbench TD, with whom he now had an uneasy relationship since Duggan had managed to assert his independence earlier in the year. A constant manipulator, Timmy had been responsible for Duggan's move to G2 from an infantry battalion and had since tried to use him in various ways.

'Still his old self,' Duggan sighed. He hadn't wanted to meet him after their previous disagreements but Duggan's mother had insisted on the annual ritual of going to Timmy's country house for Christmas dinner. Timmy had carried on as if nothing had happened between them, his usual bluff self. For which Duggan was grateful in one way: it removed the apprehension with which he had gone home for Christmas. 'How was it for you?'

'Exhausting,' McClure said. 'Children up in the middle of the night with Santa Claus. Got back to sleep again after a couple of hours but this double summer time makes you feel like you've been up for three days with only one night's sleep.'

Duggan laughed, not sure what he meant, and turned into Merrion Square at the traffic light on Clare Street. He drove by the National Gallery and Leinster Lawn and let the car coast across the street to the kerb outside Government Buildings. All the offices along the street were shut, their windows dark.

'Unusual time for a meeting, isn't it?' Duggan offered, looking for a sign of life in the building. There was none.

'Unusual times, full stop,' McClure replied as he went up the steps and pressed a large round bell. They waited in silence, McClure tapping the file with Duggan's report on the known German agents against his thigh. The street was deserted, the cowled street lights at the corners throwing down pools of feeble light. The cold air smelled of turf smoke tinged with a noxious edge of coke from the gasworks down by the river when the cold northern breeze shifted a few degrees.

The door swung open and a young uniformed garda looked at them.

'Commandant McClure and Captain Duggan for an appointment with the Secretary of External Affairs,' McClure flashed an identity card at him while Duggan held out his.

The garda nodded and let them into the small lobby. 'Hang on a second till the porter comes back and he'll bring you up.'

The porter took them along a spacious corridor with little lighting, mimicking the partial blackout in the streets, and up a stairs and down another dimly lit corridor and knocked on a door. There was a sound from within and he opened it and stood back to let McClure and Duggan enter.

It was a perfunctory office, an upright hat stand with a dark hat and heavy coat on it inside the door, and a couple of chairs in front of a desk. The only light in the room came from a green-shaded art deco desk lamp. 'Gentlemen.' The man behind the desk stood up and introduced himself as Pól Ó Murchú and gave each of them a cursory handshake. He was approaching forty, gaining weight and balding, and the world's many cares were beginning to etch his face. 'The Secretary has been delayed' – he paused as he sat down again and reconsidered the word – 'detained with the Taoiseach. He asked me to brief you.'

Duggan glanced at McClure at the mention of a briefing. McClure gave no indication of surprise as he extracted Duggan's report from his file and passed it across the desk. Ó Murchú set it down in the centre of the light like a gourmand relishing the sight of a new dish. He took his time reading it, only touching it to turn the first page.

'This man, Hermann Goertz,' he put the first page back on top again and looked up from the list. 'He's the most important one?'

'Yes, sir,' McClure said. 'As far as we're aware. He has proved to be more elusive than the others too. More competent.'

Ó Murchú read through the list again. 'What about the espionage activities of the German legation itself?'

'We're not aware of any,' McClure said. 'Not of anything untoward. They meet a lot of people and are presumably collecting information, but we're not aware that they are overstepping the line between diplomacy and espionage.'

'Hmm,' Ó Murchú sighed, 'a fine line.' He tapped the report with his middle finger. 'Do any of these gentlemen have any dealings with the legation?'

'Not to our knowledge, not on a regular basis.' McClure hesitated. 'Though their paths may cross on occasion. Captain Duggan here spotted Dr Goertz attending a reception in the German Minister's home on one occasion.'

'Ah,' Ó Murchú brightened up. 'Tell me more.'

McClure signalled to Duggan, who said, 'Dr Goertz was at a party in Herr Hempel's house last June to celebrate their victory in France.'

'And he would have had an opportunity then to speak to Herr Hempel himself?'

'I presume so, sir,' Duggan said. 'I wasn't in the building and can't confirm that he did or didn't. There were a lot of people there.'

'Indeed,' Ó Murchú nodded. 'Including some of our own.'

And ours, Duggan thought. Among those he had seen enter was Major General Hugo O'Neill, the man in charge of repelling any British move across the border. Along with some of the best-known people in the country.

'Herr Hempel is a very careful and correct diplomat,' Ó Murchú went on. 'I imagine he keeps strictly to the rules. But what about the others in the legation?'

'We try and keep track of them insofar as we can,' McClure offered. 'And insofar as can be done with discretion and without hindering their legitimate activities.'

Ó Murchú gave him a look that said, I know exactly what those vague words mean: you have no idea what they're up to.

'I'm sorry,' McClure said, interpreting the look correctly. 'We weren't aware that you were looking for information about the German diplomats. We had been told only that you wanted a report on the known German agents who've tried to operate here.'

Ó Murchú settled back in his chair and rested his elbows on its arms and pressed his palms together in thought for a moment. 'A delicate situation has arisen with the Germans,' he began. 'They want to expand the numbers at their legation, bring in three more people from Germany. Cultural attachés, commercial types, they say. In reality, of course, they are more likely to be military types, intelligence agents. In a way it doesn't matter what they are. What matters as usual is perception. And the British are almost certain to perceive any increase in German diplomatic strength here as a threat.' He paused and looked from one to the other. 'You know their attitude to the German and Italian legations?' McClure and Duggan nodded: the British demanded with monotonous regularity that both should be shut down. 'So,' Ó Murchú went on, 'they will be unhappy at what they will see as our acquiescence in a German expansion. Given their current attitude to our neutrality, that would not be helpful.'

He paused to consider something else behind his hands. 'Strictly speaking, the Germans don't need our permission to increase their personnel. As they have made clear to us in no uncertain terms. In normal circumstances it is usual to have the agreement of the host country before expanding an embassy. But these are far from normal circumstances. Regrettably, the common diplomatic courtesies are becoming a thing of the past,' he gave a nostalgic sigh in memory of a more considerate age. 'The language of diplomacy is giving way more and more to that of the bully boy.

'They have informed us of their plan and demanded that we make arrangements for the arrival of the newcomers at Foynes. Flight plans, wireless frequencies, call signs, and so on,' he waved away the practicalities with a dismissive hand.

'And the British will know about it as soon as they are filed,' McClure said. The Foynes seaplane base at the Shannon estuary was Ireland's only air link with North America and Europe through a service to Lisbon. But they were operated by the British Overseas Airline Corporation and were effectively restricted to officially sanctioned passengers. Furthermore, some of the BOAC staff there were British security agents, secretly approved by the Irish government.

'Indeed,' Ó Murchú nodded. 'If they don't know already. What is important for us is that we maintain the present status quo vis-à-vis the German legation, and that we aren't seen to be collaborating with them. On the other hand, we cannot simply reject Germany's wishes.'

He fell silent and let his information sink in. Duggan felt his stomach lurch, the return of a hollow feeling that had begun in the summer with the German successes on the Continent and the scares of an imminent invasion of Ireland as well as Britain. But this sounded even more dangerous. We're being trapped, he thought, our options closing down. The next decisive move in the war was likely in the spring, notwithstanding the battles going on in North Africa. The Germans might invade as part of the invasion of Britain. Or the British might invade Ireland to get west-coast ports and protect their Atlantic convoys. Either would make us a target, ensuring the other belligerents would then come in, and all-out war would be waged here.

After allowing them what he considered to be a suitable time for consideration, Ó Murchú added, 'And they want to fly their men in before the end of the year. Next week.'

'Can Foynes be closed?' McClure enquired.

'We can pray for bad weather,' Ó Murchú gave another hint of his wintry smile, a cultivated speciality that verged on a grimace. 'The only thing we can do is to explain to them the problems posed by their wishes and to try and delay them. We can't give them an outright "no". That could be interpreted as an unfriendly act, possibly with its own consequences. So all we can do is try and put them off for the moment. Hope they lose interest. Or other matters intervene. And in that context,' he looked from one to the other, 'it would be very useful to know if any of their existing staff was engaging in inappropriate activities.'

'The radio transmitter?' McClure offered. The German legation's radio was their only direct method of communicating with Berlin, and a regular bone of contention with the British, who wanted it put out of commission. Tracking it down was a cat-and-mouse game, with the British offering technical assistance to try and pinpoint its location.

Ó Murchú nodded. 'That's been played to a standstill, diplomatically. It would be helpful if we had any other cards. To create more diversions, so to speak.' He sat forward and tapped Duggan's report again. 'This is useful information about Dr Goertz. Do we know how often he's been in touch with the legation or its staff?'

McClure shook his head with regret. 'We've lost track of him in recent weeks,' he admitted. 'The IRA is believed to be hiding him. Perhaps others as well.'

'In this context he is of less importance than the accredited diplomats,' Ó Murchú said. 'It could be very useful if we were to find any further evidence of collusion between them and unauthorised agents.'

'I don't like deadlines like this,' McClure said when they were back in the car, lighting cigarettes before they pulled away.

'Should we drop everything else?' Duggan pointed the car towards St Stephen's Green and headed for Grafton Street.

'God, no.' McClure wound down the window a fraction to let out the smoke. 'Can't afford to do that. Just need to put our thinking caps on.'

Grafton Street was coming back to life after the holiday, cars and buses slowed by cyclists and people, heavily wrapped against the cold, heading for restaurants, gathering outside the cinema, and checking the shop windows advertising the post-Christmas sales due to begin in the morning.

'I'll have a word with the Special Branch,' McClure continued. 'See if their surveillance of the legation has thrown up anything they haven't bothered to tell us. We're not looking for much, after all. Just some people to be in the same place at the same time.'

Duggan braked gently as two middle-aged couples dashed across the street in between cars and hurried, laughing, down the laneway into Jammet's oyster bar to round off a day spent at Leopardstown races.

'That's it,' McClure clicked his fingers and brightened up. 'We need to look more closely at the Germans' IRA connections. Much easier to build up a dossier of their contacts with subversives. That'd suit Ó Murchú's purposes just as well. Allow him to have a go at the Germans for interfering in our internal affairs. Helping those who're conspiring to bring down our state.'

'He didn't say anything about them.'

'Never mind,' McClure retorted. 'We're more likely to get some quick results on that front from the Branch. They're much more interested in the local gunmen than in invasion threats.'

Freed from Grafton Street, they sped across the river and headed along the quays. McClure rolled down his window and tossed out his cigarette butt, narrowly missing a Guinness dray carrying empty barrels as they overtook it. Deep in thought, he didn't notice.

'The Branch might know who Thomsen was meeting in Dundalk,' Duggan suggested.

'They were following him?'

'I don't know. But they were at Amiens Street when he got off the train,' he paused. 'At the customs check.'

Duggan flicked out the car's indicator and turned into Infirmary Road and stopped while the sentry raised the barrier at the gate into headquarters. He parked and turned off the engine but McClure made no move to get out. Duggan waited.

'You might talk to your uncle as well,' McClure looked at him.

'Okay,' Duggan said in surprise. It was the first time McClure had ever suggested he use his family connections for work.

'He's a man about town, isn't he?'

'He's certainly that,' Duggan laughed, wondering if McClure

knew something about what his uncle Timmy was up to. Timmy made no secret of his support for Germany, though his public pronouncements were restricted by his party's insistence on strict adherence to neutrality. Timmy had little interest in Hitler's vision of a new Europe but still believed in the old Irish revolutionary dictum that England's difficulty was Ireland's opportunity and that a German victory would reunite the country. Timmy, like Duggan's father, had fought the British less than twenty years earlier in what he always referred to as 'the four glorious years'. And he continued to be friendly with some old comrades now leading the IRA campaign against the native government.

Inside, Captain Sullivan stopped Duggan in the corridor with his hand out. 'You got the money for the tickets?'

Duggan gave him one of the pound notes he had borrowed from his father and a ten-shilling note and two half-crowns. 'You got a date for me?'

'Yeah,' Sullivan smirked. 'Carmel's friend Breda. You remember her? We met them in the Carlton after that Charlie Chan picture a few weeks ago.'

'Yeah.' Carmel was Sullivan's girlfriend but Duggan wasn't sure he could remember her friend Breda.

'Don't get any ideas,' Sullivan said. 'It's not a real date. She doesn't fancy you.'

'Fine,' Duggan laughed. The feeling was obviously mutual: she hadn't made much of an impression on him either.

'She wants you to know that. She's only going with you because she wants to be there with Carmel and she's not doing a line at the moment.'

'Okay, I get the message.'

But Sullivan hadn't finished yet. 'Actually, she thinks you're a bit stuck-up.'

'She said that?' Duggan tried harder to remember her. Not a great looker, more than a bit standoffish, judgemental. Or maybe he was assuming that now. He couldn't really remember anything about her and would be hard put to recognise her in the street. They'd only met for a few minutes and he'd been hurrying away. 'Give me back half the money,' Duggan put his hand out. 'She can pay for herself.'

Sullivan laughed and walked away.

Duggan sat down at his desk, closed his eyes and stretched his neck and joined his hands behind his head. It'd been a long day, another interminable train journey back from his parents', a scramble to finish the report on German agents, which wasn't what they wanted after all, and then the meeting with Ó Murchú.

'Thanks for that note from the man in Dundalk,' a voice said behind him.

Duggan opened his eyes and twisted around. Captain Liam Anderson was standing in the doorway, as if the room was out of bounds to him. Anderson was a few years older than Duggan, a redhaired Northerner. Duggan only knew him to see, had never had a real conversation with him. 'You had no problems with him? With Murphy?'

'No. The train was very late but he was still there.'

'He's a reliable man,' Anderson nodded. 'Very interesting info.'

'Yeah?' Duggan sounded surprised. 'It all seemed a bit vague. Except for the list of damaged ships.'

'He doesn't exaggerate or speculate. Like a lot of people in this business.'

That's true, Duggan thought, thinking back to Murphy's refusal to go beyond what he had heard. 'Vague stuff about the British troops. Americans in Derry.'

'You lads in here only deal in hard facts?'

'Fair point,' Duggan conceded. 'It sounded frustrating though.'

'The important point is that these Americans were not in uniform.'

'Under cover.'

Anderson nodded. 'And the Brits have brought in another battalion. We've had corroboration from another source.'

'Not rotating?'

'No. Reinforcing.'

'Jesus,' Duggan said.

'Don't be too hard on the Jerries,' Anderson pointed a finger at him. 'We might be needing them yet.'

The day was dull and cold, a mass of threatening grey clouds pressing down on the city, dampening spirits. There was snow on the tops of the Dublin Mountains, melding them into the clouds, as Duggan cycled up Rathmines Road. The drone of a heavy aircraft grew louder and louder and passed almost overhead, hidden in the cloud, and faded away towards the mountains. A bomber, he thought, from the weight of its noise. Probably lost.

Timmy Monaghan opened the door himself. 'Hardy day,' he said. 'You're in time for the dinner.'

'No, thanks,' Duggan said. 'Love to stay but I can't.'

'On duty?' Timmy gave him a sideways look as he led him into his study. A fire blazed and the large table he used as a desk was littered with papers. He lowered his bulk into the armchair to the right of the fire, his back to the window, and Duggan sank into the other one. 'So, this is an official visit?'

Duggan shook his head. 'Not really. I just hoped you might be able to help me with something.'

'Or else?' Timmy gave him a hard stare.

'Or else nothing,' Duggan felt flustered, taken aback by Timmy's hostility. Gone was the avuncular, smiling, back-slapping host of Christmas Day. The usual Timmy, in fact. 'It's to do with work but...'

'Ah, always happy to help you lads,' Timmy said, changing his demeanour, and pulled himself up by the arms of the chair. 'You'll have another one of those cigars your father gave me.'

'No, thanks.' He's just trying to knock me off my stride, Duggan thought, unsettle me. It might've worked in the past but not anymore. I'm up to his ways. 'Too strong for me.'

Timmy took a cigar from the open box of Don Carlos Imperiales on the desk, sat back down and made a production out of lighting it. 'So,' he said through a cloud of smoke, 'the penny has dropped, has it?'

'Which penny?'

'That our neighbours will be paying us an unwanted visit any day now.' Timmy gave a crooked smile, liking his own metaphor. 'Coming in the back door without as much as a by-your-leave.'

'That's not my area.'

'It'll be everyone's area soon enough.'

'It's a complicated situation.' Duggan shifted in his chair and lit a cigarette.

'Nothing complicated about it. You saw Churchill's speech. As plain a message as anyone could ask for. You don't have to be in intelligence to read it.'

'So why would they send such a plain message if they planned to invade?' Duggan said, immediately regretting allowing himself to be dragged into a Timmy-style debate.

Timmy gave him a congratulatory nod, recognising a debating point. 'To soften us up. Prepare the ground in America.'

'The point is,' Duggan tried to get the conversation back on his track, 'that we don't want to give them any excuse.'

'When did the Brits ever need an excuse to fuck up Ireland? I marked your cards for you months ago. But you didn't want to know, for some reason.'

'Any excuse,' Duggan went on, avoiding the invitation to rehash old conversations, 'that they could use in America. That might work in America. To justify their action.'

'Like what?' Timmy demanded with the air of someone confident that there was no answer to his demand.

'Like German activities here.'

Timmy waved his cigar in the air, dismissing the idea as if it was as insubstantial as the trail of smoke left behind.

'The more reasons they have, the more likely they are to invade,' Duggan went on. 'Especially if they can point to German plots.'

'Hah. It didn't work the last time,' Timmy said, referring to the Easter Rising and British attempts to portray it as a German plot.

'Doesn't mean it won't work this time. Especially with an American president who's dying to get into the war on the British side.'

'His party won't let him. We've still got a lot of clout there.'

'Not enough clout to make him sell us the weapons we want,' Duggan shot back. 'And need.'

Timmy conceded the point with a small nod and drew heavily on his cigar. 'You know where you could've got the weapons you need. Offered to you on a plate but you wouldn't take them.'

'Your party leader turned down the Germans' offer,' Duggan reminded him. The government had rejected a German offer to supply the Irish army with British weapons captured in France.

'On the advice of you lads,' Timmy snorted. 'Are you still working with that fellow McClure?'

Duggan nodded, knowing what was to come.

'I warned you about him, too. A Prod. Father in the British army. Whose side do you think he'll be on when they come over the border?'

'On our side,' Duggan said. This wasn't going at all as he had planned. 'Listen,' he added, going straight for Timmy's weak point, his desire to be involved in every political conspiracy. 'We need your help. There is a very delicate situation at the moment.'

Timmy tried and failed to keep the flicker of curiosity from his face. Inside information was life's blood to him.

'I can't go into details,' Duggan went on, 'I'd love to and I know that you'd appreciate just how dangerous the situation is. But I'm under orders not to. The fact is that there are things happening which will make a British invasion inevitable. And the Germans will come in on our side. And then the whole country will be a battleground like France was or Greece is now. And thousands and thousands of our people will be killed and the country, this city, laid waste. It's that serious. It's one thing wanting Germany to win the war so that we have the country reunited. I understand that totally. People are entitled to support whomever they want. But having the country turned into a battleground is another thing entirely. Everybody knows this war isn't like any other. It's all about killing civilians – women, children, everybody.'

Timmy studied him as if he was seeing him for the first time as an adult, not just his sister-in-law's young fellow. Duggan returned the stare, hoping he hadn't overplayed his hand: he hadn't meant to end up appealing to Timmy's better nature. It was doubtful if such a thing existed.

Timmy finally looked away to toss his cigar into the fire. 'What is it you want to know?'

'Remember last summer,' Duggan suppressed a sigh of relief, 'you ran into a man called Robinson at a party in Herr Hempel's house?'

Timmy gave him a sly eye. So he knows now that Robinson was really Hermann Goertz, Duggan thought. 'Have you ever run into him again?'

'Seemed a decent type,' Timmy said, playing for time. 'Should be left alone. Not doing us any harm.'

He does know, Duggan thought. Maybe more than I know. 'I'm not trying to track him down. I just want to know if he's been talking to Herr Hempel or his staff again.'

'And why wouldn't he talk to Herr Hempel or anyone he wanted to? It's a free country.'

'I'm not saying he couldn't. I just want to know if he has.'

'You're not trying to catch him anymore,' Timmy gave a satisfied nod. He's heard the rumours too, Duggan thought. That Goertz's ability to evade arrest was not an accident. That he was being allowed to remain at large for political reasons. As another conduit to Germany, should the need arise. 'That's the most sensible thing I've heard in a long time.'

Duggan waited, hoping he was about to get what he wanted.

Timmy's face was a study in concentration, whether searching his memory or running through different scenarios Duggan couldn't tell. 'I haven't seen him since then,' he said at last.

'He wasn't at any other receptions in the German legation?' Duggan tried to hide his disappointment.

'I haven't put a foot inside Hempel's house since then.'

'What about the legation itself?'

Timmy shook his head.

'Have you seen him at any other things?'

Timmy pursed his lips. 'Somebody told me that they had met him at something. A few months ago.' He thought for a moment. 'At a meeting of the Irish Friends of Germany. In the Red Bank. You know the Red Bank?'

Duggan nodded. He had never been in the restaurant in D'Olier Street but he knew from reports that it was the regular meeting place for the Friends of Germany, a small group of fascist supporters.

'Any of the German diplomats there too?'

'I don't know. Somebody mentioned that they'd run into a few people there, including Robinson. Didn't know who he really was, of course. That's why it stuck in my memory.'

'When was that?

'Not that long ago. Early November maybe. Around the time they celebrate the Munich beer hall stuff.'

'Have you been to their meetings?'

'Some of them lads are off the wall,' Timmy avoided the question and waved at the pile of letters on the table. 'They keep sending me invitations. They're having something on New Year's Eve.'

'You going?'

'Mona's dragging me along to something else. But I might be able to look in for a few minutes. If you want me to.'

Duggan made a non-committal noise. He wanted information from Timmy but the last thing he wanted was to have Timmy insinuate himself into G2's operations.

Three

Duggan climbed the stairs to the Adelaide Agency, hoping he was timing his arrival right. It was almost lunchtime and he was banking on Gerda Meier's boss going out to eat to allow them to talk without hindrance. At least she hadn't gone out: he could hear a typewriter clacking as he approached the door and knocked.

She stopped typing as he came in and she said 'good afternoon' in a businesslike voice and put her finger to her lips.

He nodded and said, 'I was wondering if you've got anything new on your list this week.'

'I'm typing it now,' she said. 'There is something in Donnybrook that may suit you. Morehampton Road.'

She began to flick forward the pages of a notebook, taking her time over each page of shorthand squiggles. The door behind her opened and Montague came out, muffled against the cold with a scarf tucked into his overcoat as well as a hat. He glanced at Duggan and then glanced at him again and nodded to him; maybe he was a potential customer after all.

Gerda let the pages of her notebook fall closed after he left. 'You can't come here every week,' she said when his footsteps had faded down the stairs.

'I could meet you somewhere during your lunch break,' Duggan nodded. 'But it's better if we're not seen together.'

'Come here at one thirty then. He won't be back until one forty-five.'

'Okay. So, how did it go?'

'There were only three Germans there. A Luftwaffe crew who had to land when they ran out of fuel, Mrs Lynch said. She knew them well. One officer and two others. One of the others had an Irish girl with him and they were going to see a film. The officer reminded him to boo if there were any British newsreels, especially if they mentioned the RAF. The Irish woman said she would too.'

'Did they talk about anything else interesting?'

'No. Most of their talk in German was about the crewman's girlfriend. Not nice things.'

Duggan was about to ask her what they said but stopped himself. He could imagine.

'She didn't speak German?'

Gerda shook her head. 'Her boyfriend spoke some English. Not very good. When they left, the other two didn't talk much. A little about their families and what they do every Christmas. Did.'

Nothing much there, Duggan thought. Maybe this was a waste of time.

'Mrs Lynch told me there are usually more of them. She thought there might be something on somewhere else.'

'Like what?'

'She didn't say.'

'Do you know who the Irish woman was?'

'Her name was Patricia. That's all I know.'

'How did you know one of them was an officer?'

She gave him a withering look. 'I don't need to see a uniform to know a Nazi,' she snapped.

That wasn't the question, he thought. And being an officer didn't mean he was a Nazi. Especially in the Luftwaffe. But he let it go. 'Did Mrs Lynch know their names?'

'She didn't say.'

'Did they talk to anyone else?'

She shook her head. 'There was a man who tried to talk to them but they ignored him.'

'Who?'

'Mrs Lynch said he is an artist. From England.'

'An Englishman?'

She nodded.

'He's a regular?'

'She said he came last week the first time, just before Christmas. Asked her if he could hang some of his paintings on her wall. To sell them. She said no.'

'Did she know his name?'

'Glenn.'

'Is that his Christian name or his surname?'

'His family name. His first name is Roderick – Roddy.'

Duggan nodded. 'And what happened when he tried to talk to the Germans?'

'I couldn't hear,' she said. 'He was by himself at a table beside the window. I noticed him because he seemed to be nervous. He was playing with his cup. Twisting it,' she indicated with her two hands. 'Looking around a lot, like he was expecting somebody. Then he went over to them and said something. They didn't look pleased. Told him to go away.'

'You heard them?'

'No. But it was clear what they meant.' She gave a dismissive wave in illustration.

'Was he being abusive?'

'I don't know,' she said. 'I wasn't near the table.'

'He knew they were Germans?'

'Oh yes,' she nodded. 'They don't keep their voices down.'

'He shouted at them?'

'No. He tried to say something. But they pushed him away.' She gave the dismissive wave again.

Duggan thought about that for a moment. Something to be filed away. Maybe. But very little real information overall. 'Okay,' he said, masking his disappointment with a cheerful smile. 'Thank you very much for doing that. You'll go again next Saturday?'

'Yes.' She reached under her desk and came up with a purse, took two halfpennies from it and held them out in the palm of her hand. 'They left me a tip.'

'That was all? A penny?'

She nodded. 'You take them.'

'No. You keep them. You earned them.'

'I don't want their money.' She mocked a spit at the coins.

'I thought—'

'I changed my mind,' she interrupted. 'Here.' She pushed her palm forward, making it an order. He took the coins. 'They left their coffees too.'

'Why?'

'It tastes like piss.'

'You sound like a Cork woman,' Duggan smiled and she laughed.

On his way back to headquarters Duggan dropped the two coins into a tin cup held out by a heavily shawled woman sitting at the base of the Pillar. He typed out a brief summary of what Gerda had told him and went to McClure's office to leave a copy on his desk. McClure was standing by the window, staring out at nothing, smoking a thoughtful cigarette.

'Well?' he turned from the window, breaking his reverie.

Duggan gave him a synopsis of what he had written.

'What about the other matter?' McClure asked.

'Nothing more. I've gone through the reports of the Friends of Germany meetings for the last few months. Back to June. No mention of Robinson. Or any of Goertz's other names. Or anybody that might've been him.'

'You went through the Special Branch reports too?'

Duggan nodded. The Branch carried out surveillance outside the meeting while G2 had an informant who was a member of the organisation. Duggan didn't know who he was and didn't ask but had read his reports. They assumed the Branch also had its own man or woman among the Friends but that information was not shared with them.

'I'd be surprised if Goertz ever goes near them,' McClure said. 'Can't see that he'd have anything to gain. They're of no significance militarily or politically.'

'Some of them expect to get positions of power if Germany wins the war.'

McClure stubbed out his cigarette and went behind his desk and slumped into his chair. 'Herr Thomsen's visit to Dundalk was of no use to us either. He went to visit a German woman who's been married there for nearly twenty years.'

'Isn't that unusual? That he'd go all the way to see her? Instead of her coming to the legation, I mean.'

'Not in the circumstances,' McClure sighed. 'He went to tell her that her sister was killed in a bombing raid on Hamburg.' He paused. 'We've got nothing more for Ó Murchú.'

'The Branch have nothing on IRA men meeting the Germans?'

McClure shook his head. 'Not that they're sharing with us. Their priorities are different anyway.'

'Can we pick up Goertz?' Duggan asked.

McClure leaned back in his chair and fixed him with an inquisitive look.

'I mean,' Duggan continued, fearing that he was going out on a limb. While McClure never treated him as an underling and encouraged him to speak his mind, he was moving into unexplored waters here. 'There are rumours. That Goertz is being allowed to remain free. That it's no accident that he's always one step ahead of us.'

'Tell me more,' McClure ordered.

'Just that,' Duggan said. 'That that's why he keeps giving us the slip. Why he's never in the place that's raided. Has always just left.'

'Someone's tipping him off.'

Duggan nodded, relaxing a little. 'More than that. That the powers that be want him on the loose. As an unofficial channel to the Abwehr, the Wehrmacht. In case we need it.'

'If the British invade?'

'Yes.'

McClure put his hands behind his head and stayed silent for a few moments. 'How widespread are these rumours?'

Duggan shrugged. 'I've heard it hinted at a few times. Nobody saying it directly.'

'Around here?'

Duggan nodded.

'And outside?'

'I don't know,' Duggan said, restraining himself from pointing out that he spent little time outside the army or even G2.

'Your uncle?'

'I think so.'

'Meaning? What did he say?'

Duggan searched his memory for what Timmy had said. 'Nothing directly,' he said. Typical Timmy. As slippery as an eel. Everything was nods and winks. 'But the idea didn't seem to be a surprise to him.'

'So, it's in the political system too.' McClure straightened up behind the desk and lit himself another cigarette. 'It could work,' he said after a moment.

Duggan waited for him to elaborate but he didn't. Instead he picked up the phone and asked for the Department of External Affairs. McClure nodded to dismiss him while he waited to be put through.

Duggan was almost at the door when McClure said, 'By the way, the colonel says it's not true. We're not just going through the motions looking for Goertz.'

Duggan was hardly back in his office when McClure called and told him they were going to External Affairs. A gentle flurry of small snowflakes settled on the windscreen as he drove, turning into drops of water so quickly that they seemed like an illusion. Government Buildings was more alive this time, lights everywhere, sounds of typing behind closed doors, the corridors feeling used. Ó Murchú, however, looked like he hadn't moved since they had seen him last, still at the edge of his pool of light. He didn't bother with the perfunctory handshake this time.

'The Secretary is meeting the Germans in a couple of hours,' he said as they sat down. 'Fortunately, it's the German Minister himself, Herr Hempel. A much more civilised man to deal with. However, he's going to be looking for the details they requested. When they can fly their men into Foynes. So . . .' He held out a hand, palm up, passing an imaginary baton to McClure.

'As I said on the phone,' McClure accepted the baton, 'I believe that Hermann Goertz could be used as a counterweight to their demands.'

Ó Murchú nodded. 'Let's go through it. See where it takes us. You are sure, for a start, that this man Goertz is a spy?'

'Without doubt. He served a sentence for spying in England during the 1930s. We've found irrefutable evidence here of his activities.'

'And that he has been in contact with the German legation?'

'Yes,' Duggan said. 'We know he attended their victory celebrations last June in Herr Hempel's own house. Shortly after he arrived here.'

'And since then?'

'We don't know. But it would seem probable.'

'So we are bluffing if we complain about him?'

'To an extent, sir,' McClure said. 'Herr Hempel must know that Goertz was in his house, even if he didn't meet him himself. Which is unlikely. And he must know of their other contacts with him. So, he can't deny any knowledge of him. And he can't know what else we know.'

'Okay,' Ó Murchú nodded to himself. 'Where do we go from there?'

'Some people appear to believe that we've deliberately allowed Goertz to remain free. We can presume the German legation has heard those rumours and may believe that too. So we could suggest to Herr Hempel that we can no longer tolerate Goertz's activities. He's compromising our neutrality. And interfering in our internal affairs by fomenting subversion through the IRA.'

'So we must arrest him. As we can do at a moment's notice?'

McClure nodded.

'Really? We know where he is?'

'No, sir. But we can make an all-out effort to find him.'

'Another bluff.'

McClure conceded the point with a slight nod.

'What if they call our bluff?'

'It's unlikely. We make it clear that we must arrest Goertz and put him on trial. Which means his contacts with the legation and with the IRA will be made public. Cause a major diplomatic problem. Even justify abandoning neutrality. On the side of the Allies. Or give the British an excuse—'

A look of horror crossed Ó Murchú's face and he raised his hand for McClure to stop. 'Whoa,' he said. 'Hold your horses.' He steepled his hands on the desk and leaned his chin on them and ignored McClure and Duggan for what seemed an age. Then he sat back and placed his left hand, palm down, on the desk. 'Their request to strengthen the legation,' he said. He put his right hand, palm down, on the desk, leaving a wide gap between his two hands. 'Our concerns about Dr Goertz's activities,' he nodded, looking from one hand to the other. 'Side by side on the table. No linkage. And,' he looked up at McClure, 'no threats.'

'No, sir,' McClure accepted the reprimand.

'Thank you gentlemen,' Ó Murchú dismissed them. They stood up to leave but Ó Murchú changed his mind. 'It may help you to know how sensitive this matter is,' he said. 'They have now spoken of serious consequences if we don't make the arrangements they require.'

They waited. 'Serious consequences?' McClure prompted.

'They have hinted at breaking diplomatic relations,' Ó Murchú paused to let the implications sink in. 'It is possible, but not likely, that they are trying to engineer such a breach. Which would be very serious and probably be a prelude to military action. They insist they want us to remain neutral but who knows what their real plans are.'

McClure and Duggan remained halfway to the door. Ó Murchú ran a hand down over his face, looking tired and dropping his diplomatic demeanour. 'I don't need to remind you these are dangerous times. And of your obligations under the Official Secrets Act.'

'No, sir,' McClure said. 'Of course not.'

'I'm telling you this information so you understand the importance of what's happening. Keep it to yourselves as far as possible.' He switched back to his formal self. 'Keep me informed of any developments.'

On the way back to headquarters, McClure suggested it would be no harm to keep an eye on the Friends of Germany meeting in the Red Bank restaurant that evening. In case Goertz turned up. 'I know it's unlikely but you never know,' he added. 'He may think he's immune from arrest too. We've got to pull out all the stops.'

Duggan murmured his assent, wondering if he wanted him to do it in person.

'You're going dancing tonight?' McClure asked, confirming his suspicion.

'Bill Sullivan organised a table at the Gresham.'

'Big date?'

'No,' Duggan smiled, remembering Sullivan's advance warnings from his companion for the evening. 'Far from it.'

'Wouldn't matter then if you were a little late.'

'Not at all.'

'Good,' McClure nodded. 'You're the only one who actually knows what he looks like. Take this car,' he added. 'Hang on to it for the evening.'

The night was cold, a raw edge to it that threatened more snow than the earlier hint which had left nothing more on the ground than a wet sheen now freezing on the streets. Duggan was parked on D'Olier

Street, across the road from the Red Bank. The car's windows were steamed up and he had the driver's window open a couple of inches to watch the restaurant's entrance.

He shivered and jammed his hands into the pockets of his overcoat, trying to remember what Goertz looked like, how he walked, carried himself. A military bearing. Straight and straight-forward. A sharp-faced profile. It wasn't much to go on, unless he got a long look at him, which was unlikely at this distance and in the reduced street light. And with a hat down and coat collar up . . .

It was a waste of time. The straggle of people going in walked quickly and were huddled in overcoats and hats. Hitler himself could walk in there and you wouldn't recognise him from here, he thought.

A figure appeared at the driver's window and two eyes glared in at him through the gap, making him jump. 'Would you look at what the cat brought in?' a voice said in a Dublin accent.

Duggan watched while the figure, a shadow through the muffled windscreen, walked around the front of the car and opened the passenger door. Garda Peter Gifford sat in.

'Jesus,' Duggan breathed. 'You frightened the shit out of me.'

'So I should,' Gifford said. He was a member of the Special Branch, a couple of years older than Duggan. They had been friends since the previous summer when Gifford had helped Duggan with family problems while they were engaged in a joint operation against a suspected German spy. Their friendship contrasted with the mutual suspicion between their respective organisations. 'That's what we do to people loitering in cars on dark streets.'

Duggan turned to look back down the street and then spotted the car on the other side with a man at the wheel. The Special Branch. He hadn't noticed it earlier. Some use I am at surveillance, he thought.

'What're you doing here?' he asked, knowing the answer.

'Same as yourself,' Gifford said. 'On the punishment detail.'

'What've you done wrong now?'

'Not keeping my mouth shut, as usual. And you?'

'Keeping an eye out for our friend, Herr Goertz.'

'Mr Brandy,' Gifford nodded to himself, another of the names Goertz had used, and the one by which he was best known to the Special Branch.

'Any sign of him? I can see fuck all from here.' Duggan opened his coat and fished in his jacket pocket for his cigarette case and lighter.

'Oh, an officer and a gentleman,' Gifford smirked, catching sight of Duggan's bow tie and dinner jacket. 'This the new G2 uniform for stakeouts? Where are you on your way to?'

'The Gresham.'

'Who's the lucky girl?'

'Nobody. A friend of a colleague's girlfriend.'

'A blind date. The best kind.'

'How's Siobhan?' She was Gifford's girlfriend after flirting with both of them for a time and remained friendly with Duggan.

'She's fine. We're like an old married couple now.'

'You haven't done it yet, have you?'

'No. You'll be the first to know. Best man and bridesmaid in one.'

Duggan laughed and exhaled a stream of smoke out the window and looked over at the restaurant. The street was empty now.

'Jaysus,' Gifford muttered, shaking his head. 'Don't they teach you anything in G2? Don't blow smoke out a car window on a stakeout on a cold night.'

'It's a tactical manoeuvre,' Duggan nodded his head back towards Gifford's car. 'They'll try to avoid me and run straight into your friend's arms.'

'That's G2 all right. A distraction. Bit of a diversion.'

'Have you seen anyone interesting tonight?'

'I wouldn't recognise your man Goertz if he walked by me.'

'Anyone else?'

'Like who?'

'Anyone from the German legation? Or the IRA?'

Gifford thought about that for a moment. 'Interesting,' he said, 'that you lump them together. But no.' He nodded across at the Red Bank. 'They're a bunch of fantasists. Spend their time debating which of them will be Gauleiter for Munster or Dublin when the Nazis take over. Even the local lads couldn't be bothered with them. Never mind the Germans.'

'So why are we all sitting here then?'

'In case they're right, of course,' Gifford laughed. 'Stranger things have happened.'

Duggan tossed his cigarette end out the window and looked at his watch. It was well after eleven o'clock.

'Go up to the Gresham and thaw yourself out,' Gifford opened his door. 'I'll let you know if anything happens here.'

'Yeah?'

'Trust me,' Gifford gave him a lop-sided grin. 'Happy New Year.'

Duggan dumped his coat with a bored woman in the cloakroom and headed for the toilets. The Alex Caulfield band was playing a foxtrot, the music spilling out of the ballroom with the heat. Bill Sullivan pulled open the door of the gents as he was about to push it in.

'Hah,' Sullivan laughed. 'You're in the shithouse already.'

'Didn't you tell her I was going to be late?'

'But not nearly three hours late.'

'Fuck's sake, I told you I might be.'

'I hope it was worth it,' Sullivan pushed him out of the doorway to let someone else enter.

'What?'

'Whatever it was you were doing.'

'Where are we sitting?'

'Round to the right. At the back.'

Duggan stopped inside the ballroom and lit a cigarette, trying to identify their table. The dance floor was crowded, couples circling the room in a steady stream round the fulcrum of the revolving crystal ball, which sprayed out splashes of coloured light. A couple of the tables at the back right were empty, drinks standing like lonely sentinels, ashtrays full, but he couldn't figure out which was theirs. He turned to the bar and joined the queue and asked for a Paddy.

'Just the one?' the barman shouted at him.

Duggan nodded and leaned into the counter to pour water into the whiskey. He turned back to the dance floor and Sullivan and his girlfriend Carmel swept past. Sullivan indicated behind him with his thumb and gave him a broad wink. His would-be companion, Breda, was dancing with a tall man with blonde hair, moving fluidly and having an animated conversation. Carmel wiggled her fingers at him and gave him a sympathetic look over Sullivan's shoulder.

The music ended and couples drifted back to their tables. Duggan followed Sullivan and Carmel to a table in the corner and she greeted him with a peck on the cheek.

'Sorry I'm so late,' he said.

'You missed the dinner,' she said, looking around for Breda. A couple of their colleagues and their partners arrived at the table and greeted him.

'She's over there,' Sullivan pointed to the bar where Breda and the man she'd been dancing with were continuing their animated conversation. 'Go and get her.'

'She seems happy enough,' Duggan replied. 'It was only a matter of convenience, wasn't it?'

Carmel gave Sullivan a slit-eyed look that put him on notice of trouble later. Duggan smiled to himself, sipped his whiskey and relaxed into the warmth.

The band leader began the countdown to the new year and there was a ragged cheer, mainly from those who were already drunk, as 1941 was announced. The band broke into 'Auld Lang Syne' and they all stood and joined hands and wished each other a happy New Year, the unspoken fears of what it would bring making the atmosphere of enforced gaiety brittle.

Duggan had a couple more whiskies and danced with all his colleagues' wives and girlfriends, but Breda never came back to their table.

'You know who she's with?' one of his work colleagues whispered to him, looking over at the table she had joined. 'Somebody from the American legation.'

'Really?' Duggan followed his gaze to the distant table.

'That's David Gray, the US Minister. On the left.'

Duggan identified the elderly man on the left of the table. 'Who are the others?' he asked.

'The only other one I recognise is Chapin, the first secretary. Sitting next to Gray's wife. Don't know who your friend's with.'

Duggan was about to point out that Breda wasn't his friend but didn't bother.

She finally joined them after the national anthem marked the night's end, nodded briefly at Duggan and went off with Carmel to the ladies and to get their coats.

'Definitely want my money back now,' Duggan said to Sullivan.

'You'll have to get it back off her,' Sullivan grinned drunkenly.

When the two women came back Duggan offered a lame apology for his lateness. 'That's all right,' Breda said. 'I had a great time, thanks.'

The four of them left the hotel together, the sharp cold like an invisible wall that stopped them for a moment as they stepped out onto O'Connell Street. Taxis were lined up, a growing proportion of them old horse-drawn cabs as a result of the petrol rationing.

'Let's get a horse cab,' Carmel said.

'I've got a car,' Duggan announced, nodding across the street to where he was parked.

'How'd you get that?' Sullivan demanded as they crossed to it. 'Do they know you took it?'

'Do you want a lift or not?' Duggan said.

'Yes, please,' Carmel shivered.

Breda sat in the front with him and Duggan asked where they were going.

'Home, James, and don't spare the horses,' Sullivan commanded from the back seat.

'You can drop me first,' Breda said. 'Glasnevin. It's on the way to Carmel's.'

'You better direct me,' Duggan said. 'I'm not sure of the way.'

He felt a little light-headed from the whiskey and the car waltzed slightly on a bend and he realised the road was slippery and slowed down. In the back Carmel was giggling and Sullivan whispered something to her and she said, 'Stop that, Captain Sullivan,' in a tone that suggested she didn't mean it.

Breda leaned around her seat to look at them. 'Oh, captain, my captain,' she said and the two women burst into laughter at some private joke.

She directed him into a cul-de-sac of red-brick houses behind iron railings and small lawns and indicted where to stop. 'I'll walk you to the door,' he said, putting the car into neutral and pulling up the handbrake.

'There's no need. Thanks, I had a great time.' She turned back to Carmel. 'I'll call around tomorrow at two.'

Duggan dropped Carmel and Sullivan at her house in Mobhi Road and followed her directions back to the North Circular Road, heading for army headquarters. The road was empty, its trees spidery in the cold, the tall houses dark. He realised he was starving and lit a cigarette to kill the hunger.

He wasn't sure at first that he had heard it over the engine of the car, the flat crump-crump of explosions. He opened the window and there was a faint drone of an aircraft fading into the distance. Otherwise the silence of the road was undisturbed.

He sped up and went down Infirmary Road and turned into the Red House, seeing immediately that something was up. The sentry was already at the barrier, alert.

'What's happened?' Duggan asked.

'There's been an explosion across the river.'

'A bomb?'

'Sounded like two, sir.'

Duggan parked and hurried into the building and into the duty office where a harassed-looking lieutenant was on a phone, jotting down notes with his other hand. Another phone was ringing and Duggan picked it up and said, 'Duty office.'

'Who's that?' Duggan recognised McClure's voice and identified himself. 'What's happening?' McClure demanded.

'There seems to have been a couple of bombs.'

'Two, I think,' McClure interrupted. 'Unless there was an echo. Not far from here.'

Duggan knew he lived in Rathmines but his knowledge of the area was vague: the only times he'd been there had been to go to his uncle Timmy's house. The lieutenant, waiting for someone on the phone, signalled to him and pointed to a spot on a map of the city on his desk.

'Griffith Barracks,' Duggan said into the phone.

'What? The barracks was hit?'

The lieutenant shook his head and moved his finger a little to the right.

'No,' Duggan said. 'Near there. South Circular Road.' He twisted his head to read the street name under the lieutenant's finger. 'Donore something or other. I'll get up there.'

'Do that,' McClure said.

The lieutenant raised a finger to hold Duggan while he finished his conversation. 'Wait a moment,' Duggan said to McClure.

'There's more reports of explosions north of Drogheda and near Dundalk,' the lieutenant said, putting down his phone. It rang again immediately. 'And somewhere near Enniscorthy,' he added, picking up the phone.

Duggan repeated what he had said.

'Jesus Christ,' McClure said. 'I'm on my way in.'

Four

Duggan drove fast, his window open and collar up, listening for further sounds of planes and explosions. But the night was quiet, broken only by the distant bell of a fire engine or an ambulance. He followed the directions the sentry had given him, across Kingsbridge, right onto James's Street and left after the hospital. An ambulance bell began ringing as he got closer and then there were people hurrying along the footpath beyond Rialto. He parked the car near a cigarette factory and joined them, hurrying up the middle of the road, littered with stones and glass and bits of slate.

The street lighting, such as it had been, was out, but there were lights on the road ahead, vehicle lights and flashlights darting back and forth. The windows were gone in all the houses, curtains hanging out, and roofs blotched with random holes. Some of their occupants stood by their doors, looking shocked, overcoats and dressing gowns over their nightclothes, their breaths ballooning in the cold air, staring in silence at the centre of activity farther on. The air was sharp and bitter and smelled of gas and cordite and left a taste of dust on the tongue.

At the junction with Donore Avenue two gardaí with outspread arms were trying to keep people back. 'Please,' one of them said. 'Keep out of the way. There's still people in the collapsed houses.'

'Captain Duggan, army headquarters,' he said to him and passed by.

The litter on the road turned into a carpet of debris as he neared the centre of the explosion. A couple of the terraced houses had collapsed into a heap of rubble and rescue workers were still pulling chunks of masonry and bits of carpentry off the piles. The front walls of other houses had fallen out, exposing tilting upper floors, beds covered in plaster, dining tables, chairs smashed against walls, pictures askew. A little red oil lamp was still burning in front of a statue of the Virgin Mary on the return of a house missing the second flight of stairs.

Two fire engines were angled to cast their headlights on the rescue workers and an ambulance, lights on, waited behind them. A group of soldiers were trying to clear a path through the debris, shovelling bricks and stones and glass to one side. The only other noises were the hum of engines, the mumble of voices, and the crash of falling masonry as bits fell off some of the damaged houses and the rescue workers sifted through the demolished ones.

'Do you have somewhere to go?' an ARP warden asked a young woman with two small children hanging onto her nightdress. Her hair was covered in dust and the children's faces were streaked with dirt. 'Mrs McCarthy will take us in,' she said, on the verge of tears. 'Down the road.'

The warden called over one of his colleagues and asked him to take the woman and children to their neighbour's and ticked off a name on his clipboard. Another of his colleagues linked arms with an old woman who looked barely able to support the bull's wool army greatcoat around her shoulders. The warden stopped him and asked who she was and ticked her name on his list. Then he went to the next house and shone his torch through the hall door which was hanging half-open on one hinge and called out names. There was no response.

Duggan spotted a major dispatching more men to help the gardaí set up a cordon and saluted and introduced himself. 'Is the battalion intelligence officer here?' he asked.

'Lieutenant Kelly,' the major pointed to an officer standing by the crater in the road, stopping some soldiers from shovelling debris into it.

Duggan joined him and they swapped names. 'Might be some bits of the bomb in there,' Lieutenant Kelly said. 'Might identify whose it was.'

'Were there one or two?'

'Two. Another fell behind those houses. On the banks of the canal. Didn't do so much damage.'

'Many dead?'

'There's two children unaccounted for in there,' Kelly pointed towards one of the demolished houses where the rescue workers were lifting out a large sheet of ceiling. 'They got everyone out of the other one. A clergyman and his family. From the church down there.'

'How many wounded?'

'Don't know exactly. Ten or twenty gone to hospital. '

'Anyone see the bomber?' He looked up at the clear sky: the stars were sharp in the frosty air but were blacked out to the west by a cloud. More snow coming.

Kelly shook his head. 'Not that I know of. Heard the fucker myself. I wasn't long in the bed. Thought at first that he'd hit the barracks.' He gave a short laugh. 'Nothing sobers you up faster than that. We were here within minutes. Total chaos. Screaming and shouting. People running everywhere. Debris still falling. Choking dust.' He shook his head at the memory. 'I didn't think anyone could come out of those houses alive.'

The major interrupted them to order Kelly to get more men to clear all the gawkers back behind the cordons. 'And don't let anyone back into their houses if they're damaged. Tell them we'll keep everything safe if they're afraid of looting.'

'Yes, sir.'

Duggan wandered back towards Griffith barracks, past a Presbyterian church with all its windows gone. Its wayside pulpit still proclaimed, 'The Lord is good to all and His tender mercies are over all His workers.' Someone was inside with a flashlight and he caught a glimpse of the pews covered in chunks of plaster and dust. He came to the cordon on that side of the scene before he reached the barracks and turned back.

'They're all right,' one of the rescue workers at the demolished houses shouted. There was a ragged cheer and somebody began clapping. The ambulance moved forward along the path cleared for it and a couple of men went to the scene with stretchers. Duggan watched from a distance and then decided to go back to the Red House: he wasn't doing anything useful here.

There were fewer people in the immediate area of the bomb now as the gardaí and soldiers cleared the area. Ahead of him, Duggan saw a soldier trying to move back a young woman with an overcoat over what he thought at first was a red nightdress. She had her arms folded tight across her stomach and was ignoring the soldier and his orders, staring over his head at the rescue scene.

Duggan looked at her again and realised it was Gerda Meier. But she doesn't live here, he thought, confused. She raised a hand to push back her hair over her right ear and he saw a tear-drop earring and then a glimpse of a necklace above the top button of the coat and realised she was wearing an evening dress.

'D'you live here or what?' the soldier was saying, exasperation rising as she remained oblivious to his presence.

'It's okay.' Duggan showed him his ID. 'I'll handle it.' He waited until the soldier had moved away and said quietly, '*Was machen Sie hier?*'

She looked at him when she heard the German but gave no indication that she recognised him. 'You see?' she said in English, tightening her arms around herself. 'Even here. They're trying to kill us.'

'Who?' he asked, confused.

'The Jews. They won't even wait until they invade.' She seemed to see him for the first time, catching his confusion, and pointed to the building beside them. 'Look at the synagogue.'

Its windows were all gone and its pillars and pediment pockmarked and pitted like it had been bombarded. 'That's a synagogue,' he said, realising how stupid he sounded as soon as he said it. He hadn't really noticed it when he had arrived, presumed it was a theatre or hall or something.

'And that's the rabbi's house,' she pointed back behind him, to one of the demolished houses.

'I thought it was a clergyman,' he stammered. 'From the church down the road.'

'The other house,' she said, her look removing any doubt that she recognised him. 'Don't you know? This is where the Jews live in Dublin.'

He shook his head slightly. He had a vague memory of hearing somebody mention Little Jerusalem in some context or other but he had had no idea where exactly it was. 'No,' he admitted. 'I didn't know.'

She nodded, accepting his admission but not holding it against him.

'Do you know him?' he asked. 'The rabbi?'

'No. I don't know anybody here.' She paused. 'I don't live in this area.'

'They've all survived. Nobody's been killed.'

'Yes.' She gave a tired sigh.

A young warden ran by them towards someone up near the cordon, shouting, 'Put out that fucking cigarette. D'you want to kill us all?'

'I'll drive you home,' Duggan said.

'Yes,' she said.

In the car she remained quiet, lost in her own thoughts. Duggan tried to tread his way back to the city centre, down quiet streets that sparkled with frost in the headlights, where everyone seemed to be sleeping peacefully. But most must have heard the bombs. Are they all awake, lying there waiting for more to fall on this pretence of a peaceful sleeping city? he wondered.

'They might not have been aiming at the synagogue,' he said as they came upon Christchurch and he swung down into Dame Street.

'What do you mean?' she stirred, unfolding her arms.

'They might have been aiming at the barracks.'

'What barracks?'

'There's an army barracks just around the corner.'

She shook her head. 'I know them,' she said.

He waited for her to elaborate but she didn't. He slowed at a red traffic light and dug out his cigarette case, flipped it open with one hand and offered it to her as he edged carefully through the junction.

'I'll do it.' She took the case from his hand, extracted two cigarettes and put both in her mouth. He handed her his lighter as he sped up. She lit both and handed one to him.

'This war,' she inhaled deeply. 'This is why they started it. To kill us. They don't hide it. It's what they say themselves.'

'Did you have a bad time in Vienna? Before you left?'

'No. Not then. We left early, before they took over. My father was very wise, he saw what was coming. My uncles and aunts didn't believe him.' She shrugged. 'They know now. But it's too late.'

They went up O'Connell Street, past the Metropole and the GPO. Across the road the Gresham Hotel was dark, looking like it was unoccupied. Ringing in the New Year in the warm ballroom there a few hours ago seemed like a distant memory.

'My uncle Jacob is an obstetrician, a lovely man, so learned, civilised,' she said. 'He was one of those they made clean the footpath outside his hospital with a toothbrush. While they laughed and kicked and spat at them.' She inhaled again and waved her cigarette in a metaphorical shrug. 'You've read about all these things.'

Duggan made a non-committal noise. Yes, he had heard something about these things but it was all vague and distant and dismissed by some as propaganda. 'It must've been difficult coming here. Leaving your friends. Learning a new language.'

'Yes' she said.

'But you're safe here.' They were on Dorset Street, a railway bridge ahead of them. He looked out for Iona Road, knowing it was somewhere near here.

She gave him a curious glance that he caught. 'It's there,' she said, indicating the turn.

'I mean,' he said, 'they can't find you here now.'

She gave a bitter little laugh of disbelief.

'All the files were destroyed,' he added.

'What files?'

'About people,' he was about to say 'like you' but caught himself in time, 'about people who've come here from the Continent.'

'Destroyed by who?'

Fuck, he thought as he turned into her road. I shouldn't have told her that: it was probably secret information.

'By the government,' he said, too late to withdraw it. 'Sensitive files like that were burned last summer when people thought the Germans were about to invade.'

'That's true?' She pointed at a house on the left ahead of them and he let the car coast to the kerb.

'Yes,' he said. 'Please don't tell anybody that. I shouldn't have mentioned it.'

'I won't tell anyone,' she said in a tone that reassured him. 'But it won't matter anyway. There are always people who will tell them such things. Who will help them.'

Duggan thought of Peter Gifford's comment about the Friends of Germany dividing up the country between them under German rule. Some of them would be quick to bring an occupying force to Little Jerusalem. And Gerda's earlier remark that she didn't live there took on another dimension. Part of her efforts to hide her origins.

She pushed her cigarette into the ashtray. 'Don't speak to me in German again,' she said.

'I'm sorry,' he replied, taken aback. 'I know my accent is—'

'It's not that,' she cut him short. 'I don't want to hear it spoken.'

'What about the café? Mrs Lynch's?'

'I'll go there on Saturday. I only want to hear it from Nazis.'

'Okay,' he said, not really knowing what she meant but relieved she was continuing with the plan. 'I'll see you on Monday.'

'Yes.'

She got out of the car and took a key from her coat pocket and opened the hall door. It was closed before he had finished the first leg of a three-point turn.

The Red House was the busiest he had seen it since the summer's day when the government had ordered sensitive documents to be destroyed at the peak of a scare about a German invasion. Lights were on everywhere, men in mixtures of dress – uniforms, formal, casual – moved with purpose. The atmosphere was grim.

Captain Sullivan was in their office before him, grey-faced and dishevelled and looking like he had a premature hangover. He was on the phone, asking someone what height the planes were at when they crossed the coast. Commandant McClure came in, looking fresher than anyone else, and sank into a chair beside Duggan's end of the table. Duggan gave him a quick rundown on what he had seen and heard at the bomb site. 'Could they have targeted the Jewish area?' he concluded.

McClure rejected the idea with a shake of his head. 'They were at ten thousand feet. Could just about hit the lit-up area of the city from that height.'

So Griffith Barracks couldn't have been the target either, Duggan thought.

'But the point is that they did hit the lit-up area of the city,' McClure continued. He seemed keen to talk through what they knew. 'First time this has happened. They can't have thought they were over England since it's all blacked out. The only places in this part of the world with any lights burning are in this country.'

'And there were other bombs?'

'One north of Drogheda, another one near Enniscorthy. And the anti-aircraft unit in Dalkey saw two parachutes come down over Wicklow.'

'Parachutes?'

'Parachute mines apparently.' McClure looked at his watch. It was after six o'clock, more than three hours to daylight. 'This bloody night will never end. We haven't got any reports of explosions or where they came down yet but we'll get a spotter plane up at first light. And hope nobody stumbles across them before then.'

Captain Anderson from the British desk looked in, saw McClure and said, 'You were looking for me, sir?'

McClure waved him to another chair. 'Do we know where was hit in England tonight?'

'I haven't got a comprehensive report yet,' Anderson said. 'Seems to have been around the Severn estuary. Cardiff, Bristol.'

'So it could have been someone off course.'

'The lookout post at Carnsore said there were three planes in formation,' Sullivan had put down his phone. 'Heinkell IIIs, he thinks. There was a fair bit of cloud at the time there so he didn't get a long look at them. They were heading due north.'

'In formation,' McClure repeated to himself.

'Not a lost stray then,' Anderson said.

'You could put everything else down to someone being off course,' McClure said. 'But not hitting the lit-up city area.'

'What about the parachute mines?' Duggan offered.

'And those,' McClure agreed. 'Whoever dropped them must've seen the city lights too.'

'Were they not aimed at shipping? At Dublin bay?'

'The Luftwaffe uses them on land too,' Anderson said. 'In the London blitz. They can wipe out a whole street, no problem. There would've been a lot of deaths if they came down on the city.'

'But they haven't exploded,' McClure said, lighting himself a cigarette. 'We would've had reports of explosions in Wicklow if they had. Which suggests that their fuses were set for the sea. And that they were meant for our ships.'

'Or that they're on timers,' Anderson suggested.

McClure nodded. 'Put out a warning about timers to the ARP people, the guards. They should know not to go near them but just in case.'

An orderly came by with a tray carrying mugs of tea, a bottle of milk and a bowl of sugar. They each took one and sipped the strong tea, alone with their own thoughts for a few moments.

'Was it the same plane that dropped the bombs and the mines?' Duggan asked.

McClure gave Sullivan a questioning look. 'It's not clear yet, sir,' Sullivan said. 'Some of the reports suggest it was but we haven't got all the timings and directions straightened out.'

'So,' McClure looked from one to the other. 'What does it all mean?'

'The start of something?' Duggan asked.

'A new year,' Anderson shrugged with a twisted grin. 'Happy New Year.'

'You mean the start of an invasion?' McClure said. 'No. If they wanted to soften us up it would be with a much greater blow. Like Rotterdam. Wipe out Cork, someplace like that. To intimidate.'

'It could be a signal,' Anderson suggested. 'A message.'

'Could indeed,' McClure agreed.

'A reminder of what could happen if we give up our neutrality,' Anderson added. 'They were only small bombs on the city. They could've dropped much bigger ordnance. Like the parachute mines.'

'Let's not jump to any conclusions yet.' McClure got up and said to Duggan, 'Give Bill there a hand with collating all the reports and working out the chronology of events.'

'Yes, sir,' Duggan said.

McClure and Anderson left and Duggan moved down the table to Sullivan's space. 'At last you get to do some real intelligence work,' Sullivan passed him a wad of handwritten notes and torn-off pages from the telex.

He was about to leave and get a few hours' sleep when the phone rang at the other end of the table. He had to stand up to get it, noticing that the window was now a dull grey, no longer a darkened mirror. The tiredness hit him suddenly, his mouth felt dry and scratchy from too many cigarettes and his stomach was hollow with hunger.

'How's the captain?' a cheery voice said.

'Busy,' Duggan said, letting his shoulders sag partly at the sound of his uncle Timmy's voice.

'Yeah, yeah,' Timmy said, as if busyness was to be taken for grant-ed. 'You missed a great party last night. Drop around for the dinner and I'll tell you all about it. You'll love all this stuff.'

Duggan yawned, trying to figure out what he was talking about. Had Timmy been at the Friends of Germany event after all? Had he missed him going in? 'I'm just on my way to bed. Been up all night.'

'Wait'll you hear this,' Timmy chortled. 'It'll wake you up.'

'What?'

'Can't tell you over the phone.'

'I won't make it for dinner,' Duggan sighed, knowing that Timmy had his dinner in the middle of the day. 'Maybe later. There's a lot going on here.'

'Sure you don't know the half of it,' Timmy gave a happy laugh.

'You heard what happened last night. This morning,' Duggan corrected himself.

'You'd have to be as deaf as a Blueshirt faced with the truth not to hear it. Wasn't that far from here. As the crow flies.'

'I'll call you later.'

'Do that.' Timmy dropped his voice to underline his seriousness. 'This is more than gossip. Things you fellows need to know.'

'Like what?'

'Like don't be looking in the wrong direction.'

Duggan didn't try to hide his impatient sigh, knowing what Timmy meant. At least he was predictable. On this subject, at any rate.

'This is the time of year for pantomimes, isn't it,' Timmy's voice rose again, back to the cheery tone. 'Look out behind you!'

Duggan put down the phone and rested his hands on the table, letting his head drop down between his shoulders as the adrenaline of the last few hours ebbed. Timmy in that kind of good humour was more wearying than staying up all night. It meant only one thing: he was up to some kind of political skullduggery, deep in some conspiracy or other. That was the only thing that could make him so happy.

'Captain,' McClure snapped his fingers from the doorway. 'Go to bed. That was an order.'

'Yes, sir.' Duggan straightened up.

'And be back here by two o'clock,' McClure lightened the instruction with a grin.

'Thank you, sir,' Duggan replied, deadpan.

Five

The city seemed to be holding its breath. Air-raid wardens strolled the streets, alert for warning sounds. They had been put on standby for the night after a day of intense debate. People with air raid shelters considered spending the night in them, not wanting to overreact to one bombing, not wanting to regret their casualness later. Officials argued over whether sirens should be sounded at the approach of any aircraft. Should the reduced city lighting be turned into a full blackout? Everyone wondered if the early morning bombing had been a one-off event or the start of something. Whichever it was, the distant war had become more real.

Duggan cycled the way he had driven earlier but was stopped at a cordon blocking off the bomb site on the South Circular Road. A small group of people stood at the barrier looking past the bored young garda. There was nothing much to see: the area was lit by arc lamps and workmen moved to and fro against the sounds of hammering and sawing. He thought of using his ID to get through but decided not to: there was nothing more for him to see there. The investigators had finished their work, recovering enough fragments of the bombs to confirm that they were German.

He turned right onto Donore Avenue and crossed the Grand

Canal and cycled down by its right bank. Across the dark water he could make out the gash torn in the other bank by the second bomb. Frost was beginning to settle on the raw earth and the lights from the workmen's lamps on the road beyond shone through the gaps left in roofs and walls by the bomb. He turned onto Rathmines Road at the next bridge and pedalled as fast as he could between the tram tracks up the open road.

He still felt tired after a few hours' sleep, a brief glimpse of daylight as he went from the barracks to the Red House, and an afternoon of collating information, trying to determine the meaning of the night's events. The parachute mines had been found in farmland near Kilmacanogue and blown up by bomb-disposal officers. They were magnetic mines, intended to destroy ships.

'Did they check that they were armed first?' McClure had asked an officer from the ordnance disposal unit reporting on the mines.

'No, sir,' the officer made it clear with his tone that that would have been a crazy idea.

'So we don't know if they were armed?'

'There'd be no point in dropping them if they weren't.' The ordnance officer gave him a look that questioned McClure's sanity but Duggan, following the exchange, knew what the commandant had in mind. The Germans had dropped two small bombs on a relatively well-lit city that was easily identifiable and two parachute mines with much greater destructive capacity near the same easily visible area. If they were intended for shipping, how could they have missed the sea?

'It's looking like a message to me,' McClure said after the ordnance officer had gone.

'But what?'

McClure looked around to make sure there was no one within earshot. 'Maybe the serious consequences our friend in External

Affairs told us about last week. A warning to do what we're told about extending their legation.' McClure paused. He was looking tired now, his early morning beginning to catch up with him. 'Who knows? It could be just a reminder of our vulnerability.' He gave a weary smile. 'A sort of "Happy New Year" as Anderson said, and a "Remember to behave yourself". Or it could be an accident. But I find that hard to believe.'

It was hard to believe as well that it was still only New Year's Day, Duggan thought. The world seemed to have shifted along with the calendar. There had been so many warnings and scares and theories since the German blitzkrieg ended the phony war and overran France the previous summer that he had become fatalistic, no longer worrying so much about when the war would come here and how he would handle himself. Still, the bombing was a jolt, a reminder of how quickly things could change.

'Remember Mr Ó Murchú's warning,' McClure continued. 'Keep that speculation to yourself.'

'Yes sir,' Duggan said, aware that that was an order.

He arrived at Timmy's house feeling energised by the cycle. Timmy was still in high good humour, formally shaking his hand and wishing him a happy New Year at the door. 'Going to be an interesting one,' he added, rubbing his hands. 'The one that'll sort out a lot of outstanding issues.'

Timmy led him into the same room as before, its dining table still covered in documents overseen by a stack of free-postage Dáil envelopes that threatened to topple over. He sat down at the table, his back to the log fire, and Duggan took a chair opposite him. So this was a sort of official visit, he thought.

'You got to the party after all?' Duggan took the initiative.

'No, no. That was just in case anyone was ear-wigging on the phone. But I had a word with someone who was there. It was a bit of a damp squib. They didn't get the crowd they were expecting. No one of interest turned up.'

'I wonder what they think of their friends after last night.'

'Things aren't always what they seem,' Timmy said.

'The government has sent a formal protest to Berlin,' Duggan retorted. 'There was no doubt the bombs were German.'

Timmy snorted his disbelief and reached for a large brown envelope under his box of cigars. He took out three ten- by eight-inch photographs, looked at them, shuffled them into order, leaned across the table and placed them, face up, in front of Duggan. He took a cigar from the box and lit it slowly.

'The last of the cigars until next Christmas.' Timmy leaned back in his chair with satisfaction and blew smoke at the ceiling light. 'Unless there's something to celebrate before that. Though, to be honest with you, I'm not a great man for the cigars. An odd one is nice but I'd prefer a cigarette any day.'

Duggan was looking at the first photograph. It was of a document, taken at an angle from below, and the lighting was bad, too much on the top half, fading away lower down. He could read the headings easily, MOST SECRET and TO BE KEPT UNDER LOCK AND KEY, both underlined. But the text was more difficult as he scanned down the page, its typescript elongated by the angle and slightly out of focus. He took up the photograph, as though that would make it easier to read. Then he turned to the second and third photographs: they were also typewritten but on different typewriters and each from a different document.

Timmy watched him with an amused smile, humming a made-up tune in between blowing out streams of smoke without inhaling. 'Interesting, aren't they?' he said when Duggan finished reading and looked up.

'Are they authentic?'

'The real McCoy.'

'Have you got the rest of them?' Duggan took up the three photographs and spread them between his hands.

'There's enough there.'

There was indeed. Duggan glanced at the photographs again, reading phrases here and there. There certainly was enough there. If they were genuine.

'Where did you get them?'

Timmy gave him a disappointed look. 'You know I can't tell you that.' He straightened up and put out his cigar in the full ashtray, taking care not to push other butts and ash onto the table. 'What I want you to do is to make sure they get into the right hands.'

'Okay.'

'And I don't mean that fellow McClure.'

'He's my commanding officer.'

'I marked your card about him before,' Timmy pointed a finger. 'He can't be trusted when it comes to the Brits. He's a Protestant. Father was in the British Army.'

'He's totally loyal,' Duggan protested.

'To who?'

'To this country.'

'He'll bury them,' Timmy said with an air of certainty. 'You have to make sure they get into the right hands.'

'Whose?'

Timmy shrugged. 'I don't know. I hear there's a good lad there. From the North.'

'Captain Anderson?'

Timmy nodded. 'That could be him. A fellow with reddish hair?'

Duggan nodded and waved the photographs at him. 'Does the government know about these?'

'Don't worry about that. Or about the army brass. G2 needs to know. So you're not all looking the wrong way.'

'They're going to want to know where these came from,' Duggan said. 'That'll be their first question.'

Timmy sighed, as if his patience was being tested. 'There's always a patriotic Irishman everywhere. Even in unexpected places.'

'They're from someone in the British government?'

'Lookit,' Timmy shook his head with impatience, 'they're real. Which is obvious to anyone with a brain in his head. Churchill's made no secret of what he thinks. He wants a rematch of the War of Independence. Still hasn't got over the fact that we beat the great empire. The British gutter press is howling for our blood. They're going to try and starve us first and then invade if that doesn't get them what they want.' He pointed at the photographs. 'It's all there.'

'Okay,' Duggan nodded. 'I'll make sure they're passed on. But they'll still want to know where I got them.'

'Don't you fellows have your own sources of information?'

'Yes, but they'll want to know which one.'

Timmy grimaced, thought for a moment, and then nodded. 'If you have to,' he said. 'But only if you have to. And keep it vague.'

He tossed over the envelope and Duggan put the photographs in it. 'Jaysus,' Timmy said, business now concluded to his satisfaction. 'I forgot to ask if you had a mouth on you.'

'I'm all right. I had something to eat before I came out.'

'Are you sure now? I was always starving at your age. And look at me now,' he rubbed a hand over his bulging stomach and laughed. 'Eight months pregnant.'

'I better get back,' Duggan stood up.

'How's your father for petrol?' Timmy got up too.

'All right,' Duggan said, used to Timmy's sudden conversational swerves. 'He had more than half a tank at Christmas.'

'That won't last long now.'

'They've started already?' Duggan asked in surprise, raising the envelope of photographs. One of them contained a plan to cut off imports to Ireland of essential supplies of oil and coal and exclude other Irish supplies from Atlantic convoys.

'Maybe,' Timmy sighed. 'Word is there's going to be a shortage anyway for the next few weeks. If your father needs any more I've got a few cans. Tell him they're in the turf shed, on the left. Under the turf.'

'Okay. Thanks.'

'Don't tell him on the phone. Or in a letter,' Timmy warned.

'I don't know when I'll be down there next. You'll probably be down before me.'

'Just send word. He can just drive in and fill up himself if he needs it.'

'Thanks,' Duggan repeated, knowing that his father would walk any distance before he would ever take up Timmy's offer. His father had had a low opinion of Timmy ever since their days together in the old IRA during the War of Independence. Duggan knew why and his father knew he knew, but neither had ever mentioned it again after their one and only conversation about it.

'At least the bastards can't starve us into submission this time,' Timmy said, leading him out to the hall door. 'They can cut off the petrol and coal and tea and things. But we've got more than potatoes to eat now.'

Timmy opened the door but stopped with it half open, blocking Duggan's exit. 'By the way,' he said, 'that party last night. The Friends of Germany. Damp squib, like I told you. One of their own head bottle washers didn't even turn up. Fellow called Quinn. Lives over in Ranelagh someplace. Word was that he was too busy entertaining a VIP visitor over the Christmas.'

Duggan raised a quizzical eyebrow. Timmy raised his shoulders in a 'how would I know' gesture. Neither said anything.

'Mind how you go,' Timmy called after him as Duggan pushed hard on the pedals to get the bicycle moving through the gravel of the driveway. 'It might be a bit slippery out there.'

Duggan replayed the conversation in his mind as he cycled, his breath swept away by his speed through the cold air. With Timmy, what he didn't say was often as important as what he did say, so you had to parse and analyse everything. But Timmy's conversation faded in importance compared to the photographs in the envelope now flapping in his right hand as he gripped the freezing handlebar.

Ten divisions, he kept thinking. A hundred thousand men or so. That's what the British Army thought they'd need to capture the ports on the west coast and to hold enough of the country for the move to work. And we've got what? Fifty thousand badly-armed men, few heavy weapons, no tanks to speak of, hardly any air force. And they were bringing in the numbers already, as the man he had called Murphy in the back of the pub in Dundalk had told him.

But the information in the photographs seemed to suggest that the invasion was the third stage of their plan. The first was to reduce imports to Ireland of various things, cutting back their space on supply convoys. The second was to escalate it into an all-out economic war, adding things which Duggan didn't really understand about currencies and insurance for Irish ships. And if these moves didn't work, if they didn't persuade the government that the fate of the convoys was as essential to Ireland's survival as to Britain's, and to provide ports on the west coast, then they'd invade.

Which meant, he thought as he topped the canal bridge at Portobello and freewheeled down to Kelly's Corner, that the war was coming here. If we give the British what they want, the Germans will see it as an act of war. If we don't, the British will invade and the

Germans will come to our aid. The only choice, if there was a choice, was who to fight.

McClure caught sight of him as he came into the Red House and was stopped in his tracks by something in Duggan's face. 'I need to talk to you,' Duggan said in response to McClure's unasked question. McClure led him without a word to an unoccupied office and shut the door. Duggan handed him the envelope and tried to unbutton his overcoat but his fingers were numb with cold. He blew on them for a moment while McClure propped himself against the windowsill and looked at the photographs.

'Your uncle?' McClure looked up. Duggan nodded.

McClure held the photographs in one hand and got out a cigarette packet and shook it so he could put one in his mouth without touching it. Duggan stepped forward and lit it for him and shrugged off his overcoat and lit a cigarette for himself.

'Did he say where he got them?' McClure didn't look up this time.

'No.' Duggan watched him taking his time reading. Was Timmy right? he wondered. Could he be trusted to fight the British? Yes. He shook his head mentally, ridding it of Timmy's poisonous suspicions.

Something else Timmy had said came back to him. The Northern officer in G2, with the reddish hair. Did that mean that Timmy had met Captain Anderson? Or someone had told him about Anderson, described him to Timmy. And he could be trusted, which meant in Timmy's lexicon that he was anti-British. Of course, it struck him suddenly, that made perfect sense. Put the pro-British officers on the German desk and the pro-German ones on the British desk: both would be naturally suspicious and determined to thwart every move by their targets.

And where am I in all this? he wondered. He was on the German desk for the very simple reason that he spoke German. And to watch McClure? Was that why Timmy had pulled strings to get him moved from the infantry to G2? Were these photos a test of McClure's loyalty?

He rubbed his eyes to clear his head, telling himself to stop creating conspiracies, falling into Timmy's way of looking at the world. But where do I stand? Who do I want to win the war? He had grown up with stories of derring-do from the War of Independence, although his father refused to talk about it or his part in it: daring escapes, thrilling gunfights, brilliant tactical moves, great ambushes. Decent men forced to fight by centuries of oppression and then by Black and Tan atrocities, murders, burnings, torture. Part of him didn't want the old enemy to win. But did that mean he wanted Germany to win? He didn't really know. He just wanted to be left out of it all. Maintain neutrality.

'Does he have any more of these?' McClure broke through his reverie.

'He wouldn't say.'

'So Churchill's not bluffing,' McClure pushed himself upright and dropped the photographs on a table. 'It wasn't just rhetoric in the House of Commons. And his complaint about the ports wasn't what the government chose to interpret it as, simply a statement of fact, of the burden it imposes on the British.'

'If they're authentic,' Duggan nodded at the photos.

'They look authentic but it'd be nice to see some more. Especially the conclusions and decisions.'

'I'll ask again.'

'I presume he's given them to his political colleagues.'

'Presume so. He said he wanted us, G2, to have them. So we weren't looking the wrong way.'

'He thinks last night's bombs weren't German,' McClure said to himself.

'Timmy can't go from A to B without taking in X and Y and a few other letters in between.'

'That's a good way of putting it,' McClure gave him an approving look.

Duggan felt embarrassed: that was something his father had said about Timmy, on one of the rare occasions he mentioned him at all. 'It doesn't look like we'll be able to stay out of the war,' he said. 'One way or another we're going to get dragged in.'

'Depends,' McClure leaned across the table to put out his cigarette. 'The British would be crazy to invade and they must know that. At least the military must know that. But the politicians sometimes have different priorities. All we can do is try to make it not worth anyone's while to come here.' He stretched himself. 'It's like playing chess against two more powerful players at the same time with both chess boards linked so that your defensive moves on one creates dangers on the other.'

McClure picked up the photographs and threw the envelope in a bin. 'The colonel's called a conference for eight in the morning to draw up an intelligence assessment for the minister. I'll bring these up at it. You better be around in case they have any questions.'

'There's nothing more I can tell them,' Duggan made no secret of his apprehension at being grilled about Timmy.

'It probably won't arise. Just in case.'

There was a peremptory knock at the door and it opened at almost the same time and Captain Sullivan put his head in. 'We've just had a report from a lookout post of two Heinkels crossing the coast south of Wicklow Head.'

'Heading this way?'

'Heading north-west.'

'North-west?' McClure stopped, surprised. 'What's the target? Derry? That's probably beyond their range from that direction.'

He hurried out of the room and turned back to them as they followed. 'Get on the phones and try and chart their course as clearly as possible.'

'What was that cosy little chat about?' Sullivan demanded as they returned to their own office.

'Secrets,' Duggan smiled at him.

Back in their office Sullivan took a pound note from his pocket and put it down on the table in front of Duggan. 'Your money back,' he said. 'You owe her half a crown change.'

'You asked her for it?' Duggan looked at him in amazement.

'No. She offered. Said it was only fair. She had a great time and wouldn't have been able to go if you hadn't invited her.'

'Tell her thanks,' Duggan said, flicking a half-crown coin to Sullivan. 'That's very good of her. And tell her I'm sorry I was so late.'

'That's why she had a good time,' Sullivan sniggered as he caught the coin. 'She got to meet that fellow from the American legation. Got a date with him now.'

'Who is he anyway?'

'He's got some strange name. Max something.' He searched his memory. 'Max Linqvist.'

'What does he do in the legation?'

'Cultural attaché.'

Duggan laughed, thinking of Ó Murchú's dismissal of the extra German diplomats being described as cultural attachés when they were almost certainly intelligence people.

'What?' Sullivan gave him a sharp look.

'He didn't look very cultured to me,' Duggan backtracked. 'Looked like a bit of a chancer.'

'Oh, jealous are you?' Sullivan rubbed his hands in delight. 'Wait'll I tell Breda. She'll be even more delirious.'

The phone rang and Sullivan picked it up and Duggan heard him exclaim, 'Jesus!' as he pulled over a notepad and sat down and began taking notes. He looked up when he finished and said in bewilderment, 'They've bombed Carlow.'

'Carlow?' Duggan repeated, equally bewildered.

'Somewhere near it. Out in the country.'

'What's there?'

'How the fuck would I know?' Sullivan left the room in a hurry with his notepad.

Carlow, Duggan thought to himself. That couldn't make any sense. He suddenly remembered he hadn't told McClure what Timmy had told him about the Friends of Germany man called Quinn and his important visitor. He had been about to when Sullivan interrupted them.

McClure was in a corridor telling Sullivan to get down to the scene of the bombing as quickly as possible. 'I want to know everything you can pick up about it,' he said. 'Every little thing.'

'Yes, sir,' Sullivan said, a mixture of apprehension and enthusiasm on his face. He rarely got out of the office, one of his gripes with Duggan, who was always out of the office.

'There seems to be casualties,' McClure said to Duggan. 'All unclear at the moment.'

'There was something else I meant to mention to you,' Duggan said apologetically and told him quickly what Timmy had said about Quinn.

McClure's reaction was interrupted by someone shouting, 'There's bombs falling on the Curragh!'

There was a shocked silence around them. 'On the camp?' McClure called back, seeking confirmation that it was the military camp, the army's main base, that was under attack.

'Not sure, sir,' the voice which had announced the news said. 'HEs and incendiaries falling in the area. No reports of direct hits.' And added, 'Yet.'

McClure looked at Duggan. 'Maybe you were right. Maybe we are the target. Two nights running.' He shook his head and walked away but stopped and turned back. 'Check it out.'

'What?' Duggan asked in confusion.

'That fellow you just mentioned. Quinn.'

'Now?'

McClure nodded and walked away.

Six

Duggan felt like the pupil kept in at break time as a punishment while everyone else played outside. He was aware of the heightened background noises in the building, the phones ringing, doors banging, hurrying footsteps, urgent voices. But he didn't feel excluded, only because he knew why McClure had told him to check out Quinn while mayhem may be about to descend. High explosives and incendiaries on the Curragh, he kept thinking at the back of his mind as he turned the pages of the file on the Friends of Germany. 'Serious consequences.' The Germans hadn't been making empty threats.

It was obvious from the file that G2 had someone in the inner council of the Friends of Germany. There were detailed reports of all their meetings. He skimmed over the motions of congratulations to Adolf Hitler for his speech on the seventeenth anniversary of the Munich beer hall putsch in November, the condemnations of parliamentary democracy and capitalism for undermining the moral fibre of the Gael, and the debates on how the new European order would work in Ireland. Peter Gifford hadn't been exaggerating too much either, he thought. They were planning to turn the country into four regions, each province controlled by a Gauleiter. And some of them clearly saw themselves as in the running for the roles.

Quinn was a regular contributor to their discussions. A brief biography described him as aged thirty-nine, a clerk in the Electricity Supply Board, a devout Catholic who had wavered a little when he witnessed the German renaissance under Nazi rule while on a cultural exchange programme in Berlin. On his return to Ireland he kept up his links with the local *Ausland* branch of the Nazi party in Dublin until its effective dissolution at the start of the war when its members returned to Germany.

There was nothing in the file yet about their New Year's Eve event. Duggan lit a cigarette and sat back in his chair, half an ear still on the hubbub outside, wondering what to do. Quinn had obviously been close to the Nazi Party members in Dublin but they were all gone. He would probably help a German spy if asked. But would a German spy ask? Surely that'd be too big a risk for Goertz. On the other hand, there was no record of Quinn being arrested or questioned or kept under surveillance. He and his friends tended to be dismissed as fantasists or lunatics, an irrelevant sideshow.

Until they emerge on the victorious side, Gifford had said. Gifford, he thought. He checked his watch. It was just after midnight but there was a fifty-fifty chance that Gifford was on the night shift again. He picked up the phone and had to wait for the operator to get around to him and give him the number of the Special Branch in Dublin Castle.

To his surprise, he got Gifford on the line. 'Do you know a Friend of Germany called Quinn?' he asked.

Gifford gave a theatrical sigh. 'You're not still sitting in D'Olier Street in your monkey suit, are you?'

'He might be harbouring an interesting visitor for Christmas.'

'Christmas is over.'

'I know, but,' Duggan hesitated before committing himself, 'but there's a chance he's still there.'

'Why would you think that?'

'Information received.'

'You been reading our manual?' Gifford laughed. 'Looking for a real job?'

'Just trying to make you look good,' Duggan retorted. 'Improve your arrest record.'

'So who're we going to arrest? This Quinn fellow?'

'I'm more interested in whoever might be staying with him.'

'What's his address?'

Duggan told him and Gifford said he'd call back. He sat back, aware that he was probably exceeding his instructions. But there was no one to ask for direction at the moment. Everybody was too busy. And what if Goertz was there? And if the rumours were true? That he was being allowed to remain at liberty, as a conduit to the German military? But McClure had said that wasn't true. And they had tried to capture him several times before. All he was doing was checking out Timmy's information about Quinn.

The phone rang shortly afterwards and the sentry at the front gate said, 'Your Special Branch escort is here, sir.'

Duggan hurried out and was met by Gifford. 'That was quick,' he said.

'A few of the lads were bored,' Gifford led him towards the first of two cars on Infirmary Road. 'Dying for something to do.'

Duggan sat into the front passenger seat, Gifford into the driver's seat. 'Captain Duggan, sarge,' Gifford said to the older of the two men in the back seat and pointed a thumb at the Red House as they went by. 'The big new brain in there.'

'Another young fucker wet behind the ears,' the sergeant growled at him. He was in his late thirties and looked too big for the car, squashed beside another large man. 'Who are we apprehending?'

'There may be a German agent there,' Duggan said as they drove off.

'You have a search warrant and all that?' the sergeant demanded.

'Ah, no,' Duggan admitted. 'I thought we'd just call on Mr Quinn and talk to him.'

The sergeant snorted and the other man in the back seat gave a short laugh. 'What's the word from the Curragh?' the sergeant demanded.

'I haven't heard the latest,' Duggan admitted. 'Some high explosive bombs and incendiaries were dropped but they missed the camp. There's a full scale alert there.'

'Pity they didn't hit Tintown,' the sergeant said. Tintown was the slang for the internment camp holding IRA men. 'Solve a lot of our problems. Even better if their own friends did it.'

'They won't do it,' the other man said with a touch of regret. 'They'd only hit their own as well.' The internment camp for German combatants was beside Tintown. The one for British internees was at the other end of the military camp.

'They should move Tintown to Little Jerusalem,' the sergeant said.

Duggan was about to suggest that the previous night's bombing couldn't have been aimed at the Jews but held his breath. They crossed Charlemont Street Bridge and Gifford asked the sergeant if he wanted him to stop on the main road. 'No,' the sergeant said. 'Drive right up to the house. We only want to have a chat with Mr Quinn.' The other detective sniggered. 'But quietly,' the sergeant added. 'No lights.'

Gifford turned off the main road into a terrace of small red-brick houses behind short gardens. Duggan realised he knew this road: it was where his cousin Nuala had been staying with a friend earlier in the year. Gifford drove slowly, checking the numbers on either side and calculating where Quinn's house was. 'Should be the eleventh on the left,' he said quietly, flicking off the car's lights. He cut the engine as they approached and let the car coast to a stop outside the house. They all stepped out, leaving their doors open. The sergeant went back to the other car and sent the men from it in search of the laneway running behind the houses.

The night was calm and the road was quiet. All the houses were dark except for one opposite where there was a barely noticeable red glow in an upstairs window. A holy lamp, Duggan thought, remembering the red votive lamp in one of the shattered houses on the South Circular Road the previous night. There was no sign of life in Quinn's house. The garden in front was well tended, spiky bushes shaped and the grass trimmed around the edges.

The sergeant strolled back to them, hands in his trouser pockets, his overcoat flapping open, looking around like he had just arrived from the country and wasn't used to suburban streets. He stopped when he reached them and did a full circle, nodding at last to Gifford. Gifford opened the iron gate carefully, lifting it as it began to scrape on the ground and Duggan and the sergeant followed him up the short path to the door. The other detective stayed where he was, on the road beside the car.

The sergeant lifted the brass knocker and banged it down hard three times. The noise shattered the silence, seeming to reverberate along the street. The sergeant waited a moment, then bent down and raised the letter box flap with care and took a quick look followed by a slower one. He put his mouth to the opening and shouted 'Garda Síochána!' and hammered the door again.

In the silence that followed there was a creak above them as someone raised a stiff window. The sergeant stepped backwards to see what was happening and there was a smooth metallic click and Duggan thought, hammer, he's cocking a gun – and in the same instant the detective on the street shouted, 'Watch out!' There was a bang above them, and the sergeant hurled forward into Duggan and smashed him against the wall.

The detective on the street fired two quick shots and glass broke and shards fell around them and there was a return shot from upstairs. The sergeant had his revolver out, took a step back and fired two quick shots at the window. More glass broke. There was a moment's silence. Duggan, flat against the wall, tried to get his breath back, feeling like his ribcage had been squashed. Gifford was against the wall on the other side of the door, his revolver in hand. All three of them watched the detective leaning on the roof of the car, his gun pointed at the upstairs window, trying to read the expression on his face in the gloom. He raised his arms in a signal of ignorance.

There was a burst of shots from the back of the house, several guns firing at once, impossible to tell how many rounds. More glass shattered and a door banged and two more shots sounded from more than one gun. The detective on the road reached into the car and came through the gate at a run and kicked the hall door. The lock gave and the force of the kick bounced the door off the wall behind, knocking something over. The detective pushed the door open with his foot and dodged inside, his torch flashing from side to side. The sergeant followed and Gifford went after him but the sergeant snapped, 'Watch the car.'

Duggan bent down, his hands on his knees, catching his breath, and thinking that couldn't be Goertz. He'd know better than to try and shoot his way out. He was an experienced agent. Or would he? And hoping it wasn't Goertz, and that he wasn't dead in the back garden now. Jesus, he thought, what would the Germans do if we've shot one of their agents? Would they care that he fired first? And it was all his, Duggan's, doing.

Gifford gave him a worried look. 'You hit?'

Duggan shook his head. 'Your sergeant mistook me for a shortcut.'

'Yeah, he does that a lot.'

The door had swung half shut and Gifford pushed it open with his foot and clicked on the hall light. There was a man on the stairs in a plaid dressing gown. Gifford swung his revolver up, the hammer still cocked, ready to fire, and the man raised his hands over his head. 'Don't shoot,' he said. Duggan, outside, squinted through the gap under the door hinge and saw a slice of white face.

'Who are you?' Gifford demanded.

'Seamus Quinn,' the man said. 'I didn't know.'

'Who else is in the house?'

'Only my wife. In the bedroom.'

'Tell her to come down.'

Quinn called to her and she appeared a moment later at the top of the stairs in a pink dressing gown. She put her hands up tentatively.

'We didn't know,' Quinn said again.

'Didn't know what?'

'That Jimmy had a gun.'

'Who's Jimmy?'

'My cousin,' the woman said. Duggan breathed a sigh of relief – it wasn't Goertz.

'He's a bit hot-headed,' Quinn offered.

There were footsteps on the path outside and Gifford stepped into the hall, his back against the wall so he could glance behind. The sergeant and the other detectives were leading a man to the car. He was handcuffed and wearing only a shirt and trousers: he was shivering either from the cold or the violence.

Duggan stepped back to them and told the sergeant that the owner and his wife were in the hall and what she had said. The sergeant walked into the house and demanded, 'Jimmy who?'

'Burke,' the woman said.

'From?'

'Mayo. He's my cousin.'

'He's in the IRA.' The sergeant made it a statement.

'He's a bit hot-headed,' Quinn said again.

'He's lucky he's a shite shot,' the sergeant snorted, 'or he'd be going for the big drop. So it's only attempted murder of gardaí in the course of their duties at the moment. And you're in for aiding and abetting.'

'We didn't know,' Quinn pleaded. 'We didn't know he had a gun.'

The sergeant nodded towards the car. 'You're coming down to the station.'

'Are we under arrest?'

'Don't get fucking smart with me. Get in the car.'

'Can we get dressed?'

The sergeant thought for a moment and then said to Gifford, 'Watch them.'

Gifford followed the couple up the stairs. 'Sorry this didn't work out,' Duggan said quietly to the sergeant.

'It's worked out grand,' the sergeant gave him a crooked smile. 'Much better than some German. Another fellow for Tintown. If it's still there.' He turned back as he was leaving and added, 'Have a look around. With your search warrant.'

At the top of the stairs Gifford was standing at the half-open door of the main bedroom, watching Quinn get dressed, his wife shielded by the door. Duggan went into the small box room from which the shots had been fired. The cold night air came through the broken window. Blankets and sheet were thrown back on the single bed where Burke had jumped up at their knock and an eiderdown had slipped to the floor. A small cardboard suitcase was open on the floor, a jumble of clothes spilling out of it. Duggan rifled through it quickly and looked under the bed, pulled back all the bedclothes and lifted the mattress, went through the pockets of a jacket on the back of the door. There was nothing of interest.

He moved to the back bedroom, a bigger room with a wider bed. The top half of the window was smashed and the glass from a picture of the Sacred Heart on the opposite wall was on the floor. He looked under the bed and opened a dark wooden wardrobe and flicked through some dresses and blouses and a light raincoat. There were two pairs of worn women's shoes on the floor and beside them a brown paper parcel tied up with string. Duggan lifted it out onto the bed and tried to open the knot. His fingers were cold and he blew on them for a moment.

Outside, Gifford was saying, 'All right, come on,' and he heard them clump down the stairs a moment later.

The knot was too tight to open and he gave up on it and tried to force one end of the string over a corner. It gave after a moment and he opened back the rough brown paper. Inside were two stacks of leaflets, one in English and one in Irish. He picked up an English one and realised that they were all the same, English on one side, Irish on the other.

He scanned it and then sat down on the bed to read it. 'Soldiers of Eire,' it was headed. 'We have come to help you in your historic struggle against the British warmongers. Do not resist us. Come to us. Keep your weapons. Join us in the fight against the common enemy. Together we will free Ireland from the imperialism which has oppressed you for centuries.' It was signed *Oberkommando der Wehrmacht* and decorated at each corner with crossed flags, the Irish tricolour and the German swastika.

Duggan was scanning the Irish version, an accurate and good translation, when Gifford came in and picked up one of the leaflets. He gave a quiet whistle. 'That's not Jimmy's work,' he said.

'Wouldn't think so,' Duggan said.

'They're all gone to the Bridewell,' Gifford said. 'The sarge said we were to stay here until some uniforms arrive. Apparently Mr Quinn is very worried about the security of his property. So,' he looked around, 'we might as well have a look-see.'

They took their time going through the rest of the house, looking in and under drawers, in and behind wardrobes and cupboards, pulling up carpets, checking behind pictures, poking in the barrel of soil holding a Christmas tree, but found nothing more. A uniformed garda arrived to take up a position outside the broken door and Gifford asked him where they would get a lift back to the Bridewell. He laughed at him and told him to walk, young fellows like them. Duggan parcelled up the leaflets again and carried them under one arm as they walked through deserted streets. Frost sparkled in the pools of light from the occasional street lamps and the silence was broken only by their footsteps.

Gifford stopped on the canal bridge and sniffed, closing his eyes and letting his head tilt backwards. 'Does that remind you of home?'

'What?'

'The turf smoke.' Gifford sniffed again at the faint smell from the previous night's fires.

'I didn't notice,' Duggan shrugged.

'Jaysus,' Gifford started walking again. 'Culchies. You'll have us all smelling like bogmen. And we won't even know it.'

'Here,' Duggan handed him the packet of leaflets. 'You carry them for a bit.'

Quinn was still in an interview room when they got to the Bridewell. Gifford took a couple of leaflets from the package and showed them to his sergeant who gave them a cursory glance. 'Can we talk to him?' Gifford asked.

'You and him?' the sergeant inclined his head towards Duggan. Gifford nodded. 'All right. He says he knows nothing about anything.'

'We'll see what he knows about this.'

Quinn was slumped in a chair behind a scarred wooden table, huddled into himself. He was dressed now in a dark suit with a V-neck pullover and a shirt and tie but they all seemed to be too big for him. His head hung down, dark wavy hair facing them, and his hands were joined loosely between his legs. He didn't look up when they came in and took the chairs across the table from him.

Gifford and Duggan studied him. He didn't look much like a Gauleiter, Duggan thought. Or like the man who had firm political opinions at the Friends of Germany meetings. He looked more like a man in shock.

Gifford slid one of the leaflets across the table under his eyes. 'You know what this is?'

Quinn didn't raise his head and they couldn't tell if he could see the leaflet.

'I'll tell you what it is,' Gifford paused, waiting for a reaction. There was none. 'Do you want me to tell you what it is?'

Quinn gave a barely perceptible shrug.

'Treason.' Gifford waited a moment than added, spacing out the words. 'Straight. Forward. Treason.'

Quinn looked up, bewildered, and then dropped his eyes to the leaflet.

'A hanging offence,' Gifford continued. 'Pure and simple.' He let Quinn read through the leaflet. 'Inviting the Defence Forces of this country to surrender to a foreign power. Treason. Pure and simple.'

'They're not invaders,' Quinn said.

'Oh?' Gifford masked his delight with mock surprise at having engaged him. He tapped the leaflet under Quinn's nose. 'Where does it say "Thanks for the invitation, we came as soon as we could"?

That's not what it says though, is it? It says, "Surrender now, or else." '

Quinn shook his head.

'So, when are they coming?' Gifford demanded. 'When's the invasion?'

A brief look of interest – maybe hope, Duggan thought – flashed across Quinn's face and he straightened a little. He said nothing.

'When were you going to distribute these?' Gifford continued.

'What?' Quinn looked bewildered again.

'As soon as the invasion started? Just beforehand?'

'Look,' Quinn sighed. 'I've never seen this before.'

Gifford gave a cynical laugh. 'The man who knows nothing. Who didn't know his wife's cousin was an armed IRA man. Who didn't know his German friends were coming. Even though,' he picked up the leaflet and waved it in Quinn's face, 'he was preparing for their arrival.'

'Where's my wife?'

'Next door,' Gifford snapped. 'Having her neck measured for the rope.'

'Look, she—'

'Once the questioning is finished that'll be that,' Gifford interrupted him. 'Charged with treason. Up before a military tribunal. Only one possible sentence.' Gifford gave a harsh laugh. 'You think there'll be mass prayer vigils outside Mountjoy jail the night before the two of you are hanged? People on their knees in the street, saying the rosary? Calling on Jesus and his Holy Mother to save you with a last-minute reprieve? To save a couple who did their best to bring the war here? You're out of your fucking mind.'

'She knows nothing. She's not involved in anything.'

'Oh for fuck's sake,' Gifford groaned. 'Don't give me this gallant shite. She's as guilty as you are. It's in her house as well as yours.'

'What?'

'This,' Gifford waved the leaflet.

'I never saw it before,' Quinn pleaded.

'He thinks this is a game,' Gifford said to Duggan. 'He things he's in the pictures. Up on the big screen. Cary Grant. A hero protecting his wife. Hundreds of these leaflets in their house and he's going to do the manly thing.' He threw his hands up in despair.

Duggan kept his eyes on Quinn, realising that Quinn had not seen him before. '*Wo ist Ihr besonderer Weihnachtsbesuch?*' Duggan demanded. Where is your special Christmas visitor?

Quinn's eyes darted to Duggan and fixed on him with a look of horror.

'*Sie verstehen die Frage,*' Duggan said evenly, a statement. You understand the question.

Quinn seemed unable to break the stare but he wasn't really seeing Duggan.

'He left the leaflets in your house,' Duggan switched to English. 'In the wardrobe in the back bedroom. Where he stayed.' He took Quinn's silence as confirmation and nodded to Gifford. He turned back to Quinn. 'When is he coming back for them?'

Quinn said nothing.

'Or were you to deliver them to somebody else?' Duggan continued.

Quinn remained silent. Gifford sighed with impatience. 'I'm fed up with this shite,' he pushed his chair back and yawned. 'Let's get them charged. Hand them over to the military tribunal. We get to bed. They get hanged.'

'Give him another minute,' Duggan said. 'He needs time to think.'

They both stared at Quinn, who dropped his head. Seconds ticked by slowly. Quinn didn't move. Gifford looked at Duggan and shook his head. Duggan nodded. They both pushed back their chairs noisily and stood up.

As they walked out the door Gifford said to Duggan, 'We'll charge her first. Get her before the tribunal today.'

Quinn muttered something and Duggan paused. '*Ich wusste es nicht*,' Quinn repeated.

'Don't waste your time,' Gifford snorted and walked out, letting the door bang behind him.

'What didn't you know?' Duggan asked in German.

'That that was in the house,' Quinn nodded at the leaflet. He seemed more willing to talk in German.

'He didn't tell you?' Duggan said. 'He didn't trust you.'

Quinn winced, like he'd been poked in the ribs.

'Did Herr Goertz trust you with his real name?'

Quinn glanced up quickly and Duggan tried to decipher whether that meant a yes or a no. Or just that he knew who Goertz was.

'*Ich wusste es nicht*,' Quinn repeated, more an admission to himself that he had been used than a reply to Duggan. He dropped his head and shrank into himself again.

Gifford was waiting outside in the corridor and gave him an enquiring look. 'I don't think he knew those leaflets were there,' Duggan said. 'But he knows who Goertz is. And there's a strong chance Goertz was the one staying with him over Christmas. He knows more than he's telling us.'

'Such powers of deduction,' Gifford exclaimed. 'You ever thought of becoming a detective?'

Duggan ignored him. 'We should go back and keep an eye on the place. See who turns up.'

'Nobody's going to turn up. The word will be out that we were there. That we've got Quinn.'

'If we got the guard away and propped up the hall door—'

'And put some Christmas paper over the bullet holes in the window,' Gifford interrupted, shaking his head. 'A waste of time. Nobody'll turn up now.'

Duggan stopped to light a cigarette. He was right. But this was the best lead they'd got on Goertz in months. They couldn't just let it go. 'I've got to phone the office,' he said.

He waited for Commandant McClure to come on the line, working out a brief report in his head. 'I'm sorry, sir,' the orderly on the switchboard at headquarters came back, 'the commandant is not here at the moment. Will anyone else do?'

'It's all right,' Duggan said. 'I'll be back in a little while.'

He replaced the receiver and put out the cigarette and looked up to find Gifford staring at him. 'What?' Duggan demanded.

Gifford was sitting on a table, his feet on a metal chair, hands in his trousers pockets. 'You need to get some sleep,' he said, amused.

Duggan shrugged. His body ached with tiredness but his brain was still too active to allow sleep. Go back to the office and write a report while it's all fresh, he told himself. Aloud, he said, 'Where are the leaflets?'

'Station sergeant has them.'

Gifford's sergeant looked into the room. 'Stop playing with yourself and come on,' he said to Gifford. 'Jimmy boy has given us another address.'

Gifford dropped his feet to the floor and raised his eyes to Duggan as he went past. The sergeant looked back into the room and said to Duggan, 'If we find any Germans we'll bring them back to you.' An unseen detective in the corridor gave a single loud laugh.

When they had gone Duggan went to the station sergeant and asked him for the package of leaflets they had left with him. 'No can do,' the sergeant, an elderly man in uniform, said. 'It's in the evidence locker with the gun and a few other things.'

'But I need it for my superiors.'

'Too late,' the sergeant shook his head. 'It's entered in the book now.'

Duggan didn't move, a wave of tiredness breaking over him. 'There's a few of them here,' the sergeant offered, taking a clutch of the leaflets from a drawer in his desk. 'How many do you want?'

'All of them,' Duggan said, too tired to disguise his demanding tone.

The sergeant held his gaze for a moment and then handed them over. 'Are they real?' he asked, no longer sounding official.

'I don't know,' Duggan said, subconsciously repeating Quinn's mantra. *Ich wusste es nicht.*

Seven

Captain Sullivan came into the office, ashen faced, and sank down behind his typewriter. Duggan looked up from the previous night's reports and stared at him. Sullivan stared back.

'Give me a cigarette,' Sullivan said.

Duggan slid his cigarette case down the table to him, followed by his lighter. Sullivan didn't normally smoke. He coughed and made a face as he inhaled too deeply.

'You just back from Carlow now?' Duggan had already read the preliminary report on the bombs which had fallen in County Carlow. One had hit a farmhouse, killing two women and their niece in their beds.

Sullivan inhaled again, more cautiously, and nodded. 'Car skidded on a patch of ice. Had to wait for a transport truck to come and pull me out of the ditch.' He put the cigarette in his mouth and placed two sheets of carbon paper between three sheets of typing paper, straightened them, and rolled them into the typewriter. The smoke drifted into his eyes and he rubbed them. 'You heard what happened?' he looked at Duggan, red-eyed.

Duggan nodded.

'I mean it's the middle of fucking nowhere.' Sullivan shook his head. 'A farmhouse on the side of a hill. The middle of nowhere.' He took another cautious drag and stubbed out the cigarette. 'From higher up the hill you could look down and see where all the bombs landed. Black holes in the snow. In a straight line. One after the other.' He indicated with his hand, like he was beating out music. 'And the house in the middle of it. One bomb hit the end of it. Totally destroyed the bedroom where the women were sleeping. Probably never knew what hit them. I hope so anyway.' He paused. 'I mean it's the middle of nowhere,' he repeated, emphasising every word.

'It was a German?'

'Yeah, yeah,' Sullivan waved with impatience, as if that was of no importance. 'No doubt.'

'A clear night?'

'I've never seen so many stars in my life. I don't know what the fucker thought he was doing.'

'Dumping his bombs?' Duggan asked, still concerned with the reports he was reading from the coastal lookout posts.

Sullivan looked at him like he was a bit slow, missing the point. 'They lived in the middle of nowhere. It really is the middle of nowhere.'

Duggan nodded, realising what he was saying. The shocking randomness of war. The carelessness with which it rained down death and destruction. How could anyone be safe when it could reach into the middle of nowhere and kill you? For no reason. Without a thought.

'You see the bodies?' Duggan gestured at his cigarettes.

'Jesus, no.' Sullivan slid the case and lighter back to him. 'Where's the commandant?'

'Still in conference with the colonel.'

Sullivan began to poke at the typewriter and Duggan lit himself a cigarette and went back to his reports, trying to figure out the bombers' intentions from the courses they had followed. The two

Heinkels had crossed the east coast south of Wicklow Head, apparently heading north-westerly. One had dropped its bombs in Carlow, the other to the north of it on the Curragh. Nobody had been injured in the Curragh: the high explosives had fallen on open ground near the racecourse, one incendiary had set fire to a hay barn in a stud farm.

Two Heinkels had been logged crossing the south coast near Helvick Head within a few minutes of each other shortly afterwards, heading south-easterly. Back to Bordeaux or around there, he thought. Maybe to the base from which they flew their Condors up the west coast to Stavanger, looking for British convoys.

Duggan jumped as someone poked him in the back. 'How's about you?' Captain Anderson from the British desk announced himself. 'Very interesting photos you got about the Brits' strategy.'

'Yeah.'

'Be great to know the source,' Anderson sat back against the table. 'I mean the original source.'

'I know. But my source won't say.'

'You could ask him again. Explain that it's in the national interest that we talk directly to that person.'

'I can try,' Duggan agreed, thinking that he knows it was Timmy. 'But he wouldn't budge the last time.'

'He might change his mind when he realises just how important it is.'

'He knows how important it is. But I'll explain to him again.'

Anderson clapped him on the shoulder and left. Duggan felt that he had been patronised but shrugged mentally. At least McClure had wasted no time passing on the information. So much for Timmy's insinuations.

The commandant himself arrived and said to Sullivan, 'Good work last night. You're putting it all on paper?'

'Yes, sir,' Sullivan looked up, a hint of satisfaction crossing his grey face.

'Well?' McClure turned his attention to Duggan.

Duggan told him of the flight paths of the Heinkels. 'No indications that they were in trouble,' he added. 'So they didn't jettison their bombs for that reason. Unless they were short of fuel to get back home.'

McClure shook his head. 'Shouldn't have been. So,' he paused, summing up. 'Clear night, perfect visibility. They fly up the Irish Sea. Can't mistake that. Drop their bombs on open ground. Drop incendiaries on open ground. What appeared to be open countryside. Turn around and fly home. Mission accomplished. But what was the point of it? What was the mission?'

Duggan wasn't sure if that was a rhetorical question but said nothing.

'Were they trying to hit the Curragh camp?' McClure continued. 'They had to know it was there. Why would you drop incendiaries on open ground?'

'Another message,' Duggan offered.

McClure nodded. 'But it kills two women and a girl. Inadvertently.' He glanced at Sullivan who had stopped typing and was following the conversation. 'Come with me.'

Duggan followed him into his office. McClure sank into his chair with a sigh and waved Duggan to another chair. He caught sight of one of the leaflets Duggan had found in Quinn's house and picked it up from the desk. 'Where are the rest of these?'

'The guards have them. In the Bridewell. In their evidence locker.'

'We should get them back. We don't want them floating about.'

'I asked. But they wouldn't give them back.'

'We'll ask again.' McClure let go of the leaflet and watched it float to the desk. 'Things are balanced' – he paused – 'so delicately.' He picked up the leaflet and let it fall again. 'That's all it might take. For one side or the other to make a move.' He watched it for a moment, then reached for a cigarette and lit it. 'Looks like we're in a situation where both sides are looking for an excuse to invade. Or, even better for them, trying to provoke the other into doing it first.'

'I'll go down to the Bridewell again and try and get them back.'

'Your information about the British plan is on the nail,' McClure went on, as if he hadn't heard. 'They've told the Department of Supplies that they have to cut back on the coal they can give us. And the oil and fertilisers and other things. Because of the losses on their convoys. Barely enough supplies getting through to maintain themselves. And their war effort.'

'The first part of their plan,' Duggan nodded. So, it was starting. Regrets at first. You have to understand our problems, the way things are. Then up the pressure. You've got to help us, it's in your interest too. We both need to secure these convoys and your western ports are the only way to do it. Then, it's a matter of life or death. We must have those ports to survive. So we have to take them by force if you won't let us have them. No choice.

'Exactly,' McClure nodded. 'There are talks still going on between officials. They say they're sorry but that's just the way it is. Have to concentrate on providing for their war needs. And their own population. No mention of quid pro quos. Or of retaliation for neutrality or not giving them access to the ports or anything like that.'

Duggan lit a cigarette too and they smoked in silence for a moment.

'What about all the food we're sending them?' Duggan said.

McClure shook his head. 'We don't want to escalate the situation with threats of retaliation. Just play into the hands of those who want to invade, get it over and done with.' He leaned back and stretched his arms above his shoulders and then straightened up at the desk. 'Anyway, that's none of our business. A matter for officials and diplomats and the government. But it's a hell of a situation. Very dangerous.'

'What can we do?'

'Our jobs,' McClure sighed and gave him a grim look. 'Gather the best intelligence we can. Make sure that whatever happens doesn't happen by accident. By people getting the wrong end of the stick. Misinterpreting something.'

Duggan half stood to reach the ashtray on the desk and stub out his cigarette. 'What do you want me to do?'

'Keep on the Goertz trail for the moment. Your man Quinn is the best lead we've got on him for a while.'

'Could I just ask you something?' Duggan said. 'Just to be absolutely clear. We are trying to catch him, aren't we?'

McClure looked at him for a moment. 'Let's put it this way,' he said. 'We want to find him. We want to know what he's up to. When we know where he is and what he's doing, someone will decide what to do with him. Okay?'

'Yes, sir,' Duggan stood up and went towards the door.

'And,' McClure stopped him with a wintry smile, 'we shouldn't really speculate about the bigger picture. The country has enough armchair generals and strategists without us adding to their number.'

Duggan cycled along Benburb Street and then cut down to the quays and the raw east wind pushing the tide up the Liffey hit him in the face. He lowered his head into it, pushed harder on the pedals, thinking about what McClure had said. And Sullivan. Both had seemed shocked in their own way, McClure by the evidence that the British were really following a plan that would lead to invasion. Sullivan by coming close to the reality of the war, seeing where people had died, in the middle of nowhere. Randomly. For no reason.

In the Bridewell, the station sergeant gave him a disgruntled look and said something into a phone. 'This is against regulations, you know,' he said to Duggan as they waited. 'Once something goes into the evidence locker it can't come out again.'

Duggan nodded, rubbing the backs of his hands, trying to warm them up, not caring about the sergeant's problems. Whoever McClure had talked to had obviously overruled him and his regulations.

A young guard arrived in the office with the package of leaflets and handed it to Duggan. 'And Mr Quinn?' Duggan prompted.

'He's waiting for you,' the sergeant said. 'That's against regulations too. He's been charged so he can't be questioned again.'

'I'm only going to talk to him,' Duggan said. 'Not question him.'

'I can only do what I'm told,' the sergeant said, almost to himself, as if preparing for a defence barrister demanding to know why he had allowed evidence to be removed. He nodded to the young guard who led Duggan out of the room.

'What's he been charged with?' Duggan stopped at the door.

'Offences Against the State,' the sergeant said. 'Harbouring a member of an illegal organisation.'

'What'll he get for that?'

'Six months.'

'His wife? Has she been charged?'

'Not yet.'

Duggan thought for a moment. 'Could I make a quick phone call?'

The sergeant raised his eyes, sighed, then nodded at the guard who showed Duggan into an empty office. Duggan phoned McClure and asked him if he could offer Quinn the release of his wife if he cooperated.

McClure thought about it. 'I'll get onto it,' he said. 'But don't offer any cast-iron guarantees.'

Quinn was at the same table in the same interview room. His arms were crossed on the table, his head resting on them. Duggan thought at first that he was asleep but he raised his head slightly when the door opened. He looked exhausted, dark circles under his eyes, and his hair was spiked up from the way he had been resting his head.

Duggan took off his overcoat and placed it and the parcel of leaflets on the spare chair at his side of the table. He offered his hand to Quinn. After a moment, Quinn gave it a perfunctory shake and straightened up.

'Have you been here all night?'

Quinn shook his head.

'Did you get any sleep?'

'Not much,' Quinn said in a hoarse voice and coughed to clear his throat.

'I'd like to have a talk with you,' Duggan said, settling himself on the chair. 'Unofficially. Nothing said here will be used against you in court or anything like that.'

'*Wer sind Sie?*' Quinn coughed again.

'*Ich heiße Paul Duggan.*'

'Are you a policeman?' Quinn continued in German.

Duggan shook his head, offered nothing more, intrigued by Quinn's switch into German. Did he feel more comfortable speaking German? Like earlier when he'd been more forthcoming in German? But why? Was he distancing himself from his current predicament? Living in some fantasy world where Germans already ruled?

They looked at each other in silence for a moment. Duggan reached into his inside pocket and took out their only picture of Hermann Goertz, the British police one taken when he'd been jailed in England before the war for spying. He placed it on the table facing Quinn. 'Was this man your Christmas visitor?' he asked in German.

Quinn took his time responding. Then he nodded.

'What's his name?'

'I don't know. He never told us his name.'

'Had you ever met him before?'

'No.'

'Did he ever come to the Friends of Germany meetings?'

Quinn shook his head.

'How did he come to spend Christmas with you?'

'Someone asked if he could stay with us for a few days.'

'And you didn't ask who he was?'

'No,' Quinn shrugged.

'But you knew he was a German?'

'Yes.'

'And he spoke German to you?'

Quinn nodded. 'And English to my wife. She doesn't speak German.'

'She's not in the Friends of Germany?'

'She's not interested in politics.'

Duggan took out his cigarette case, offered him one but he shook his head. Duggan lit one for himself and pulled the tin ashtray within reach. 'So what happened then?'

'We had a lovely Christmas,' Quinn said. 'He told us all about growing up in Germany. Christmas in Germany. Sang all the songs for us. '*Tannenbaum*'. '*Stille Nacht*'. He has a lovely voice.'

'You know he's a German spy?'

'He's not a spy.'

'What do you think he's doing here?'

'He's here to help us.'

'Help us?' Duggan prompted, expecting to hear that Goertz's mission was to help defend Ireland against a British invasion.

Quinn nodded, enthusiastic now. 'Help us adjust to the new Europe. Make sure that the transition works for us after the war. So that we can take full advantage of all the opportunities we will have.'

'What opportunities?'

'To be really free at last. To get out from under the British shadow.

And be able to live our own lives like Herr Hitler has shown the German people how to live their own lives in their own culture. To respect our own culture and grow strong and get rid of the talking shops and the Bolsheviks and the moneylenders and all the parasites who feed off us and keep us weak.'

Duggan took a deep drag on his cigarette, taken aback with this sudden speech but recognising its echoes from the reports of the Friends of Germany meetings. 'And he said all this? That's why he's here?'

Quinn nodded.

'Not to get us to give up our neutrality?'

'Oh, no. The Fuhrer wants us to remain neutral. He was sent here to help us as well, if the warmonger Churchill attacks us.' He made it sound like Hitler had personally sent Goertz to Ireland out of his personal concern for the country.

Duggan resisted an impulse to get involved in a political debate. 'So what happened after Christmas?'

'He left.'

'Where did he go?'

Quinn shrugged, showing his disappointment. 'I don't know.'

'He didn't say?'

Quinn shook his head.

'What if you wanted to contact him again?'

Quinn said nothing, clearly hiding something.

'Tell me,' Duggan ordered, hearing the demanding tone of his old German teacher in his own voice. *Sagen Sie mir.*

'He didn't say goodbye,' Quinn admitted. 'He went out for a walk the day after Stephen's Day and he never came back.'

'Something happened to him?'

'No. She said he was okay. He just had to move. For security reasons.'

'Who said? Who's she?'

'The woman who came to collect his clothes.'

'Wait a minute. Tell me, step by step.' Duggan crushed his cigarette butt in the ashtray.

'He went out for a walk and didn't come back,' Quinn said with a hint of impatience. 'Two days later a woman came to collect his clothes. She said he had to move for security reasons and that he had said to thank me very much. That he enjoyed our discussions.'

'Who was she?'

'I don't know.'

Duggan gave him a sceptical look.

'I never saw her before,' Quinn said. 'She didn't tell me her name.'

'What'd she looked like?'

'Well dressed. She had a fur coat. Well spoken.'

'By herself?'

Quinn nodded. 'She drove herself.'

'What kind of car?'

'I didn't see it.'

'You saw her driving it,' Duggan pointed out.

Quinn dropped his head.

'Listen,' Duggan said. 'They haven't charged your wife yet. They're still deciding what to charge her with. I can have a word with them.'

Quinn raised his eyes and stared at Duggan for a moment. He took a deep breath. 'A Wolseley,' he breathed out.

Duggan reached for another cigarette to cover his satisfaction. There weren't too many Wolseleys around. There shouldn't be any problem finding the woman. A fur coat and a Wolseley: she had to be well off. She mustn't have known about the leaflets, just gathered up Goertz's things, hadn't looked closely at the side of the wardrobe with Mrs Quinn's clothes.

'You must've been worried when Herr Goertz went out for a walk and didn't come back,' Duggan backtracked.

Quinn nodded.

'What did you do?'

'Nothing. There was nothing I could do.'

'You could've talked to somebody. To whoever brought him to you in the first place.'

'He was away. For Christmas.'

'Who is he?'

Quinn half shook his head. 'He doesn't know anything either.'

'He brought Herr Goertz to you.'

'He didn't know who he was.'

'You asked him?'

'He didn't know.'

'Who brought Herr Goertz to him?'

Quinn thought for a moment. 'A woman.'

'The woman in the Wolseley?'

'Could be. I don't know.'

'You haven't asked him?'

'I haven't seen him. He's still away.'

'Who is he?'

Quinn dropped his head and shook its crown at Duggan.

'A friend of yours,' Duggan said, as if he was talking to himself, a statement, not a question. 'Okay. I can understand that.' He paused. 'And your wife's cousin? The IRA man? Did he meet Herr Goertz?'

'Oh, no,' Quinn's head shot up. 'He's a foolish young lad. Hasn't a brain in his head.'

'So he wasn't there when Herr Goertz was there?'

'No, no. He turned up on New Year's Eve. Invited himself to stay.'

'What was he doing in Dublin?'

'I don't know. We didn't want him there but we couldn't refuse, you know? Family.'

'Yeah, I know,' Duggan agreed with a heartfelt sigh. 'So what did you and Herr Goertz discuss?'

'Germany. How it's been transformed. Have you been there?'

Duggan shook his head.

'You should go when the war's over,' Quinn's voice became more animated with enthusiasm. 'What Herr Hitler's done is extraordinary. Raised a whole nation off its knees. After everything the French and British imperialists threw at them. Did their best to grind them into the mud. And one man put a stop to it. One man.' He raised a finger and shook his head in amazement. 'And look at them now.'

'You knew who he was, didn't you?' Duggan tapped Goertz's photo.

'I wasn't sure,' Quinn flashed a sly smile. 'There'd been talk about him.'

'What talk?'

'You know, a special representative of the Reich.' *Ein Sondergesandter des Reiches.*

'And you'd heard him mentioned by name?'

'There were rumours.'

'What does he think of the IRA?'

'Not a lot.'

'But he's working with them?'

'Not really,' Quinn dismissed them with a wave of his hand. 'They'll be put in their place when the time comes.'

Duggan put out his cigarette with slow stabs at the ashtray. 'Okay,' he switched back to English as he put the photo of Goertz in his inside pocket. 'Thanks for talking to me.'

'My wife?' Quinn asked in English, sounding more uncertain, almost as if it was a second language to him.

'I'll have a word with them.' Duggan gathered up the parcel of leaflets and his overcoat.

'I wouldn't like her to go to jail.'

'I understand.'

'I know it wouldn't be for long,' Quinn looked up at him. 'It won't take much longer now. One more push and it'll be over. The English can't hold out. The U-boats are sapping their strength and the axe will fall in the spring.'

Duggan nodded, thinking of McClure's admonishment about armchair generals and strategists. 'That's what Herr Goertz says?'

'It'll be over by the summer,' Quinn nodded with satisfaction. 'We'll be able to assist them in governing England. Who knows better than we do all the devious English ways?'

Duggan almost smiled at the neat symmetry of the idea, revenge for all those centuries of English rule in Ireland, but stopped himself in time. Quinn was serious. 'You discussed this with Herr Goertz?'

'He thought it was a very interesting idea. Worth looking into.' Quinn watched him move to the door. 'And there could be interesting positions for a man like yourself. In the new order. An intelligent man with good German.'

Duggan turned back to him at the door and said, '*Auf Wiedersehen.*'

'I enjoyed our talk,' Quinn relapsed into German.

Outside, Duggan stood on the Bridewell's steps and inhaled the cold air. The temperature was dropping as the sun went down and the dark bulk of the Four Courts lay before him. 'I hope you've got what you wanted,' the station sergeant had said as he left and he'd muttered a 'yes, thanks'. But all he'd really got was a well-off woman in a fur coat and a Wolseley car. And a bizarre job offer to help the Germans run Britain. He shook his head to try and clear it, disconcerted by the realisation that he'd left Quinn a happier man than he had been before.

Eight

Commandant McClure was coming out the door of the Red House as Duggan parked his bike. 'Just in time,' McClure tossed him a bunch of car keys. 'We're going to External Affairs.'

'Will I leave these inside?' Duggan caught the keys and took the parcel of leaflets off his carrier.

'Bring them with you. It's what we're going to talk to Mr Ó Murchú about.'

In the city centre the footpaths were filling up with people leaving work, muffled against the cold, some carrying torches in the gloom of the half-blackout. The traffic moved sluggishly, cyclists weaving among the buses and trams and cars. Duggan filled McClure in on what Quinn had said, his preference for speaking German, his description of Goertz as a special representative of the Reich.

'Huh,' McClure snorted at that. 'Interesting to know if that's how Goertz is describing himself.'

'I'm not sure,' Duggan cast his mind back. 'I think that may just be how Quinn sees him.'

'Even so. That could be useful for Ó Murchú in his dealings with the German legation. As in, who are we supposed to deal with? You or this man who claims to represent your government and is actively conspiring with our internal opponents to undermine our government?'

Duggan nodded at the thought, watching in his rearview mirror for a tram to lumber past so he could overtake a dray. 'What's Germany like?' he asked as they got clear and moved up Westmoreland Street to the next blockage in College Green.

'It's a few years since I was there,' McClure shrugged. 'Like Quinn told you. An extraordinary transformation. If you're prepared to overlook the price of it.'

'How do you mean?'

'No room for any dissent. Do what you're told, think what you're told to think, or get beaten up and thrown into a concentration camp. It's got worse by all accounts.'

'I thought it was only the Jews.'

'No, not just them. They're the scapegoats for everything that's gone wrong for the Germans.' He paused. 'The Germans can be full of self-pity and self-righteousness at the same time. Love to have someone to blame for their own problems.'

A thicket of cyclists slowed them again as they waited to turn into Merrion Square. They parked and stood to one side, waiting to enter Government Buildings as a group of young women came chattering down the steps. Ó Murchú was standing at his window, looking out on the deserted forecourt of the College of Science next door when they were shown in. 'Gentlemen,' he turned, indicating chairs, and sat behind his desk. 'Well?'

McClure gave him a concise report of the previous night's bombings, the evidence that they were German and their latest information about Hermann Goertz, and handed over a leaflet from the package Duggan held on his knee. Ó Murchú placed it on his desk and read both sides, rubbing the backs of his hands in an unconscious gesture. 'Somebody who knows their Irish well.' He looked up. 'And there's no doubt these were in the possession of this man whose host thinks he was a special representative of the German government?'

'No, sir. No doubt.'

'Good. That's very useful. Can you leave me some of them? I'm sure the Taoiseach will like to see them.'

Duggan placed a fistful of the leaflets on the desk.

'Have you seen this?' Ó Murchú held out a sheet of paper torn from a telex machine. McClure took it and held it so that Duggan could read it at the same time.

It was a report from the American news agency Associated Press in Berlin, quoting a German government spokesman. Asked about the bombs dropped in neutral Ireland he replied: 'Those bombs are English or they are imaginary. Our fliers have not been over Ireland, and have not been sent there, so someone else will have to explain those bombs.'

McClure gave a short laugh and shook his head.

'You find it amusing?'

'No, sir. Just hard to credit.'

'There are people who will believe it.'

'Not that the bombs were in our imagination.'

'That they were English,' Ó Murchú watched him closely.

'Yes, sir.'

'We're considering whether to allow the newspapers to print it. What do you think?'

McClure glanced at the sheet again and left it on the desk. 'I think you should.'

'Why?'

'Because those who think the English are dropping German bombs from German planes will think so anyway. Everybody else will be taken aback at the dismissive way they treat the deaths and damage they've caused here.'

Ó Murchú nodded. 'Not very diplomatic of them to suggest we are imagining such things. As I'm sure Herr Hempel will agree when we point it out to him. And,' he tapped the Goertz leaflet, 'it'll be interesting to see how he equates this with his government's support for our neutrality.' He stood up and they stood as well. 'Thank you, gentleman. Your information is very useful.'

Back in the car, McClure said, 'You better follow up on the woman with the Wolseley.'

'With the guards?' Duggan drove faster now, as the rush hour had tailed off and the streets had emptied.

'They'll probably be able to tell who she is just from the description. One of those well-off women who support the IRA. Who've been looking after Goertz since he arrived.'

'Why is he so popular with them?'

'Politically or personally?'

'Politically I can understand. But he's nothing much to look at.'

'Ah,' McClure grunted. 'They probably love his *Mitteleuropa* formality. Heel clicking. Bowing. Hand kissing. All that. It's not all about looks with women.'

Duggan shot him a glance to see if he was joking but he was looking at the road ahead, unsmiling. 'Check as well,' McClure said, 'if the guards raided any of these women's homes just before Christmas. He seems to have gone to Quinn's house on the spur of the moment. He may have been flushed out of somewhere else.'

'They needed somewhere new for him in a hurry,' Duggan nodded.

'Yes. And all the usual haunts were not available for some reason.'

'And why did he leave Quinn's so suddenly? Without any notice?'

'Perhaps they didn't have much confidence in Quinn. Or in the Friends of Germany.'

'And now they've got him back in their own circle.'

'Could be they've got him back in some place that was raided recently by the guards. And they think lighting won't strike twice.'

Duggan pulled into army headquarters and waited for the sentry to raise the barrier.

'Could be all wrong,' McClure said as he got out of the car and they walked into the Red House. 'But you might have a chat with that Branch man you're friendly with.'

'Peter Gifford?'

McClure nodded. 'He seems to be the kind of fellow who can think sideways.'

Duggan smiled to himself and filed the comment away to tell Gifford. Inside, an orderly stopped them to hand a message to Duggan. 'Contact Miss Maher urgently,' it said.

'Did she leave a number?' Duggan asked him.

'No, sir,' the orderly said, glancing at McClure, who had also stopped. 'She said you knew where to find her.'

Duggan looked at his watch. It was almost seven thirty. She'd be gone from her office by now. And he realised he didn't have a number for her digs, or even know if there was a phone there. He passed the note to McClure.

'She rang three times,' the orderly said and added, with another glance at McClure, 'She said it was urgent and' – he hesitated – 'that you knew where she lived.'

'Thanks,' Duggan said. The orderly hurried away, thinking he had dropped Duggan in an embarrassing position in front of his superior officer. 'I've no idea what this is about,' Duggan added to McClure.

'Only one way to find out,' McClure said. 'Take the car.'

Duggan turned left at Phibsborough and went over the canal and turned right into Iona Road and idled along, trying to remember which house was Gerda Meier's digs. The street lights were out, apart from the cowled lamp at the corner with Botanic Avenue. Thin strips of light showed around blinds in a few windows. He parked and got out and looked up and down. This one, he decided, picking the second of a pair of semi-detached houses.

The house seemed to be in darkness but he opened the iron gate and knocked twice. A light flicked on in the hall and a middle-aged woman in a wrap-around housecoat opened the door. 'Come in,' she said before Duggan managed to say anything. 'She'll only be a few minutes.'

'Ah, Gertie?' Duggan managed to stammer as he stepped in, not sure he was at the right house.

'You know what the girls are like,' the woman said, closing the door behind him and opening another one into a parlour. It had the cold air of an unused room and the woman bent down to plug in an electric fire. 'Titivating herself,' she added with a smile. 'She'll be ready in a few minutes.'

She straightened up and looked him in the eye. 'Paul, isn't it?'

Duggan nodded. So he was at the right place.

'You're in the army?'

'That's right,' he said.

'Did you know Gertie in Cork?' She folded her arms, settling in for a long interrogation. The electric fire burned off the dust on its element, adding to the disused atmosphere. The room was almost cold enough for them to see their breaths.

'No,' Duggan said. 'I'm from the west.'

'What part?'

'Galway.'

'Oh we have a Galway girl here too. You might know her. Maureen Mannion?'

'No, I don't think so.'

'She's from Galway city. Salthill.'

'I'm not from the city.'

'Oh, what part—'

She was interrupted by the door opening. Gerda stood there, her face made up, black hair glowing, set off by a silver slide above her left ear. She was wearing a well-cut navy dress, scooped at the neck and tight at the waist, under an open gabardine overcoat. A necklace and broach matched the silver slide in her hair. 'I'm ready,' she smiled at Duggan, belting her coat.

'You look lovely,' he said.

The woman pushed him out the door of the parlour and opened the hall door for them. 'Enjoy the picture,' she said, seeing them out.

Duggan followed Gerda to the gate and she waited for him on the footpath. He glanced back at the house and caught a curtain falling back into place in an upstairs window.

'I hope you're not angry,' she said.

'No, of course not,' he indicated the car.

'I had to say you were a boyfriend.'

'How did you know I'd turn up?'

'I didn't.'

'And what if I hadn't?'

'Then they would all have been sad for me,' she gave him an impish smile. 'And we would have had a nice night in, complaining about men. You can't rely on them.'

Duggan laughed and walked her around to the passenger door to open it for her. Like Hermann Goertz would do, he thought. *Mitteleuropa* formalities. He shook his head in wonder at this sudden jump from the world of spies and politics and diplomacy and war to ... what? He sat into the car and was aware of her proximity and the clean smell of bath salts.

'Will you drive away a little bit, please?' she asked.

He started the car, twisted on the headlights to dim and edged into the road.

'I was in the restaurant today,' she said, all business now. 'Mrs Lynch asked me to come in because someone was sick. Nobody wants to rent flats at the moment so Mr Montague said I could leave. So he could leave early too, I think.'

Duggan dawdled along, waiting for her to tell her story.

'It wasn't very busy. There were no Germans there. But that English painter I told you about was there again. You remember? Roddy Glenn?'

Duggan nodded. 'The one who was trying to talk to the Germans last time.'

'Yes. He tried to talk to me but I ignored him at first. But then I couldn't ignore him all the time. He told me he wants to meet some important Germans. But they won't talk to him. The German prisoners won't talk to him. They think he is an English provocateur. He asked me to tell them that he's not. And that he has very important information for them.'

'What?' Duggan let the car coast to the kerb and faced her.

'I asked him but he wouldn't say. He asked would I tell them, the Germans, that he is not a provocateur or a spy. That he is an artist and a pacifist. He is opposed to the war.'

'Do you think he knows? That you speak German?'

'I wondered about that. But I don't think so. I asked Mrs Lynch about him and she said he has been talking to all the waitresses. She said she's going to ban him if he doesn't stop pestering everybody.'

'What's he saying to them?'

'The same thing, I think. Mrs Lynch nodded her head again and again when I told her what he was saying. That's when she said she'd ban him.'

'Has she banned him?'

'No, not yet anyway. I said it was all right, I didn't mind him talking to me.'

Duggan struggled to fish his cigarette case out of his jacket pocket from under his overcoat and offered it to her. She took one and he lit their cigarettes and opened his window a little to let the smoke out.

'He said there's a group of English artists here. All pacifists. They came here because they are against the war. All war.'

'And he's one of them?'

She shrugged. 'I presume so.'

'Is there ever anyone else with him?'

'He's always alone when I've seen him.'

'Strange,' Duggan inhaled and gave a short laugh.

'What?'

'We should send your landlady down to talk to him.'

'She was questioning you?'

'You rescued me just in time. She was about to reach down my throat and extract the contents of my stomach.'

Gerda laughed. 'She is a busybody. That's what you say? A busybody?'

'That's exactly what she is. If you could survive her questioning you'd never need to worry about a *Sicherheitspolizei* interrogation.'

Gerda inhaled deeply, closed her eyes and exhaled, letting her body slump a little with the expelled air. Duggan caught her reaction and cursed himself. 'Sorry,' he said quietly. 'That was a stupid thing to say.'

She acknowledged his apology with a slight nod. They sat in silence for a while.

'What do you want me to do?' she asked at last. 'About Roddy Glenn?'

'Keep an eye on him,' Duggan shrugged. 'Try and find out what information he has. Maybe ask the other waitresses if he's told them anything.'

'All right.'

'What does he look like?'

'He's about twenty. Light brown curly hair, long, needs to be cut. About one metre seventy-five.'

'What's that in feet and inches?'

'A bit shorter than you.'

'Anything else?'

'Well dressed. Polite. A little shy, I think. An English accent, but I don't know what kind. Maybe the other girls would know. '

Duggan nodded. 'And ask Mrs Lynch not to ban him yet.'

'You think she will do what I tell her?' she said, an edge to her voice.

'You having problems with her?'

'She doesn't trust me.'

'She say something?'

Gerda shook her head. 'She keeps me at arm's length. She is very wary of me.'

'I'm sorry,' Duggan said. 'You don't have to do this if you'd prefer not to.'

'It's all right. I am not there to be her friend.' She stubbed out her cigarette in the ashtray and opened her door.

'Where are you going?' Duggan asked in surprise.

'I'll go for a walk.'

'You can't go back in now.'

'I'll go for a long walk.'

'You can't walk round here,' he indicated the dark street, 'for a couple of hours.'

'I like walking in the dark,' she said, with a faint smile. 'It's all right.'

'No, that's ridiculous. What picture are we supposed to be going to?'

'Aren't you on duty?'

'I don't know,' he said, wondering whether he was or not. 'I haven't really been off duty since Christmas. It's time I had some time off.'

She opened her door wider to close it with a sharp tug. 'All right,' she said.

'What do you want to see?' he turned on the car's headlights and let the clutch rise.

'Every time I leave my office I see the poster for Deanna Durbin in *Spring Parade* across the road at the Savoy. It's been there for weeks now.'

'What's it about?'

'It's a fairytale musical,' she said. 'Set in Vienna.'

'Okay,' he said without much enthusiasm.

'You decide what we go to.'

'Actually,' he said, feeling hungry. 'I'm starving. I haven't eaten. Have you?'

'Yes. But I'll watch you eat.'

'Oh, no,' he grinned at her as he stopped at the end of the road, before turning into Drumcondra Road and heading for the city centre. 'That's not a good idea. You might be disgusted. I'm really hungry.'

'I'll avert my eyes if it gets too disgusting.'

They parked in Cathedral Street and walked around the corner into O'Connell Street. The night was clear, the air crisp under a moonlit sky and the brighter stars were visible through the subdued city lighting. There were few people about in the in-between hour after the early cinema showings had begun and before the final showings. A ticket tout leaning against a doorway near the Savoy offered them tickets for Sunday night in a half-hearted way, not bothering to move from the wall.

'Are you sure you don't want to see it?' Duggan asked as they turned into the cinema and passed by the poster showing a large picture of Deanna Durbin against a black and white background of a ball scene in a stately building.

'I'm sure,' she said.

They climbed the stairs up to the restaurant and found a table at the back, away from the windows. It was still busy, mostly with couples finishing their meals and probably waiting for the next showing of *Spring Parade*. A middle-aged waitress took Duggan's order for a mixed grill and Gerda ordered tea.

'Would you like some dainties, dear?' the waitress asked.

Gerda glanced at Duggan. 'Cakes,' he said. 'Pastries.'

'No, thank you.'

'We'll still have time to see the film if you change your mind,' he said when the waitress had gone.

'I've seen it,' she shook her head.

'Oh,' he said, presuming she'd been to it with someone else. Whoever she'd been at the New Year's Eve dance with. A real boyfriend.

'In Vienna,' she added. 'It was an Austrian-Hungarian film then, called *Frühjahrsparade* and my mother brought my sister and I to it. It was our last Hanukkah there. Like your Christmas,' she looked at him in explanation, 'but not the same.'

The waitress came back with a plate of white bread and cups and saucers and cutlery. They waited for her to place them.

'It's a fairytale,' Gerda continued. 'A farm girl discovers her prince through some songs. It was a silly film then and it is probably more silly now that Hollywood has made it again.'

'What's Vienna like?'

'A place where fairytales can come true. Like in the film. We didn't want to leave. We cried and cried, my mother and my sister and I. We didn't want to leave our friends and our nice gentile neighbours. That was when we still believed in fairytales.' She paused. 'Now it's a place where nightmares come true.'

'It must've been very hard adjusting to here.'

'My father wanted to go to England, to London. But he couldn't get permission. We thought Ireland was the same thing.'

'So you ended up in Cork.'

'That was an awful shock to the system, boy,' she said in an exaggerated Cork accent.

Duggan laughed. 'You've adjusted very well.'

The waitress brought his mixed grill of sausages, rashers, a fried egg, a lamb cutlet and some fried potatoes and came back a moment later with a large teapot. Gerda poured for both of them.

'Time to avert your eyes,' Duggan said, slicing a sausage.

'Don't they feed you in your army?'

'Yes, but I didn't have time to eat. Meetings.'

'Preparing for war.'

'Trying to avoid it.'

'You can't avoid it.'

'We've avoided it so far,' Duggan drank some tea and buttered a slice of bread.

'Because they've let you.'

'This is the disgusting bit,' he dipped his bread into the yolk of the fried egg and raised it, dripping, to his mouth.

'Ugh,' she smiled. 'Is that the worst?'

He nodded, doing it again.

'That's not too bad. I think I can keep my eyes open.'

They lapsed into silence for a moment. She sipped at her tea and he cut the meat from the cutlet.

'We're not entirely helpless,' he said, continuing their serious conversation.

'You can't stop them.'

'Militarily, no. But it's not all about military action. There's a lot of strategy and politics involved.'

'Politics,' she dismissed it with a shrug.

'War is just an extension of diplomacy. Of politics.'

She shook her head. 'It's hatred allowed to run free.'

'After it starts,' he said. 'But before it starts, it's politics.'

'And you think you can stop it with your politics?'

'It's the only way we can stay out of it. It's not really in either side's interest to fight here. They've nothing much to gain. And we have to keep making that clear to them. Keep things balanced that way.'

'That's what you do?'

'Me?' he said in surprise. 'No, I'm only a small cog in the machine.'

'And what these Germans say to each other in Mrs Lynch's can make a difference?' she made no attempt to hide her disbelief.

'Yes,' he said with a realisation and a conviction that surprised him. 'The smallest things can make a big difference. That's what I've learned. Am learning. That might sound stupid but it's true.'

'But it won't make any difference if they defeat the English,' she said, almost an apology. 'They won't even have to fight you then.'

Duggan conceded with a nod, thinking of the knock-on consequences of a British defeat and of Quinn and his friends ready to offer to help the Germans rule Britain, not to mention Ireland.

'We can only do what we can do,' he said, offering her a cigarette. He stretched over to light it for her and she steadied his hand with her own.

The waitress came back and cleared away his plates. 'Would you like some fresh tea?' she inquired. Duggan said yes and she offered to get Gerda a clean cup to replace her half-full one.

'No, thanks,' Gerda said and added when the waitress left. 'It tastes like piss.'

'I thought that was the coffee.'

'That too. Dublin tea is horrible. Not like Cork tea.'

'You've really turned into a Cork woman,' he smiled.

'Do you know Cork?'

'No. I've never been there.'

'Or to Vienna.'

'Or to Vienna,' he agreed.

'So where have you been?'

They were the last to leave the restaurant, joining the crowd emerging from the cinema downstairs after the final show. The temperature had dropped some more and the windscreen of the car was clouded and beginning to freeze. Duggan wiped it with the cuff of his overcoat and they drove in companionable silence back to Iona Road. He parked a little beyond her digs and switched off the engine.

'That was a very nice surprise,' she said, touching the back of his hand. 'Thank you.'

'I really enjoyed it. Being a pretend boyfriend.'

'Maybe we can pretend again sometime.'

'Yes. Definitely.'

They got out of the car and walked, hand in hand, back to her house. The street was dark and still, the silence broken only by a car passing on Botanic Road. As its engine faded another engine took its place, the drone of an aircraft not too far away. They stopped and listened for a moment and she gave him a quizzical look. The noise wasn't getting any louder and he shrugged and opened the iron gate in the railings. She took her key from her pocket and turned to him and the crump-crump of two quick explosions sounded, dulled by distance.

She looked at him, horror on her face, and her body slumped and she let her head fall onto his shoulder. He put his arms around her and felt her shudder as he drew her close.

'They're coming,' she said in a quiet voice beside his ear. 'Aren't they?'

'I don't know,' he whispered back, her hair soft against his cheek.

Nine

'Where did they fall?' Duggan asked the first person he saw after he sped back to the Red House.

'Terenure, sir,' the orderly replied and saw Duggan's uncertainty. 'Out beyond Rathmines, Rathgar.'

Near Timmy's house, Duggan thought, as he ran up the stairs to his own office. McClure beckoned to him in the corridor. He looked stressed, his tie pulled open sideways, a cigarette in his hand. Duggan followed him into his office. 'You want me to go out there, sir?'

'Sullivan's gone.' McClure closed the door behind them with a backward kick.

Fuck, Duggan thought, I shouldn't have disappeared for four hours. But McClure had other things on his mind. 'Once,' he said, pacing the room, 'could be an accident. Twice, a coincidence. But three times . . .' he stopped and stared at Duggan. 'Three nights in a row. We need to know what the fuck is going on. And we need to know now. We can't be waiting while the diplomats dance their minuets. We need to talk to someone who can give us a straight answer.'

'Goertz,' Duggan said, catching his train of thought.

McClure nodded. 'We don't want to arrest him. We want to talk to him. Maybe he knows. Maybe he doesn't. Maybe he is a special representative of Germany. Or just an ordinary spy. I don't know. But we've got to find someone who can tell us what this is all about. If it's retaliation for not allowing the Germans to bring in more people to their embassy, that's fine. If it's a warning about not giving into British demands for the ports, that's fine too. But we need to know what they think it's about. Otherwise we can't be sure we're reacting the right way. Or even to the right thing.' He went behind his desk, lit another cigarette off the last one, and sat down. 'Things can get very dangerous when people act and react at cross purposes.'

Duggan lit himself a cigarette and inhaled a deep lungful of smoke. 'Can I say something? Something that may be out of order?'

'Yes, of course,' McClure glanced at the door to make sure it was closed. 'You know that by now.'

Duggan took a deep breath, without smoke this time. 'Some of our superiors are said to be close to the Germans. Maybe they could make inquiries outside the diplomatic channels.'

'Major General McNeill,' McClure nodded. Hugo McNeill was the deputy chief of staff and commander of the first brigade, tasked with securing the border area against a British invasion; he was a regular visitor to the German legation's events. 'But I can't go questioning a general. Never mind giving him orders.'

'Maybe the colonel could talk to him.'

McClure nodded, as if confirming that he'd already had that discussion with the head of G2. 'I don't know what's going on above our heads. But we're the ones supposed to be providing intelligence on German intentions and activities. They're dropping bombs on us and we don't know why. Probably a message. But about what? We can speculate but we don't know. And until we know what the message is, we don't know how we should respond.'

Duggan sat down and they smoked in silence. 'Is there a barracks near Terenure?' Duggan asked after a while.

'In Rathmines,' McClure said. 'Not far as the crow flies.'

'Maybe they are targeting barracks,' Duggan harked back to his theory after the first bombing on the South Circular Road. 'Which means they're targeting us, the Defence Forces.'

'So it's a military message. Aimed at us, not at the diplomats and politicians.' McClure thought about that and asked rhetorically, 'And what are we doing that they don't like?' He leaned forward and rested his arms on the desk and answered his own question, 'Christ.'

'The liaison officers,' Duggan said. British Army officers from the North had become regular visitors to the Red House as both forces drew up joint plans for resisting a German invasion of Ireland. 'They're still here?'

McClure nodded.

'And they're also planning an invasion if the pressure over the ports doesn't work,' Duggan said, trying to square the two things in his own mind.

McClure nodded again.

'That's fucking mad,' Duggan blurted. 'We're probably giving them information that'll help them invade us.'

McClure nodded for a third time. 'It's a delicate situation.' He put his hand perpendicular to the desk and bent it slightly one way, then the other. 'We have to prepare for all eventualities. No good seeking British help after an invasion if there aren't plans already in place. Logistics, command structures, areas of operation, battle plans. Otherwise it'd be more of a hindrance than a help. Be falling over each other.'

'Could the Germans know about it?'

'Entirely possible. It'd be a major breach of security.' McClure paused and then gave a crooked smile. 'But it mightn't be a total disaster if they did. They'd know how serious we are about resisting an invasion, serious enough to be planning to call on help from the old enemy. And it keeps the British happy that we will resist the Germans with all our might.'

Duggan closed his eyes and shook his head to try and clear it.

'All in line with government policy,' McClure smiled. 'Neutral with a certain consideration for Britain, as Mr de Valera says. We'll fight any invader and we won't allow our territory to be used to attack Britain.'

'And if the British attack us?'

'We'll fight them.'

'With German help?'

'With any help we can get, I presume.'

'But it wouldn't be much use if there weren't plans in place already,' Duggan said. 'Would it?'

McClure stared back at him for a moment. 'That's another question we'll put to Herr Goertz when we find him.' He stood up and came around the desk. 'Keep after him.'

'Now?' Duggan stood as well.

'Yes.'

They went out into the corridor and McClure put his head into another office and asked if there were any casualty reports from Terenure. 'Nobody killed, sir,' a voice said. 'A couple of minor injuries. A Jewish family and another taken to hospital.'

'Jesus,' Duggan said, feeling again the shudder in Gerda's body and hearing the resignation in her voice as she whispered 'they're coming'.

'What?' McClure turned to him.

'They're targeting Jews.'

'Those bomber boys have trouble hitting a haystack, never mind a needle in it. Besides, I doubt there are any Jews in County Carlow or even the Curragh,' McClure dismissed the idea and then remembered Gerda. 'By the way, what was Fraulein Meier's urgent information?'

Duggan told him about the English artist, Roddy Glenn, hoping McClure wasn't going to ask why it had taken him so long to get that information. 'Odd,' he said. 'But it doesn't sound very urgent. Certainly not as urgent as Goertz.'

Duggan coasted up to the gate of Dublin Castle, standing on one pedal. It was chained shut and there was no one visible but he knew the guardroom was hidden from his view, to the side. 'Hello,' he called, his voice sounding loud in the frosty midnight silence.

'What do you want?' a voice responded after a moment.

'Captain Duggan from army headquarters to see Garda Gifford in the Special Branch.'

'Throw your identity card through the gate and put your hands up on the bars.'

For fuck's sake, Gifford thought as he fished out his card, tossed it on the ground and raised his hands to hold onto the vertical bars of the gate. Security was all very well – the IRA had bombed the Special Branch headquarters the previous spring – but Gifford might have told them I was coming.

A uniformed guard came from one side of the gate and a plain-clothes man carrying a Thompson submachine gun from the other. The guard picked up the ID and studied it and then nodded to the other. 'You armed?' the plainclothes man asked.

Duggan shook his head.

'Open your coat and turn around slowly.'

Duggan did as ordered and the guard opened the gate and let him through. 'You know where to go?'

'Yes.' Duggan got back on his bike and cycled across the lower castle yard and around the back to the Special Branch offices.

Peter Gifford had his feet up on a battered wooden desk and was reading the first edition of the *Irish Independent*. 'You might've told them I was coming,' Duggan said.

'Sorry,' Gifford dropped the paper and got to his feet. 'Got immersed in Curly Wee and Gussy Goose. Didn't realise the time.' He opened the drawer in his desk, took out his revolver, broke it, spun the chamber to check it was fully loaded and snapped it shut. 'So who're we shooting up tonight?'

'Nobody.'

Gifford replaced the revolver in the drawer with the dejected air of a thwarted schoolboy. 'Cup of tea then?' he brightened up. 'The height of the night's excitement?'

'That'd be lovely.' Duggan pulled over a chair and sat down while Gifford took a cup from his desk and disappeared out the door. Across the squad room another man in shirtsleeves had his chair tilted back against a wall and was reading the *Irish Press*. He gave Duggan a sour glance as he turned a page and disappeared again behind the paper. Duggan picked up the *Irish Independent* and read its front page: there was nothing about the latest bombing but it carried the German denial of the earlier ones. They decided to let it be published, he thought.

Gifford came back with two mugs of tea. 'No bikkies,' he said. 'You'd miss the woman's touch.' He settled himself down. 'So? You want to share my lonely vigil?'

'I'm looking for a woman who drives a Wolseley and wears a fur coat.'

'Too old for you,' Gifford shook his head. 'And way above your pay bracket.'

'She collected Goertz's things from Quinn's house.'

'Ah, the Brownshirt Pimpernel,' Gifford smiled. 'I'm beginning to wonder if that fellow Goertz really exists. Or if you lads in the hothouse haven't invented him so you can run around pretending to do something useful.'

'He exists,' Duggan said, not really in the mood for Gifford's flippancy after his conversations with Gerda and McClure. 'You saw those leaflets.'

Gifford took a slow sip of his tea, changing tack. 'And you think she might have come to the attention of the Garda Síochána?'

'She could be one of those republican women.'

'The irreconcilables,' Gifford looked over Duggan's shoulder and raised a finger. 'The very man.'

Duggan turned and saw the Special Branch sergeant from the previous night crossing the room towards them.

'What?' the sergeant barked.

'He's looking for a woman with a fur coat who drives a Wolseley,' Gifford explained.

'You went over our heads,' the sergeant said to Duggan, ignoring Gifford. 'I don't appreciate that.'

'What?' Duggan asked, flustered.

'You got that bitch released.'

'Mrs Quinn?'

'She might fool your lot with her I-know-nothing innocence but she doesn't fool us. That whole family are up to their necks in irregular activity. Every single one of them. Not just her thick cousin.'

'I didn't know she had been released,' Duggan said, surprised that his recommendation had had such an immediate effect.

The sergeant snorted. 'What's the number?'

'The number?' Duggan repeated.

'Of the Wolseley?'

'I don't know.'

'What you do know?'

'It's black.'

'Jaysus.' The sergeant turned to Gifford. 'You brought him in. Give you something to do. Look up the records and find all the black Wolseleys whose drivers wear fur coats. That probably includes men as well.'

'Yes, sarge,' Gifford said. 'You know I hang on your every word.'

The sergeant narrowed his eyes and pointed a warning finger at him and walked away.

'Sorry,' Duggan said to Gifford when he had gone.

'Not to worry. It's not as meaningful as Curly Wee but it might be more useful.'

'Hold on a minute,' Duggan said. 'He's given me an idea. Don't bother doing anything.'

'Whatever you say, sir. A captain always outranks a sergeant.' Gifford paused. 'You're going to talk to her.'

Duggan nodded.

'Want me to come?' Gifford made a theatrical move towards his desk drawer and froze halfway. 'Shoot out her other windows?'

Mrs Quinn took her time opening the door. She was wearing a faded apron over a flowered dress and her face was scrubbed and without make-up. She looked like she hadn't slept much. Duggan told her his name without his rank and asked if he could talk to her.

'You're the German,' she said, a statement to herself.

'No,' he said. 'I'm not German.'

'I mean the one who was talking German to my husband.'

'Yes. Can I have a word with you?'

She hesitated a moment and then opened the door. 'He said you had come to an arrangement with him. To have me released.'

'They let you see him?' Duggan stepped in and paused in the hallway.

'When they let me go,' she nodded towards a room at the back of the hall and he went into the kitchen ahead of her. 'They were moving him to Mountjoy.'

'He shouldn't be there too long,' Duggan offered, thinking of Quinn's belief that the Germans would release him when they achieved their final victory in the spring.

'Would you like a cup of tea?' she gestured towards the table and he took a seat.

'No, thanks. Don't go to any trouble.'

She sat opposite him and folded her arms, waiting.

'Your husband was telling me all about Herr Goertz,' Duggan began. 'The man who was here over the Christmas.'

'There's nothing more I can tell you about him then.'

'What was he like?'

She shrugged. 'He hardly spoke to me at all. They talked in German all the time.'

'You don't speak German?'

She shook her head with a touch of impatience.

'He didn't talk to you at all?' Duggan tried again.

'Only "please" and "thank you" and that sort of thing. Very polite.' The way she said it was not a compliment.

Duggan picked up on her tone. 'He left without telling you.'

'Without a word of thanks. Just disappeared.'

'But he sent his thanks. Through the woman who collected his things.'

'Mrs O'Shea,' she sniffed.

Duggan kept his face straight, hiding both his delight and a flash of anger. That bastard Quinn had been lying to him, saying he didn't know who she was. He'd have to think again about everything he'd said. 'You met her?' he prompted.

'Yes. I had to bring her up to the bedroom to collect his things. While she looked down her nose at everything.'

'What did she say?'

'About the house? Oh, nothing. But she didn't make any secret of what she thought of it.' She raised her head in another unconscious sniff. 'All beneath her.'

'What did she say about Herr Goertz?'

'Just that he sent his thanks. That's all. No mention of all we had done for him. Given him Christmas dinner and everything.' She paused. 'Just "thanks". That was all. Offhand. Like I was one of her servants.'

'You know her?'

'I know of her. And her type.' She stood up and got a packet of Sweet Aftons from a counter. She offered him one and he lit both. 'All airs and graces. You should hear her accent. She was only a nurse when she married Surgeon O'Shea. But you should hear her now. All hoity-toity.'

'Surgeon O'Shea?' he said, like he was trying to place him.

'You know him?'

'I don't think so.'

'You'd know if you knew him,' she nodded to herself. 'If you know what I mean. He hobnobs with all the powers that be these days. Knows all the so-called right people. From the old days.' She looked him in the eye, squinting through a plume of smoke. 'The glorious years.'

He nodded. The War of Independence years, she meant. Before it all ended in civil war.

'He was a young doctor then. Treated more than a few lads who couldn't go to hospital with their wounds. Then went with de Valera.'

Duggan put the politics of it together without even thinking. O'Shea had been close to the IRA, opposed the treaty, but followed de Valera when he founded Fianna Fáil and came into the Dáil and then into government. Like Timmy, he thought. And the Special Branch sergeant was probably right: Mrs Quinn was one of the irreconcilable opponents of the treaty and of those who had given up the fight. Not so innocent, he thought. Like her husband.

'And where are they living now?' he asked, as if he used to know where they lived.

'Rathgar,' she said, an unspoken 'where else?' attached to it. 'A big house on Rathgar Road.'

'And your husband had a word with her too,' he prompted.

'Aw,' she gave a humourless laugh. 'He was afraid of her. Kept out of the way. Let me bring her upstairs and collect the things.' She took another drag and picked a loose piece of tobacco off her lip as she exhaled. 'He's an innocent when it comes to politics, you know. He got a job on the Shannon scheme when he left the tech. Siemens brought him to Germany to train some of them on the electricity-generating equipment. He's been back and forth a few times and every time he goes he loves it even more. I think he wishes he was born a German.'

'He told me he had interesting political discussions with Herr Goertz.'

She dismissed that with a shrug, not interested in German politics. 'He knows nothing about politics,' she repeated, meaning local politics. 'He's really only interested in engineering and machines. Germany is just a fairyland to him.'

Duggan put out his cigarette in the ashtray and stood up. 'Thank you very much for your time,' he said.

He went ahead of her to the hall door and turned on the doorstep. 'Sorry about your windows,' he looked up at the plywood nailed over the bedroom window above.

'Thugs,' she said and added quickly, 'You're not one of them, are you?' He shook his head. 'Just thick, ignorant thugs.'

Duggan started pedalling with one foot and threw his other leg over the saddle and cycled away slowly, keeping to the tracks where the light shower of snow had been turned to slush by car wheels. He almost felt a twinge of sympathy for Quinn, who was trying to ignore the political tensions under his nose by moving his interests into a political fantasy land. And there was Gerda, too, trying to shake off the world she'd been born into, but with greater reason. And the O'Sheas, now among the powers that be. And maybe harbouring Hermann Goertz.

The morning was brisk, the sun bright and the air still sharp. Ranelagh was busy with Saturday shoppers, the footpaths more crowded than the roads. He sped by, weaving behind two women pushing prams across the street and headed back towards the city. He was about to cross the humpback bridge at Charlemont Street when he thought he should let Gifford know that he'd found out who the woman was and turned onto Canal Road. The canal was still, reflecting back the sky's blue and hiding its usual murkiness. The snow lay pristine on its far bank.

Gifford's flat wasn't far away, in Heytesbury Street, and he crossed at the next bridge and freewheeled down to Harrington Street and turned right at the church. He propped his bicycle beside the railings outside the house and realised it was too early to knock on the door: Gifford would still be asleep after his night shift. He tore the back off an envelope and wrote a message and pushed it through the letterbox of the basement door. A noise inside stopped him as he was about to turn away and he waited for a moment, undecided. There was no further sign of life, so he left.

Captain Sullivan raised his head from his arms resting on top of a typewriter and gave Duggan a bleary look as he came into the office.

'Been up all night again?' Duggan asked, tossing his overcoat onto a spare chair.

Sullivan straightened up. 'Got a few hours' sleep but I'd be better off if I hadn't got any.'

'Any more news from Terenure?'

'German bombs again,' Sullivan shrugged.

'But nobody dead this time.'

'They were lucky. Especially one family, who used to live on the South Circular. In one of the houses that was bombed the other night.'

'You're joking me,' Duggan looked at him in astonishment.

Sullivan shook his head and gave a mirthless laugh. 'It's true. I wouldn't want to live near them wherever they move to next. It looks like Adolf has personally targeted them.'

'Fuck's sake,' Duggan shook his head. 'That's ridiculous.'

'Would you like to live beside them?'

'I mean the Luftwaffe can't be targeting a single family.'

'I wouldn't want to take any chances. Would you?' Sullivan paused. 'You know the other house hit belonged to Jews.'

'Jesus,' Duggan said, thinking of Gerda and how she would take that news. 'They can't be targeting them. A needle in a haystack.'

'Maybe someone's pinpointing them.'

'Even so,' Duggan said. 'How could they hit specific houses?'

'Maybe they have a secret weapon of some kind. Like the British with their radio detection thing.'

'And why would they have hit that house in Carlow if they had? Killing people in the middle of nowhere.'

Sullivan was about to answer but his gaze shifted and Duggan felt a slap on his back. 'You got something for me?' Captain Anderson from the British section said as he turned.

'Not yet,' Duggan said. 'My source is down the country.'

'Doesn't he have a phone?'

'He doesn't like talking on the phone.'

Anderson gave a short laugh. 'Wise man. When's he back?'

'Monday, probably.'

'You'll talk to him then,' Anderson's Belfast accent made it sound even more like an order. 'Impress on him the importance of linking us up with his source. In the national interest.'

Duggan nodded, curbing his instinctive reaction that Timmy didn't need to be told by Anderson what was in the national interest. 'By the way,' he said instead, 'do you know anything about an Englishman called Roderick or Roddy Glenn?'

'Doesn't ring any bells.' Anderson propped himself against the desk.

'He's an artist.'

'One of the conscientious objectors? The group of English artists who've come here to avoid the war. Say they're pacifists or conscientious objectors. Maybe just dodging conscription.'

'I don't know,' Duggan said. 'He's hanging round a café used by the German internees. Keeps trying to talk to them. '

'Ah,' Anderson nodded in satisfaction. 'An agent provocateur.'

'Says he has information for them. But they won't talk to him.'

'Yeah,' Anderson nodded again. 'They're right. Brits love that sort of stuff. Psychological operations, they call them.'

'So he's a British agent,' Sullivan intervened. 'You should be keeping an eye on him.'

Anderson gave him a scathing glance over his shoulder and said to Duggan, 'We're up to our necks at the moment. Fishermen flooding in.'

'Fishermen?'

'Retired English colonels pretending to be here for the start of the salmon season. Going around the west trying to catch German submarines refuelling in quiet bays.'

'I thought they'd given up on that,' Duggan said.

'They'd still love to catch us out. Really put the cat among the pigeons.'

'But it's not true,' Duggan protested. 'There are no U-boats coming ashore.'

'Doesn't matter,' Anderson shrugged. 'We have to keep an eye on them anyway. See where they're going. Who they're talking to. Some fuckers down there'll tell them anything for a few pints. Or just for the hell of it.' He paused. 'You're from down there, aren't you?'

'Sort of,' Duggan admitted. 'Nowhere near the coast though.'

'So you know what I mean,' Anderson straightened himself up. 'What's his name again? That English artist?'

'Roddy Glenn.'

'You have someone covering that café, don't you?' Anderson waited for Duggan to nod in agreement. 'Keep an eye on him. And let me know if anything transpires.'

'We've got our hands full with the Germans,' Sullivan interrupted. 'You might have heard they're bombing us every night.'

Anderson gave him a sardonic wink, clapped Duggan on the shoulder and left.

'Fucking northerners,' Sullivan grunted. 'Think they can come down here and order everyone around.'

'You better get used to it,' Duggan laughed. 'Partition's not going to last forever.'

Sullivan snorted and asked him for a cigarette. Duggan lit one for himself and slid his case and lighter down the table. 'Where's the commandant?' he asked through the smoke.

Sullivan lit his cigarette before replying. 'At another meeting with civil servants. Trying to decide whether to sound air raid sirens or not the next time a plane approaches Dublin.' He slid the cigarette case and lighter back to Duggan.

'What're they going to do?'

'Who knows. The boss thinks they shouldn't unless a fleet of bombers approaches. Anyway, who's going to sleep in their beds tonight if they've got a shelter? And if they haven't . . .' Sullivan shrugged the thought away. 'By the way, he wants everyone on stand-by for another raid. So no more of your sudden disappearances.'

Duggan grunted. 'Are you finished using that typewriter as a pillow?'

'It's all yours.'

Duggan carried it back to his place and put in two sheets of paper with a carbon between them and typed the details of his conversation with Mrs Quinn. The next move was obviously to put surveillance on Mrs O'Shea, let her lead them to Goertz. Or maybe talk to her about his whereabouts. Her husband's connections made either option sensitive, but they needed to talk to Goertz, as the commandant had said, see if he could explain what the bombing was all about. Which didn't mean they had to talk to him in person. Indeed, it might be better if they didn't, keep him at arms length in case the British found out about it. If they talked to him through an intermediary. Like Mrs O'Shea.

He finished typing his note about Mrs Quinn's information, stubbed out his cigarette and leaned back and closed his eyes and thought of Gerda and her head on his shoulder and his arms around her.

Ten

Duggan chained his bicycle to a lamp standard across the road from the Ha'penny Bridge and walked along Liffey Street, taking his time. People hurried by him in the gloom, trying to pick their steps carefully on the slush and snow, well wrapped against the cold. The lights were going out in shops and the crash of shutters coming down broke the sound of hurrying feet. At the corner of Abbey Street he bought an *Evening Herald* from a newsboy and crossed, timing his way between cyclists and stepping over two lumps of horse shit, still steaming as a dray clomped westwards.

The lights were on in Mrs Lynch's café and he glanced in as he went by. An elderly couple were at a table, eating a fry, and a young man sat alone reading a newspaper, his cigarette lying in an ashtray. He reached a slow hand for it without looking as Duggan passed. A waitress was sweeping the floor around tables whose chairs had been upended on their tops. There was no sign of Gerda. Maybe she had left already, he thought, as he crossed the road and continued on to the corner of Henry Street.

He stopped and opened the paper and glanced at the headlines and then folded it and put it in his overcoat pocket. He lit a cigarette and stomped his feet against the cold, a man without patience waiting for someone. This was probably a bad idea, he told himself again.

He shouldn't be seen anywhere near the café. You'd never know who else could be watching it, who might recognise you. He could put Gerda at risk. He exhaled a cloud of smoke made bigger by the cold air and dismissed the thought. He was just a pretend boyfriend waiting for a pretend girlfriend.

A young man came out of a jeweller's across the road, carrying a metal screen which he fixed to one side of the shop window. He went back in and came out with another one. The Angelus bell sounded from a nearby church, the pauses filled in by another one like an echo from a more distant church. An older man came out of the jeweller's and shot home some bolts and locked them. He grabbed the screen with both hands, shook it to make sure it was secure and cast a suspicious eye across at Duggan before going back inside.

The elderly couple emerged from Mrs Lynch's café and were followed a moment later by the young man. Could that be Roddy Glenn? he wondered. The couple came towards him and he watched them, having learned that people weren't always what they seemed to be, but they appeared to be what they were, a couple going home after an afternoon's shopping, the woman carrying a large shopping bag. The young man went the other way and the lights in the café dimmed.

He flicked his cigarette butt into the gutter and its glow died with an instant fizz and when he looked back at the café three women were emerging. Two of them came towards him and he recognised Gerda. She was wearing her gabardine coat and a scarf covered her hair and she carried a handbag. He caught her eye as she approached and she stopped and said hello when she reached him, as if she had expected him to be there.

'See you next week,' she said to her companion.

'Cheerio,' the other girl smiled, glancing from Gerda to Duggan and back again.

'Something has happened,' Gerda said when she had gone, somewhere between a question and a statement.

'No,' Duggan said, suddenly at a loss for words.

She gave him a quizzical look. 'You are on duty?'

He nodded twice, an expression of regret.

'So we pretend,' she said to herself and slipped her arm under his and they began to walk up Henry Street. 'You can come and visit me in the café any time now.'

'How do you mean?'

'Yvonne will tell everyone you're my boyfriend.'

He gave a light laugh. 'Still not a good idea for us to be seen together there. In case someone adds two and two and gets the right answer.'

'And how would they do that?'

'Because I look like a soldier,' he said, remembering how Gifford's girlfriend, Sinead, had immediately identified him the first moment she set eyes on him.

'So?' Gerda shrugged. 'The whole world is full of soldiers now.'

'I don't want to put you in any danger.'

'How am I in danger?'

'If it was realised you were helping us. There are people—'

'The Nazis are that powerful here?' she let go of his arm and stopped and stared at him.

'No,' he said, taking her hand and starting to walk again past the GPO arcade. 'But there are people playing their own games. Like the IRA.'

'You really think it's dangerous?'

'No, not really.'

'So,' she said, squeezing his hand, 'you just don't want to lose your spy. And then have to find another one.'

'That's true,' he smiled at her and stopped outside a bar near the

Pillar. Snowflakes began to fall, spaced out and hesitant. 'Would you like a drink?'

She looked at his left eye, then his right. 'You're on duty.'

'I have to go back. But not yet. We're on standby for tonight.'

'More bombs?'

'Maybe.'

'You know something?'

'No. It's just in case.'

'Okay,' she said.

The bar was jammed and the small lounge was also full, a group of men from the radio station across the road in the GPO spread around three tables covered in pints of Guinness and glasses of whiskey. The air was heavy with the smell of pipe smoke and the sudden heat was oppressive. They found a spot against the panelled wall at the side and Duggan shrugged off his overcoat as he asked her what she would like.

She untied her scarf and let it fall around her neck and asked what he was having.

'A hot whiskey,' he said, prompted by the Bunsen burner hissing behind the bar beneath a glass jug of bubbling water. 'Very medicinal.'

'I'll try that.' She shook her hair and ran a hand through it.

Duggan waited impatiently while the barman topped up a line of pints of porter and a man beside him took three at a time and carried them over to the crowded tables with the care and solemnity of a religious ritual. Duggan gave an apologetic glance back at Gerda. She was leaning against the wall, holding their coats, her dark eyes unseeing, deep in her own thoughts.

'Yes,' she made a face after the first sip of the hot whiskey. 'Like medicine.'

'Yeah, you'll never get drunk on it.'

'Can you hold it for a moment?' she asked, passing him her glass.

She opened her handbag and took out a folded brown envelope and gave it to him as she took back her glass. He unfolded the envelope, the size of a normal sheet of typing paper. It was sealed and had nothing written on it.

'What's in it?' he raised the envelope, feeling its weight. Whatever was in it was not very bulky, but substantial enough.

'You don't know?'

'No. How would I know?'

'I thought it was why you were waiting for me.'

'No,' he shook his head, perplexed. 'I just wanted to see you.'

She gave him a fleeting smile and touched the back of his hand and then was serious again. 'That English painter gave it to me,' she dropped her voice. 'Roddy Glenn. He asked me to give it to a German officer.'

'What is it?' Duggan dropped his voice too and they moved closer, facing each other, their shoulders against the wooden wall.

'He would only say it was important, very important for peace. He said that a number of times. It's very important for peace that the Germans get it.'

'Why didn't he give it to them himself?'

'That's what I said too. He said they wouldn't take anything from him. Or talk to him.' She took a sip of her hot whiskey. 'I know that's true. I've seen them telling him to go away. To fuck off. They think he's an English spy.'

'Was that him in the café before it closed?'

'No,' she said. 'He was there this morning, before I arrived. Yvonne told me he had tried to talk to one of the Nazis but the Nazi spat on his shoe. Mrs Lynch was afraid there was going to be a fight and she told the Englishman to leave and not to come back.'

She took another sip of her whiskey. 'He was waiting for me when I arrived,' she continued, recounting the story in a quiet, matter-of-fact voice. 'Stopped me on the street before I got to the café and gave me the envelope. He said, "Give it to an officer or just leave it on their table, for an officer." I said, "I can't." And he said, "Please, it's very important for peace." And I said, "What is it?" And he said, "I can't tell you but it's very important for peace. For ending the war."'

'For ending the war?' Duggan repeated with a sceptical tone.

'That's what he said. And then he pushed it into my hand and as soon as I took it he walked away in a hurry. Nearly running.'

Duggan looked at the envelope. It was farcical to think that something in it could end the war. Anderson was probably right: Glenn was some kind of low-level British agent, trying to feed disinformation to the Germans.

'He seemed nervous,' Gerda added. 'Like he had to go away quickly.'

'Like someone was after him?'

She nodded. 'That's what I thought.'

'Did you notice anybody else hanging around?'

'No. I called after him to wait but he kept going.'

Duggan tried to juggle his overcoat and his drink and get a cigarette and Gerda took his glass to help him. 'Thanks,' he said, lighting the cigarette and taking back the glass. 'Do you think he knows you're a'– he stopped himself just in time from saying German – 'who you really are?'

'No,' she dragged out the word in an unconscious exaggeration of her Cork accent.

'Why would he give it to you?'

'Because I'm the only one there who was friendly,' she shrugged. 'No one else gives him the time of day.'

'So he can't go back there. But I still don't see why he's trying so hard to pass information to the German internees. Why not go to the German legation?'

'Maybe he's afraid it's watched.'

'Could be,' Duggan said, knowing that it was. And that any new caller to the German legation would interest the watchers and someone would want to know who he was and what his business there had been. Mrs Lynch's café and its German clientele was a less conspicuous way of passing information. Unless he used the IRA and its links to the Germans and their spies. But the IRA would be very suspicious of any Englishman offering information.

'They are collecting information there,' Gerda said, as though she was thinking along the same lines.

'In the café?'

'There are some silly girls who come in and talk and drink coffee and go to the pictures with them. One of them was saying today that her brother is working in England and her mother's very worried about him even though he didn't work in a bomb factory. They kept asking her questions, pretending they were worried too. And she told them he works for Electrolux and there is also a factory in the area making tanks and another one making some parts of planes for their air force. So he's afraid the area will be bombed and she and her mother are praying every night that he'll be safe. And they kept her talking and said, "We'll tell our comrades to leave that area alone. Where is it?" And the stupid girl said,' Gerda paused and shut her eyes to remember the unfamiliar name, '"Luton".' She paused. 'Where's that?'

'Somewhere near London, I think.'

'And then one of them said to their flight captain' – she leaned in close to whisper – '"*Das ist eine für Henning nächste Woche.*"' That's one for Henning next week. She move back and searched his face to see that he understood.

'That's the name he used? Henning?' It had to be Henning Thomsen, the counsellor in the legation. He visited the Curragh camp every week.

She nodded.

'Do you know if this Henning ever turns up in Mrs Lynch's?'

'I don't know. I haven't heard anyone use that name there.' She sipped her drink. 'I wanted to slap her in the face and tell her to shut her stupid mouth.'

'People don't think,' Duggan said. 'It all seems so far away. Hard to imagine.'

'What's hard to imagine?' she shot back in anger. 'They bombed some more Jews here last night.'

A burst of loud laughter came from the group of Radio Eireann men as one finished a joke. Gerda glanced across at them and Duggan swallowed the last of his whiskey, picked a clove from his lips and dropped it in the empty glass.

'I'm sorry,' she said.

'You're right,' he said. 'People can be stupid sometimes. Unthinking. Just concerned with their own problems.'

'Like this country. So concerned with the bad English and their little border.'

'There's a lot of good reasons for that,' he said. 'Centuries of reasons if you—'

She put her finger on his lips to stop him. 'I'm sorry,' she repeated in a whisper. 'You didn't want to see me to hear my anger.' She leaned forward and kissed him on the mouth and drew back. 'Was that why you wanted to see me?'

'Yes,' he drew her head to him for another slow kiss.

She put her hand flat on his chest and pushed him back. 'Are you trying to ruin my reputation?' she smiled. 'Kissing and drinking in a pub.'

'Don't they do that in Cork?'

'Oh God, no. Pubs are serious places in Cork. For talk about hurling. Do you play hurling?'

'Sometimes.'

'Are you any good?'

'Not bad.'

'A back or a forward?'

'A forward. Sharpshooter.' He tilted his head to one side in a quizzical look. 'What are you, an expert?'

'I can talk hurling all night. How are your shins?'

'Would you like to see them?'

She gave him a coy smile and sipped her drink.

'Would you like another?' he pointed at the glass.

'Are you trying to get me drunk?'

'Of course not.'

'I think you are.'

'Maybe.'

'Maybe I will only get more angry when I get drunk?'

'I'll take that chance.'

She looked around the pub. 'It would be lovely to stay here and forget everything,' she sighed. 'You shouldn't be drunk going back to work.'

'Hot whiskey won't make me drunk.'

'It's medicine.'

'For the cold.'

She kissed him quickly. 'You should have a clear head for your work.'

Outside, the snowflakes were coming down faster and thicker and beginning to cover the tyre tracks and pedestrian paths, muffling the fading sounds of the teatime city. They muffled up too: she pulled her scarf over her head and knotted it under her chin and he pulled up the collar of his coat. They held hands and turned up O'Connell Street towards her bus stop.

'I love snow,' she said. 'There should always be snow in the winter.'

'Remind you of home?'

'Of being a child,' she corrected him. 'I hope it snows for days.'

'I hope not,' Duggan laughed. 'Makes everything harder. Harder to walk, to cycle, get around.'

She gave an exasperated sigh. 'Everybody here talks like this is real snow and they go into a panic.'

'You should tell them what real snow is like.'

'I can't,' she said, as they stepped into the doorway of her office opposite the bus stop and faced each other. 'I'm Gertie from Cork. What would I know about real snow?'

He looked into her eyes and put his arms around her and they kissed. She slid her arms inside his overcoat and they held each other. 'You're the only one who knows who I am,' she said into his chest and he held her tighter for a moment and then tipped her head back to kiss her again and saw the moistness in her eyes.

'It's hard having to pretend all the time,' she said in answer to his unasked question. 'To always be careful and not betray myself.'

'You don't have to pretend with me,' he said.

She nodded and tried to smile.

'Or with your family.'

She shook her head.

'What?' he asked, pulling back a little.

'My parents want me to stay away from them.'

'What?' he said. 'Why?'

'For my own good,' she added quickly. 'My own protection. It's better that I be Gertie Maher than be the daughter of Herr and Frau Meier. That's how everyone knows them in Cork. They can't hide.'

She saw the shock in his face and tried to lighten it. 'And not be drinking and kissing in pubs. Like . . . I don't know what. Not a good Catholic girl from Cork anyway.'

'But what do your parents tell people? Everyone must've known about their children too.'

'They say we've gone to England. To work. Like everyone else.'

He went to say something but she cut it off with another kiss. 'You Irish,' she said with a sad smile, 'you think you're the only ones with history.'

They held each other in silence until her bus came up the street, moving slowly, and they crossed to the stop and its indicator flicked out. She gave him a last kiss and stepped onto the platform at the back and the conductor hit the bell twice.

He cycled slowly through the pristine snow, alert for hidden tram tracks and potholes. The flakes still came down in languorous flurries, some heavy, some light, teasing. The streets were empty except for a few boys pelting each other with snowballs on Arran Quay. They turned their attention to him as he passed and he ducked and sped up and felt a couple of snowballs on his back. He shook a fist above his shoulder and they shouted in delight and another snowball went by his ear. He laughed, still cocooned in the warmth of the pub and Gerda's embraces.

He stopped on the steps of the Red House to brush the snow from his shoulders and shrugged off the coat as he went up the stairs to his office. Sullivan was slouched at his desk, his eyes half closed. 'The commandant was asking where you were,' he said.

'What's happening?'

'Nothing,' Sullivan said, straightening himself. 'I told him you were skiving off as usual. He said a week's detention would put a stop to your gallop.'

Duggan laughed as he sat down and took out the envelope Gerda had given him and smoothed it on the desk.

'And there's a message for you for from your so-called cousin Peter,' Sullivan added. 'I don't know why that smart-arse Special Branch friend of yours bothers with his bullshit.'

'What?' Duggan opened the envelope carefully and took out the contents.

'You're to pick him up at home in the morning, in time for ten o'clock mass at the Church of the Three Patrons.'

There were twenty pages of Photostat paper inside, streaked with vertical lines and the type already beginning to fade to sepia. It was a letter, beginning 'My dear Mr President' and he scanned through the pages, catching phrases, his heart racing faster, until he got to the signature at the end.

Winston S. Churchill.

'Holy fuck,' he exclaimed.

'What?' Sullivan demanded.

'Is the commandant in his office?' Duggan was already on his feet and heading for the door before Sullivan nodded.

He knocked on McClure's door and went in and handed him the Photostats and explained quickly how he got them. McClure glanced through them and swore softly.

'Can it be real?' Duggan asked.

'Looks real,' McClure started reading it again with greater care. 'Sounds real.'

'But how could—' McClure raised a finger to stop Duggan's questions while he continued reading.

'Yes,' McClure said when he finished and reached for the cigarette smouldering in his ashtray. 'How could this young English artist get a copy of a letter from Churchill to Roosevelt?'

'And why is he trying to give it to the Germans? I mean, Captain Anderson thought he was trying to feed them disinformation or propaganda.'

'The best lie is often the one closest to the truth,' McClure stood up and came around his desk. 'There's all sorts of implications to this. I better show it to the colonel.' He stopped at the door. 'Don't go away.'

'No, sir.'

Duggan wandered back to his office, thinking it couldn't be what it appeared to be. How could a young English painter – if that's what he really was – end up in Dublin trying to give such a letter to Luftwaffe internees? Who was Roddy Glenn? Was he really a painter? He had pictures that he wanted Mrs Lynch to put on her walls and sell. But that didn't mean anything. He had to be an agent of some kind. But for whom?

He carried a typewriter over to his desk, sat down and lit a cigarette, lost in his thoughts.

'Penny for them,' Sullivan said.

Duggan held out a hand, palm up.

'Ah, they're not even worth that.'

'What was the name of that church again?'

'Church of the Three Patrons,' Sullivan said. 'In Rathgar.'

'Who are the three patrons?'

'Fucked if I know,' Sullivan stood up and stretched himself. 'De Valera, Aiken and Lemass, I suppose.'

Duggan laughed and Sullivan went over to the window and squinted through a crack in the shutters. 'Still snowing out there,' he reported. 'We could go home to our beds and have a decent night's sleep. There won't be any bombers about tonight.'

'You should tell the commandant that.'

'What'd he say to you?'

'He said I was to stay here.'

'Really?' Sullivan laughed. 'Confined to barracks?'

'Yeah,' Duggan tipped his chair back and threw his feet onto the desk beside the typewriter. 'You were right.'

'About time too,' Sullivan said.

'Gifford say anything else?'

'Some shite about your mother being worried you were neglecting your religious duties. Why do you listen to all his bullshit?'

'He's all right,' Duggan said, remembering how much help Gifford had given him in the past. 'A free spirit.'

'My arse,' Sullivan snorted.

Duggan stretched out an arm and pulled the phone towards him by its cord. He asked for the Dublin Castle number and then for Garda Gifford when he got through. 'Who wants to know?' the Branch man who answered the phone demanded.

'A confidential source,' Duggan said.

'Call back tomorrow,' the voice said and hung up.

'It's catching,' Sullivan wagged a warning finger. 'You'll end up as bad as him if you're not careful.'

Gifford must have something for me, Duggan thought. Nothing to do with going to Mass. Hopefully something to do with Mrs O'Shea and Goertz.

He dropped his feet from the table and settled at the typewriter to record everything Gerda had told him about Roddy Glenn and the German internees and about their plans to pass on to Henning Thomsen their information about tanks and aircraft being made in Luton. He hadn't finished when his phone rang and the switchboard told him he was to go to the colonel's office. On the stairs he met Anderson who gave him a quizzical look. 'You know what this is about?' Duggan asked.

'Just been hearing about it,' Anderson said. 'That fellow you were telling me about?'

'Roddy Glenn,' Duggan confirmed.

They reached the colonel's office and Anderson knocked and they went in. The colonel was standing in front of his desk, talking to Commandant McClure and Commandant Egan, the head of the British section. 'Okay, gentlemen,' the colonel said, waving them towards a table. He took his place at the head of it with McClure on his right and Egan on his left. Duggan sat beside McClure, facing Anderson beside Egan.

'Let's go through this,' the colonel said, placing the Photostat of the letter in front of him, a vertical palm on either side of it as if to contain it. 'What we have here is a copy of a letter purporting to be from Mr Churchill to President Roosevelt setting out some of Britain's plans for 1941, primarily its needs for more American supplies of aircraft and munitions, and the vital importance of keeping the north Atlantic route open. There is also highly valuable information about its naval forces, convoy losses in recent months, the tonnage of supplies that Britain needs, and the shortfall at the moment. And there is a somewhat desperate appeal to the Americans to lend Britain some of its surplus naval ships and new materiel because it is running out of dollars with which to pay for them.'

The colonel looked up from the page. 'There is a lot of information clearly of military value to an enemy and, also, by implication, a lot of political information about the behind-the-scenes contacts between Mr Churchill and President Roosevelt. Some of which, I imagine, would be damaging to the president if it were to be revealed publicly, especially after his pre-election promises that he wouldn't involve America in any foreign wars. But, in the way of politics, I suppose it is not as damaging now as it would have been before the election.

'And then,' the colonel sighed and turned over the pages until he got to it, 'there is section twelve. About us. He's asking the US to either lease our western ports for itself or to use its influence to persuade us to make them available to Britain. In the first instance, he says, trade between America and Ireland would be trade between two neutral countries and the Americans would be entitled to protect it with their navy without the Germans claiming that to be an act of war. And, in any event, he says the Germans won't make the mistake they made the last time of declaring war on America.

'In the second instance,' he continued, paraphrasing the letter, 'if the Americans persuade us to give southern or western ports and airfields to the British, he promises that Britain would defend Ireland if Germany saw that as a hostile act. And he suggests an all-Ireland defence council from which' – he paused and read the phrase – 'the unity of Ireland would probably emerge in some form or other after the war.'

He placed the pages back on top of each other. Nobody said anything for a moment as they tried to absorb the implications. 'It obviously requires more considered study,' the colonel broke the silence. He looked from McClure to Egan and back to McClure, 'But what are our initial thoughts? Is this genuine or is it a forgery?'

'The content suggests that it is genuine,' McClure said. 'But the source raises doubts.'

The colonel turned to Egan. 'I agree,' Egan said. 'We know that the convoys from America are Churchill's main preoccupation at the moment. It ties into that, and into the other information we've received about their plans to pressure us over the ports. It raises the question of whether the source is the same for all these documents,' he glanced across at Duggan, a question in the statement.

Shit, Duggan thought. That hadn't occurred to him. But how could Timmy and this Roddy Glenn be connected? He cleared his throat to say something but the colonel interrupted him. 'Leave that to one side for a moment,' he said. 'Let's just consider first whether this is genuine or whether it is disinformation.' He scanned through the pages again. 'It says the British have lost 420,300 tons of shipping in just five weeks,' he looked up to allow that to sink in and then looked down again. 'They need forty-three million tonnes of supplies a year to survive and the shortfall is running at about five million tonnes. And then there are the naval details, the fact that the German battleships *Bismark* and *Tippitz* put them on a par with the Royal Navy and even give them an advantage. Can this be disinformation?'

'It could be exaggerating their losses, sir,' Anderson offered.

'Or minimising them,' Egan suggested.

'Either way,' the colonel said, 'I don't see the point if this is intend-ed to mislead an enemy.'

'Lull them into a false sense of superiority?' Anderson said.

'Surely this information would be more likely to boost German morale and encourage them to greater effort,' McClure said. 'Whether it's minimising or exaggerating Britain's dilemma.'

'Indeed,' the colonel nodded. 'It doesn't appear to make any sense as an attempt to mislead the Germans.' He took out a tobacco pouch and began to fill his pipe. 'So, let's consider another option. That this document is not intended for their eyes at all. But for our eyes.'

'That's possible,' Egan nodded. 'It ties in with the other docu-ments we've received and with their campaign to pressure us to hand over the ports. That would explain the concentration on the losses and the importance of the convoys. And it could also be a warning to us that they'll get the Americans on their side to pressure us on the ports as well.'

The colonel nodded through a cloud of smoke as he got the tobac-co burning. He shook out his match and dropped it in an ashtray. 'That could make sense of almost everything. But it then raises the question of their method of giving us this document. Let's look at the source.'

Everyone looked at Duggan who gave a résumé of what little he knew about Roddy Glenn. Young English painter, initially asking to sell his works in the café, then hanging around and trying to talk to the German internees who frequented it on their parole days, culminating in the spitting incident today and Mrs Lynch barring him from the café.

'That's all we know about him?' the colonel asked.

'So far,' McClure replied. 'Up to now he appeared to be an irritant rather than anything else.'

'Have you seen him?' Egan asked Duggan.

'No, sir. I haven't gone in there.'

'We're keeping our distance,' McClure explained. 'Relying on our source to keep us informed of anything of interest. As she has done.'

'It's a woman who works there?' Egan said.

McClure nodded.

'We all know the conduit for the earlier documents you've brought us,' the colonel said to Duggan. So they all knew about Timmy, Duggan thought. 'Is there any connection between him and Roddy Glenn?'

'Not that I know of, sir.'

'Is it possible?'

'I wouldn't have thought it likely but I don't know for certain.'

'Or between the conduit and your source in the café?'

'No, sir,' Duggan shook his head.

'You're sure of that?'

'Certain, sir.'

The colonel reached for his matches again to relight the pipe. 'We should bring her in and debrief her properly,' Anderson said to him.

'That's not a good idea,' Duggan retorted, horrified at the idea of Gerda being interrogated and the effect it might have on her. Everyone turned towards him and he felt his face redden. 'I mean—'

'There are extra sensitivities involved,' McClure interrupted, coming to his rescue.

'What sensitivities?' Anderson demanded.

'There are reasons to keep her identity as secure as possible,' McClure addressed the colonel, ignoring Anderson.

The colonel sucked in and puffed out a series of small clouds of smoke. 'Very well,' he said and then looked at Duggan. 'You will talk to her and find out everything you can about Glenn.'

'Yes, sir,' Duggan replied, deciding that the colonel knew who Gerda was.

'We need to know everything we can find out about Glenn,' the colonel said to the table at large.

'We could ask Captain Collison,' Egan said with a dry laugh. 'In his capacity as passport-control officer.' Collison was the British official in charge of issuing permits for travel to and from England but his real job was as MI6's man in Ireland, running the British covert intelligence service.

'That's an idea,' the colonel gave a dry smile. 'Perhaps it would be best if the request came from the guards rather than us. As a follow-up to a complaint about some minor indiscretion, a little public drunkenness or something of the like.'

The colonel pushed back his chair, indicating that the meeting was over, and everyone got to their feet. 'By the way,' he added, 'you can stand down everyone except the normal staff. There won't be any bombers tonight.'

Eleven

Duggan drove as smoothly as he could, taking care to ease the car into gear with every change and braking with caution only when he had to. There were few tracks in the snow along the quays and he held his breath as the car climbed the hill at Christchurch and went under its arch, and again as it picked up speed downhill on the other side, past St Patrick's Cathedral. People were emerging from a morning service and he drove slowly, rounding the bend into Kevin Street and then right into Heytesbury Street.

Gifford was waiting for him, leaning against the railings outside his flat, his hands deep in the pockets of an overcoat the same navy as a guard's uniform. He came around the back of the Ford Prefect as it slid to a stop, and sat in.

'This the best you could do?'

'What?' Duggan asked.

'I expected a larger limousine.'

'With pennants on it?'

'Something appropriate to our importance.'

'It is appropriate to our importance,' Duggan said. 'Where're we going?'

'Rathgar,' Gifford clapped his hands and rubbed them, like the destination was a special treat. 'Didn't you get my message?'

'I didn't assume it was about going to Mass.' Duggan got the car moving again.

'Never underestimate the truth as a form of deception,' Gifford said. He waited while Duggan nosed the car onto the South Circular Road, checked there was nothing coming, and crossed into Stamer Street. 'The new love of your life, the woman in the fur coat and Wolseley, goes to half-ten Mass in Rathgar every Sunday. So this is your chance to see her in person. Unfortunately, she will also be *en famille*. That won't upset you, will it?'

'No,' Duggan drawled as he turned at the canal and went up to the bridge. 'I'll punch the husband in the nose, grab her hand and run away with her.'

'Won't work,' Gifford said, with mock sadness. 'She'll never get into a Prefect.'

'I see your point,' Duggan laughed as he went over the humpback of the bridge. The car gathered speed and waltzed to the right and then to the left before it recovered traction on untouched snow near the pavement.

'Of course,' Gifford observed in a disinterested voice, 'we may not live long enough to get to Rathgar.'

They parked facing up Rathgar Road before a line of shops and the crossroads beside the church. The kerbs were beginning to fill up with parked cars and groups of families moved towards the church. There were ten minutes to go to Mass time.

'Let's walk up the road a bit,' Gifford suggested. 'The O'Sheas live up that way. With any luck they'll be bringing your German friend to Mass with them.'

'I doubt he's a Catholic.'

'Of course not. He's a heathen. Probably sex-mad as well, like our old friend Hans Harbusch.' Harbusch was a German spy, now interned, whom they had watched the previous summer before his arrest.

They got out of the car. The footpath on this side was almost empty, people going to Mass crossing towards the church.

'You might get lucky,' Gifford continued in a conversational tone. 'Herr Goertz might think it polite to accompany his hosts to Mass. If he's staying with them.'

'I'd say he's too careful for that,' Duggan said, watching the families streaming towards the church. Its bell began to peal, giving five minutes' warning.

'You never know,' Gifford shrugged. 'When in Rome . . .'

They crossed Frankfort Avenue and were facing people coming from the other direction towards the church across the road, some hurrying as the bell stopped. 'There they are,' Gifford said, keeping his tone conversational. 'The couple with the three children.'

Duggan glanced across. The man was tall and upright, wearing a well-cut dark overcoat with a fur collar and a hat and gloves. The woman had on a brown fur coat, a felt hat of similar colour, matching gloves and handbag. Ahead of them were three boys of different heights, as formally dressed as their parents. They were not hurrying.

'Do you know anything about him? O'Shea?' Duggan asked as they continued.

'A pillar of the community.'

'Pro-German?'

'Maybe. Maybe not,' Gifford said. 'But well got with the people in power. Which should be your main concern.'

'I know,' Duggan looked sideways at him. McClure had already warned him to be careful how he followed up the information about Mrs O'Shea. 'Not a man to cross.'

'Unless you want to get back to the infantry. Sleeping in tents, crawling through muck and all that.'

'He must know about Goertz if his wife is ferrying him around the place,' Duggan was thinking out loud.

'That's a non sequitur. These Germans have a way with women. Like dear old Hansi.' Gifford paused. 'I feel sorry for him, separated from the lovely Eliza in their lonely prison cells. In Athlone, as if internment wasn't bad enough.'

'They're lucky they weren't hanged as spies,' Duggan said.

Gifford gave a short whistle. 'Heartless bastards, you lot.' He nodded across the road. 'That's the house over there.'

The house was a substantial three-storey with a well-tended garden and a Wolseley and a Jaguar parked in front. There was smoke rising straight up in the calm air from two chimneys. 'Coal,' Gifford sniffed the air. 'A proper fire. None of that sodden culchie bog stuff for them.'

'There must be somebody in,' Duggan offered. 'Probably a maid.'

'Or two. Do you want to go over?'

'What, knock on the door? Ask for Herr Goertz?'

Gifford sighed like he was dealing with a slow student. 'Shout *"Heil Hitler"* through the letterbox. And listen.'

'For what?' They stopped as they came to a bus stop.

'For his heels to click as he jumps to attention and shouts *"Heil Hitler"* in return. And, if you're lucky, he might overturn a table or smash some crockery as his arm shoots up automatically.'

'And then what?' Duggan gave a short laugh and got out a cigarette.

'Then he realises he's been tricked and runs out the back door and I nab him.'

'So you get the glory.'

'I'll share it with you.' Gifford bowed twice like he was in front of an audience and addressing it. 'Thank you, thank you, but let me say first that this remarkable achievement would not have been possible without the support and help of my slow-witted assistant from what is jokingly known as military intelligence.'

Duggan bent down, scooped up a handful of snow and threw it at him. 'Actually,' he said, 'we mightn't get any credit for arresting him. Maybe the opposite.'

'Oh,' Gifford cocked his head to one side. 'Tell me more.'

'I'm supposed to find him. Then await further instructions.'

'Interesting. We can't just shoot him on sight.'

'That's why we're in intelligence, not the Special Branch.'

'Cheeky,' Gifford nodded to himself as if Duggan had confirmed something. 'Make a culchie a captain and that's what happens.'

'That's for your ears only,' Duggan said. 'That we're just trying to find him, not take any action.'

Gifford made the sign of the cross over his heart. 'So he has the ear of the men as well as the eye of the women?'

'I don't know that for a fact,' Duggan shrugged. 'But I wouldn't be surprised if he's more than a simple spy.'

'There's such a thing as a simple spy?' Gifford inquired.

'You know what I mean.'

They began to saunter back down the road again, watching the house and the twin columns of grey smoke rising into the brighter grey of the sky.

'By the way,' Gifford said, 'you put the heart crossways in Sinead yesterday.'

'How?'

'Pushing notes through the letterbox.'

'She was there?' Duggan remembered the sound he thought he had heard in Gifford's flat when he had left him the note about Mrs O'Shea the previous morning. 'I didn't knock because I thought you'd still be in bed.'

'Yeah,' Gifford laughed. 'She was terrified you'd look in and see her.'

Duggan flicked his cigarette butt down the path ahead of them, realising what Gifford was telling him. 'She's living with you?'

'Only for the weekend. Her flatmates think she's gone down to culchie land. "Back home" as you lot call it.'

Duggan squashed the butt into the snow with his toe as they walked over it.

'She's afraid you'd think less of her if you knew.'

'Why should I?' Duggan said, trying to come to terms with the information. He didn't know of anyone who'd spent a night with their girlfriend, never mind a weekend.

'See her as a fallen woman,' Gifford shrugged. 'She's terrified that anyone will find out.'

'So why are you telling me?'

'So I can reassure her that you won't think less of her. She still has a soft spot for you. A soft spot in the head, if you ask me.'

'Of course not,' Duggan said. 'Maybe we could all go out for a drink later?' And invite Gerda, he thought.

'Not during the weekend,' Gifford said. 'She won't go out at all during the weekend in case anyone sees her.' He gave a dirty wink. 'Which is fine with me.'

They were passing the church and Duggan stopped and said, 'I'm going to have a look inside.'

'Okay,' Gifford looked at him sideways. 'I'll keep an eye out in case any Germans try to sneak away early.'

Duggan handed him the car keys.

'You've got to live while you can these days,' Gifford said, taking them. 'You never know when . . .' He made a whistling sound and sketched a falling bomb with his thumb and forefinger and added, 'Boom.'

Duggan crossed to the church and tried to inch his way into the porch through the group of men packed into it. Two of them had one foot on the step outside, cigarettes cupped in their hands away from the building. He managed to slide through the door and the porch and sidled to one side to a narrow space amongst those standing against the back wall.

The church was packed and an almost continuous series of coughs and snuffles sounded like an accompaniment to the mumble of Latin coming from the altar. He recognised from the well-known ritual that it was coming up to the communion and moments later the first pews began to empty into a line in the aisle. Some of those around him shuffled out the door and he knew the porch would empty in a moment as most of the men there left for the pubs that would be open illegally behind closed doors.

He watched the line of communicants returning from the altar, wondering what was the best way to follow up the O'Shea lead. The obvious thing was to try and follow Mrs O'Shea and hope she'd lead them to Goertz. But that could take a lot of time and effort. And upset some powerful people if she realised what was happening. A better option was to approach Mrs O'Shea directly, he thought. We know for a fact that she knows Goertz, whether her husband does or not. Even better if he doesn't know. Something to use as a lever. Get her to pass a message to Goertz. Ask him what was going on, why the Luftwaffe were bombing Dublin and other Irish targets. Then he'd know they were after him, but he knew that anyway. And it would be interesting if he didn't know the answer to the question. He wouldn't be what they thought he might be, just a low-level operative.

He tired of watching the slow-moving line of communicants and joined the stealthy movement of men out the door.

Gifford was leaning against the driver's door of the Prefect, his arms folded. He raised an inquisitive eyebrow as Duggan approached. Duggan shrugged and shook his head and joined him, leaning against the car. They watched in silence as men left the church in dribs and drabs until the Mass ended and crowds began to pour from the main door and side doors.

'There they are,' Gifford muttered as the O'Sheas emerged from the door on their side of the church.

They watched Mr O'Shea move slowly through the throng outside, his wife and children hidden until they came out to the footpath and turned towards their home.

'What do we do now, general?' Gifford demanded, handing him back the car keys. 'Come between them and the Sunday roast? Or escort them safely home?'

'I don't—' Duggan cut short what he was about to say as the O'Sheas stopped to talk to a woman in a fur coat with two teenage daughters. 'Fuck me,' he breathed.

Gifford followed his gaze. 'What?'

'That's my aunt,' Duggan said, watching his aunt Mona smile at something Mrs O'Shea said to her.

'Timmy Monaghan's wife?' Gifford sounded aghast. 'And your cousins?'

Duggan nodded, his mind going into overdrive. Mona knew the O'Sheas? Which meant that Timmy knew them, too. So, did he know Goertz as well? Was he part of a group who were protecting the German? Wouldn't surprise him at all.

'Ah Jaysus,' Gifford sighed, turning his back on them. 'I'm out of here. I'm not getting involved in another Timmy Monaghan fuck-up conspiracy.'

O'Shea raised his hat to Mona as the two families separated and the Monaghans crossed the road towards Frankfort Avenue. Duggan turned away from them, bent his head to open the driver's door and sat in. The Monaghans disappeared into the avenue and he breathed a sigh of relief, sure they hadn't seen him.

Gifford sat in and asked, 'Was one of them the lovely Nuala?' She was Timmy's eldest daughter and the cause of a lot of previous trouble.

'No,' Duggan replied. 'She's working in London.'

'Jaysus,' Gifford repeated. 'The English are in more trouble than I thought.'

Gerda's landlady opened the hall door and told Duggan to come into the parlour. 'She's titivating herself again,' she added in a conspiratorial tone.

'I better not,' he said. 'I left the car engine running.'

'Aren't you the lucky man that doesn't have to worry about wasting petrol these days,' she said, masking her disappointment in disapproval.

'I'll wait for her in the car,' Duggan said, happy that his ploy had worked. He had avoided another interrogation.

'I'll hurry her up,' the landlady said in a curt tone.

Duggan sat back into the car and left the engine ticking over. Gerda came out a few minutes later, smiling, and kissed him lightly on the lips when she sat in. 'She said you were in an awful hurry. What did you say to her?'

Duggan told her and she laughed as he drove off.

'The girls are all jealous,' she said. 'That I have a boyfriend who's an officer and has a car.'

'Which part of that is the more important?'

'The car, of course.' She punched him in the shoulder, her Cork accent turning more pronounced.

'But they know it's not mine.'

'They think you must be very important to have a car at your disposal. And not just one car. Cars.'

'But they don't know what I do?' he asked, a note of caution entering his voice.

'No,' she said. 'And they don't care either. Just that my boyfriend must be important.'

'That's okay,' he smiled, stopping at the junction with Drumcondra Road and checking the traffic.

'My pretend boyfriend,' she looked at him. 'Are we still pretending?'

'No,' he turned his attention to her. 'Are we?'

She shook her head and leaned towards him and they kissed lightly. 'Where are we going?' she asked, as he turned towards the city centre.

'For a walk on the beach,' he said,

'Are you mad? In this weather?'

'It'll be lovely. Blow the cobwebs away.'

'I don't have any cobwebs.'

'You don't want to do that?' He turned left into Clonliffe Road, driving gingerly on the packed-down tracks of previous vehicles.

'I don't mind. Whatever you want to do.'

They drove in silence for a while. The road was deserted, people huddled inside in a Sunday afternoon slump. The only sign of life was the smoke coming from chimneys.

'There's something I have to ask you,' he said. 'For work.'

'Hmm,' she mumbled, as if her thoughts were miles away.

'I need to know everything you can tell me about Roddy Glenn.'

'That letter was important?' She sounded surprised, brought back to the present.

He nodded to her, taking his eyes off the road for a moment.

'Really important?'

'Could be,' he nodded to himself. Especially if it's real, he thought. And even if it isn't real. He had come to realise that everything could matter, that a lie was as important as the truth in this business. The difficulty was in telling them apart and then interpreting them correctly. 'Yes,' he corrected himself. 'It is. Really important.'

He felt rather than saw her inquiring look but ignored it; he couldn't tell her anything about the letter.

'It's hard to imagine,' she said after a moment. 'That he really knows anything important.'

'Why?'

'He seems . . . harmless really,' she said, thinking. 'He's young. Nervous. Unsure of himself. Not like a spy.'

'He is an agent of some kind.'

'You're sure?' she shook her head in disbelief.

'Yes. Do you have any idea where he lives? Where he's staying?'

'No. Mrs Lynch might know. He might have told her when he was trying to sell his paintings.'

That's a possibility, he thought, nodding in agreement. 'Did he ever mention anything?'

'About what?'

'Anything that would give us a hint about where he lives?'

She thought for a moment. 'No.'

'Ever have anybody with him? A girlfriend? Other artists?'

'No,' she repeated, still thinking. 'He was always alone when I saw him. He seems a little lost. A lonely person. Uncomfortable.'

'Yeah?' he encouraged her, turning left at Fairview and heading out the coast road to Clontarf, following the map he had memorised before leaving the office.

'A loner. In a strange place. Strange to him, I mean.' She paused and then added, 'Not like a man carrying out a mission.'

But he is a man carrying out a mission, he thought. The question was on whose behalf. 'We have to find him again,' he said. 'And he can't go back to the café since Mrs Lynch barred him.'

'It's important that you find him?'

'Yes.'

'And the information he wanted to give to the Nazis? That was important too?'

He nodded.

'What will you do with it?'

'That depends,' he said. 'That's why we have to find him. Find out who he's working for.'

She turned sideways in the seat and her tone sharpened. 'You might give this information to the Nazis?'

'No, no,' he glanced at the sudden anger in her face. 'It's important for us. For Ireland. For our neutrality.'

'And it would help the Nazis?'

'It could.' He slowed in the centre of the road to turn onto the Bull Wall. 'But we won't give it to them.'

'You are sure?'

'Absolutely,' he said with more confidence than he had any reason to feel. They won't, he told himself. They can't. It'd be a huge breach of neutrality.

'I don't understand,' she said. 'Why do you need to find this man then?'

'To see who he's working for. Find out if his information is accurate.'

'What does it matter if it is accurate if you're not going to tell the Nazis?'

'Because it has implications for us too.' He let the car glide to a halt, pulled up the handbrake, switched off the engine, and turned to her in the silence. 'And as long as he's free he could always tell the Germans again. Find another way of getting the information to them.'

She nodded. 'I've told you everything I know about him.'

'Would you describe him to me again?' he turned the question into a request, thinking of Anderson's suggestion that they bring Gerda in for a debriefing. An interrogation.

She described him again: about twenty, one metre seventy-five, light brown hair, sandy really. Usually wore a tweed jacket and cavalry twill trousers, open-necked check shirts, polite, well-mannered, English accent.

'What kind of English accent?' he prompted.

She gave him a look that said you're asking the wrong person. 'I don't know. It's not hard.'

'By the way,' he said. 'We're very grateful for all you've done. It's really appreciated.'

'I haven't done anything much,' she shrugged.

'Yes, you have.' He put his hands on her shoulders and looked into her deep eyes. 'Let's go for a walk. Blow all those cobwebs away.'

She held his gaze for a moment, then gave a barely perceptible nod.

The wind was stronger than they had expected and they had to catch their breaths against the cold as they got out of the car. They turned up their coat collars and he took her hand and put it with his into his deep coat pocket and they walked into the wind, heads bowed, close together.

The beach was deserted apart from a distant figure with a dog which chased back and forth after a stick or ball they couldn't see. Loose sand skimmed along its surface towards them and the incoming tide broke in nonchalant waves, following their own rules. Beyond it, the flashing light from the Poolbeg lighthouse at the mouth of the port was beginning to become visible, an advance warning that the winter daylight was beginning to wane.

They walked in silence, slowed by the wind and their closeness, deep in their own thoughts. She leaned her head against his shoulder and they slowed to a stop and she turned to him, her hair blowing forward to narrow her face. He kissed her frozen forehead and the tip of her icy nose and found her warm mouth. She slipped her hands between the buttons of his overcoat and under his jacket and around his back.

After a long moment they turned and were hurried by the wind back towards the car.

'What's a metre in feet and inches?' Duggan asked Sullivan, stopping in the middle of typing Gerda's description of Roddy Glenn.

'A bit more than a yard,' Sullivan yawned.

'How much more?' Duggan scratched his head.

'Three foot and something inches.'

'Yeah, but how many inches?'

Sullivan shrugged. 'What do you want to know for?'

'That's classified information,' Duggan turned back to the type-writer. He didn't want to write Gerda's estimate of Glenn's height in metres as that would make it clear that his informant was from the Continent. She had said before that Glenn was a couple of inches shorter than himself. Estimated height, five feet nine to ten inches, he wrote and tried to decide how to describe Glenn's English accent. Not hard, Gerda had said. What did that mean? She was no expert on English accents. But neither was he. Soft English accent? Was there such a thing? Undetermined English accent, he wrote.

'Can I bum another cigarette?' Sullivan asked.

Duggan slid his cigarette case and lighter along the table to him. 'When are you going to buy some?'

'I'll buy you a packet next time I'm out.'

'Buy one for yourself, too.'

'Ah, I don't really want to start smoking,' Sullivan lit a Sweet Afton and slid the case and lighter back to Duggan.

'Smoking other people's is still smoking,' Duggan flicked his lighter to a cigarette.

'I'm just bored,' Sullivan sighed and rolled his eyes. 'This Mulhausen fellow's broadcasts are boring as hell. Only talks about the

Black and Tans and the lovely days he had in the *currach* and bits of old Irish poetry. It's like listening to the old man. Without the *currachs* and the poems. I prefer Haw-Haw any day.'

'They could be coded messages,' Duggan said idly. 'The poems.'

'That's what the commandant said.' Sullivan took a pull on the cigarette and blew out the smoke without inhaling it. 'Had me looking them up, to see what they were about. All double Dutch to me.'

Duggan rolled the paper out of the typewriter, took the carbons from between the sheets and dropped them in a waste basket. He looked at his watch.

'You off again?' Sullivan sighed.

'No rest for the wicked.' Duggan stood up and put his overcoat on his arm and took the report and copies he had typed.

'You'll come back with a whiff of perfume again?'

'Goes with the job,' Duggan sighed like it was a burden. 'There's not going to be any raid tonight, is there? What's the weather forecast?'

'That's classified information,' Sullivan smirked.

'I'll be back anyway.'

'I won't be here,' Sullivan said. 'Got a big date tonight. A foursome. We're going out with your friend Breda and her new beau.'

'The American?'

Sullivan gave him a meaningful nod. 'She's eternally grateful to you for not bothering to turn up on time that night.'

'Tell her I'm very happy for her,' Duggan said, meaning it, still feeling Gerda's hands on his skin and the taste of her lips.

'*An bhfuil sé fein sa bhaile,*' Duggan asked the young maid who opened the door of Timmy's house.

'*Tá sé ina sheomra*,' she inclined her head towards the room Timmy used as his office.

Duggan heard music from inside as he knocked on the door and opened it after a moment. Timmy was sitting at the table, his jacket off and the collar of his shirt freed from its studs and open like two wings from his thick neck. His sleeves were rolled up and he was writing with a fountain pen on a sheet of lined foolscap. There was a well-stacked coal fire behind him and a wind-up gramophone was playing a tenor singing 'Love Thee Dearest' at high volume.

'Well, 'tis yourself,' Timmy grunted, leaning back in his chair.

'I'm not interrupting, am I?'

'What?' Timmy waved at the gramophone. 'Turn that down a bit.'

Duggan stepped over to it and twisted the volume knob.

'Have you heard him?' Timmy's casual words were at odds with his cautious eyes. 'The new McCormack. Michael O'Duffy.'

Duggan shook his head and slipped off his overcoat as sweat broke out on his forehead.

'That's what your mother gave me for Christmas,' Timmy repeated.

'You're just back from home,' Duggan said, half statement, half question, glancing at what Timmy had been writing. He knew he was jotting down notes of requests from constituents and other bits of political information from his weekend down the country.

'Aye,' Timmy said, still cautious. 'They're all well.'

'I'm sorry for interrupting,' Duggan waved towards Timmy's notes. 'But I need your help.'

'Half the fucking country wants my help all of a sudden.' Timmy screwed the top onto his fountain pen and placed it on the foolscap page with an air of finality. He didn't seem perturbed by the idea. 'You'll have a drink?'

'Yeah, thanks.' Duggan took off his jacket and hung it on the back of the chair facing Timmy's across the table. He wondered what the temperature in the room was.

Timmy went to the sideboard and took out a bottle of Paddy whiskey and two glasses. Then he changed his mind and left back one glass. He dropped on one knee to peer into the cupboard and pulled out a bottle of Guinness and a half-pint glass.

'Better not feed you whiskey,' he said, putting the bottles and glasses on the table, 'or your mother will have my guts for garters.'

'You see them?'

'Just coming out of Mass,' Timmy handed him the bottle of Guinness. 'There should be a corkscrew somewhere in there.' He pointed to a drawer in the sideboard. 'They're in grand form. I told your father where to get the petrol if he needed some.'

Duggan found the corkscrew and opened the bottle of Guinness and poured it slowly into the glass. Timmy half-filled his glass with neat whiskey, raised it, said '*Sláinte*' and drank half of it. They sat down. 'Now,' Timmy said, putting his glass down and tossing Duggan a cigarette.

'First of all, thanks for the information about Quinn,' Duggan leaned across the table to light Timmy's cigarette and then his own.

'That's not a good place to start.' Timmy held up his cigarette between two fingers and waved it at him. 'You didn't have to lock up the harmless little fecker.'

'Wasn't our doing,' Duggan protested. 'That cousin of his wife's started shooting at the Special Branch.'

Timmy sighed as if that was a minor matter. 'There's still too many Blueshirts in that outfit,' he muttered, his usual comment about the Special Branch. 'Should've been cleared out properly long ago.'

Duggan inhaled a lungful of smoke. 'You know Surgeon O'Shea?'

Timmy gave a half nod at the sudden change of direction.

'And his wife?'

'Why?' Timmy cut to the chase.

'I think they might be able to help us,' Duggan took an unconscious deep breath. He didn't like doing this, letting Timmy in on any information. But he had to use any avenues open to him. 'Get in touch with a German intelligence officer.'

'Well, now.' Timmy emptied his glass and reached for the Paddy bottle and poured himself another one. 'You want to lock him up too? Like you did with the others?'

'We want to get a message to him.'

'Seen the light, have ye?'

'I don't make the decisions,' Duggan kept his voice even, determined not to get into an argument with him. 'We just want to ask him a question.'

'What question?'

'Why they have been dropping bombs on us for the last week.'

Timmy gave a short laugh. 'Don't you fellows read the papers? It was there in black and white the other day for everyone to read. From the horse's mouth in Berlin. They haven't dropped any bombs on us.'

'Our people have no doubt that they did. The bombs were German.'

'But who dropped them?' Timmy wagged a finger.

'The Luftwaffe. From Heinkels.'

'Did you see them?'

'Enough people did,' Duggan took another drag to calm himself. 'It's not that hard to tell planes apart.'

'And who was flying them?'

'Where would the British get Heinkels even if they had German bombs?'

Timmy shook his head, unconvinced. 'You couldn't be up to the fuckers.'

'How well do you know the O'Sheas?' Duggan tried to get the conversation back on track.

'I know him to say hello to. He was very helpful to us in the old days, when he was a medical student. Patched up a few lads who couldn't go near hospitals. He's got a bit lah-di-da since then. Now that he's qualified, raking in the money.'

'What about her? Do you know her well enough to have a quiet word with her?'

'Mona'd know her better than me. They're in the same bridge club. And something to do with the church. Altar committee or something.'

'Maybe I should talk to her.'

'What are you saying?' Timmy narrowed his eyes.

'Mrs O'Shea is in touch with this German. Hermann Goertz.'

'Well, now,' Timmy said, with a slow smile. 'Isn't that something?'

Duggan drank some of his Guinness, wondering why Timmy was smiling and what machinations were going on in his head. He couldn't avoid the feeling that this information meant more to Timmy than he knew. But then, he reminded himself, Timmy was an expert in appearing to be more knowledgeable than he was. It was part of his stock-in-trade to appear to always know more than anyone else. 'Could you ask aunt Mona to ask her to pass the question on? Ask him why they've been dropping bombs on us?'

'It's her?' Timmy raised an eyebrow. 'Not him?'

'Definitely her,' Duggan said. 'Could be him too, but I don't know that for a fact.'

'And who would we say wanted to know?'

Duggan shrugged. 'We wouldn't have to say, would we? You're a member of the government party.'

Timmy gave him a slow smile. 'You're getting to be a crafty little fucker,' he said, a compliment. 'But we'll leave Mona out of it. You don't want too many middlemen. Or middle women. So what's the question again?'

'Why are they bombing us? Is it in response to something we've done or are doing?'

'Like what?'

'That's what we want to know. If they're sending us a message we want to know what it is.'

'I could give you a few reasons why they mightn't be happy with you lot.'

'We want to hear it from them,' Duggan cut him short.

'Fair enough. We'll see what we can do.' The look on Timmy's face showed that he was already thinking about the possibilities this request opened up for him. Duggan didn't want to think too deeply about what they might be.

The spinning record on the gramophone, its song long ended, broke into the sudden silence. Timmy stood up and lifted the needle with care and settled the arm back on its rest. He tossed his cigarette butt into the fire and shovelled some coal from a scuttle onto it. He stood in front of the fireplace with his thumbs under his braces, the lord of the manor.

'There's something else,' Duggan said, putting out his butt in the full ashtray.

'Jaysus,' Timmy gave him a happy grin. 'You're a mine of information all of a sudden.'

'Do you know someone called Roddy Glenn?'

'Roddy Glenn?' Timmy rocked back and forward for a moment, then shook his head. 'Where's he from?'

'I don't know exactly.' He doesn't know, Duggan thought. There hadn't been the slightest flicker of recognition. So Roddy Glenn wasn't the source of the photographs of the British government documents that he had. At least not directly.

'Glenn? Glenn?' Timmy shook his head. 'Another intelligence fella?'

'I don't know,' Duggan said truthfully. 'Just a name that came up and I wondered if you might've heard of him. You come across so many people.'

'Glenn? Is he Irish?'

'I know nothing about him.' Duggan stood up and put on his jacket. 'I better let you get back to work.'

'It's more or less done. Finish your drink.'

Duggan poured the remainder of the bottle into the glass and waited it for it to settle. 'By the way, they're very interested in the photographs you gave me.'

'You passed them on.'

'I gave them to Commandant McClure.'

'And?'

'They've had several meetings about them. They're convinced they're genuine.'

'Of course they're genuine.'

'They want to know where they came from.'

'And what'd you tell them?'

'Nothing.' Duggan drank most of the Guinness in his glass. 'But they know you gave them to me.'

'How would they know that?'

'They know we're related,' Duggan shrugged. 'I didn't tell them and they didn't ask. But I know they know.'

Timmy nodded, not unhappy. That was exactly the sort of conclusion that he would have reached in their situation. Imparting information without saying anything was another of his specialities.

'And they want me to ask who the original source is,' Duggan continued. 'And if he will talk to them.'

Timmy switched his hands to his pockets as if to hide them. 'I can't tell you that,' he frowned.

Can't or won't? Duggan wondered. Can't because he doesn't know. Or won't because it's a suspect source of some kind. A German?

An IRA man? But the documents seemed to be real. And sources were often suspect. 'Captain Anderson is handling it,' he said. 'The man you mentioned to me.'

'The northern fella with the reddish hair?'

'That's him. He'd like to have a word with you about it.' Anderson hadn't said any such thing to him but it was a fair assumption. And a way of keeping Timmy at arm's length.

Timmy rocked back and forth on his heels, attracted by the prospect of having another contact in G2, cautious of the pressure it might put on him. 'No, no. We'll just leave it as it is,' he said at last with a hint of regret. 'Anything I come across I'll pass on through you. And if they want to jump to conclusions about where it came from we can't stop them.'

'They're going to keep on at me about it,' Duggan sighed and drained his glass. He didn't relish the prospect of continuing as the go-between. 'It's important that they know.'

'Tell them you can't get blood out of a stone,' Timmy gave him a crooked smile. 'They'll just have to accept it for what it is.'

Twelve

Duggan reversed the car over to the steps of the Red House and kept the engine idling as he waited for Commandant McClure. He watched Captain Anderson come in the gate past the sentry and catch his eye. Both held their stares as Anderson approached and Duggan began to wind down his window.

"Have you ever seen this Roddy Glenn character?' Anderson demanded without preliminaries.

Duggan shook his head.

'How do you know he exists?'

'What do you mean?'

'How do we know this source of yours hasn't made him up?'

'Why would she do that?'

Anderson gave him a withering look. 'You trust her?'

'Others have seen him,' Duggan retorted.

'Who?'

McClure bounded down the steps with a buff folder in his hand. 'Any response from Captain Collison?' he asked Anderson over the roof of the car.

'He says the name doesn't ring any immediate bells. But he'll investigate.'

McClure gave a sardonic laugh, sat in the car and Duggan drove away.

'He's still trying to find out about Gerda,' Duggan said as they went along the quays and told McClure what Anderson had been hinting at. That Gerda might be feeding information to them.

'Is that possible?' McClure asked in an even voice.

Duggan glanced at him, taken aback that McClure would even raise the question. 'No,' he shook his head to emphasise his reply.

'Agreed,' McClure said. 'I've had a word with Mrs Lynch and she confirms Glenn's existence. But she doesn't know where he lives or anything else about him. Except that he's a troublemaker and she has barred him.'

'So Gerda was telling the truth,' Duggan said with an unconscious hint of victory.

'Did you have reason to doubt it?'

'No, no,' Duggan glanced at him again, wondering why he was raising the question again. McClure had a way of discomfiting him like this now and then. Perhaps to keep me on my toes, he thought. 'Absolutely not.'

'I doubt he'll go back to Mrs Lynch's again. It's a dead end for him. He can't sell his paintings there, if he really is an artist. And the German internees won't talk to him. So there's no point going back.'

'So what do we do?' Duggan turned onto O'Connell Bridge and stopped at the signal of the garda on point duty.

'Circulate your description of him and hope someone picks him up somewhere. He might try and contact the German legation directly now if all over avenues are closed.'

They watched the garda trying to hurry along the cross traffic with fast waves of his baton. Most of it was made up of cyclists and drays: there were noticeably fewer cars on the roads with the new year's shortage of petrol. The city itself was sinking back into his mid-winter torpor, the last signs of Christmas disappearing from shop windows. There were few people on the streets, moving fast against the penetrating damp.

'Does Captain Collison really run MI6 here?' Duggan asked, seeing an opportunity to inquire. McClure was always more discursive on these car journeys.

McClure grunted an affirmative.

'So they're spying on us while we're cooperating with them?' Duggan looked at him.

'That's it,' McClure gave him a wan smile. 'But different organisations. MI6 runs their spies abroad. MI5 tries to catch foreign spies. Like us. So we have a common interest with them. Up to a point.'

'That's mad,' Duggan let up the clutch as the garda waved his baton at them. 'So we should be chasing them at the same time as we're cooperating with them.'

'We are,' McClure said, indicating the corner of College Street and Westmoreland Street with his thumb as they went by the statue of Tom Moore. 'Their main undercover operation is based in that building over there. The StubbsGazette offices.'

'Really?'

'A good cover,' McClure added. 'They can go around asking questions while people think they're just checking out creditworthiness and business matters. Of course,' he gave a dry chuckle, 'it'd be an even better cover if we didn't know about it.'

'And we're just letting them do it?'

'If we close it down they'd only set up another operation. Better that we know what they're doing than waste time trying to uncover their next effort.'

'And what are they doing?'

'Trying to find German submarines harbouring along the west,' McClure laughed as if it was a joke.

'Ah,' Duggan said, remembering what Anderson had told him. 'The fishermen?'

'Them as well. Wasting their time looking for something that isn't there. But it keeps them out of harm's way.'

'What if they find a U-boat?'

'Then we'd be in trouble, wouldn't we?' McClure smiled, still treating it as a joke.

Duggan gave him a sharp look, not seeing the humour.

'There are no German submarines there,' McClure smiled back at him. 'Anyone who gives it a moment's thought knows that.'

'How can you be so sure?' Duggan let the car idle behind a couple of cyclists until a tram had gone by and he could overtake them.

'U-boats don't use petrol or diesel. They usual a heavy oil that we don't have in this country. Besides, who controls all the oil we do have?'

'The British,' Duggan nodded as he sped around the cyclists. 'So why do they go on about it, then?'

'Politics. Propaganda,' McClure said as though they were the same thing. 'The only way the Germans could refuel U-boats in Irish harbours would be from their own tankers. Not from some fishermen giving them a few cans of petrol. And they couldn't bring their own tankers there on the Q.T. for long.'

'That's as mad as us cooperating with them while letting them spy on us.'

'Now you have it,' McClure clapped him on the back as they came to a stop outside Government Buildings. 'There's no point having the left hand and the right hand wasting time doing the same things. Anyway, it's better sometimes to keep the real issues out of sight.'

They climbed the steps into the building, passing the bored garda outside, and waited while the porter checked with someone on the phone. Pól Ó Murchú was sitting back in his chair when they were shown into his office, looking like the cares of the world had crushed him into the back rest. His face was pale in the gritty twilight and there were dark rings under his eyes. He made no effort at formality this time, merely indicating the chairs facing his desk with a tired hand.

McClure placed the file on his desk and sat down. 'We are making some progress in the search for Dr Goertz,' he said. 'We hope to close in on him shortly. Or at least find out what, if anything, he knows about Germany's current intentions.'

'Tonight will tell the story,' Ó Murchú said in a gloomy tone. 'I gather the weather is clearing from the west.'

'Tonight or tomorrow night,' McClure corrected him, his good humour ebbing away. 'It's doubtful if it'll have cleared enough by tonight for their bombers.'

'And do we have any more cards in our hand?' Ó Murchú stared at the 'SECRET' stamp in a red box on the file cover.

'We have evidence of German internees collecting intelligence of military value while out on parole and passing it to the German legation.'

'Good, good,' Ó Murchú nodded a couple of times. 'The more breaches of diplomacy we can throw at them the better. Though it won't make much difference at the end of the day, if they've decided to make an issue of expanding their legation.'

'Have they?'

'That's the question. We're getting mixed signals. Herr Hempel says the bombings are accidents. Flyers off course, confused by our air defences shooting at them. That sort of thing.' He gave a hollow laugh. 'Like it's our fault. Apparently the Irish Sea is very difficult to see from up there. No mention of it being retaliation for us dragging our heels over flying their men into Foynes. And we haven't made any overt linkages either.'

He straightened himself in the chair as if it was more a mental effort than a physical one. 'And we now have to worry as well about the British, about their multipronged campaign against us and their efforts to mobilise President Roosevelt against us.'

'Yes, sir,' McClure said.

'This sudden' – Ó Murchú opened his hands in a search for an appropriate word – 'influx of information about high-level British plans. Are we to take it all at face value?'

'We are operating on that basis. But we are still trying to assess the sources.'

'Sources?' Ó Murchú picked up on the use of the plural with alacrity.

'Yes, sir.'

'I understood it all came through one source.'

'No sir. It all came to the attention of Captain Duggan here but from two different sources.'

Ó Murchú turned his attention to Duggan.

Duggan cleared his throat. 'The British government plans came from one source, sir. The letter to President Roosevelt from another. As far as I'm aware, they did not originate from the same person.'

'That seems hard to credit,' Ó Murchú said drily. 'That there are suddenly two sources with access to top-level British government information and both are willing to share it with us at the same time.'

Duggan reddened under his stare, wondering if he should point out that Churchill's letter to Roosevelt was not intended for them but for the Germans. He half-expected McClure to explain but the commandant said nothing. 'We're trying to trace the original sources of both sets of documents, sir,' he kicked to touch.

'In the meantime,' Ó Murchú went on, 'we have to deal with the unpalatable fact that these documents, whether they are authentic or forgeries, do express the known and likely sentiments of the people concerned. And they pose another series of grave threats to us.'

Nobody said anything and a clock marked time in the silence, emphasising the air of gloomy fatalism that seemed to have inhabited Ó Murchú's office and settled on his shoulders. He stirred himself after a moment and added, 'The Minister for Defence Co-Ordination, Mr Aiken, is going on a critical mission to Washington shortly. To procure arms for you people. Perhaps his visit will throw more light on the threat we face from the Americans.' He gave McClure an inquisitive look. 'And there are reports of Americans moving into Derry.'

'So I understand, sir.'

'How reliable are they?'

'I couldn't say, sir. That's not our section.'

Ó Murchú gave a humph, as if to say that he wasn't surprised at McClure's response, that this was the type of inadequate help he had to deal with to do his job.

McClure lit an inevitable cigarette as soon as they got back into the car. 'That wasn't exactly encouraging,' he wound down his window an inch and blew a stream of used smoke at the gap.

'What do you mean?' Duggan looked over his shoulder to check the traffic and did a quick U-turn, bumping over the ridge of frozen snow in the centre of the road.

'He sounds like he's given up the ghost,' McClure said. 'Like it's getting to be too much. Trying to keep all the balls in the air.'

'He seemed more concerned about the Americans than the Germans or even the British.'

'He is. They are,' McClure inhaled. 'It's much harder to resist pressure from the Americans about the ports. We're friendly nations, in every sense, not just diplomatically. Both neutrals. How can we not help them make sure their shipping isn't being sunk in the Atlantic?'

'But it's not their shipping.'

'It's their cargoes, exports, supplies.'

'But they're for the English.'

'Yes,' McClure agreed. 'For their friends and allies. Part of the group of democratic nations opposed to the dictatorships. As we are too. So we have a community of interests and friendships. And some of those supplies are for us. So how can we not help them?'

'It all goes back to partition,' Duggan suggested. But that wasn't of much interest to the Americans, apart from the Irish-Americans, of course.

'Yeah,' McClure sighed. 'And now the Americans may be moving into the North. Into our national territory, without the courtesy of even an advance warning.'

Jesus, Duggan thought, realising the dilemma that created for the government. Should they protest? And create bad feelings with the Americans? Or should they just ignore it? And accept that the US was also part of the partition problem, actively supporting the British position?

'Which increases the pressure on us to provide the Americans with port facilities,' McClure continued, thinking aloud. 'To keep in their good books. And it's only a small step from that to transhipping supplies across the country to Britain. And for the Germans to see that as a hostile act and to start bombing the transhipment routes. Roads, railways, ports.'

'And then we're in the war.'

'Yep.'

'Christ,' Duggan sighed. You do need three-hundred-and-sixty-degree vision, he thought. And end up spinning in circles and getting dizzy. 'We can't keep out of it forever, can we?'

'Depends,' McClure shrugged. 'The Germans don't want to declare war on the Americans but there's probably a limit to the amount of provocation they'll take. Now that Roosevelt's been re-elected he's going ahead with his lend-lease plan to increase supplies to the British. As long as the Americans are officially neutral, we might have some protection, I suppose. But I can't see that lasting long if we're directly providing supplies to the British in a way we didn't before the war. It's all right to go on exporting cattle to them as we always did. Turning Galway or someplace else into a big transatlantic port is another matter.' He wound down his window some more and flicked out his cigarette butt with his thumb. 'It really all depends on what happens next. When the Germans make their move on Britain.'

Back in headquarters Captain Sullivan was going into the Red House as they parked, and followed them in. 'What's up?' he demanded in response to their sombre faces as he and Duggan went into their own office.

'Nothing.'

'Come on,' Sullivan persisted. 'You two look very serious.'

'Just got a grilling from External Affairs,' Duggan said. 'Because we couldn't answer all their questions about Adolf's plans.'

'Hah,' Sullivan gave a short laugh. 'Tell them to talk to my old man. He'll know exactly what Adolf's going to do next.'

'The whole country thinks it knows what's going to happen next,' Duggan said. 'Without knowing half of what's going on.'

Sullivan picked up a message and waved it at Duggan. 'Your girl-friend's looking for you again.'

Duggan glanced at the handwritten note. 'Please contact Gertie as soon as possible.'

'Can't get enough of it, can she?' Sullivan sniggered. 'What does she see in you anyway?'

'No point trying to explain it to you,' Duggan smiled, as he picked up his phone, 'if you can't see it yourself.' He glanced at his watch: it was just after half-four. He put the phone back on its cradle before the switch answered, deciding he'd call around to Gerda in person. He grabbed his coat, wondering if he should take the car again. He still had the key in his pocket. It was tempting. This was probably work, though he hoped it wasn't. Or not entirely.

'Is this Gertie a real person?' Sullivan watched him with a crooked smile. 'Or just another code name for that fucker Gifford?'

'Can't talk now,' Duggan put on his coat. 'Got to run.'

'You're not a pair of homos, are ye?' Sullivan said as he left and shouted after him. 'Don't worry, your secret's safe with me.'

Duggan paused a moment in the corridor to reach back his arm and give Sullivan a backwards victory sign through the open doorway. Sullivan's laugh followed him out.

He took his bicycle, reckoning it could be quicker as the evening traffic built up, and wanting some exercise. He cycled fast on the tracks cleared in the snow by the metal-rimmed wheels of carts, along by the tenements on Benburb Street, by the back of the Four Courts, by the deserted markets, and up to O'Connell Street. He chained his bike to a lamp post outside Gerda's office, glancing up at her window. The reflection from a shop's lights across the street bounced off it and he hurried inside, fearing he was too late. She was at the top of the stairs, locking her office door, and turned and looked down as she heard the street door close. A slow smile spread over her face. He went up the steps two at a time and took her in his arms.

'You were running,' she said when they broke apart.

'Cycling,' he said. 'Just got your message.'

She opened the door and they stepped inside and she locked it behind them. Neither said a word and she took his hand and led him into the inner office. He shrugged off his coat and she undid the knot in her scarf and shook her black hair free and he opened the buttons on her overcoat as she gave him a series of urgent kisses on the lips. When they had undressed each other they spread his coat on the cold linoleum, she rolled up her coat as a pillow and they lay down.

'Is it safe?' he murmured before he entered her.

'*Keine Sorge*,' she whispered. Don't worry.

Afterwards, he lay on his back and she rested her head on his shoulder. He became aware of their surroundings as their bodies cooled and he ran his fingertips up and down her back, onto the hollow of her waist, over the hump of her hips and down the outside of her leg, feeling the firm smoothness of her skin. The corner of her boss's desk loomed over them in the murky light and cinders glowed through the ashes of the dying fire. From outside came the sounds of the evening rush hour, hurrying footsteps, a newsboy's repeated shouts of '*Herald!*' or '*Mail!*', an occasional door banging, the screech of bus brakes, the metal grind and clang of a tram, and the clip-clop of a trotting horse.

After a while she raised herself and went onto her hands and knees towards the fire. 'Don't look at me,' she said over her shoulder and she picked up a poker.

'You're beautiful,' he said, watching her.

She shook the poker at him and then prodded the fire to bare the burning coals. She exchanged it for a tongs and hovered over a coal scuttle. 'Will we risk some more?' she turned to him, holding up a small lump of coal.

'Hmm,' he agreed. 'What's the risk?'

'I think Mr Montague counts the lumps of coal.'

'You're joking.'

'I'm serious,' she looked at the lump of coal. 'He's very careful. Counts the pencils and paper. I have to ask for a new one and explain what happened to the old one if I've lost it.'

'I don't believe you.'

'It's true.' She dropped the coal on the fire. 'There. We've done it. Will we risk another one?'

'Yeah,' he raised himself on an elbow and sifted through the pile of clothes, looking for his jacket pocket. 'Or maybe it'd be safer to burn the pencils.'

'Oh, no,' she picked up another lump of coal and dropped it on the fire. 'How would I explain the missing pencils?'

'How are you going to explain the missing coals?' He found his cigarette case and felt for the lighter in the other pocket.

'How would I know what happened to the coals?' She dropped a third coal onto the fire. 'There,' she said with satisfaction and crawled back to him. He flicked open his cigarette case and held it out to her.

'We can't smoke,' she lay down and snuggled up to him again.

'Why not?'

'Mr Montague hates cigarette smoke.'

'He won't notice.'

'Oh, he will. He notices everything.'

'You're pulling my leg.'

'No, I'm serious.'

'No, you're not.'

She raised her head to look him in the eye. 'Yes, I am.' She bent forward to kiss him lightly. 'Are we having our first fight about Mr Montague's nose?'

He laughed and she put her hand on his stomach and said, 'Do that again?'

'What?'

'Laugh.'

He laughed and she pressed her hand on his stomach. 'It's nice to feel a laugh as well as hear it,' she said.

'You're great,' he said.

'What I am is cold,' she replied.

'We'll get under the coat,' he said, and they rolled off it and back under it again.

'Ouch,' he said as the linoleum touched his skin. 'That's colder.'

She rolled on top of him and said, 'That's better.'

'For you.'

'And not for you?'

'Yes,' he pulled the coat over her and slid his hands under it. 'For me too.'

They made love again and then lay as they were, their feet cooling beyond the cover of the coat. Flames licked around the new lumps of coal, casting jumpy shadows around the room while the sounds from outside eased. The traffic noises had become more sporadic and the newsboys' cries had been replaced by a ticket tout outside the window offering tickets for the main evening showing at the Carlton cinema.

'I do have something to tell you,' she said. 'Why I called you.'

'I thought you just wanted to see me.'

'That's why you came in a hurry?' she smiled.

'Of course.'

'And I wanted to see you too.' She moved off him and onto the floor with an intake of breath as her side touched the cold lino. He turned on his side and moved back, letting her share the area his body had warmed. 'But there is something to tell you too.'

He said nothing, closing his eyes, not wanting to come back to the real world with its uncertainties and dilemmas and threats. She said nothing either and he opened his eyes after a few moments and she was looking into them in empathy. They kissed slowly, a confirmation of mutual understanding rather than passion, and then he said, 'Tell me.'

'I got a phone call from Yvonne,' she sat up.

'Yvonne?' He sat up beside her.

'You met her. A waitress in Mrs Lynch's? Who saw you when you were waiting for me outside?'

He nodded, remembering.

'Roddy Glenn stopped her in the street today when she was out shopping during her break. He said he wanted to contact me. Asked her where I live.'

Duggan nodded, aware this could be a breakthrough, but still reluctant to break the passing moment. He sighed and asked what Yvonne had told Glenn.

'She said she couldn't tell him where I live because she doesn't know. But that she would give me a message next time she saw me. He was very insistent, she said. Kept saying it was important, very important, that he see me again. As soon as possible.'

'Where was this?'

'Down in Mary Street. Around the corner from the café. You know?'

He nodded.

'She said she'd give me the message when she saw me but she didn't know when that would be as I didn't work there all the time. She asked him how I would get in touch with him.'

'And?' Duggan felt his interest come fully alert.

'He said he was moving digs at the moment and it'd be easier for him to contact me.'

'So he is in hiding,' Duggan nodded to himself.

'She wanted to know what she should say to him if he contacts her again. I said I'd think about it and asked her to call me tomorrow. And then I called you.'

Duggan stared at the fire, repressing the urge to have a cigarette and trying to focus on the best thing to do. The obvious thing was to arrange a time and place for Gerda to meet Glenn and nab him. Which might put her in danger, depending on who Glenn really worked for. She didn't have to turn up but that wouldn't ensure her safety: Glenn and his masters would know who had set him up.

'When's she going to meet him again?'

'I don't know. I don't think they've any definite arrangement.'

The best thing was to find out when Yvonne was meeting Glenn: surveillance could pick him up then. That'd get them onto him and keep Gerda out of it.

'Yvonne thinks he fancies me. That's what it's about.' Gerda put her head to one side and gave him a wry smile. 'Would that make you jealous?'

'Yes,' he said. 'I'll beat him up the first chance I get.' She looked shocked and he gave her a broad smile and added, 'Everything that keeps us apart make me jealous.'

'That's a better answer,' she kissed him, partly with relief.

They stood up and dressed and she looked around the room to make sure nothing was disturbed. In her office, she tied the scarf under her chin and asked him what she should tell Yvonne when she called.

'Let me think about it,' Duggan said. 'I'll call you first thing in the morning.'

'I can meet him again,' Gerda looked him in the eye. 'And get more information.'

'It could be dangerous.'

'Why? Who do you think he is?'

'I don't know. That's what we need to find out.'

'I'll ask him.' She shrugged like it was the most obvious thing to do.

Duggan shook his head. 'Let's think about it overnight.'

'You have to talk to your superiors,' she said, a statement of realities.

He nodded. 'But I want to think about it myself first. I don't want you to be in any danger.'

'I don't think he's dangerous. He's harmless.'

'Maybe. But the people he's working for may not be.'

'Why do you think that?'

'Because he has very serious information.'

'What?' she asked in surprise.

'Very secret documents.'

'For the Nazis?'

Duggan nodded. 'For everybody. For the Americans, too.'

'What have the Americans got to do with it?'

He kissed her to stop her questions, not wanting to refuse her anything. She responded but when they had finished she was still giving him an inquisitive look, not diverted. He shook his head in a silent apology.

'I understand,' she said. 'It's important.'

'I just don't want you to be in danger,' he repeated. 'Of any kind.'

She gave him a grateful look and he followed her down the stairs and onto the footpath and waited while she locked the outer door. The air was cold and sharp, tinged with turf smoke and the acrid smell of the city's gasworks drifting up from the docks. The ticket tout made for them but Duggan shook his head while he was still at a distance and he veered away towards another couple. Duggan glanced at the sky to see if it was clearing but couldn't make out anything above the haze of the limited city lights.

'Are they coming again tonight?' Gerda asked, following his glance.

'I think we'll be all right,' he said. 'The weather isn't due to clear yet.'

'Just in time,' she said, catching sight of her bus approaching and moving towards the stop

'I'll give you a lift,' he said.

'I thought you were cycling.'

'On my bike.'

She gave him a soft punch in the arm. 'I'm not getting up on any fella's crossbar,' she laughed, putting out her hand to stop the bus. 'I'm a respectable woman from Cork.'

The bus pulled in and she placed her open palm on the side of his face and stepped onto the platform. The conductor hit his bell and the bus got into gear and heaved itself away, leaving a belch of oily exhaust smoke behind. She remained on the platform and he watched her recede until the bus went into Parnell Square and he couldn't see her any more.

He cycled back along the quays, feeling his feet were barely pushing the pedals, tasting the hint of snow on the air, savouring the limited lights and wider shadows, energised. He took his time, smoking as he cycled, but seemed to get there faster than ever, pushing up the last stretch of hill, in the gate and back around to the Red House.

His office was empty, Sullivan's end of the table cleared of everything, indicating that he had left for the night. He found Commandant McClure in his office, twiddling a pencil instead of his usual cigarette and frowning at a page of what Duggan knew from the flimsy paper was a carbon copy of a garda report.

Duggan told him of Glenn's attempt to contact Gerda and McClure leaned back in his chair and tossed the pencil on the desk with relief. 'What do you think we should do?' he inquired.

'Pick him up when he contacts the other waitress,' Duggan suggested.

'Arrest him?' McClure said in surprise.

'I mean put surveillance on him.'

'And how do we know when that'll happen?' McClure sounded disappointed. 'When he'll approach her again.'

'We don't know exactly,' Duggan admitted, aware how weak the idea sounded.

McClure stared at him for a moment, increasing his discomfort. 'Is our friend willing to meet him?'

'Yes.'

'And do you think she could handle it?'

Duggan nodded.

McClure lapsed into silence again, keeping his eyes on Duggan. 'What do you think of her?'

Duggan shifted in spite of himself, not wanting to have this conversation but unable to stop himself signalling his feelings. 'She's reliable. Observant. Reports regularly and accurately. As far as I know.'

'Intelligent?'

'Yes.'

'Motivated?'

Duggan nodded.

'Trustworthy?'

Duggan nodded again.

'Attractive.' It wasn't a question this time. McClure modified his stare with the hint of a grin and added, 'At ease,' although Duggan was not at attention. He stood up and stretched himself.

Duggan relaxed, realising how tense, and probably transparent, he was. He got out a cigarette. 'I don't want to put her in any danger,' he said as he lit it.

'No, of course not.' McClure picked a cigarette from the box on his desk. 'But you think she would be willing to meet him?'

'Yes. She really hates the Nazis.'

'With reason,' McClure grunted.

'Have you met her?' Duggan asked, seeing an opportunity to find out something he'd wondered about.

'Only once and then briefly. To see if she'd do what we wanted.'

'How did you find her?' Duggan gave vent to his curiosity and then regretted it as McClure gave him a silent stare. 'I'm sorry, I don't . . .'

McClure waved away his apology. 'I sent a circular around battalion IOs, asking if anyone knew of a female German speaker who'd be willing to help us. One of Southern Command's lads told me about her. And she agreed. Motivated, as you say.'

Thirteen

'Adelaide Agency,' Gerda answered the phone.

'How are you today?' Duggan said, the sound of her voice filling him with affection.

'Yes, sir,' she said in an efficient tone. 'I'm sure we have something suitable.'

'You can't talk.'

'We have excellent properties in all the best locations in the suburbs.'

'Okay,' he said. 'Tell Yvonne to give our friend your phone number.'

'Yes, sir, that's a very popular location.'

'And arrange a meeting if he wants to see you.'

Gerda made a sound of approval.

'But don't go to meet him until I've seen you first.'

'We have several properties that would meet your requirements.'

'That's very important.'

'Can I send you a copy of our list?' she asked.

'Anyway,' Duggan dropped his voice as Sullivan came into the office. 'That should be done as soon as possible.'

'Yes, we're open from nine to five, apart from the lunch hour.'

'Thanks for your help,' Duggan said, hoping that she would understand the reason for his change of tone.

'Good day to you,' she said and then dropped her voice to the barest whisper, little more than an exhaled breath. 'I love you.'

Duggan wasn't sure he heard it, or even that she said it. He grappled with a response, aware of Sullivan's presence, but she hadn't waited. The phone line was dead.

'Are you still talking on that thing?' Sullivan nodded towards the phone that Duggan was still holding.

'No,' Duggan dropped the receiver onto its cradle. 'Do you want it?'

Sullivan shook his head and opened the file before him. 'The mammy's been right all these years,' he said.

'What?'

'The power of prayer,' Sullivan looked at him as if the answer was obvious. 'It's shifted the wind back to the east so the clearance from the west isn't happening. And I had the night off.'

'I was wondering how you managed that.' Duggan thought of Ó Murchú in External Affairs hoping for bad weather to keep the Germans from pushing their demand to be allowed to fly more 'diplomats' into Foynes. Maybe Mrs Sullivan was one of a battalion he had praying for bad weather, like the church did for the farmers threatened with drought in the summers.

'There won't be an invasion either,' Sullivan smiled. 'The mammy's been sending up prayers against it. Like a rapid-firing Bofors.'

'Have you written a report on that? Calm everybody down.'

'You think I should?'

The phone rang before Duggan could answer him and he picked it up and gave his name.

'The very man,' Timmy said in his ear. 'Buswell's. Half an hour.'

'What?'

'Great things happening in our time,' Timmy said, almost breathless with excitement.

'What?' Duggan repeated.

'On your bike,' Timmy chuckled and hung up.

'For fuck's sake,' Duggan muttered as he replaced the receiver again. Timmy in a state of excitement filled him with instant caution. His idea of great things happening wasn't necessarily anyone else's idea of greatness. Still, he probably had some news of Goertz. Unless it was some other conspiracy altogether.

'What's the problem?' Sullivan asked. 'More women chasing you?'

'That's it,' Duggan said, getting up and retrieving his coat from the stand. 'I've got to go out.'

'Jaysus,' Sullivan said, his shoulders drooping over his file. 'I'm going to get the mammy to start praying that you'll do some work around here.'

The bar in Buswell's Hotel was quiet, grey light seeping in from the morning outside as if it was afraid of what it might illuminate. A mixture of stale smoke and spilt beer from hundreds of raucous drinking nights suffused the unnatural silence. A man sat at one end of the bar, an *Irish Press* open on the counter before him with a pint of untouched Guinness half-covering its main headline. His head rested on his arms and he was snoring, making a delicate, almost elegant sound. There was no one else there but the barman, running a desultory cloth over a shelf of spirit bottles.

Duggan was about to take a seat at the bar when he saw Timmy passing the window, coming across from his office in Leinster House. Timmy nodded to him as he came in and said, 'Hardy day, Johnny' to the barman who reached automatically for a bottle of Paddy and poured some into a measure.

'Bottle of Guinness?' Timmy asked Duggan.

'No, thanks. Too early for me.'

'Give him a lemonade,' Timmy told the barman.

'Will we have more snow, Mr Monaghan?' the barman asked as he set up the drinks.

'I don't know,' Timmy said, giving the question an unexpected gravity. He seemed in sombre mood, not at all what Duggan had expected after the ebullience of his phone call. 'Hope not. I'm fed up slipping and sliding about the place.'

They took their drinks over to a corner table and lit cigarettes. Timmy looked around the bar as if he had never been there before, uncomfortable with its emptiness and its early morning atmosphere.

'Maybe we should go somewhere else,' Duggan broke the silence. 'Go for a walk.'

Timmy gave him a stare that suggested he was mentally deficient and splashed a practised dash of water into his whiskey. 'I met the Doc,' he said in a low voice.

'Surgeon O'Shea?' Duggan leaned forward into a conspiratorial huddle.

'No, the Doc himself.'

'Who?' Duggan asked, confused.

'Mr Robinson,' Timmy dropped his voice even more.

'*Goertz*?' Duggan asked, astonished. He hadn't expected that. He had hoped, at most, that Timmy would give them another lead to follow, not take them directly to the German spy.

'Whatever you call him,' Timmy inhaled a stream of smoke, followed it with a mouthful of whiskey, and exhaled. 'I only know him as Henry Robinson. That's how I was introduced to him.'

'At the German Minister's party last year?'

Timmy nodded. 'They call him the Doc.'

'Who does?'

'The people who look after him. He's a doctor, you know.'

'He's a legal doctor,' Duggan said. 'Not a real doctor.'

'What the fuck's that?'

'A lawyer.'

Timmy picked up his glass, like the wind had been taken from his sails. He finished off his drink and raised the glass to catch the barman's attention. Keep your mouth shut, Duggan told himself, let him tell it the way he wants to. Timmy liked to do things his own way, didn't like other people stealing his thunder.

The barman put another glass of Paddy on the counter and Timmy heaved himself off the chair and went to get it. Duggan took a drink of the red lemonade and watched him, keeping his impatience and excitement under control.

Timmy came back with his whiskey and another bottle of lemonade. He took his time stubbing out the butt he had left burning in the ashtray. Then he watered the whiskey, raised his glass and said, '*Sláinte.*' Duggan touched it with his glass and they drank in silence.

Timmy put down his glass and leaned forward. 'I ran into Mrs O'Shea, *moryah*, the other night as she and Mona were leaving the altar committee meeting. Told her I needed a private word with her about a sensitive matter. She nearly fell off her high horse when I said it was about our German friend. An unofficial official inquiry, just between us, blah, blah, blah. To cut a long story short, she sent me a message yesterday, asking me to call round to a certain address at nine o'clock last night.' Timmy paused for a drink but really for dramatic effect. Duggan resisted the temptation to ask where.

'And there was the man himself,' Timmy resumed his narrative. '"Mr Robinson," I said, "we've met before." "We have indeed," he said, "and I'm very pleased to meet you again. I've been hoping to talk to an emissary from your government." "Hold your horses now," I said, "these are very dangerous times and I'm on an unofficial mission here." "Like myself," he said, "but it's important that we understand each other." "I couldn't put it better myself," I said.' Timmy stopped for another sup of whiskey.

'Anyway. I asked him the question. "What's all this bombing about?" And he said he didn't know but we shouldn't assume that it was the Luftwaffe. "My own sentiments entirely," I told him. Then he said he's been hounded from pillar to post by you fellows and the Blueshirts in the Branch. That he can't communicate with his people. And nobody in official circles will talk to him. That he's the best friend Ireland ever had. He's tried to get in touch with a senior military man who said he'd love to have a talk with him but he'd have to do his duty and arrest him if they met.' Timmy lit a cigarette, while Duggan tried to remember every detail of what he was hearing, automatically filtering Timmy's phrases and his beliefs out of his account. He doubted if Herr Goertz had complained about the Blueshirts in the Special Branch.

'He has a good point,' Timmy continued, going off on another tack. 'The German legation doesn't have a military attaché here and the British one does. They've a whole lot of spies in their place. What kind of neutrality is that? So the Doc has to do the job of a military attaché but he hasn't the facilities to do it. Can't communicate with his people. Hounded from pillar to post. Living on the run. It's not fair. And it's not in our interest. The best friend Ireland ever had.'

Timmy sat back, finished. Does Goertz know about the German demand to increase the numbers in its legation? Duggan wondered. It sounded like he did. And that put a whole new complexion on his relationship with Herr Hempel and his role in Ireland. It also means he knows if the bombings were meant as a message. But he couldn't ask Timmy directly about this without revealing more than he should.

'That's great,' Duggan said. 'Very useful information.'

'You should talk to him yourself. You'd like him. An intelligent man. A decent sort.'

'Would he talk to me?'

'If you guarantee not to have him arrested.'

'I don't think I could do that,' Duggan said, wondering if it might be possible. He could put it to McClure. 'I can ask.'

'Do that,' Timmy nodded. 'That'd be a good day's work for the country.'

'What exactly did he say when you asked him about the reasons for the bombing?'

'He said he didn't know, only what he read in the papers. And he explained why he didn't know. Because he can't contact his people.'

'Doesn't he have a radio?'

'He lost it along the way. The IRA was to get him one but they haven't managed it yet. He's a bit fed up with them lads actually.'

'He's still involved with them?'

'Yeah, but he says they're very inefficient. Fighting with each other and whatnot. He's actually trying to leave the country.'

'He is?'

'Been trying for months,' Timmy nodded. 'Get a boat that'll take him back to France.'

'That's interesting,' Duggan said, beginning to see how things might look from Goertz's perspective.

'That's the least you could do for him,' Timmy went on. 'Help him get back home and he'll be a great contact there.'

'Spy for us?' Duggan couldn't help smiling.

'He's not a spy,' Timmy snapped back. 'He's a representative of the German high command. Help him go home and he'll be able to answer all your questions. Ireland has no better friend than him. His own words. And we'd have him there in Germany if we needed him. Right at the top.'

'He's carrying on with the IRA,' Duggan pointed out.

'Never mind that,' Timmy waved his objection aside. 'He's no time for them anymore. Says the high command needs to know the truth about them. The Germans think they're a serious force but he says they're a waste of time. Messers.' Timmy gave him a questioning look, as if to wait for the penny to drop about the advantage of letting Goertz go. 'And,' he leaned forward in a more confidential pose, 'he could get us the arms that you fellows need to resist an invasion.'

Duggan was already shaking his head. They had been down this road before. Germany had offered to supply captured British arms to the Irish army after the fall of France the previous year. The offer had been turned down by the government on the grounds that it would be seen as a breach of neutrality by the British and would put Ireland in the Axis camp. But Timmy had been arguing, even conspiring, in favour of accepting it.

'Hear me out,' Timmy raised a finger. 'It could be done right. So that the Brits wouldn't know.'

'They'd know very fast if we suddenly had a lot of their old rifles. And be very angry.'

Timmy waved his finger at him to stop him. 'Suppose the rifles were sent in a shipment from France. A boat from Brest to some quiet spot on the south coast. It'd be for the IRA, *moryah*. But you lads would've happened to hear about it. And you'd be on hand to grab it as it came ashore.' Timmy sat back with a smile. 'And you'd have a few thousand more Lee Enfields.'

Duggan shook his head in admiration at the deviousness of the plan. 'This your idea?'

'And the Doc's,' Timmy beamed. 'Neat, isn't it?'

Duggan nodded. 'But it's still dangerous. If it went wrong.'

'How could it go wrong?'

'If people got to hear about it.'

'Wouldn't matter. You could even tell the Brits. Look what we've done. Stopped those nasty IRA chappies getting your old guns,' Timmy laughed. 'Even offer to give them back. But that might be seen as a breach of neutrality by the Germans. So it'd be better for everybody if we held onto them ourselves. Nobody need know the real plan. Except you and me and the Doc. Be a feather in your cap.'

Jesus, Duggan thought, he's indefatigable. I'm not getting involved in any conspiracies with Timmy and German agents. 'Too risky,' he said. 'What if the British decided that it proved the IRA was a real threat and working with the Germans? And used that as an excuse for an invasion?'

'They don't need an excuse to invade us. They'll just make one up.'

'Besides,' Duggan said. 'Mr Aiken is going to America to get us the supplies we need.'

'Is he now?' Timmy looked at him with a triumphant smile, delighted to hear something that wasn't yet general knowledge. 'No better man,' Timmy added. 'Frank'll mark the Yanks' cards all right.'

'Are you meeting Goertz again?' Duggan changed the subject, cursing himself for telling Timmy something he didn't know, but there was no way to take it back.

'Depends,' Timmy said. 'You have any more questions for him?'

'Not at the moment. Where was the meeting?'

'Now, Paul,' Timmy wagged his finger at him. 'You know better than that. Anyway, it wouldn't do you any good if I told you. He's long gone from there.'

'How do you know?'

'Because he's being hounded from pillar to post. Like I keep telling you. Everyone who's helping him is being harassed by the Branch. So he's having to rely on other people. Less reliable people.'

'Like who?'

'There's never been any informers in our family,' Timmy gave him a cold stare. 'And I hope there never will be.'

'Okay,' Duggan nodded, anxious now to get away and write all this down as soon as he could.

'If you've any more questions,' Timmy took the hint and stood up. 'I'll see what I can do.'

'Thanks. I appreciate you help.'

The man at the bar raised his head and looked around, sleepy but not surprised at his surroundings. 'Timothy,' he called over, 'you'll have a drink.'

'Later, Charlie,' Timmy slapped him on the back as they passed. 'Got a meeting.'

'Sound man,' the man called after them.

'Poor fucker,' Timmy muttered as they left the hotel. 'Got a bit of a drink problem.'

Back in the office Duggan typed a report as fast as two fingers would allow but he was making so many mistakes he had to stop and start again. He didn't mention Timmy's name or, as was usual practice, his initials, and just typed G for Goertz to speed up the report. When he'd finished he read over it again, corrected some typing mistakes by pen on the top sheet and on the carbon copies and put his initials at the bottom.

'Big news?' Sullivan had been watching, noting his concentration.

'Yeah,' Duggan screwed the cap back onto his fountain pen. 'Message for your mother from Adolf. Please tell Mrs Sullivan to stop attacking me with her prayers.'

'Laugh all you want,' Sullivan said. 'It's all that's between us and some fuckers raining down bombs on us for no reason.'

Duggan glanced at him, surprised at the fatalism in his voice. It wasn't like Sullivan to sound like that but he'd been a different person since he'd been in Carlow and seen the effects of a bomb on a farmhouse in the middle of nowhere. Sullivan caught his look and shrugged. He took a small packet of Sweet Afton from his pocket and tossed it down the table to Duggan. 'I took two out of it,' he said.

'Thanks.' Duggan pocketed the cigarettes and took his report to McClure's office.

'This from who I think it's from?' McClure asked as he scanned quickly down the page. Duggan nodded and McClure wrote a faint TM in pencil on the top of the page. 'Good work,' he said when he had finished reading it again. 'So our friends in the Branch have been after the right people. But need to extend their search to the wider circle of hangers-on.'

'Seems like that,' Duggan agreed.

'Useful.' McClure muttered. 'But nothing here to answer our main question or to help Mr Ó Murchú.'

'No,' Duggan said. 'Unless he was lying when he said he knew nothing about the bombing. But why would he do that if he did know? It'd be in his interest to explain if they wanted something.'

'You'd think so,' McClure agreed. 'This idea of importing arms under cover of IRA smuggling, was that from Goertz?'

'I'm not entirely sure,' Duggan admitted. 'My source wasn't too clear about that. He was trying to take some of the credit.'

'Is he trying to get himself into trouble again?'

'He's just . . .' Duggan shrugged, stopping himself from adding 'Timmy'. That was enough of an explanation to him but he didn't want to name Timmy out loud. Anyway, it probably wouldn't mean anything to McClure to tell him that Timmy was just Timmy, how he could never leave well enough alone, always conniving and conspiring over something. Instead, he pointed out Timmy's suggestion that they help Goertz escape, have a friend in Germany.

'Interesting idea,' McClure said without committing himself. 'Would require careful consideration.'

'Dangerous if it backfired in some way.'

'Everything's a risk these days,' McClure stretched himself.

'What about offering to meet Goertz?' Duggan asked.

'To talk? Or to arrest him?'

'To arrest him.'

McClure gave him one of his long disconcerting stares, thinking. But Duggan had the impression that it was tinged with disapproval this time. 'Everything's risky these days,' McClure repeated at last. 'It's best if we play straight. Don't create any unnecessary bad feeling.'

Duggan nodded, chastised.

'Straightish, anyway,' McClure gave him a crooked grin and stood up. 'Meantime, our friend at Mrs Lynch's gave me a call.'

Duggan stared at him, taken aback. Why was Gerda calling McClure?

'She was looking for you. Asked for me when you weren't here. She said she didn't trust anyone else to give you the message.' McClure put a question mark at the end of the sentence. Duggan made a helpless gesture with his hands. Why didn't she trust Sullivan? he wondered. Probably because he's been making some smart comments to her.

'Anyway,' McClure continued. 'This Glenn fellow called her.'

'That was quick.'

'A man in a hurry,' McClure nodded. 'He wants to meet her. So she said she'd meet him outside the Savoy cinema. At a quarter to eight.'

'Tonight?'

McClure nodded. Shit, Duggan thought. He'd told her not to agree to anything until they'd worked out what she was to say. 'We could put some people onto him,' McClure was saying. 'Though I don't think we've enough available to do a proper job. The guards say they can't spare anyone. They've enough on their own plates, and they're doing a job for us down the docks this evening.'

'But it could be dangerous for her. To be alone.'

'She doesn't seem to think so,' McClure said, pacing around the room. 'Neither do I. As far as he's concerned she's a waitress who was friendly to him in an unfriendly place. And a link to the Germans he wants to communicate with.'

'But we don't know what he's up to. Other than passing secret British documents to the German.'

'This is our chance to find out. It's too good to pass up.'

Duggan shook his head, following his own thoughts. It was still dangerous. Glenn had top-secret documents. It hardly mattered whether they were real or false. Either way, he had to be working for some organisation. Either passing secrets or sowing disinformation. And Gerda was in danger of walking into the middle of something very dangerous if they found out what she was really up to.

'Also,' McClure was watching him closely, 'it's safer for her if we don't try anything. In case he has someone watching his back.'

Duggan shook his head again. 'That's what I'm worried about.'

'Then it's best that she be exactly what she appears to be,' McClure said in a patient voice, aware that Duggan's concern were not just about an operation. 'A helpful waitress. A nice, decent girl who's taken pity on someone who's been treated badly. Nothing more, nothing less. That's her best protection.'

Duggan accepted the logic of that. As long as her feelings about the Nazis didn't get the better of her. And cause her to say something. 'What does she say to him?' he asked, as they slipped into playing out the meeting, with Duggan standing still in the unusual role of throwing the questions at his superior who continued to walk around the room.

'She says she's given the envelope he gave her to one of the Luftwaffe officers. He took it but didn't open it in front of her. She doesn't know what he's done with it. She hasn't seen him again since.

But, mainly, she listens. Glenn's asked to meet her, so . . .' McClure spread his hands, inviting Glenn to make the next move.

'And what if he asks her to do something else?'

'Depends what it is. If it's to deliver another message to the German internees, she takes it.'

'And if it's to do something else?'

'What else could it be?'

'Meet someone else, maybe.'

'She acts the innocent. Who is this person?'

'Go to the German legation for him?'

'Why would he want her to do that? Why couldn't he do that himself?'

'And if he doesn't buy her response?'

'She doesn't agree or disagree to anything on the spot. She indicates without saying so that she's not keen to be involved in anything. She has to think about it. He can call her tomorrow. Or the day after. She kicks to touch. That's her basic position.'

'As long as she doesn't lose her temper with him.'

McClure stopped pacing. 'Why would she do that?'

'Because she really hates the Nazis.'

McClure nodded to himself and walked back behind his desk. 'You impress on her the danger in doing that.' He sat down. 'She's got to be what she appears to be.'

Duggan tried to think what else Glenn might want and a hint of a smile crossed his face. 'What?' McClure caught it.

'Maybe he just wants to buy her a drink,' Duggan said.

'I'm sure she can handle that.'

Duggan stood in the queue at the bus stop on Upper O'Connell Street, facing back down the street but really waiting for Gerda's boss,

Montague, to leave his office. The night was cold again, the street busy with the last hour of business, the old snow now blackened with grit and smuts. The pedestrians were in a hurry and wary at the same time, cautious of where they put their feet. The street was oddly empty of voices, people waiting to get home, waiting for the snow to go away, waiting for January to end, spring to come. Waiting.

A bus pulled in and half the queue got on, filling the last few seats inside and jamming the aisle. A haze of cigarette smoke, accentuated by the reduced blue lighting, shifted back and forth beneath its ceiling as it accelerated away. He checked his watch again. Almost a quarter past five. Maybe Montague had left before five, like he'd done yesterday. He glanced up at the window of Montague's office but the bottom half was blocked by the sign for Adelaide Apartments and the top half was opaque in reflected light.

He left the queue and went to the door and ran up the steps, noting the light under the door at the top.

Gerda stood up and came around her desk as soon as he came in, flicked off the light by the door and turned the key in the lock as she put her arms around him. She stepped back and poked at his side. 'What's that?'

He put his palms on either side of her face and kissed her and she unbuttoned his overcoat and held it open and broke away from the kiss. She looked at the binoculars hanging over his right shoulder and felt under his jacket to the butt of the revolver under his left arm. 'Later,' he said in response to her inquiring look.

She took a patterned rug from behind her desk and led him into Montague's office where the fire was still bright. 'I put on a big fire when he was out earlier,' she giggled. 'He gave out to me for wasting coal and I had to say I was distracted and forgot it was so late in the day.'

They undressed each other, she leaving it to him to shrug off the holster with the heavy Webley and place it on the desk. They settled down on the rug, into the warmth of the fire and of each other and made love. They lay in each other's arms for a long time, communicating with their fingers on each other's bodies.

She shivered and he shifted to pull his coat over them and said, 'You should've talked to me before you agreed to meet him.'

'I know,' she said with a sigh after a long pause, dragging herself back to the present from somewhere else. 'But he said it had to be today.'

'Why?'

'I didn't ask.'

She raised herself on her elbow and the flames flickered sideways in the dark depths of her eyes. He combed his fingers through her black hair, raising it and letting it fall.

'You're going to protect me,' she said, amusement mixing with gratitude and tenderness.

'You haven't made it easy,' he grunted. 'We could've picked a better place to meet if we'd had time.'

'Like where?'

'I don't know,' he watched her hair rise with his fingers and fall away. 'We could've come up with something better, safer.'

'It's safe over there. Always people around the cinema.'

She lowered her head onto his chest and they didn't talk again for a while. The fire cast its teasing flickers along the underside of the mantelpiece and the ceiling and the outside world went through its rush hour and settled into its early night mode, unnoticed. He wasn't sure if he dozed a while or not but he came back to the present when she moved her leg over him and they made love again.

Afterwards, he looked at his watch and she asked him what time it was and he told her it was just after seven.

'You will be careful,' he whispered to her. 'Won't you?'

'*Keine Sorge*,' she whispered back. Don't worry.

He smiled, remembering the last time she had said that. 'Seriously,' he added. 'I know you think he's harmless but we don't really know who he is. Who he belongs to or what they're up to.' She made a line of kisses across his chest. 'Just be who he thinks you are,' he closed his eyes, 'Gertie. Not Gerda. A nice waitress.' He went on, murmuring McClure's instructions. Don't ask him anything. Let him make the running. And don't agree on the spot to do anything else for him, other than give more envelopes to the German internees.

She gave no indication that she had heard him at all and he shifted onto his side and looked into her eyes. 'Okay?' he asked.

'Hmm,' she nodded.

'These are instructions from Commandant McClure,' he said, trying to impress on her the importance of what he was saying.

'Does he know about us?'

'No,' Duggan said, though he wasn't sure. He hadn't yet decided after nearly a year working with McClure whether he really knew more than he ever said or whether he just gave the impression of knowing more than he did. A bit like Timmy. 'Why did you call him?'

'Because they said you were not there. And I didn't want to talk to the other man who usually answers your phone.'

'Bill Sullivan?'

'He's not friendly,' she said.

'Why? What'd he say?'

'Last time he asked me was I the latest.'

'The latest what?'

'He didn't say.'

'That's just a bit of banter between us.'

'You make love to all your agents?' she asked with an impish grin.

Duggan began to laugh, thinking of Timmy and Gifford and all the other people he came across. 'You should see them,' he chortled.

'I love your laugh,' she said, serious. 'We don't laugh enough.'

'No,' he agreed. 'But we will. When we've put all this behind us.'

They got dressed and she watched him pick up the revolver and put the holster over his shoulders. 'Is that loaded?' she asked.

'No point carrying an empty gun,' he said.

'You're going to follow behind me?'

'No,' he said. 'It's too dangerous. We don't know who might be with him, watching his back. And if they saw me, they'd know you were a plant.'

'A plant?' she repeated, confused by the word.

'A spy. Working for somebody. Not who Glenn thinks you are.'

She nodded, the possible danger of the situation now beginning to sink in for the first time. 'A plant,' she repeated, trying out the word, a new description for herself.

He put his hands on her shoulders. 'Remember,' he said. 'You are Gertie Maher, a part-time waitress. You're not interested in the British or the Germans or what's going on in the war. You couldn't care less really. Nothing to do with us, we're neutral. It's just a' – he searched for the right word – 'an inconvenience.'

She nodded, searching his eyes, very serious now. A wave of tenderness overwhelmed him and he kissed her softly.

'I'll be watching from here,' he inclined his head towards the binoculars on the floor. 'Afterwards, you come back to the bus stop and get on your bus when it comes. Get off the third time it stops. Not at the third stop, but the third time it actually stops. Walk about fifty yards up the road and then turn around and come back to the stop, like you changed your mind. Wait at the stop again and I'll pick you up in the car. Okay?'

'Okay,' she said.

'Don't agree to go anywhere with him. Under any circumstances. Not even into the Savoy café. Nowhere.'

She nodded.

'If he asks you make some excuse. Someone's waiting for you.' He looked at his watch: ten minutes to go. She put on her overcoat and tied her scarf under her chin. 'Go down the road and cross at the Pillar,' he said. 'And come back the same way. And don't tell him where you work or live. Except in a general way. If it arises naturally.'

'Don't worry.' She put a finger on his lips. 'I will be very careful.'

He helped her fold up the rug and she checked that everything was as it should be in Montague's office. The fire had died down and the room was beginning to cool. He followed her out to her own office and she put away the rug behind her desk and picked up her handbag. 'Good luck,' he said at the top of the stairs. She kissed him on the cheek and he watched her go down the stairs and out the street door. She didn't look back.

Fourteen

Duggan smoked at the top of the stairs, hearing the street door still bang in his mind. He topped the half-finished cigarette onto the floor, rubbed out the burning coal with his shoe, went back into Gerda's office and took up a position a step back from her window. He scanned the other side of O'Connell Street with the binoculars, moving slowly down the street, pausing at a few people standing in doorways and those at bus queues. The street wasn't busy but there was a steady stream of couples and singles passing up and down.

He picked up Gerda as she came into view and held the picture steady as she passed through it, watching everyone who came after her, trying to pick out their features. That was impossible, he realised. Everyone was swathed in coats and hats and scarves and the dim streetlight was made more dense by the binoculars' magnification. He caught up with Gerda again as she reached the Savoy and then the statue of Father Mathew in the centre of the street blocked his view. He cursed and willed her to go further and breathed with relief when she reappeared and stopped at the cinema, her back against the wall. Another woman waited near her and a man was standing at the other end of the building.

Duggan studied him for a moment, a dark hat over a brownish scarf and a black overcoat. He couldn't make out any of his features under the shadow of the hat, made impenetrable by the light from the cinema entrance behind him. He scanned back down the street again, pausing at any of the men who were alone and whose posture suggested they were not old. He swung back up the street to the Savoy and his pulse quickened. There was a man talking to Gerda, his back to the street.

He was wearing a tweed cap and a tweed coat down below his knees. Duggan could see hair under his cap but couldn't tell if it was black or brown. He was taller than Gerda, thin, and stood straight but moved from foot to foot as if he was cold or impatient. Where had he come from? He hadn't seen him approach.

Duggan watched them for a few moments, catching glimpses of Gerda's face over Glenn's shoulder as they shifted their positions. She was listening to whatever he was saying, then said something short, a couple of words. The man put his right hand into his pocket, took something out and gave it to her. At least Duggan assumed he gave it to her. His arms were beginning to ache from trying to hold the binoculars steady and he forced himself to breathe slowly to minimise the movement.

He scanned back down the street, trying to spot anyone who might be watching the meeting. A man in a doorway was facing the other way. There were two men separated by a middle-aged woman with a shopping bag in the middle of a bus queue, all facing up the street towards the oncoming traffic and the cinema. A bus pulled in and Duggan waited impatiently for it to take on the passengers, scanning back to the cinema to make sure Glenn and Gerda were still there.

The bus pulled away at last and there were a few people left at the stop, including one of the young men and the middle-aged woman. Duggan tried to make out his features but could see little other than an impression of his profile underneath a dark cap: he had his hands in the pockets of a dark overcoat and was rocking back and forth on his heels. A sign of nerves? Or just impatience?

Duggan swung back to the Savoy and Gerda was just walking away. Glenn turned to look after her and then looked up and down the street a couple of times. He's alone, Duggan thought: he wouldn't be looking around if he knew he was being backed up. The brim of his cap and the cinema's lights shadowed his face but Duggan caught a hint of a sharp chin. Glenn walked up the street, hurrying in the opposite direction, and Duggan cursed as he went outside his vision.

He scanned the street again once or twice but nobody caught his interest and he put the binoculars back in their case and put on his overcoat, ready to leave. He waited until he saw Gerda come up the street underneath the window to her bus stop. He locked the door behind him, went down the steps, and then locked the street door behind him. He sauntered down the street, not looking towards Gerda but trying to check out anyone coming towards him. He stopped under the canopy of the Pillar Picture House and looked at a poster of Bing Crosby and Gloria Jean without taking in the details, crossed Henry Street and stopped under the portico of the GPO and lit a cigarette, waiting for her bus to come up the street.

As soon as it passed him, he walked around the corner into Henry Street to where he had parked the Prefect and edged slowly into O'Connell Street. The bus was pulling away from the kerb and he followed it, keeping his distance, as it went up Parnell Square and North Frederick Street. He stopped every time it stopped, watching the traffic in front of him and behind. There were few cars on the streets and some cyclists. None of them seemed to be trying to match the bus's progress.

The third time it stopped was near Phibsborough. A couple got off, followed by Gerda. They crossed the road behind the bus and came back down the road towards Duggan. He watched them go into a house almost opposite him and waited until they had opened the door and closed it behind them. There was no sign of anyone taking an interest in the bus, Gerda or himself.

She had walked away from the bus stop, as instructed, turned and was now approaching it again. He waited until she got there, pulled out onto the road and drove up to her. She sat in, let out a deep breath and untied her scarf and shook out her hair.

'Okay?' he asked.

'Whew,' she nodded. 'Is it all right?'

'Nobody followed you.'

She poked him in the side with her finger. 'See?' she said. 'I told you he was harmless. You had me all worried someone would follow me home. Kill me in my bed.'

'Just being careful.'

'Are you always so careful?'

'I don't want anything to happen to you,' he said truthfully, but wondering if she'd forgotten that he was working.

'Then you better get me some food before I starve to death.' She was in a giddy mood, the release of tension giving way to a mild euphoria.

'Me too,' he said. 'There's a chipper back down there.'

'Ugh,' she laughed.

'You don't like fish and chips?'

'It's disgusting. But I'll eat anything now.'

'He is harmless,' she said as he did a three-point turn and drove back past the Mater hospital to Dorset Street. 'I answered all his questions. Did you give the letter to the Germans? I did, to an officer. What did he say? Did he open it? No. Who was he? I don't know, just one of the Germans. Have you seen him again? No, I only work there some of the time. Will you give them another message?'

'Ah ha,' Duggan sighed with satisfaction.

'Tell him I'd like to meet him?' she continued her staccato report. 'I don't know when I'll see him again. But tell him when you see him. All right, I said. Then he asked me to send a postcard to a woman in England.'

'What?' Duggan glanced at her.

'He asked me to send a postcard to a woman in England,' she repeated, opening her handbag. 'Gave me the postcard and what to write on it.'

Duggan coasted to a stop just before the chipper on Dorset Street and turned off the engine. Gerda handed him a postcard, a black and white photograph of O'Connell Street on one side, the back blank. Then she handed him a folded sheet of paper from a young child's copybook. It had a name on it, Mrs Agnes Smith, an address in Chelsea, London, and a message written crossways over the red and blue guidelines: 'Dear Aunt Agnes, I'm having such a nice time here I'm staying another week! Hope all the family are well. Love . . .'

Duggan read it again. 'Love, who?'

'He said to sign it with any name I liked. A woman's name. My own if I wanted. But any woman's name.'

'Why doesn't he write it himself?'

'I asked him that. But he wouldn't give me a straight answer. Said it'd be better if someone else did it. And would I please. Then he said he had to go. And I tried to give him back the card and note and he pleaded with me. So I kept it.' She paused. 'You told me not to argue with him.'

Duggan nodded absently, wondering what this meant. It didn't make any sense at all. Why would Glenn want her to send a postcard for him? With an apparently harmless message? Which was almost certainly a prearranged code for something. But why want a woman to send it? Just so it had a woman's writing on it?

'What about the other message? You said he wanted you to give the German airmen another message?'

'He said he'd ring me in a day or two when it was ready.'

'When it was ready? Did he say what that meant?'

'No,' she shook her head. 'You told me to be a silly girl and not ask questions. I could've asked him a whole lot of things but you told me not to.'

'You did a great job. Following orders.'

'Yes, captain, sir,' she gave him a mock salute. 'Am I a good soldier?'

'You're a real trooper.' He bent forward to kiss her.

'Do I get my dinner now?' she demanded when they broke apart.

Duggan put the postcard and note into his inside pocket and went into the chipper. He stood by the window and lit a cigarette while the deep fat fryer burst into life when the heavy man behind the counter threw a few handfuls of chipped potatoes and two battered fish into it. The shop was steamy with the heat, its window fogged with condensation. He rubbed a clear circle but it fogged over again almost immediately.

An ad on the corner of a folded *Evening Herald* caught his eye with its black silhouette of a bomber. 'Last week you had a vivid reminder,' the copy said, 'so store food now: perhaps you will not get another chance.' He turned over the paper and scanned the headlines: the Dáil was being summoned back next week to discuss shortages and the government had slashed the petrol ration. A two-gallon coupon was now worth only half a gallon, the story said, effectively putting an end to private motoring. A black box carried a Press Association report quoting Berlin radio saying that a Swedish newspaper reported that Britain would invade Eire in a few weeks.

Dúirt bean liom go ndúirt bean léi . . . he thought of the dismissive saying about secondhand gossip, shaking his head involuntarily. So the British were implementing their plan, turning the screw on supplies to bring home to Ireland its refusal to help the Atlantic convoys with port facilities. The first part of the plan that ended with invasion.

But they'd hardly move that quickly. Surely they'd give the shortages more than a few weeks to work before . . .

'Vinegar and salt?' the counter man interrupted his thoughts, pointing to the bottle and large salt shaker as he wrapped the fish and chips in two sheets of old newspaper.

'Hold on a moment,' Duggan said and went out to the car to see what Gerda wanted.

'Only salt,' she grimaced.

He bought two bottles of red lemonade as well and they ate in the car, wolfing down the food with their fingers.

'Maybe it's not too disgusting,' Gerda conceded, wrapping the newspaper around her remaining chips.

'Even better after a few pints,' he said.

'Or a little spying,' she giggled.

'Are you not finishing those chips?'

She unwrapped them again and held them out for him to finish.

'Do you want me to write the postcard?' she asked.

'We need to think about it first.'

'Or will you get some of your other women to do it?'

'That's a possibility too,' he smiled at her. 'Maybe I'll run a competition to see who has the nicest womanly writing.'

She took a small handkerchief from her handbag and tried to wipe her fingers, making little progress. He took her hand and licked her fingers. 'Now you're eating my fingers,' she said. 'Are you still hungry?'

'I can't resist the taste of vinegar and salt.' He took her other hand and sucked each finger.

'I'll keep some salt and vinegar in the office from now on,' she laughed.

'Oh, no,' he rolled up the used newspapers and tossed them onto the floor in the back of the car. 'Mr Montague'd know there was something fishy going on if his office smelt like a bag of chips.'

She rested her head on his shoulder as he drove towards her digs and parked short of the house, in a dark area. They held each other for a while, contorted in the cramped space.

'I had an idea,' she said slowly. 'How I could get all the information. I could tell him I am German. Then I can—'

'No, no,' Duggan recoiled. 'No.'

'He would tell me everything he wants to tell the Germans. I could ask all the questions.'

'No.' Duggan was still shaking his head. 'It's too dangerous.'

'But you said he's all alone.'

'He seems to be. But he's got very important information. Stuff that could affect the whole course of the war. Not just the British and the Germans. The Americans too.'

'*Him?*' she looked sceptical.

'Yes. Him. I know it sounds unlikely. But you've got to believe me. His information is very important.'

'To Ireland?'

'Yes, to Ireland. But to everyone else as well. It's about getting America into the war. And it could stop that happening if it got into the Germans' hands.'

She stared at him as if he was indeed mad. 'This man? Roddy Glenn?'

'Yes,' he nodded his head with emphasis, repeating his usual refrain. 'We don't know what his game is. Who he's working for. But he's playing for really high stakes. That's if he knows what he's doing. We don't even know that, if he really does know what he's doing.'

He held her startled gaze until she blinked and lowered her head onto his shoulder. 'So,' he continued in a calmer voice, 'we've got to take it slowly. Not rush him. Or frighten him off. Until we can find out what he's up to and who's behind all this. He can't have come across this information by himself. Somebody must have given it to him. And he's not harmless. He can't be, with that kind of information.'

She thought about that for a while and then raised her head. 'What will I tell him when he phones? About a meeting?'

'Tell him you haven't seen the German officer yet. Until we decide what to do.'

Commandant McClure peered at the front and back of the postcard with a magnifying glass. He shrugged when he was finished and replaced the magnifying glass in the drawer of his desk. 'Nothing obvious,' he said. 'We'll see if there's something written on it. Invisible ink.'

Duggan gave a laugh. 'Invisible ink?'

'Have to check all possibilities.' McClure looked at the handwritten note on the copybook page. 'Maybe ask the British about this address.'

'What if it's one of theirs?'

'Then they'll say that this Mrs Agnes Smith is an upright citizen, above suspicion.' McClure gave a hint of a grin. 'And we'll know it's one of their accommodation addresses.'

'But why would they be leaking their own secrets to the Germans?'

'Captain Anderson seems convinced that it's a devious ploy. To try and get them to declare war on the US. Push the Germans' patience with the Americans over the top.'

'Could that be true?'

'Certainly it's what the British want more than anything else, to involve the Americans in the war. That'd change the odds. Maybe even turn the tide. Like it did last time.' McClure stifled a yawn and stood up and stretched himself. 'Still,' he said. 'I'm inclined to think Glenn's documents are real. They smack of the truth, from everything we know.'

'The best lies are the closest to the truth,' Duggan said, repeating what McClure had said to him when they'd first discussed these documents.

McClure nodded in recognition. 'But sometimes it's best to take things at face value, not build up huge conspiracies. Occam's razor.'

'How can you tell one from the other? I mean I can't see why Glenn wants Gerda to write this card for him.'

'The obvious explanation is that he's trying to recruit her,' McClure said. 'Ask her to do one or two simple things. Things that seem pretty harmless. Suck her in and then involve her more and more in his operation. That's the only way it makes sense.'

'But what's his operation?' Duggan protested. 'And why her? As far as he's concerned she's just a part-time waitress. No interest in politics. Or in the war. Unless he knows more about her. But he can't.'

'I don't see how he can.' McClure began leafing through a stack of papers on his desk. 'It doesn't seem to make any sense.'

Duggan was about to tell him of Gerda's suggestion that she hurry things up by telling Glenn she was German. But McClure had found what he was looking for and held out a Photostat to Duggan. 'Recognise this?'

It was a copy of a page with a column of nine letters, all handwritten in capitals, without any breaks or punctuation. 'A coded message,' Duggan stated the obvious.

'The interesting thing,' McClure nodded, 'is that Dr Hayes thinks it's the same code the guards found last year among Goertz's things when they missed him in the raid on Stephen Held's house.' Dr Richard Hayes was the head of the National Library and G2's unofficial cryptographer.

'What does it say?' Duggan scanned down the letters.

'He's still trying to break the code but he recognises the patterns. He's ninety-percent certain it's the code used by Goertz. Which means there's either someone else operating here with the same codebook or, more likely, that this message was coded by Goertz.' McClure reached for a cigarette and tossed one to Duggan.

'This was found on a sailor on one of the ships that goes back and forth to Lisbon. We'd had a tip-off that he was hanging around with some Germans while they were in Lisbon. So we asked our Special Branch friends to have a chat with him this evening while he was on his way to his ship. And they found this on him, in his pocket. Looked like he had just received it. Hadn't had time to put it away, hide it in his things.'

Duggan flicked his lighter for both of them. He was aware that the Dublin-to-Lisbon sea route was one of the few still open to Irish ships, although they were required by the British to call into an English port on the way for a permit to get through their naval block-ade of the Continent. And that neutral Lisbon was also a hotbed of spies, infested by everyone's intelligence services watching each other, trying to steal secrets and plant lies.

'He huffed and puffed,' McClure exhaled. 'Got it from a man in a pub who asked him to do a favour, take a message to a woman friend in Lisbon. Never saw him before. Usual stuff. Didn't impress the Branch, of course. They threatened to charge him with treason and he caved in pretty smartly. He's now on his way to Lisbon, working for us. Or, at least, for the Branch.'

'With the message?' Duggan asked in surprise.

McClure nodded. 'We had to make a quick decision. His ship sails about now. But the balance of advantage lay with letting him deliver his message and bring us back the reply. Be a great help to Dr Hayes to have both sides of a correspondence.'

'He might jump ship,' Duggan said. 'Stay in Portugal. Or even go over to the Germans.'

'That's a possibility,' McClure conceded. 'But I doubt it. He's got a wife and children here. There's no sign he wants to do a runner on them. But that'll all take time. Up to six weeks to get to Lisbon and back between one thing and another. If they don't get caught up in any trouble. If he comes back. What's of more immediate interest is who gave him the message.'

Duggan's pulse quickened. He could tell from McClure's demeanour that he was enjoying this narrative and hadn't yet reached the punchline.

'You ever heard of an unsavoury type called Benny Reilly?' Duggan shook his head and McClure went on. 'An opportunist and unscrupulous character who's on the fringes of everything – the IRA, politics, crime, business. You name it, he's on the fringes of it with only one thing in mind, making a few easy pounds. The guards keep an eye on him now and then but have never been able to pin anything much on him. He tried to blackmail the Hospital Sweepstakes a while back. Threatened to give the FBI a list of their American agents unless they paid him off.'

'How did he know who they were?'

'He worked for the Sweeps himself for a bit.' McClure gave him a knowing look. 'Anyway, the Sweeps dealt with him in their own way, didn't want the guards involved. He's shifted his interest to the black market since the war started. Involved in smuggling both ways across the border but was warned off by the local border gangs who don't like anyone interfering in their business. Apparently, he'd been trying for some time to get our new sailor friend to bring him cigarettes and tea from Lisbon. Offering him a fifty-fifty partnership, big profits.'

'And he's the one who gave him the coded message?'

'Yep,' McClure nodded with satisfaction. 'It ties in with the information from your,' he paused for a moment, stopping himself from saying uncle, 'informant that Goertz is running out of helpers and having to rely on less trustworthy types. Reilly is just the type of character who'd love to get involved with him. Especially if he thought Goertz had lots of reichsmarks.'

Does Timmy know Reilly? Duggan wondered. Almost certainly yes. He was just the type of character Timmy would know. Or, to be fair to Timmy, Timmy was just the type of person that someone like Reilly would go out of his way to know. And was Reilly actually the person Timmy had in mind when he told him that Goertz was having to rely on untrustworthy people? That should be easy to check.

McClure took another sheet of paper from his desk. 'Reilly's home address in Clontarf and the address of a yard where he keeps a horse and cart on the edge of Raheny.' He sighed. 'We're trying to get the guards to keep an eye on both but they say they're too stretched. They said they can only spare one man, your friend Detective Gifford.'

Duggan looked at him in surprise. Were McClure and the guards up to something? Why were they throwing him and Gifford together?

'You get on well with him,' McClure made it a statement, reading his mind. 'And you did a good job together on Harbusch.'

Duggan nodded, wondering, not for the first time, if McClure knew more about the other things they had gotten up to as well.

'Have a word with him, flesh out the details about Reilly,' McClure continued. 'In case there's anything that slipped their minds in the official report.'

Duggan checked the sky as he waited at the door to Gifford's flat. As far as he could make out it was still grey with clouds; at least there was no sign of stars or the moon. So they were still safe from the bombers.

The city was quiet around him, the flipping of the letterbox flap still resounding in his ears. He was about to leave when Gifford opened his hall door and glowered at him. 'Don't you ever sleep?' he said in a sour tone.

'It's not even eleven o'clock,' Duggan protested.

'Fucking culchies,' Gifford held the door open for him.

'I can go away.' Duggan waited, unsure whether Gifford was really unhappy at his presence. 'See you tomorrow.'

Gifford nodded him in. 'Been a long day,' he said. 'Run off my dainty little feet.'

They went into the living room where a radio was playing some *céilí* music. 'I hear you were down the docks this evening,' Duggan said.

'Good news travels fast,' Gifford grunted and left the room. He returned a moment later with two bottles of stout and a corkscrew and handed them to Duggan. 'You open them. I don't have the energy to pull anything, never mind a cork.'

Duggan dropped his voice. 'Sinead still here?'

'Another late-night merchant,' Gifford shook his head. 'She had me up till two o'clock the other night, waiting for her train to come in. The train she was supposed to be on coming back from culchie land. Where she was supposed to be. We had to hang around Amiens Street till it came in, nearly four hours late. And she could then pretend to get off it and go back to her digs. In case anyone wondered how she got back so early when the train was so late.'

Duggan handed him the open bottle and set about opening his own.

'What has you so perky?' Gifford demanded.

'We're closing in on Goertz.'

'The sarge is right,' Gifford raised his bottle in a toast. 'You fuckers don't seem to realise there's a war on. Demanding this, that and the other. Wanting round the clock surveillance on every Tom, Dick and Benny.'

'That's because there is a war on.'

'Not that war. Who cares about the Brits and the Jerries beating shit out of each other?' Gifford dismissed it with a wave of his bottle. 'There's a war on right here and now. That's what the sarge is concerned about. There are feckers shooting at us day in, day out.'

'So that's why he's assigned you to us,' Duggan smiled. 'To keep you safe, out of the firing line.'

'That's it,' Gifford sank into a battered armchair, little tufts of horsehair emerging from the side of the cushion as his weight squashed it. 'I'm like a son to him. He's only worried about my welfare.'

Duggan eased himself onto the edge of the matching chair, taking care that it could take his weight before committing himself.

'Actually,' Gifford said. 'It's a test.'

'Of what?'

'Loyalty. I have to give him a daily report of everything you're up to.'

'Everything?'

'Every single thing.'

Duggan took a swig from the bottle, not sure whether Gifford meant that literally or not. The Branch hardly cared about him personally, probably wanted to know what G2 knew. Unless. A sudden thought occurred to him. Unless Timmy was up to something again and they thought that he knew about it or was even involved.

Stop building conspiracies, he told himself. 'Tell me about Benny Reilly,' he said.

'A wily lad. Lives by his wits.' A touch of admiration entered Gifford's voice. 'Though he'd never have come to your attention without my help.'

'How do you mean?'

'We stopped the sailor man on his way to the boat on the North Wall. As per orders from your betters. The sarge frisked him and we looked in his sailor's bag but found nothing. Don't know what the sarge thought we were looking for. That he'd be smuggling bottles of Guinness to Portugal or something. He was all ready to let him go when I said, "Not so fast there now, my good man." And I looked in his pockets and found the letter. I knew immediately that a string of meaningless letters was just the sort of thing that'd send you fellows into paroxysms of delight. You love all that Boy Scout stuff.'

Duggan laughed, thinking how he could complete Gifford's day by telling him about the postcard which might have a message in invisible ink. But he resisted the urge.

'See? You admit it,' Gifford grimaced at him. 'You'll get another badge for your uniform now.'

Duggan leaned back until he was almost horizontal on the chair. The national anthem came from the radio, followed by a hum and then static as the transmitter was shut down. 'So what do we do now?'

'You fuck off back to your monastery or wherever you rest your head,' Gifford yawned. 'And let me get some sleep.'

Fifteen

'Another hard night?' Duggan gave Sullivan a sympathetic look.

'Jaysus,' Sullivan scratched the right side of his head. 'She had me up till four. Decided it was time we had a serious talk. Wants to get engaged.'

'Congratulations,' Duggan offered.

'Fuck's sake,' Sullivan snorted.

'You don't want to get married?'

'What would I want to get married for?'

'Is that what you said to her?'

'No,' Sullivan twitched and twisted his shoulder muscles as if he'd been on a twelve-hour route march with a heavy pack. 'Had to go through the whole rigmarole. Take it seriously. She says you can't let things drift these days. You never know what's going to happen. We could all be dead and gone in the morning.'

'You told her about the bomb in Carlow.'

Sullivan nodded. 'Should've kept my big mouth shut. You know what I think?'

'What?'

'She sees herself as a grieving widow. Wants to get married as quick as possible in case I'm killed.'

Duggan laughed.

'Seriously. A young widow, waiting for the compo.'

Duggan laughed. 'Did you tell her she could be waiting a long time? I can't see the Germans or the British paying compo for shooting us.'

'No, of course not. She didn't . . .' Sullivan paused as he looked over Duggan's shoulder. Duggan was about to look around when a balled-up old newspaper bounced on the table in front of him with a smell of vinegar.

'I hear this is yours,' Captain Anderson said as he came around beside him. 'Left it in the Prefect last night.'

'Yeah,' Duggan picked up the balled paper and tossed it towards a bin in the corner. It bounced off the edge and fell on the floor.

'Has Gertie come up with the goods yet?' Anderson gave him a crooked smile as he perched himself against the table.

'We're working on it,' Duggan kept his face straight while cursing inwardly. So Anderson knew who Gerda was, or at least knew that Gertie Maher was his source in Mrs Lynch's café. That wasn't surprising, as her initials were in earlier reports, but he'd have preferred to keep everything about her secret.

'I haven't seen any more paperwork,' Anderson said.

'Nothing definite to report yet.' Good, Duggan thought: McClure hadn't passed on the report of Gerda's meeting with Glenn.

'Have you checked out this Montague fellow she works for?'

'What do you mean?'

'Not exactly sound on the national question, is he?'

Duggan shrugged to suggest that wasn't very significant though he was already wondering otherwise. So Montague was probably a unionist, or ex-unionist, and probably pro-British. But that didn't make him what he knew Anderson was hinting at, a British agent. Still, it was something that should be checked out. Anyway, Montague had had nothing to do with putting Gerda in contact with them.

'By the way,' Anderson pushed himself upright and gave him a humourless smile, 'you'd want to be more careful about using that car. If anyone looks at the log book they might think you're using it as your own personal passion wagon.'

'What was that about?' Sullivan demanded when Anderson left, his interest piqued.

'I don't know,' Duggan lied, cursing inwardly.

Duggan made a point of seeking McClure's permission to take the car again before collecting Gifford and driving northwards. It was another grey day, clouds like dirty rags sitting on the city, the snow turning filthier on the ground. Their progress was slow, their speed set by drays and bicycles. The number of cars on the roads had dropped dramatically with the new petrol ration and most garages remained closed. A middle-aged man sitting on a sidecar with a briefcase under his arm turned to give them a dirty look as Duggan waited to overtake it.

Gifford interrupted his tuneless humming. 'We're upsetting the populace,' he said, staring back at the man until he looked away. 'Young pups flying round in luxury while respectable citizens have to travel in the open, exposed to all weathers. 'Tis unnatural. The world's upside down.'

'Just thinking that,' Duggan said, accelerating past the sidecar as a tram from Howth glided by. 'We won't be able to use the car for any undercover work soon.'

'Proper order. The soothing clip-clop of horses. It'll be just like the old days.' He inhaled a deep breath. 'The smell of horseshit and turf smoke everywhere. The world like God meant it to be. Before cities started all this rushing and fussing about.'

'You've the most sensitive nose I've ever come across,' Duggan laughed as they went by Fairview.

'An essential prerequisite for the superior detection agent. I fear you'd never cut the mustard.'

'I could smell it though.'

'There's hope for you yet.'

'Where do we go now?' Duggan asked as they went under the railway bridge onto Clontarf Road.

Gifford gave a theatrical sniff. 'I smell salt water. The sea.'

'You should be a navigator in a bomber.'

'Tut, tut.' Gifford unfolded a map onto his knees. 'No need for insults. I know perfectly well where I am.'

He guided them into a long avenue running inland from the bay and then into a succession of right turns until Duggan thought they were turning back on themselves. 'Here,' Gifford said as they turned into a short road of new semi-detached houses. Duggan slowed to get a better look and navigate the snow-covered road with care. A group of young boys were running and sliding along the ice they had created on the footpath with a bucket of water the night before. One fell on his backside and went careering off the path into the gutter. The others laughed and Duggan swore as he swerved to avoid him.

'This one,' Gifford looked to their right at a house like all the others, distinguished only by an old Austin van in the driveway. 'Benny must be at home.'

'What should we do?' Duggan asked himself as much as Gifford.

'Fuck all we can do,' Gifford muttered. There was nowhere they could stop and keep an eye on the house without advertising who and what they were. The road was too short and too open, the young trees on the edge of the footpath offering no cover.

'Where's his stables?' Duggan asked as he turned into another avenue.

Gifford unfolded his map again and plotted a route with his finger.

'What should we do?' Duggan repeated. 'I don't want to call on him in case Goertz is there. We can't watch the house.'

'Take the next right,' Gifford said, looking up from his map. 'Maybe have a chat with Benny when he leaves home.'

'But how'll we know when he leaves home?'

'That would be a dilemma,' Gifford offered and yawned, signalling another change of direction with a lazy finger.

They drove through Raheny village and a train went by ahead of them, its smoke interrupted by the bridge over the railway. The Belfast train, Duggan thought, and remembered his visit to Dundalk and the man in the pub telling him about the Americans in Derry. There had been some headline in the paper last night about President Roosevelt and Congress, but he hadn't had time to read it in the chipper.

'Jaysus,' Gifford muttered to himself as the houses ended suddenly and they found themselves on a country road lined by skeletal trees etched against the billowy clouds. Two tracks were cut into the snow by cartwheels and Duggan kept the car on them, hoping that nothing would come in the opposite direction.

'Make you nervous?' Duggan smiled at Gifford.

'There could be savages,' Gifford said, watching the ditches as if he expected attackers to come from behind the tracery of the leafless bushes. 'Do we have enough petrol to get back?'

Duggan laughed and asked him how much further it was. Gifford consulted the map again and directed him into a lane. The hedges closed in and the snow was still marked by cart tracks and an occasional tyre print where a car had edged out of the rut.

'How are we going to turn back?' Gifford demanded.

''Tis a long road that has no turning point.' Duggan laughed, beginning to wonder if Gifford was really nervous about being in the open countryside.

'Fuck's sake,' Gifford muttered. 'Don't go all culchie cute on me now.'

'That must be it ahead,' Duggan said of a ramshackle-looking building near the top of an incline. Gifford consulted his map again and grunted his assent. Duggan let the car slow and dropped it into second gear and went up the incline, holding his breath and hoping that the tyres wouldn't lose their grip on the compacted snow. He exhaled as they reached the building and he turned into its open gateway.

A woman was pushing the bolt closed on the shed door and stopped mid-action and turned to look at them in surprise. She was of indeterminate middle age with a knitted cap on her head and wearing a worn tweed coat that stretched down to the top of her black Wellington boots. By her side stood a metal bucket that she had put down to shut the door.

'Interesting,' Gifford muttered without moving his lips.

Duggan turned the engine off. He opened the door and stepped out, tasting the crisp air and noting the silence broken only by cattle lowing with hunger in the distance. He glanced around the yard and knew it was normally a sea of muck, now frozen. A cart was tipped up by a wire fence, snow icing its upper edges, its once-blue shafts pointing skywards back to the east like twin anti-aircraft guns.

'Hello, ma'am,' he said as he walked towards her, hoping his shoes wouldn't break through the frozen crust.

She nodded to him and glanced back at the car, at Gifford who was still in the passenger seat.

'We were hoping to find Mr Reilly,' Duggan said.

'He's not here,' the woman said.

'We have a problem,' Duggan scratched his head and furrowed his forehead. 'We're trying to get back down home but we're running short of petrol. We have the coupons and all but they've cut the ration and now we don't have enough to get us there. And someone said that Mr Reilly might be able to help us out.'

The bucket by her foot was half-full of horse manure, a faint column of steam rising from one side of it. From inside the shed the horse shifted on a straw bed. The woman glanced back at Gifford again and said nothing.

'We had to bring the mother up to hospital for an operation,' Duggan continued, falling deeper into his country accent, 'and then they changed the petrol ration without warning yesterday and we have the coupons and all but they're not enough to get us home now and we can't leave the car in Dublin and get the train back.'

'Where're you from?' the woman asked, caught up in his story.

'Roscommon,' he said. 'A few miles from the town, out in the country. You can see the problem, like. We can't just leave the car in the city, it'd never be there when we get back, would it? And we don't want to set off without knowing we won't be able to get home and have to abandon it in the middle of the country. That'd be nearly as bad. Maybe worse.'

The woman gave a half-nod.

Duggan picked up on it and moved to the point. 'There was a man in the hospital, visiting his wife, in the same ward as the mother, and he said to contact Mr Reilly. That he might be able to help us out. That he's a decent man. Do you a good turn.'

'He's not here.'

Duggan let his shoulders droop, defeated. 'I can see that,' he sighed. 'Sorry for troubling you. We'll have to go back into the city, I suppose, and try and find someone else. I don't know.'

'You'll find him at his office.'

'Mr Reilly?'

'He has an office in the North Lotts.'

'The North Lotts?'

'I don't know where it is exactly,' the woman said. 'Somewhere near O'Connell Street.'

'We can always stop and ask somebody. The North Lotts.' Duggan repeated, memorising it.

'He's always there between four and five,' the woman said. 'In his office.'

'Thanks very much for your help, ma'am.' Duggan turned away, exultant, and then turned back to her again. 'Can we give you a lift anywhere?'

'No, I'm only going down the road.'

Just as well, Duggan thought as he got back in the Prefect. Don't want the smell of horse shit in the car. Though it would get up Anderson's nose next time he used it. Give him something to really complain about.

The woman went back to locking the stable door as he reversed out into the lane.

'Well?' Gifford demanded as they went down the incline.

'Benny's got an office in North Lotts. Where's that?'

'Of course,' Gifford clicked his fingers and pointed his index finger at the road ahead. 'That's right.'

'You knew that,' Duggan shot him an angry glance.

'In the deep recesses of my mind. It's not an office, just a lock-up.'

'Fuck's sake,' Duggan felt deflated. 'I had to spin her a cock and bull story about our mother being in hospital to get that out of her. And you knew all along.'

'Sorry,' Gifford hung his head. 'My brain's addled. Must be love.'

'Bollocks,' Duggan shook his head.

'What's bollocks?'

'It doesn't addle your brain.'

'What doesn't?'

'Love.' Love, if that's what it was, energised him, sharpened all his senses. The opposite to addling the brain. Duggan fumbled in his pockets for his cigarette case.

Gifford leaned against the door to get a better look at Duggan. 'Tell me more, Casanova,' he said.

Duggan clicked open the cigarette case, found his lighter and tried to hold the flame steady against the cigarette end. He had no intention of telling Gifford what he was thinking. The car slid sideways on a patch of ice and he cursed and gave up the attempt and concentrated on the road. The tyres gripped on the frozen grass verge and he guided the car back onto the centre.

'Do I know her?' Gifford took the lighter from his hand and held it to Duggan's cigarette.

Duggan shook his head and took the cigarette from his mouth. 'I thought we might all go out for a drink some night. With Sinead and her.'

'Good idea. Stop Sinead asking about you.'

'What do you mean?'

'She still has a thing about you. Be good to show her you've moved on. Found another culchie.'

Duggan gave a short laugh. 'Still worried about the competition?'

'Course not,' Gifford dismissed the idea. 'Just don't like to see people living in fantasy lands.'

Commandant McClure had his eyes closed and gave no sign that he had heard Duggan's knock as he had tapped the door and opened it in one move. Duggan cleared his throat and McClure opened an eye and said, 'Well?'

Duggan told him what had happened and concluded, 'I don't think we should raid Benny Reilly's house until we're sure Goertz is there. It'd only tip him off and he'd disappear again.'

McClure nodded and straightened himself behind his desk.

'I suggest we put surveillance on Reilly,' Duggan continued.

McClure gave him one of his disconcerting silent stares but Duggan was used to them by now and waited for him to speak. 'Take too long to set up properly,' he said at last. 'From what you say about the house.'

'We could detain him over his black-market activities. Question him then.'

McClure picked up his cigarette lighter and tossed it into the air a couple of times. 'Better to talk to him,' he said. 'Hold the threat of arrest over his head. He's a man who understands self-interest.'

Duggan turned towards the door but McClure interrupted him. 'We may be running out of time. Our friend in External Affairs, Mr Ó Murchú, has been on to me. The Germans are pressing their request for landing details at Foynes, to bring in their extra staff. And this weather isn't going to last forever.'

So we'll find out soon if the German bombings were accidents or a message, Duggan thought. 'How soon?' he asked.

'Who knows,' McClure shrugged. 'But Ó Murchú says he can't keep stalling them indefinitely. Got to give them a yes or no soon. And he'd like to have something more on the table when he says no.'

Duggan remembered something Timmy had said to him about Goertz, that he saw himself as the German military attaché in Dublin as there wasn't one in the legation. He mentioned it again to McClure.

'Which suggests that Goertz knows about the legation's demand for more staff,' McClure nodded. 'Which means he's in touch with them. While conspiring at the same time with the IRA against our government. Which is not the activity of a supposedly friendly nation. Trying to involve us in a war in which they say they support our neutrality.'

'I don't see how catching Goertz can help with this,' Duggan said. 'Apart from anything he can tell us about the reasons for the bombing.'

'Ó Murchú sees him as a counterweight,' McClure lit himself a cigarette. 'We can threaten to put him on public trial, expose his IRA activities and Germany's hypocrisy towards our neutrality. Which could be an excuse for us to join the Allies. So,' he gave a friendly grin, 'please don't do anything to upset the delicate balance of the apple-cart like insisting on your right to bring more spies into your embassy right now.'

Duggan lit a cigarette and sat down opposite him. 'Will it work?'

'Why not?' McClure reached for a slim folder. 'But that's only one of Mr Ó Murchú's current concerns. He has also become more interested in the Glenn document, the letter from Churchill to Roosevelt and where it came from. Mr Aiken is heading off to Lisbon on his way to Washington in a couple of days and wants to know more.' He opened the folder which contained only a few documents: Duggan recognised the top one as his last report on Gerda's meeting with Glenn. The post-card Glenn had given her was clipped to it and McClure slid it free.

To Duggan's surprise, two postcards came away, both the same black and white view of O'Connell Street. McClure pushed them across the desk to him. Duggan picked one up and turned it over. The back was filled in, the message and address Glenn had given to Gerda written with a clear flowing hand: 'Dear Aunt Agnes, I'm having such a nice time here I'm staying another week! Hope all the family are well. Love, Marjorie'.

Duggan picked up the other postcard and turned it over. The back was blank except along the top and left edge of the message area. Brown letters, crudely written, said, 'contact made need more docs'.

Duggan gave a quiet whistle in surprise. 'Invisible ink?'

McClure nodded. 'Milk,' he said.

'Milk?' Duggan laughed.

'Very basic. But it works. Just heat it up and that's what happens,' he pointed towards the card still in Duggan's hand.

'And this one?' Duggan pointed at the addressed card.

'That's the one we're posting.'

Duggan picked it up and looked at the edges where the hidden message had been on the other one. There was nothing visible.

'We've copied the message onto it,' McClure said. 'As similar as possible. Using the sharp end of a broken matchstick to write it. That's what they think he used. Or something like it.'

McClure reached for the addressed card and put it to one side. He took the original from Duggan's hand and slipped it back in the file under its paperclip. 'No word from Glenn?' he asked.

'No. Gerda will contact me as soon as he calls.'

'Good.'

'He's probably waiting to get more documents. So he won't call for a while.'

McClure nodded. 'We need to hurry things up.'

'How? We can't contact him.'

McClure sighed with a stream of cigarette smoke. 'Tell Gerda to seek an immediate meeting as soon as he contacts her. That's all we can do.'

They smoked in silence for a moment. Duggan debated whether to voice an idea that had been coming back to him since Gerda's meeting with Glenn. 'Suppose she tells him that the Luftwaffe officer has agreed to meet him,' he said. 'Sets up a meeting and I go along as the German.'

McClure laughed and shook his head.

'Why not?' Duggan felt mildly affronted. 'I can speak German and ask him all the questions we want answered.'

'And put on a phony German accent while speaking English?' McClure smiled.

'Maybe he speaks German.'

'Maybe he knows all about bombers and he asks you a question about the stall speed of a Heinkel with a full load of bombs.'

'Okay,' Duggan admitted. 'A stupid idea.'

'No,' McClure replied. 'Just too risky. Until we know more about him.'

'He must be an amateur if he's using milk as invisible ink.'

'Or he wants everyone to think he's an amateur.'

'But he doesn't know we're on to him.'

'No. But he may want the Germans to think he's an amateur. The ideal informant: an innocent, well-meaning person who comes across information whose significance he doesn't really understand. Every intelligence agency's dream.'

'But they'll be suspicious. It's too good to be true.'

'Exactly.'

'So what's the point?'

'Depends,' McClure leaned forward to stub out his cigarette. 'If it's a British operation they may be leaking true information in order to discredit the same information the Germans have got from another source. To undermine a *really* dangerous spy.'

'Jesus,' Duggan scratched the back of his neck. 'That's complicated.'

McClure found another file on his desk and stood up. 'Spend too much time thinking about these things and you'll end up in Grangegorman babbling about conspiracies and double and quadruple agents. Be dismissed as a harmless lunatic.'

'So what about Mrs Agnes Smith in Chelsea?' Duggan got to his feet too.

'The British haven't come back yet with any info about her.'

'But they know we know about Glenn. If he's one of them.'

McClure came around his desk. 'Yep. But we're not likely to upset their operation. And the fact that they know we know gives us another card to play if we need it for something else.'

Duggan laughed, thinking Timmy was wasted in politics: he'd love this stuff. He opened the door for McClure to pass through.

'Meanwhile,' McClure paused. 'Talk to Benny Reilly. Keep it informal. We're just suspicious, don't really know anything.'

'Who's Marjorie?' Duggan asked as they went down the corridor.

'My wife.'

'Oh,' Duggan said, embarrassed that he had gone too far. He knew nothing about McClure's life outside the office. They had never shared any personal information.

'She wrote the card,' McClure stopped outside Duggan's office. 'Her name's actually Caroline. You must come around to the house and meet her some day.'

Sullivan was smirking at him as he came into the office. 'What?' Duggan demanded, aware he had heard McClure's parting comment.

'Like I said,' Sullivan said. 'The commandant's pet.'

Duggan grunted at him, a dismissive sound.

'I had to tell him,' Sullivan dropped his voice to a contrite note. 'He put a gun to my head.'

'Who?'

Sullivan looked at the open door behind Duggan and waited for him to close it. 'Anderson,' he said. 'He was asking about you.'

'Asking what?' Duggan demanded, wondering if Sullivan knew Gerda's real identity and had told Anderson.

'Asking what you were up to. Why you spent so much time out of the office. Using cars like they were your own.'

'What did you tell him?'

'The truth. I had to,' Sullivan widened his eyes with innocence. 'That you're the commandant's pet. He lets you do whatever you want. Swan around town. Not have to sit here doing the hard work all day.'

Duggan wondered if Anderson had actually asked Sullivan anything or if Sullivan was just voicing his own views. 'What else did he ask?'

'Nothing. Said it was strange that no one seemed to know what you were up to. But I didn't mention a word about your homo friend.'

Duggan laughed with relief. 'I thought you didn't like Anderson.'

'Pushy fucker,' Sullivan said. 'That's why I didn't tell him about Gifford. What's he up to anyway?'

'He thinks we're holding back information about someone he thinks might be a possible British spy,' Duggan shrugged.

'You wouldn't do that,' Sullivan looked shocked.

'Of course not,' Duggan said. 'But he's got a bee in his bonnet about it for some reason.'

A cold wind came up the river with the tide, bringing the acrid smell of the gasworks farther inland to mix with the bitter tang of hops from the Guinness brewery. Duggan cycled along the northern quays through the afternoon darkness, wishing he had taken a car again and to hell with Anderson. The road was treacherous for the bicycle, the limited lighting making it difficult to distinguish between hard-packed snow and yielding drifts. He hit the side of what he thought was a ball of snow but turned out to be a stone or a frozen lump of horse shit. The front wheel jerked to the right, threatening to unbalance the bike and he slid his foot along the ground to keep it upright. He recovered his equilibrium and pushed on, following the tracks of a horse and cart ahead of him: two messenger boys hung onto its stubby back shafts with a hand, their other hands struggling to keep their handlebars balanced.

Gifford was waiting for him at the corner of O'Connell Street, between Kapp and Peterson's tobacconists and Harris's radio shop, his back against the wall under the unlit neon signs. He had his hands in his pockets, watching the parade of passers-by with the half-sneer of a practised corner boy. Duggan was breathing hard with the extra effort and concentration as he stopped in the gutter and tried to get a stable foothold on the path.

They went back down Bachelors Walk a short distance and into a narrow laneway that cut through to Middle Abbey Street. Duggan told him his instructions in a low voice as they walked and they worked out how they were going to get Benny to reveal Goertz's whereabouts without telling him they knew that he was in touch with the German and that he had passed on his coded message to the sailor en route to Lisbon.

They turned into North Lotts, an unlit laneway of former stables, now mainly stores, their eyes adjusting to the gloom. Above them, the clouds seemed brighter with a dull reflection of the city but there were few lights visible here, an odd pool from a printer's window or store door ajar. There was no one in sight and the lane's length was broken only by the shadow of a vehicle a third of the way down. It turned out to be what they hoped it was. Benny Reilly's van.

A faint light showed between the cracks of the double doors behind it. Duggan put his bike against the next entrance and nodded to Gifford who knocked on the wicket door. There was a shuffling noise inside, the sound of a latch lifting, and the small door opened inwards. The man inside had to bend down to look up at them. 'Lads,' he said, glancing from one to the other, identifying them as policemen.

'Mr Reilly,' Gifford said as if he had found a long lost friend. 'Can we come in?'

Reilly opened the door and they bent down to step through it. There was a bench running around two sides of the garage and various implements and horse harnesses hanging on the third wall. A high barstool stood before the bench at the back wall, close to a lit oil lamp. A closed ledger and an open ink bottle and pen were on the bench in front of the stool. There was a paraffin oil heater on the ground nearby, its dome glowing red, the distinctive smell of its fumes all pervasive.

Gifford closed his eyes and inhaled. 'Ah, the smell of paraffin,' he said. 'They say it'll be rarer than perfume in a few months.'

'Aye,' Reilly nodded as if he had heard a piece of inspired wisdom. He was in his mid-forties, about five foot eight, wiry, and had a deeply furrowed forehead from exaggerating what he thought was an honest face. There was a cigarette propped behind his left ear.

'Surprised you're wasting it like that,' Gifford rubbed his hands in front on the heater. 'But makes it very cosy in here.'

'You have to have a bit of heat and light,' Reilly pointed to the ledger. 'Just doing up the accounts. Maybe for the last time.'

'Really?' Gifford encouraged him.

'The haulage business is fucked, if you'll excuse the expression. That van outside's only a liability now.'

'No petrol?'

Reilly shook his head in affirmation. 'Only scrap metal without the juice. And I wasted two hundred quid on it last year.'

'You were robbed.' Gifford said in sympathy.

'I was and all. Nothing but trouble since I got it.'

'I was reading in the paper that there's a special petrol allowance for lorries and vans that keep essential supplies moving.'

'For farmers and the like,' Reilly dismissed the idea.

'I'd have thought a man like yourself would be able to get extra petrol for that.' Gifford moved away from the heater and ran his hand along the bench at the side of the shed, looking at the jumble of items on it.

'That'd be only for the big operators,' Reilly watched him.

'Essential supplies, though. You're used to carrying them.'

'In a small way. But you know how it is. It all depends on who you know. Pull.'

'True for you. But you must know lots of people. People you've done favours for.'

'I'll apply anyway and see if anything comes of it.' Reilly turned to look at Duggan, who was standing in the centre of the floor with his hands in his pockets. Duggan stared back at him.

'You always have the horse and cart.'

'Thank God for that.' Reilly switched his attention back to Gifford.

'We were out there this morning.' Gifford stopped beside a weighing scales and took a small rusty weight off one side of the balance. The scales tipped slightly to one side. 'Tut, tut,' Gifford smiled at him and hefted the weight in the palm of his hand. 'Yeah,' he continued, 'we were running short of petrol. The woman there said you'd be able to help us.'

Reilly shook his head in sadness. 'God love her. She's a bit simple. Doesn't keep up with the news.'

'Ah, well,' Gifford took another weight off the bench and balanced it against the one in his other hand. 'We made it back anyway. Just about.'

Reilly glanced at Duggan as if he might like to confirm their safe return. Duggan stared back at him. Gifford put down one of the weights and pulled open a drawer beneath them and took out a handful of unused paper bags, all folded flat. 'So what are you hauling about these days?'

'Anything people want me to,' Reilly folded his arms, a gesture that said he could go on playing this game for as long as it took. 'Furniture, stones, clay. Whatever people want me to bring from one place to another. There's a lot of people moving around these days. You'd be surprised.'

Gifford touched a box under the counter with his foot and raised his eyebrows in surprise when it did not sound hollow. He bent down and pulled a tea chest part way out and looked into it. 'Well I never,' he said. 'A tea chest with tea in it.' He straightened up and looked at Duggan. 'Have you ever seen a tea chest with tea in it?'

Duggan kept his face straight but Reilly didn't bother looking at him. 'Fill a bag there for your mother,' Reilly said to Gifford.

'I don't have a mother,' Gifford pushed the tea chest back with his foot.

'She's gone to her reward. Sorry to hear that.'

'No.' Gifford dropped the paper bags into the drawer and shoved it closed with his hip. 'Never had one. I was found under a head of cabbage in the Castle garden.'

'I know some of the lads there,' Reilly said. 'In the Castle.'

'Really?' Gifford sounded interested. 'Who?'

'What branch are you in?'

'The Branch.'

'Ah, no,' Reilly said, relaxing. 'I wouldn't know any of you lads.'

Gifford hefted the weight in his hand. 'You know any of the lads from weights and measures?'

'I bought those weights from the fucker who sold me the van,' Reilly flicked another glance at Duggan.

'Him there,' Gifford nodded at Duggan, picking up on Reilly's thoughts. 'He's from another world altogether.'

'Really?' Reilly turned to Duggan, knowing that they had come to the point at last.

'These are unusual times,' Duggan said, taking his hands from his pockets. 'Dangerous times. And we need all good patriotic Irishmen to keep their eyes open. Especially men who know a lot of people, who move around a lot. To alert us to anything we should know about. Anything out of the ordinary. Especially people out of the ordinary.'

Reilly nodded his head up and down as if this was all a revelation to him. 'I know what you mean. We have to protect our position, neutrality.'

'Exactly. So we're asking people who know what goes on around town to keep us in the picture. About strangers, for instance. For everyone's sake.'

'Those bombs last week,' Reilly bit his lip at the memory. 'We don't want any more of that here.'

'And we don't want anyone taking chances with our neutrality. We want to keep out of this war. And we want to know of anything that threatens that. Anything at all.' Duggan took a piece of paper with a phone number on it from his breast pocket and passed it to Reilly. 'Would you call me if you come across anything? Ask for Robert.'

'That's you?' Reilly took the page and mouthed the number.

Duggan nodded.

'Just Robert?'

Duggan nodded again. 'You can rest assured that anything you tell me will be kept totally confidential. If I'm not there you can leave a message.'

Reilly folded the note and slipped it into the top pocket of his jacket.

'Okay,' Gifford interjected, replacing the weight on one side of the balance and watching it fall to the counter with a thud. 'We're all clear here?'

'Definitely,' Reilly patted his top pocket. 'Couldn't be clearer.'

'Right,' Gifford nodded to Duggan.

Duggan put out his hand and shook Reilly's, as if they were sealing a deal. 'We're counting on people like you in this emergency.'

Reilly shook his hand and his solemn face broadened into a grin. 'I'm sure your mother would appreciate a little extra tea.'

'Jaysus,' Gifford interjected. 'Fellows like him never have mothers.'

'Another cabbage man?'

'God, no,' Gifford shuddered. 'He's one of those fellows you hear about from Russia. Make them in factories. Not an ounce of human feeling in them. Just mechanical parts. Chop up their own mother for spare parts without a moment's hesitation. If they had one.'

'Best of luck now,' Reilly said with a laugh that contained little humour and maybe a touch of nervousness as he showed them out and closed the wicket behind them.

'He'll do it,' Gifford said as they emerged from the lane onto Bachelors Walk.

'You think so?'

'We've threatened him three ways. At least.'

Duggan straightened his bicycle alongside the footpath, pointing back down the quays. 'I better make sure that phone line is set up,' he said.

'It'll take him a day or two,' Gifford said. 'To stumble across Goertz, accidentally like. An amazing coincidence.'

'As long as he tells us where he is. Not where he was two days ago.'

'He'll give him up,' Gifford nodded to himself with conviction. 'Benny's got to live here. And with us. Interesting, his reference to knowing lads in the Castle.'

'What? He was just trying to figure out who you were.'

'He was trying to figure out if I was one of the competition. Some lads in the detective branch are running their own black market operation. He wanted to know whether we were with them.'

'Jesus,' Duggan sighed. 'How long's that been going on?'

'Since the shortages began to bite and the black market began to explode.'

'And they're getting away with it?'

'Not for much longer. There's an inquiry under way. All very hush hush as usual. Benny probably doesn't know that. Did you notice how the fucker relaxed a little when he realised we weren't there to put the squeeze on him over his supplies of oil or tea.'

Duggan shook his head. He was so immersed in his own world that it was almost a shock to hear about ordinary venality.

'There's always someone at it,' Gifford pursed his lips and exhaled loudly. 'In the land of saints and shysters.'

Gerda's landlady tightened her lips in a sign of disapproval when she opened the hall door to Duggan. She said nothing, just turned and shouted 'Gertie' up the stairs. She waited until Gerda came down and said, 'This is a respectable house. We don't allow unannounced callers at this hour of the night.'

Gerda lifted her overcoat off the hall stand and walked around her. The landlady closed the door behind them without another word and Gerda mimicked her, '*This is a respectable house*' in a low voice as they went down the path.

'It's not that late,' he said as they sat into the car. It was nearly nine o'clock.

'This better be important,' she said.

'Yes, it is.'

'What?' A shadow of concern crossed her face.

'I wanted to see you.' He leant across and kissed her on the lips. She kissed him back quickly and put her palm on his chest and pushed him away.

'Jesus, Mary and Joseph,' she said, exaggerating her Cork accent. 'You want her to think I'm a right whore altogether.'

'Is she watching?' Duggan started the car.

'Of course she's watching.'

He drove down Iona Road. 'Where're we going?' she asked.

'You have the keys to your office?' he asked back.

'You should have phoned me.'

'You don't?'

She fished in her coat pocket, dangled a ring of keys before his eyes, and rested her head on his shoulder. He leaned his head over to rest on hers and they drove in silence to the city centre. He went down O'Connell Street and turned into Cathedral Street to park. O'Connell Street was busy with people hurrying for their last buses and trams and they threaded their way through a long bus queue and skipped across the road in front of a tram.

In her office they dropped their coats on the floor and embraced, cold hands reaching under clothes. 'Aah,' she shuddered at the touch of his hand on her bare back. 'Wait a minute. I have a present for us.'

She went behind her desk and opened a cupboard and took out a folded blanket as well as the rug and held it up in one hand like a trophy. She came back to him and rubbed the soft wool against the side of his face.

'Only nineteen and eleven,' she said. 'On sale in Todd Burns'.'

'A bargain.'

'Reduced from two pounds ten.'

'You couldn't resist it.'

'How could you resist that?' she smiled and they both laughed at the ease in which they had slid into an old married couple routine.

The fire in Mr Montague's office was dead, the few sparks dying almost as suddenly as they were exposed from the ash as he poked at it. She spread the rug on the floor and folded her overcoat into a pillow and they undressed quickly and lay beside each other on the rug and pulled the blanket over them. It was too narrow to cover them completely.

'Won't work,' he whispered. 'My turn to be on top.'

He shifted position and she tucked the blanket in at their sides and held him tight while they made love. They stayed like that until she said, 'You're getting heavier,' and then they swapped positions, she half-lying on him, her head on his chest and a hand stretched out to his other hip. He dozed off and when he woke again she was still in the same position, breathing in a smooth rhythm. He tried not to move, not sure whether she was awake or asleep, and he listened to the night-time stretches and contractions of the building and smelled the polish of the linoleum, thinking idly that someone had cleaned the office recently. There were no sounds now from the street outside.

His shoulder bone under her head was beginning to ache and he tried to shift position without waking her but she raised her chin onto his chest and looked at him, her dark eyes dreamy. He kissed each eye and she smiled and lowered her head onto his chest again.

'I can hear your heartbeat,' she murmured.

'Beating for you.' He ran his fingers through her hair. 'I hope it's a nice tune.'

'It sounds like men marching.'

'No, no,' he said sharply. 'Forget about that.'

She raised her head to look at him. 'How can I?' she said in a hopeless voice.

He put a finger on her hips. 'Let's talk about afterwards. After the war. What we'll do.'

'You think the war will end?'

'All wars end some time.'

'In our lifetime?'

'Yes, of course.'

'You've heard of the *dreißigjähriger Krieg*?' The Thirty Years' War. He nodded. 'That was different. Total war like this can't go on that long. There'd be no one left alive.'

'Maybe that's how it'll end.'

He shook his head at her, wishing the war away.

'And who will win this short war?' she continued.

He shifted his body and eased her onto him, trying to change the subject, but she held his gaze, her question demanding an answer.

'It could be a stalemate,' he sighed. 'England won't be beaten and there will be a peace treaty with Germany and we'll be protected by it. It will be all right.'

'That's what your spy bosses think?'

'I don't know what they think,' he said. 'I think that's one possibility.' Maybe the best possibility we can hope for, he thought. Not wanting to think now about all the uncertainties and the prospect of a new spring offensive by Germany against England, continuing where it had left off last year. And maybe against Ireland. If the British hadn't come here first.

She closed her eyes for a moment and then said in a lighter voice, 'And after the war? What will we do?'

'You can be yourself again. And we can have children.'

'And what will they speak?' Her eyes brightened as if a shadow had passed.

'They will speak German. And English. And Irish.'

'So. This is not just sex?'

'No,' he shook his head.

She nodded, as if he had confirmed something. She bent forward to give him a slow and tender kiss and then raised her body to put her hand down between his legs and guide him into her.

He fell asleep afterwards and when he awoke she was looking at him, her dark eyes deep and dreamy again. 'What time is it?' he asked.

'Late,' she said.

He closed his eyes again. 'What time does Mr Montague come in?'

She poked him in the ribs. 'We have to get up. It's half-eleven.'

'Not that late.'

'Do you want to make me homeless?' She rolled away from him and shivered with the cold as she stood up. 'That bitch will throw me out if I'm not back soon.'

'Then we could live here.'

She gave him a loving laugh and began to dress herself.

'We could even lie in late on Sundays. When Montague doesn't come in.'

'Get up,' she prodded him in the side with her toe and bent down to pull the blanket off him and tried to tug the rug from under him.

He rolled off it and put on his clothes quickly, holding his breath against the cold. He looked out the window and he had a sudden sensation that they had slept for years and the city had become a ghost town. There was nobody on the street, no traffic, no sound at all. Snow filled the hood of the Father Mathew statue and was draped on its shoulders and along its outstretched, soothing arm. The tram lines shone in the weak light amid the black ruts cut in the dirty snow. It was like the black-and-white postcard that Glenn had given Gerda.

'We've posted that card,' he turned back from the window.

'You got another woman to write it?' Gerda handed him his overcoat.

'Yes. One that won't upset the King's English with *umlauts* and *eszetts* and other funny symbols.'

She threw the folded rug at him and he caught it with a laugh.

Sixteen

'What's the point of that?' Sullivan aimed a finger at the sign saying 'DO NOT TOUCH' on the new phone on the desk.

Duggan looked up from the paper where he was reading a report on a murder trial in Tipperary. He had his chair tipped back, his feet on the table, and a cigarette in his ashtray sent up a column of smoke that split in two as it ascended. 'It's a direct line, bypassing the switch. For incoming calls only. One incoming call.'

Sullivan stared at the phone as if he expected it to ring. 'A special phone for just one call?'

'A call to tell us where Goertz is.'

'Jaysus,' Sullivan snorted. 'You think someone's going to call and tell you where he is? Just like that? After all this time?'

'Yes,' Duggan leaned forward for his cigarette, took a slow drag, and replaced it in the ashtray. He felt relaxed, on top of everything. Just a matter of being patient: Benny Reilly would call; Glenn would come back to Gerda with more information. And Gerda . . . Gifford was totally wrong about being addled by love, he thought.

'You praying for a miracle?' Sullivan was saying. 'Doing a novena like my mammy?'

'A man will call and ask for Robert. And tell us where Goertz is.'

Sullivan shook his head with a laugh and sat down at his end of the table. 'After all these months running around in circles, getting nowhere, you think someone's going to call you and tell you where he is? Just like that?'

Duggan gave him a serene smile and picked up his paper again.

'Does he even exist?'

'Who?'

'Goertz?'

'You've seen him yourself.'

'I saw a man you said was a German spy called Goertz,' Sullivan waved a correcting finger at him. 'Months ago. Last summer. And you haven't seen him since.'

'Other people have.'

'You mean other people have seen a man you say is a German spy called Goertz,' Sullivan smirked. 'Don't automatically believe anything anyone tells you, the commandant always says. Actually,' he paused, 'I think you and he have just made up this Goertz character. So you can spend all your time pretending to do some work around here.'

Duggan turned a page and scanned the foreign headlines. The RAF had bombed Italian bases in Libya; Churchill said Britain's future depended on the US; and Democratic Party leaders in Washington were discussing a bill to lend and lease war material to countries fighting the Nazis.

'So who's going to call?' Sullivan persisted.

'A man's going to call, asking for Robert. If I'm not here you're to offer to take a message. And he'll tell you where to find Goertz.'

'And who's this fella that's going to call?'

Duggan tipped the side of his nose twice with his finger.

'How'll I know he's the right one? Not some hoaxer?'

'He's the only one who has the number.'

'And you really think he's going to tell you where Goertz is?'

'I hope so.'

'Ah, hope,' Sullivan said, like a man who'd given up on that commodity years ago.

The phone rang and they both stared at the new receiver but it was their ordinary extension. Duggan picked it up and gave his name and the switch told him it was his cousin and plugged Gifford into the line.

'We need to talk,' Gifford said without preliminaries.

'There are developments?'

'There's a café near O'Connell bridge. Berni's. I'll be there in half an hour.'

Gifford hung up and Duggan stared at the receiver for a moment, taken aback at Gifford's tone, before putting it down. It didn't sound good. What could Benny have done?

'Lover's tiff?' Sullivan smirked.

'That reminds me,' Duggan folded his paper and stubbed out the already dead butt in the ashtray. 'Have you popped the question to Carmel?'

Sullivan tapped his finger against his nose.

Duggan laughed as he put on his overcoat

'Why am I stuck with all this shit?' Sullivan groaned at the file of overnight reports from the lookout stations around the coast.

'Because you're so good at it.'

'There's nothing happening. No air activity for the last week. Just more bodies and stuff washed up in Donegal.'

'Remember,' Duggan pointed at the new phone. 'Robert.'

He got to the café five minutes early but Gifford was already there, sitting at the far side of a table, facing the door and window. He was ordering as Duggan sat down opposite him and asked for a tea. 'One poached egg and tea for two,' the uniformed waitress confirmed.

'Very late for breakfast,' Duggan said. 'I hope you're not skiving off now that you're working for the army.'

'You fellows don't know how well off you are. Don't have to worry about meals, clothes, shelter. Nothing.'

'You should join up.'

Gifford grunted. He didn't seem to be in his usual form this morning. The waitress came back with cutlery and cups and saucers. When she had gone again, Gifford glanced around the café. It was empty apart from them, waiting for mid-morning shoppers in need of a break. He steepled his elbows on the table, rested his chin on his hands, and leaned forward.

'Are in you in trouble again?' he dropped his voice.

'Me?' Duggan sat back in surprise. 'No.'

'On another solo run?'

Duggan shook his head. 'Why?'

'Gertie Maher,' Gifford said in a soft voice.

Duggan froze. He hadn't told Gifford her name.

'Your new girlfriend?'

Duggan nodded, a feeling of dread hollowing out his stomach.

'What do you know about her?'

'Enough,' Duggan shot back in anger. 'What the fuck . . .'

The elderly waitress came back with a tray and put a double pot of tea on the table along with Gifford's poached egg on toast and two more half-slices of toast in a triangular silver-plated holder. 'Anything else now?' she asked.

'No, thanks,' Gifford smiled at her. He held up a calming palm to silence Duggan as she went away. 'She's under surveillance. And your name has come up as a result.'

Christ, Duggan thought, his mind racing. Were they watching us last night? Have they been watching us all along? Have they been talking to Gerda's landlady? Was that why her demeanour had changed? Why she was so unfriendly last night? And what had they been saying about Gerda?

'I don't know what the fuck's going on,' Gifford said. 'I just over-heard one of the lads talking about it, complaining about how he had to follow this woman.'

'When?'

'When what?'

'When was he following her?'

'Yesterday.'

'And?'

'And,' Gifford shrugged, 'he was just complaining to one of the other lads. That this was another G2 waste of fucking time operation because this woman was hanging out with another guy from G2. And what were those fuckers playing at? Were they spying on each other now?'

A G2 operation. Spying on me. 'Jesus Christ!' Duggan snapped his lighter to a cigarette.

Gifford poured two cups of tea and gave him a wary look as if he was afraid that Duggan would do something rash. 'I couldn't butt into the conversation in my usual manner,' he went on in an apolo-getic tone. 'I'm not sure if these lads know that I know you but too many people do. So I couldn't ask any questions.'

Duggan nodded, his mind elsewhere. Anderson, he thought. This was an Anderson operation. Pursuing his theory that Gerda was a British spy or a patsy for one. For Montague or Glenn. Or both of them. He took a furious drag on the cigarette, turning its hot tip into a flaming coal.

'The other lad said there's something fishy about the Maher woman,' Gifford continued. 'There's no trace of her in Cork. Where she's supposed to come from.'

No, Duggan felt like shouting. Dear God, no. Don't let the fucking

Special Branch go near her. After where she's come from. It'd terrify her. Like Vienna again. He took another drag to try and calm himself. 'I know where she comes from,' he said, trying to keep his voice as even as he could. 'What else?'

'That's it,' Gifford said. 'That's as much as I heard. I couldn't—'

'I know,' Duggan cut him off. 'Listen, thanks for telling me. You better eat your breakfast.'

Gifford took up his fork and stabbed the yoke of the poached egg and a stream of yellow sank into the toast. Duggan's gaze focused on the egg but his mind was elsewhere, wondering how long they'd been watching Gerda, how often they'd seen them together, what their reports said. And, he closed his eyes at the thought, what else they'd found out about her. Nothing, he told himself. There was nothing to find out that he didn't already know.

'Do you know who in G2 they're reporting to?'

Gifford shook his head, his mouth full of food.

'I think I know who it is anyway,' Duggan said. Would Anderson have ordered the surveillance himself? Possibly, he thought. Otherwise, it would have had to be his commandant, Egan. And would they have had the colonel's approval? His heart sank again. Did McClure know about it? Were they all just using him?

Gifford wiped his plate with a triangle of toast, poured himself another cup of tea and sat back. Duggan hadn't touched his. He lit another cigarette off the butt of his previous one.

'Problem?'

Duggan inhaled the fresh nicotine and waved the cigarette in a noncommittal gesture. 'It's another operation,' he said.

'Nothing to do with Goertz?'

'No.' Although, Duggan thought, everything's tied up together.

'So you are just carrying out your orders.'

Duggan nodded.

'But,' Gifford flashed him a pale imitation of his usual grin, 'you weren't ordered to seduce her.'

'Is that what their reports say?'

'I don't know.'

'It wasn't like that, anyway.'

'You want to tell Father Petey? Confess all?'

Duggan gave a short laugh. 'You promising absolution?'

'That's my role in life. Wipe out all your sins.'

'Listen, thanks for tipping me off.'

'You can handle it?'

'I think so.' Duggan put out his half-finished cigarette and took a six-penny piece from his pocket and left it on the table. 'For the tea.'

Gifford flicked it back at him with his index finger. 'You forgot to drink it.'

The day seemed to have become duller as he cycled back to headquarters, knowing what he had to do. He covered the distance at speed, spurred on through the mixture of slush and horse manure by anger, not wanting to think of what Anderson might have been reading about him. And what his innuendoes and smirks about using the car might have been based on.

Commandant McClure was reversing a car as Duggan swung his leg off the bike and came to a sudden stop outside the Red House. McClure raised a hand to signal him over, got out of the driver's seat and went around to the passenger side as Duggan approached.

'We've been summoned,' he sat as they both sat in. 'To meet the Minister.'

'The Minister for Defence?'

'No,' McClure replied. 'Mr Aiken.'

Duggan gave a whistle of surprise. Aiken, the Minister for

Defence Co-ordination, was generally seen as the second most important man in the government: a former IRA leader, hard man, and one of Timmy's heroes. And about to go the US on an arms buying mission.

'In Leinster House,' McClure added. 'He's at a cabinet meeting in Government Buildings and wants to see us in his office there.'

'About what?' Duggan let up the clutch and moved off. The windscreen began to steam up from the heat of his body and he rubbed at it.

'The Glenn document. He wants a personal briefing before he leaves for Washington.'

Duggan paused at the bottom of Infirmary Road and turned left towards the city centre.

'No further word from him? Glenn?' McClure rolled his window down a little to let in some raw air in preparation for lighting a cigarette.

'No, sir,' Duggan said with unusual formality.

McClure gave him a sharp glance. 'Something up?'

'Yes, sir.' Duggan took a deep breath. 'I've just learned that the Special Branch has Gerda under surveillance. At the request of G2.'

'Fuck's sake,' McClure said. 'Who requested that?'

'I don't know.' Duggan told him what Gifford had said.

'Jesus Christ,' McClure shook his head when he had finished and took out his cigarettes. He passed one to Duggan and lit it for him and one for himself.

Duggan relaxed slightly. At least McClure wasn't involved. 'She can't be involved, can she?'

'You mean as an agent for the British?'

'Yes.'

McClure looked at the Four Courts, still closed up for its Christmas break, as they went by, thinking. 'No,' he said, at last. 'I don't see how.'

'Or the man she works for?' Duggan sought further reassurance.

'Don't know anything about him. But she didn't come to us through him.'

'I think Captain Anderson suspects her,' Duggan said cautiously, not wanting to make any direct accusations.

'Hmm,' McClure muttered, lost in his own thoughts.

'He's mentioned the possibility to me once or twice,' Duggan went on. 'And he keeps dropping hints about her.'

'Hmm,' McClure repeated, indicating he had heard him.

Duggan took the hint that McClure was thinking something through and remained silent as they came up to O'Connell Bridge and joined a line of carts waiting for the policeman on point duty to let them cross. A stream of pedestrians passed in front of them, muffled against the damp cold and trying to pick their steps carefully through the mix of muck and melting snow. The thaw had already turned the gutters into liquid.

'It's not impossible,' McClure sighed, 'that her boss is an agent. That they waited for us to find her and ask her for help. And that she came to our attention independently and reports everything to him as well as to us.'

Duggan's heart sank, his mind disputing everything McClure was saying. The line of traffic began to move and he followed it across the bridge.

'Which would mean what about Glenn?' McClure shook his head, thinking aloud.

'I don't think her boss knows who she really is,' Duggan said.

'You're probably right,' McClure conceded, rolling down his window further to toss his cigarette out. 'In any event, the main point is that we shouldn't be cutting across each other. The British section shouldn't be interfering in our operation.'

Duggan felt a weight lift off his shoulders as he threw his butt out the window too. 'She would be very upset if she knew the police were following her,' he said. 'Even more so if they were to approach her. Or her family.'

'Leave it with me,' McClure nodded agreement.

'Her relations in Austria are having a very hard time,' Duggan said, feeling a sudden urge to talk about her. No more than Gerda herself, he realised that he had nobody to whom he could really talk about her, about her true identity.

'She talks about that?'

'She has no one else to talk to. Nobody else knows who she really is, except us. And if the guards keep making inquiries in Cork, they might come across her family and if they call on them . . .' Duggan let the thought hang there, as though it didn't bear thinking about. 'I mean, she's very sensitive about the—'

McClure raised a hand to stop him. 'Don't tell me anything that I might have to report.'

'Sorry,' Duggan muttered, realising that his sudden enthusiasm to talk about her had probably already confirmed McClure's suspicions about his relationship with Gerda. He slowed down on Nassau Street and waited to turn into Kildare Street.

'It's not a good idea to become too close to agents,' McClure said, his tone mild to lessen the rebuke. 'As a general principle. It can lead to complications.'

Duggan parked outside the National Library and they got out and walked past the closed gates of Leinster House. 'I'll try and have the surveillance lifted,' McClure said in a quiet voice as they entered the pedestrian gate to the reception hut. 'We can't be operating at cross purposes.'

The snow shrouding the statue of Queen Victoria in front of the building was beginning to drip and pool onto her lap as they walked around it and went through the main entrance and were put in a waiting room to one side. They sat on two chairs and McClure drew a sheet from the file he carried and passed it to Duggan. 'He'll want to know about this as well,' he said.

It was a report confirming from several unnamed sources that American naval or military personnel were active in Derry, apparently preparing facilities there for a possible base. So, that man in the pub in Dundalk, whatever his real name was, was right, Duggan thought.

'You been reading the papers?' McClure asked in a low voice.

'Just the headlines,' Duggan admitted.

'President Roosevelt is going ahead with his plans to lend and lease more supplies to Britain. So, it's probably only a matter of time before something happens to involve them directly in the war. One too many U-boat attacks on one of their ships or on a passenger liner like the Lusitania in the last war, or something like that. And then they'll base destroyers and men openly in the North. Without giving us advance notice, never mind consulting us or asking our permission.' McClure raised an eyebrow to see if Duggan realised the implications of that.

Duggan nodded. At its extreme, it was tantamount to an American invasion of our national territory, he thought, albeit territory already occupied by the British. At the very least, it isolated Ireland, leaving it the only democracy in the English-speaking world to remain neutral. The only neutral democracy of any kind, apart from Sweden and Switzerland. And the Americans could exert a lot more moral pressure than the British.

He was about to say something when the door opened and a hard-faced woman of indeterminate middle age held it open for them. She didn't say a word and led them silently through empty corridors, their stagnant atmosphere waiting for a summons to action, and up a back stairs to a small office where there were two desks at right angles to each other and a couple of chairs against a wall painted a washed-out green. She took her place again behind one desk and began typing with hardly a pause. The man behind the other desk, balding prematurely, looked them up and down with the air of disapproval that civil servants always seemed to adopt towards military men and said: 'The Minister's been delayed.'

McClure and Duggan sat down and waited. The civil servant sorted through a pile of papers, ticking some, passing others to his secretary's in tray. The secretary paid no attention to the growing heap, maintaining the fast rhythm of her typing, the heavy key strokes broken only by the tinkle of the warning bell as she came near the end of a line and the crash of the platen rolling up to another as she flicked it across with her left hand.

The room was stuffy and Duggan found his eyes getting heavy with the heat and the steady sound of the typing. He tried to think about the Goertz operation and whether there were any other leads that he had overlooked. Having everything dependent on a shifty character like Benny Reilly was far from ideal. It was too much to hope for that he would simply give up Goertz. Assuming that he really knew where he was.

But he kept coming back to the sickening thought that Anderson had had the Special Branch spying on him and Gerda. Though they couldn't have actually seen them in Montague's office. Or could they? Even if McClure had the surveillance called off, would Anderson accept that? Or would he go a step further and have someone question Gerda? Which would devastate her. Probably encourage her to go to England, join her sister there. Never seeing her again was not something he wanted to think about.

The only way to be sure of stopping further investigation is to wrap up the Glenn mystery as soon as possible, he thought. This whole thing had started off as a low-level operation, just keeping an eye on the German internees. But now it had reached the stage where it involved the Minister on his way to see President Roosevelt. He had to find out what was going on, who Glenn was and what he was up to, as soon as possible. So they would leave Gerda alone.

Fifty minutes later the phone on the civil servant's desk rang. 'Yes, Minister?' the man said, listened a moment, and then added without a question mark, 'Yes, Minister.'

He put the phone down and said to McClure, 'The Minister has important government business to conduct and cannot see you now.'

McClure and Duggan stood up and the civil servant held out his hand. 'You have a report for us.' McClure handed over his file. 'You can find your way out,' the civil servant said, somewhere between a question and an order.

'Yes, sir,' McClure said and they retraced their steps down the staircase to the ground floor, down a narrow corridor behind the empty Dáil chamber and turned a corner into the stately original building. Timmy Monaghan was coming towards them, his hands in his trouser pockets, like the lord of the manor taking a leisurely stroll around his home, admiring the family portraits and checking on the cleaning staff.

'Fuck,' Duggan breathed.

'How's the men?' Timmy beamed from one to the other, blocking their way.

Duggan introduced McClure and Timmy to each other. 'Ah, yes,' Timmy shook McClure's hand. 'I've heard a lot about you.'

Oh, Jesus, Duggan squirmed, unconsciously moving from foot to foot, trying to flee.

'All good,' Timmy was still shaking McClure's hand. 'All good.' He paused as a thought struck him. 'I'm just going down for a bit of grub. Would you lads like to join me? Get a change from army cooks.'

'That's very generous of you, sir,' McClure said. 'I have to go to a meeting. But Paul here is free for lunch.'

'When I was his age you couldn't keep me fed,' Timmy said to McClure, as if Duggan wasn't there. 'Eating morning, noon and night. If I got the chance.'

McClure gave a polite laugh. 'A pleasure to meet you.' He held out his hand to Duggan who took a moment to realise what the gesture meant. Duggan handed him the car keys and caught the hint of a wink, the flicker of an eyelid, as McClure took them and turned away. Only someone who knew his customary unblinking stare would have noticed it.

'So,' Timmy said as they went towards the members' dining room, 'you trust that fella?'

'*Yes*,' Duggan sighed with emphasis, not wanting to have this conversation again.

'I warned you about him before, didn't I?' Timmy ignored him.

'What are you doing here?' Duggan changed the subject.

'Getting out of the house,' Timmy laughed, as if his explanation was the most obvious thing in the world. He put on a sombre face. 'And preparing for next week's emergency sitting about the shortages, of course.' He gave a delighted laugh. 'We'll watch the Blueshirts getting upset about their Brit friends trying to put pressure on us by cutting our supplies.'

'Are you going to use those documents about the British plans?'

'I'd use them in a shot,' Timmy retorted. 'If it was up to me. Show up those fuckers at their devious tricks again.'

So the government knew about them and wasn't going to use them, Duggan thought. Interesting. Probably don't want to create any anti-British feeling. But it meant that Timmy had handed them over to his political masters as well. Or, he thought, the other way round. Maybe they've had them all the time and Timmy somehow managed to get his hands on them.

He was trying to work out what that could mean as they went into the dining room. It was almost empty. A group of six men were gath-ered at a table inside the door, laughing over the punchline of some joke, and two other men faced each other in an intense discussion halfway down the room.

'Men,' Timmy waved at the bigger group as they passed by. Duggan recognised Frank Aiken, the Minister, among them. Important government business, he thought. Another of the group was starting another story, 'That same lad was going up to Carlingford one time . . .'

They took a table at the back, Timmy facing the room to keep an eye on everything. A waitress came over with a menu. 'Well, Betty,' Timmy ignored the menu. 'What do you have for us today?'

'The bacon and cabbage is very nice, Mr Monaghan,' she said. 'And the oxtail soup.'

'That'll do us nicely,' Timmy rubbed his hands.

'It's a good thing I ran into you today,' Duggan said as the waitress left, trying to seize the initiative.

'Why's that?' Timmy gave him a suspicious look.

'I have to know where those documents came from.'

'You're a persistent little pup,' Timmy said without antagonism, taking a half-slice of slightly grey bread from a plate and buttering it.

'You know how it is,' Duggan said, encouraged. 'Information itself is one thing. Where it comes from is another. And just as important.'

'True, true,' Timmy folded over his half slice of bread and bit into it.

Duggan waited for him to chew. Timmy took his time, as if he was chewing on something hard. 'All I can tell you is that those docu-ments are the real McCoy,' Timmy said at last.

'I know. But it's still important to know where they came from. And why. What if we aren't being shown the missing pages because they might make the overall meaning different?'

'The meaning is perfectly clear. The Brits are preparing the ground for an invasion. To play the game all over again. Churchill won't take his beating from the Paddies. That's the beginning and end of it.'

'I know,' Duggan agreed, realising that he had struck a productive line: Timmy himself would never be satisfied with a piece of information without knowing its source and building a conspiratorial motive into its dissemination. 'But knowing the source would help us in all sorts of ways. You know that.'

The waitress came with their deep dishes of thick brown soup. 'And we'll have a glass of milk too, Betty,' Timmy said as she put them down. He took a pinch of salt from an open bowl and scattered it on his soup. He tasted a sample, licked his lips in approval, and set to eating.

Duggan did likewise, wanting to ask him who Aiken was with. The Minister's group was laughing again. It didn't sound like they were discussing important matters of state.

'Strictly between ourselves,' Timmy laid down his spoon and dropped his voice. 'I don't know where those documents came from.'

Duggan looked at him in surprise, his spoon halfway to his mouth. He hadn't expected that: Timmy was never one to admit to ignorance of anything.

'I mean,' Timmy corrected himself, 'I know where I got them, of course. From a reliable man. But I don't know how they got into the system.'

'The system?'

Timmy waved a hand, indicating their surroundings.

'The government?' Duggan asked.

Timmy shrugged, uncomfortable, and turned his attention to Aiken's group.

'You mean the government had the documents first? You didn't give them to them?'

Timmy nodded, his gaze still focussed on the other end of the room.

'And where did they get them?'

'You don't think they're going to tell anyone that,' Timmy turned his attention back to Duggan. 'Least of all a humble backbencher.'

The waitress came back with two glasses of milk and took their soup dishes away.

'Actually,' Timmy continued when she had gone, 'I'm sorry I ever told you about them. But I thought you fellas should know what was going on. So you won't be caught napping when the Brits stab us in the back.'

Duggan sipped at his milk, realising that there was a layer of things going on of which he knew next to nothing. That G2 was operating at one level but the politicians were the people with all the cards, playing a much higher game. 'Where do you think they got them?' he asked, certain that Timmy had a theory and would want to share it now that he had admitted his own minor role.

'That's the question,' Timmy gave a serious nod. 'Those fellas in External Affairs have a lot of sources. Their man in London knows everyone there. He used to work for them, you know. Very high up in their civil service before independence.'

'You think he got them? The High Commissioner?'

Timmy shrugged. 'The thing is,' he added, 'they're genuine, whoever got them. We have the proof of it now. They're cutting our supplies. Following their plan. And unless we give them the ports, they're going to try and take them by force. But you fellas will stop them. Give them another bloody nose like we did in our day.'

It'll be a different kind of war, Duggan thought but said nothing, wondering instead why Ó Murchú had seemed to treat the documents as new information when he had got them from him. Perhaps he wasn't high up enough in the hierarchy to have received them in his own right. Still, it made him doubt Timmy's version of events.

The waitress brought two plates with thick slices of boiled bacon and a metal dish of cabbage and boiled potatoes. 'Would you like apple sauce?' she asked.

'Lashings of it,' Timmy laughed, inviting Duggan to help himself to the vegetables. 'By the way,' he said after she brought the apple sauce, 'did your father ever get the petrol I told you about?'

'I haven't talked to him since.'

'Well, it's still there for him.' Timmy piled the rest of the potatoes and cabbage onto his plate.

'Have you seen the Doc again?' Duggan asked casually, intrigued by Timmy's change of demeanour. He wasn't his usual blustering self, treating him more as an equal.

'How would I see him?' Timmy shot back. 'When you fellas are chasing him from pillar to post?'

'That's only because we want to talk to him. About the bombings.'

'I told you, he knows nothing about that. If they were German bombs.'

'They still want to talk to him. Think he knows more than he says.'

'Don't we all?' Timmy laughed. 'Know more than our prayers.'

Behind him, Duggan heard the scrape of chairs on the floor and the conversation died and the room went silent with the bang of the door. He didn't know whether the other two diners were still there or not. 'Who was that with the Minister?' he asked in a quiet voice.

'Some of his old cronies from Louth.'

'We were told he was busy with important government matters,' Duggan said, deciding to offer Timmy some information.

'You two were here to see Frank?'

'Ahead of his visit to America,' Duggan nodded. 'But we didn't get to meet him.'

'I could've introduced you if you'd told me.'

'Jesus, no,' Duggan said with horror. 'That wouldn't have been right.'

'No harm letting everyone know who you are,' Timmy said. 'Not just some young gobdaw up from the country.'

They ate in silence for a while and then Duggan asked if he'd ever come across Benny Reilly.

'Keep away from him,' Timmy sighed. 'You'll never have a minute's peace if you have anything to do with him.'

'What do you mean?'

'He's like a leech. Ask him for a little favour, do you a good turn, and he'll suck the blood out of you forever after.'

'He's running some kind of black-market operation.'

'What are you fellas doing with the likes of him?'

'His name came up in relation to something or other.'

'You met him?' Timmy asked a direct question.

'Just very quickly.'

'He give you his "wise virgins" speech?'

Duggan shook his head.

'Ask him where he got all the tea or cigarettes or petrol and he goes into this bullshit about how he saw the shortages coming and like the parable of the wise virgins he saved up everything and did without while everyone else was carrying on like there was no tomorrow. And now he's got all this stuff and people keep asking him for favours and he can't refuse them. For a price.'

'You've had some dealings with him?'

'I sent a man who was short of something to see him once. And the eejit mentioned my name to him. So he contacted me and wanted me to do some favours for him. I told him if he ever came near me or mentioned me again I'd wring his scrawny fucking neck and his body'd be found in the Liffey at low tide.'

Timmy drained his milk.

'Why don't the guards arrest him?'

'They say they can't get any evidence against him.'

'Gives them his "wise virgin" speech,' Timmy nodded. 'And no one he's done a favour for will give evidence against him. Of course, you'd have to be a right bollocks to do that.'

Seventeen

Duggan pushed on the pedals and swung across the thin film of surface water coming down the hill against him and slowed as he went through the gates of army headquarters and ducked under the pole as soon as a sentry raised the barrier high enough. Captain Anderson was coming around the corner of the Red House and raised a finger to stop him. Duggan slowed but didn't stop.

'Fuck you,' Anderson growled, punching him in the shoulder as he went by.

The bike almost fell over as Duggan lost his balance but he got a foot on the ground and came to a halt. Anger smothered the pain in his shoulder as he turned back and shouted, 'What the fuck do you think you're doing?'

Anderson stepped up close to him. 'You shouldn't go telling tales.'

'And you shouldn't go round spying on other people's operations.'

'I'll do whatever I think's necessary to get the job done properly.'

'Stick to your own job. Stop trying to fuck up other people's.'

Anderson shook his head in wonder. 'Have you stopped for a minute to wonder how she knew she was being followed?'

Duggan laughed in his face. 'You haven't a fucking clue what's going on.'

Anderson raised a threatening finger and Duggan slapped it away, hard. 'Just mind your own fucking business,' he snapped and pushed a pedal to coast away. In the background he caught sight of two privates at the sentry post smirking at the young officers' spat.

His face was still flushed with anger when he got into their office and Sullivan gave him an enquiring eye.

'Anderson,' he muttered as he threw his overcoat on the table and slumped into his chair. At least, he thought, he really doesn't know what's going on. Thinks Gerda had spotted his surveillance on her.

'Don't give that fucker an inch,' Sullivan said.

Duggan grunted and lit a cigarette. But he's going to go on pushing things, he thought. Even though he must've been ordered to keep out of it. But it mightn't stop him. He could always get some friendly guard to go on harassing Gerda. Even have someone pull her in, question her. The only way out of it was to bring the Roddy Glenn case to a quick conclusion. Find out what he was up to. And put a stop to it.

'Your boyfriend left a message,' Sullivan was saying. 'Said your friend's in the Bridewell.'

'What friend?'

'Didn't say,' Sullivan smiled. 'Probably one of the friends you two know from the public toilet in College Green.'

'Fuck off,' Duggan muttered, in no mood for the usual banter. It couldn't be Goertz, he thought, or Sullivan would know about his arrest. So it had to be Benny Reilly. Fuck. 'Has he been arrested?'

Sullivan shrugged, turning his attention back to the file he had been reading.

'Thanks,' Duggan said, an oblique apology, and went to find Commandant McClure. Off to tell tales again, he thought. But he had to get Benny out of the guards' clutches. Even if Benny was willing to cooperate in custody, Goertz would probably find out quickly that he'd been picked up and cut all links to him. Probably knew already.

McClure was on the phone, saying 'Yes, sir' as Duggan entered, and raised the pen in his other hand to detain him as he went to leave again. 'Safe journey, sir,' he concluded and put the receiver down.

'The colonel's on his way back from London,' he leaned back in his chair. 'Top-secret meeting. With MI5. He asked them casually about a Mrs Agnes Smith in Chelsea who had come to our attention in passing.' McClure threw his pen onto the desk and reached forward to replace it with a cigarette. 'That apparently caught their attention. He wants to see us as soon as he gets back.'

Duggan gave a quiet whistle. 'She's one of theirs? So Glenn is one of theirs?'

'I don't know,' McClure stood up and stretched his shoulders. 'The colonel wasn't very talkative on the phone. Made it sound like it was something very casual we'd come across that would require a little further investigation. But he did say,' he reached for a sheet of paper on which he had written a date, 'to check the newspapers for this date. There might be something relevant there.'

Duggan took the sheet of paper and glanced at the date: 8 November. 'What am I looking for?'

'Something relevant,' he said. 'That's all I know.'

Duggan folded the sheet of paper in half. 'There's something else. I think Benny Reilly might've been arrested.'

'I've heard.' McClure sighed a stream of smoke. 'One hand not knowing what the other's doing again.'

'Can we get him out? I don't think we'll get anything out of him while he's in the Bridewell.'

'I've set it in motion,' McClure nodded. 'The powers that be have ordered a clampdown on the black market. Worried about popular unrest if people see others able to buy their way around the new shortages. All the main black marketeers were rounded up this morning.'

'I'll try and be there when he comes out,' Duggan said. 'Make it clear that he owes his freedom to us.'

'Good idea. But don't be too specific with him. About anything.'

'No,' Duggan nodded. 'By the way, I hear that some guards are involved in the black market too.'

'That's being taken care of too. They've put in a senior officer to clean it up.'

Benny would know about that too, Duggan thought. Help him realise what a favour they were doing him. And that they expected results.

'By the way,' McClure said as Duggan head for the door. 'Not a word to anyone about the colonel's travels. I don't need to tell you how sensitive that is.'

'No, sir,' Duggan said. He could imagine there'd be hell to pay if Timmy and some of his colleagues found out about it. Not to mention how the Germans might react if they knew. They could use the secret collaboration with the British as an excuse for an invasion if they wanted to.

Dangerous games, he thought as he collected the three daily newspapers for 8 November from the library, glancing at the front page of the *Irish Press*, the only one with news on the front, as he walked. 'May Be Facing Crisis Says Taoiseach' the main headline said, reporting de Valera's reply to Churchill's warning that the withholding of ports facilities in Ireland was a heavy and grievous burden.

Another headline above the fold stopped him in his tracks: 'London Spy Trial Disclosures' and underneath, 'Secret USA Papers Stolen At Embassy'. He scanned down through the report quickly, thinking, that's it. That's where Glenn's letter from Churchill to Roosevelt came from. The US embassy in London. So there's no doubt about its authenticity. Glenn was part of some kind of spy ring involving the two people mentioned in the story, a Russian woman and a US diplomat. And trying to pass on the stolen information to the Germans in Ireland. Fucking hell.

He turned in to his office and Sullivan was on the phone. 'Hold on,' he said, looking up. 'He's just come rushing in. Can't wait to talk to you.'

He handed the phone to Duggan. 'Our friend's about to be released,' Gifford said in his ear.

'Right now?'

'Throwing the poor man out on the street without his dinner.'

'Are you there? Can you delay it till I get there?'

'How long do you want?'

'Fifteen minutes,' Duggan said, thinking. 'I'll be waiting outside for him.'

'Okay, boss,' Gifford sighed. 'I'll try to pull your rank.'

Duggan put down the phone and grabbed his coat off the table. 'Don't let anyone move those papers,' he said to Sullivan as he pulled on the coat and turned to go.

Sullivan gave a silent two-fingered salute to his back as he left.

He cycled quickly along the quays, taking the longer route to give himself time to think about what he'd read, slotting all he knew about Glenn into the new context of the London trial. The day had brightened as the cloud base lifted and let more sunlight through. The weather was changing; the forecasters now thought it was only a matter of a day or so until it cleared from the west and the sky was open again to the air forces. As if to underline the thought, a rumble from the west grew into the drone of an aircraft coming from behind him. It passed almost overhead, a twin-engined Avro Anson, and he recognised it as one of the Air Corps' patrol planes. He watched it follow the Liffey to the sea and then bank across the bay and head southwards along the coast.

Glenn was obviously an accomplice of the Russian woman, Anna Wolkoff, a daughter of a former Czarist admiral, who'd tried to send secret documents from the US embassy to Lord Haw-Haw in Germany. And of the American diplomat with the triple name, Tyler something Kent, who'd given her the documents. Which must have included the letter from Churchill to Roosevelt, though the report didn't mention it. Or did it? Details of the evidence given at the secret trail had not been reported, only the guilty verdicts, the judge's comments and the jail sentences, ten years for her, seven for him.

He needed to read it again, more carefully. To try and tease out what was between the lines. And hear what the colonel had to say when he got back from London. Clearly, he knew something more about this secret trial. It all suggested that Glenn was an amateur agent. Which fitted in with everything they knew about him. Unless he was part of a double operation to sow disinformation among the Germans. In which case, he was a British agent. And Anderson would've been right. Partly. But not about Gerda. He was sure of that.

He turned into Church Street, following the track cleared in the slush by a heavy vehicle, and crossed the road onto the footpath beside the Four Courts. He chained the bicycle to the railings and checked his watch. Five minutes to go before Benny Reilly was released if Gifford kept to their timetable. He walked around the corner towards the Bridewell garda station and leaned against the railings across the road from its entrance and lit a cigarette, still thinking about Glenn and Gerda and how to make sure she wasn't exposed to Anderson's blundering.

A line of empty carts went by, heading back towards the country from the markets up the road, their drivers well wrapped up and probably half-drunk after spending the morning in the area's early opening pubs. He watched the building, idly trying to translate the Latin inscription under its pediment. Something about letting the heavens fall.

Benny Reilly appeared on the steps, blinking in the dull brightness, and looked from side to side as if he expected an ambush. A cart carrying empty milk churns clanged by with two young boys scutting on its tailgate and they caught each other's eyes across it. Duggan raised his cigarette hand and Benny crossed to him, taking his time.

'You're a lucky man,' Duggan said.

'How's that?' Benny stopped in front of him.

'The government's locking up all the black marketeers.'

Benny turned and spat into the gutter. 'Very foolish of them. They'll have riots in the streets if people can't get a little extra tea here or there for special occasions. From people who saw all this coming and were wise enough to put some aside.'

'And you're one of the wise virgins,' Duggan laughed. 'And one of the lucky ones. Because it's more important that you stay out of jail. For the moment.'

'I don't know where he is,' Benny gave him an anguished look. 'I swear to God.'

Duggan shrugged and flicked his cigarette butt into the gutter beside Benny's spit. 'Enjoy this little taste of freedom,' he straightened up. 'It could be your last for a while.'

'Ah, Jaysus,' Benny shook his head. 'I'd help you if I could. But, honest to God, I don't know where he is. He could be anywhere by now.'

Duggan repeated the phone number he had given him before and walked away. Benny looked after him for a moment and then went in the other direction. He was going into Hughes's pub on the corner of Bull Lane as Duggan went by on his bicycle on Chancery Street. There was a horse and cart tied to a lamp post outside it. Give him another day, he thought. Two at the most. If he didn't come up with something by then he never would.

He headed for the city centre, freewheeling through the water and slush beside the markets where a man was washing out the floor, forcing out a pool of water with a heavy yard brush. He went on up to

Middle Abbey Street and turned into O'Connell Street and cycled up to Gerda's office. He clumped up the stairs but the door at the top was locked. Gone to lunch, he realised, retracing his steps. He stopped on the footpath, wondering where she might have gone, and went up to the Monument Café. There was a queue inside the door and he scanned the crowded tables but saw no sign of her. He went on up past the Carlton cinema to the Cabin Café and tried to look through its steamed-up window. He stepped inside the door but she wasn't there either.

He went as far as the Aer Lingus office and couldn't see any more cafés. He crossed the street to Findlater's, weaving his way through the bicycles and drays, and went down past the Gresham Hotel and into the Savoy restaurant above the cinema but she wasn't there. He gave up the search and went back towards her office and waited outside the Carlton a few doors away for her to come back. The footpath was crowded and he only caught sight of her as she turned into her office, a shopping bag swinging from one hand. He scanned the people behind her but there was no point trying to spot if anyone was following her: there were too many people around, most moving with purpose, some idling by windows and bus stops. Besides, there was no need for anyone to follow her here: the guards would know as well as he did that she'd come back to work.

He hurried after her and she heard the front door open and close as she was halfway up the stairs. She glanced back and a smile softened her face. 'Well, hello,' she stopped and he went up to the step below her. She leaned down to kiss him, then continued up to her office. Inside, they kissed again.

'When will he be back?'

'Any minute,' she said, breaking apart and taking off her coat and hanging it on the back of the door.

'I don't know where you go to lunch.'

'I didn't today,' she said, putting her shopping bag under her desk. 'I went shopping instead.'

'What'd you buy?'

'You'll see,' she gave him a coquettish smile. 'Sooner or later.'

'No call from our friend?' he asked, anxious to get down to business before her boss returned.

She shook her head.

'There's a new plan,' he said. 'When he calls, tell him that you've spoken again to the German internee and he's set up a meeting for him with another German.'

'Who?'

'Me.'

'You?' She stepped back from him in disbelief. 'You're going to pretend to be a Nazi?'

'You tell him that you speak German and that you'll translate between us. And I'll only speak German.'

She shook her head with a dismissive smile. 'You don't look like a Nazi.'

'What does a Nazi look like?'

'Arrogant.'

'All of them?'

She nodded.

'It doesn't matter,' he said with a touch of impatience. 'He wants to pass information to the Germans. And I will be the German he's looking for. I don't have to do anything, say anything much. Ask a few questions. Speak German only. You will translate. And we'll find out what we want to know.'

'What if he speaks German too? And knows from your accent that you're not one?'

Duggan took a deep breath. 'We'll take that chance. Even if he does, he's unlikely to be able to tell I'm not a native speaker.'

She stepped close to him. 'You said it was dangerous,' she searched his eyes.

'We need to know what he's up to.'

'You said he's not alone.'

'It'll be all right,' he put his arms around her. 'And once this is over you shouldn't go back to Mrs Lynch's anymore.'

'Why not?'

'Because you need to forget about all that stuff. About the war. What they've done to your relations. All that.'

She dropped her head onto his chest and he kissed her hair and the street door banged and heavy steps came up the stairs. They stood unmoving for a moment, listening, then broke apart and she sat down behind her desk. Duggan stepped in front of it and she was handing him a typed list of flats to rent as Montague came in the door and saying, 'That's our up-to-date list.'

Montague nodded to him, showing no sign of recognising him from his previous visits, and went into his office and closed the door. Duggan waved the list in front of Gerda. 'Could we use one of these for a quiet meeting?' he asked in a low voice.

She stared at him for a moment, then fished out another list, picked up a pencil and circled one line and handed the page to him. He glanced at it. It was a list of houses to rent. He didn't recognise the address she'd circled but knew the area vaguely. Sandymount.

'It's very quiet there,' she said. 'I had to show it to somebody but they decided against it. It was too quiet.'

'You have the keys?'

She opened the shallow drawer in front of her and picked a set of keys from the rows there, all of them with a little cardboard tag. She held them up and he went to take them. 'No,' she said. 'I better keep them. In case someone looks for them.'

'Okay,' he said, 'Tell him to meet us there.'

'When?'

'The evening he calls. Whatever time suits you.'

She stared at him, still holding the keys.

'What?' he held her gaze.

'It's dangerous. He's a fascist.'

'You needn't come,' he said, leaning his hands on her desk and bending forward.

'Then how will you pretend to be a German?'

'I just will. Speak English with a German accent.'

She shook her head with a short laugh.

'What's so funny? You pretend to speak English with a Cork accent.'

She punched him on the shoulder and he caught her wrist and pulled her towards him.

The colonel sat ramrod straight behind his desk, his posture at odds with the grey exhaustion on his face and the dark circles under his eyes. 'At ease,' he waved at a couple of chairs behind McClure and Duggan as they stood to attention.

They relaxed and pulled forward two chairs. 'Long journey, sir?' McClure asked as they sat down.

'Endless delays on the trains,' the colonel said. 'Stuck near Crewe for a couple of hours. They had to hold the Aer Lingus plane an hour for me in Liverpool.'

'How does London look?'

'Didn't see much of it. Damage is terrible. Morale all right, apparently. But some concerns about people becoming fatalistic. The growing number who don't bother taking shelter during raids anymore. Feel if they're going to die, they're going to die.' He shrugged. 'You look up those newspaper reports?'

'Yes, sir,' Duggan said, leaning forward to place the copies on the desk. He had gone through them more carefully earlier, reading the most detailed one in the *Irish Press* first. But it was as his hasty first impression had suggested: there were no details of the information Anna Wolkoff had tried to send to Berlin to Lord Haw-Haw or of what Tyler Kent had taken from the US embassy. The judge had said that Kent's offence did not relate to any actual military or naval movements but to four highly confidential documents. He saw Wolkoff's offence as more serious because she had tried to send a document to a traitor in Berlin. He had added, 'I take into consideration the fact that you have undoubtedly been led to do this by this anti-Jewish obsession on your part, a virus which had got into your system and had destroyed your mental and moral fibre.'

The reports in the other papers had been less detailed but one line in the *Irish Independent* had caught Duggan's attention. Tyler Kent was believed to be partly of Irish ancestry, it said. Which led Duggan to wonder if that was why Roddy Glenn was in Ireland.

The colonel read through them and put them aside. 'Right,' he steepled his fingers. 'I mentioned to our friends over there that a Mrs Agnes Smith in Chelsea had come to our attention. As part of routine checks on the mail. Their ears pricked up at that, though they pretended at first that the name didn't mean much to them. But,' he gave a wry smile, 'they came back to Mrs Smith again later. In a casual way.

'Anyway, the story came out finally. This Mrs Smith is on the periphery of a group called the Right Club, led by a Conservative MP from somewhere in Scotland. A Captain Archibald Ramsay, who was interned last summer because of his anti-Semitic views and his support for Hitler's thesis that the war is the result of a Jewish conspiracy. He had gathered some like-minded people around him, notably this Wolkoff woman, and they had caught the interest of the young American diplomat, Kent, who began to provide them with information about secret correspondence between the British and the Americans. Or, more precisely, between Mr Churchill and President Roosevelt.

'Wolkoff tried to send some of these messages to Lord Haw-Haw to get the Germans to publicise them. And to let Americans know that Roosevelt was playing a double game, telling his voters before the election in November that he would not involve them in the European war while plotting with Churchill to give Britain more support and even to become involved.'

He paused and looked from one to the other. 'Wolkoff and Kent were arrested and the Americans waived his diplomatic immunity and put both of them on trial in October in the final weeks of the US election campaign, as the Right Club increased their efforts to contact German agents and other intermediaries. You know the result,' he waved an index finger towards the newspaper reports.

'Why is Roddy Glenn still trying to get these documents to the Germans?' McClure asked. 'The election's over now. Roosevelt's back in office. Even Wilkie's on his side now.'

'And increasing the pressure on the Germans,' the colonel nodded. 'But things like the Churchill letter we've seen could still embarrass him. And perhaps even block his current efforts to have his lend and lease plan put through Congress at the end of the month. There've been reports about it in the last few days.'

Jesus, Duggan thought, remembering the headlines he had scanned but hadn't read. He dragged up his shadowy mental picture of Glenn across snowy O'Connell Street, talking to Gerda. It was hard to imagine he could really have an effect on the war. But he could.

'Glenn is a member of this Right Club?' McClure was asking.

'We can assume that for the moment,' the colonel said. 'But I don't know for a fact. I haven't told our London friends anything about him. Just that something about a postcard to Mrs Smith had aroused our mail censors' suspicion. I didn't know what exactly. And I didn't have a copy of it with me.'

'They'll probably pick it up on their side,' McClure offered. 'If they're keeping an eye on her.'

'Indeed,' the colonel said. 'And we can presume they've concluded that we know more about this than we've let on at the moment.' He rubbed his face in is hands but failed to bring any colour back into it. 'This Right Club has caused a lot of gossip in the inner circles over there about who belongs to it. Some important people, apparently, who want Britain to make peace with Hitler. Maybe even join him in an anti-Bolshevik crusade. A list of its members was apparently found in Kent's flat when they arrested him. Set the cat among the pigeons. You can imagine the rumours about who's on it. A veritable fifth column of possibly influential people.'

'We don't know if Glenn is on it?'

The colonel shook his head. 'That's one of the possible lines of inquiry. If and when we tell the British about him.' They lapsed into silence again, broken by the colonel saying, 'Your thoughts?'

'It'd be interesting to see more of Glenn's documents,' McClure said. 'Now that we have confirmation that they're authentic.'

The colonel nodded and looked at Duggan.

'One of the newspaper reports said Kent might have Irish connections,' Duggan offered.

The colonel nodded with a sigh. 'I don't know anything about that. That's another line of inquiry we can pursue with the British if and when we tell them about Glenn.'

'I hope he's not a relation of Father Coughlin,' McClure said. The Irish-American Father Charles Coughlin was one of the leaders of the isolationist campaign in the US to keep America out of the war. 'That wouldn't help us with President Roosevelt.'

'Which reminds me,' the colonel said. 'External Affairs wants a final briefing from us in the morning. Before Mr Aiken leaves for Washington the day after tomorrow.'

'I presume we don't need to tell them about the Right Club,' McClure said.

'Not at this stage,' the colonel agreed. 'Just that we are confident that this letter from Churchill to Roosevelt is genuine and the Minister can expect to be pressured about the ports issue.'

'We're hoping Glenn will come back to us with more documents in the next few days, sir,' Duggan said.

'I doubt he'll have anything more to give us,' the colonel said. 'I'd be surprised if MI5 will let Mrs Smith send him any more. Or more genuine ones, at any rate. Assuming the British have intercepted the postcard to her and read its secret message.'

'You think this could still be a disinformation operation, sir?' Duggan continued.

The colonel thought for a moment. 'I don't think it has been up to now. But that could change. The British now know that there is someone acting on behalf of the Right Club in Ireland. They don't know yet that we know who it is. And I suggest we try and find out as much as we can before we alert them to Glenn's identity. If we ever do. Meanwhile, we'll send them a copy of the postcard sent to Mrs Smith. Which, as you say, they've probably intercepted.'

'But it'll show willing,' McClure smiled.

'Perhaps,' the colonel reciprocated with a wry smile and pushed his chair back. 'Thank you, gentlemen.'

'Jesus,' Duggan muttered as they went headed for the stairs down to their own floor.

'What?'

'This is a tricky business.'

'I thought you'd realised that months ago.'

'Yes, I did,' Duggan said. 'But maybe not just how tricky.'

'The higher the floor,' McClure took the top step first, 'the trickier it gets.'

Maybe it's the other way around, Duggan thought as he followed him. The higher up, the clearer the view. And the lower down the more confusing everything appeared.

He thought of telling McClure about his plan to meet Glenn but he was in two minds about it. Fear that McClure would veto it had stopped him so far. Or, even worse, that he would use it as part of a full-scale operation with the guards to pick up Glenn. Which would involve Gerda, revealing her true identity to a wide range of people. Unless he could keep her away from it altogether. But Glenn would be suspicious if she wasn't there. Might not appear at all.

At least it was clear now that Glenn wasn't a British agent: if he was he wouldn't have been trying to send amateurish messages to a Right Club contact. So there was little or no risk in his plan; the worst that would happen would be Glenn seeing through his impersonation of a German and refusing to talk. Which wouldn't leave them much worse off than they were.

He was still trying to work out all the angles as he arrived in his office. Sullivan was standing over the table, his palms flat on its top, and reading the *Evening Herald*. He straightened up as soon as Duggan entered and checked his watch. 'Good,' he said.

'Nothing?' Duggan nodded at the special telephone.

'Not a peek,' Sullivan was all dressed up, wearing a smart suit with a red tie and his hair had been Brylcreemed with care.

'Big date?'

Sullivan gave a half-shrug, an embarrassed confirmation. 'Going to get one of the old hansom cabs from the station. Pick her up in about forty minutes.'

'Where're you taking her?'

'Jammet's.'

Duggan gave a low whistle. So it was a big date.

'Finally got her on her own,' Sullivan said. He didn't seem in a great hurry to leave. 'She and Breda are like Siamese twins. And that American fellow keeps tagging along too.'

'That's still going strong?'

'Missed your chance there,' Sullivan said.

'Story of my life,' Duggan said, without meaning, as he sat down and the realisation struck him. 'You're going to pop the question.'

'I'm wondering whether to do it in the cab,' Sullivan shifted from foot to foot. 'On the way there.'

'Why not in the restaurant?'

'Lot of people there.'

'It's an expensive place, isn't it?' Duggan had never been there. 'Surely there's lots of room between the tables.'

'Maybe. I haven't been there before.'

'And if that doesn't work, do it in the cab on the way home.'

'Maybe.' Sullivan looked undecided.

'Show me the ring. You got it there?'

'Fuck off.'

'Congratulations anyway.'

'She hasn't said yes yet.'

'Why wouldn't she?' Duggan smiled. 'Aren't you good for the widow's pension?'

'Jaysus,' Sullivan gave a mirthless laugh and checked his watch again. 'Wish me luck.'

'Good luck.'

Sullivan left, like a reluctant volunteer going on an unwelcome mission. Duggan shook his head with a smile, wondering why Sullivan was so uncertain about it. If I was heading off to propose to Gerda I'd be in seventh heaven, he thought. He looked at his watch and considered calling around to her. But he couldn't afford to leave the phone unattended. He had better wait for a couple of hours anyway. And, by then, it would be too late to call on her.

He lit a cigarette, tipped back his chair, threw his feet up on the table, and watched the smoke curl to the yellowed ceiling. Wouldn't it be great if they could just go out on a date, he thought. Without work or Glenn or the German internees or the war hanging over their every meeting. It was never far away, even when they were lost in each other. But then he would never have met her. The real her, the one she kept hidden from everyone.

He inhaled some smoke and let it drift back out of his mouth. The thing now was to get her away from all of that as soon as possible, help her to forget her own past. And protect her public identity. The moment of truth was probably coming in the war. In the spring. When the Germans made their next move. Which would have to be the invasion of Britain. And maybe of Ireland. But they wouldn't even need to invade Ireland if Britain fell. Unless it could all be decided in North Africa. But that was unlikely. It would have to come back to Europe. And if Britain fell the Germans could just dictate terms to

Ireland. Which would leave Gerda in a dangerous position if her real identity was known to many people. Who knew who would side with the new order once it became established?

The only way to protect her was to get her away from the Glenn business as soon as possible and as discreetly as possible. And the only way to do that was to wrap it up quickly without the involvement of anyone who didn't already know her true identity. Which, as far as he knew, was only McClure and probably the colonel. And the intelligence officer in Southern Command who had first put them onto her.

He leaned forward to stub out the butt in the metal ashtray and a thought struck him. He pulled the phone over by its cable and asked the switchboard for the main telephone exchange. When he was put through he asked for the supervisor, identified himself, gave the supervisor Gerda's office number.

'Is there an intercept on that line?' he asked.

'Hold on,' the man said.

Duggan twisted the phone cord around his finger while he waited for him to return.

'No,' the man said when he came back. 'Will you be wanting one on it?'

'Ah, no,' Duggan said. 'Thanks.'

At least Anderson hadn't gone that far in his pursuit of Gerda. There was no need to worry that he would overhear any arrangements she made with Glenn.

He dropped his feet to the floor, stood up and went to a cupboard to find the Ordnance Survey map covering the Sandymount area. It took him a while to find the address of the house for rent that Gerda had given him. He memorised its location and how to get there and decided to drive by it later. It was better than sitting here, just waiting. And it was never any harm to reconnoitre the ground.

Eighteen

'Flights are resuming from Foynes to Lisbon tomorrow morning,' Pól Ó Murchú said in the formal manner of a head waiter laying out the evening instructions for staff. He was in a brisk mood this morning, no longer under the burdens that seemed to have oppressed him during their last meeting. 'Mr Aiken will be on the first flight out, stay a day or two in Lisbon and be in Washington at the start of next week.'

'Yes, sir,' McClure said. He and Duggan were across the desk from him, in their usual chairs in his office.

'His main task is to buy the weapons and military supplies and ships we need. But,' Ó Murchú picked up the copy of the letter from Churchill to Roosevelt, 'his most difficult task will be to counter the British attempts to get the US to put pressure on us over the ports. We know from some of our friends in the Democratic Party that the President is somewhat impatient with our position. Even though it's the very same as his own official position, neutrality. Mr Aiken will have his work cut out to explain it to him.'

He paused and looked at them in silence for a moment. 'You have nothing more to add to this document?'

'I'm afraid not, sir,' McClure said. 'We were hoping to get further information, documents, but that now appears unlikely. But we may be able to learn some more from the source of this letter.'

'Like what?'

'We don't think he has access to any more similar documents but he may have seen some others. Or at least heard people talking about them.'

Ó Murchú gave that a moment's consideration. 'In what way do you think he might add to our knowledge about the situation?'

'I can't say, sir,' McClure shook his head. 'I can't even be sure that he will add anything to our knowledge. All we have confirmed at this stage is that the letter to President Roosevelt is genuine.'

'We've assumed that all along,' Ó Murchú sighed with disapproval at their failure to tell him something new. 'It chimes with everything we know about both Mr Churchill and President Roosevelt. Anything new on this German parachutist?'

'We're hoping for a breakthrough in the near future.'

Ó Murchú gave a harrumph.

'Christ,' McClure sighed as they sat into the car and lit cigarettes. 'Just as well we're not looking for promotion in the foreseeable future.'

'Maybe we should've told him about the Right Club and all that,' Duggan ventured as he did a U-turn and headed back the way they had come.

'You heard what the colonel said,' McClure shrugged. 'And it wouldn't have been of any practical use to him or Mr Aiken. The Americans obviously know all about it already. And they might be none too happy to have us sticking our oar into it. Until we have something definite to contribute. Like Glenn.'

The thaw was now well established, turning the air raw with dampness and the streets into a shallow stream of muck. The few pedestrians about crossed the streets paying more attention to where they put their feet than to the sparse traffic.

'I'm going to meet Glenn myself next time he contacts Gerda,' Duggan said, deciding it was time to tell McClure. 'That'll speed things up. Get us the answers we need from him.'

'Good idea,' McClure said. 'We'll work out a plan.'

'I already have one.' Duggan spelled out what he intended to do.

McClure went into one of his silences. They crossed O'Connell Bridge and turned onto Bachelors Walk. Peter Gifford was just turning into Bachelors Way, leading down to Benny Reilly's place in North Lotts. Duggan let the car coast to the pavement and told McClure why. 'I'll just go check with him for a moment,' he said. McClure nodded.

Duggan tossed his half-finished cigarette away and went after Gifford. He found him hammering on Benny's door. 'Fucker's disappeared,' Gifford said, giving up as Duggan reached him.

'Fuck,' Duggan echoed.

'Last seen in Hughes's pub last night. Pissed out of his mind. Tried to pick a fight with some of the lads from the Bridewell. Singing, "Take it Down from the Mast, Irish Traitors".'

'They didn't throw him in a cell somewhere?'

'They threw him into the street. Hasn't been seen since.'

'Fuck,' Duggan repeated.

'Didn't go home last night. No sign of him at his usual haunts.' Gifford kicked the door of the garage for emphasis.

'Hope he didn't fall in the Liffey.'

'No bodies washed up yet,' Gifford said, cheering up as they turned away. 'Anyway, life goes on, whether Benny remains in the land of the living or not. Sinead wants to meet this friend of yours. Give her the once over. See if she passes muster.'

Duggan couldn't help laughing at the sudden change of mood. 'We'll get together at the weekend.'

'No can do.'

'She's going home for the weekend?'

'Yes,' Gifford dragged the word out and raised the first two fingers of each hand into inverted commas. 'She's going "home" for the weekend.' He dropped his hands. 'Which means she won't leave the flat for a minute in case anyone sees her. And I'll be as limp as a wet rag by Monday.'

'Better start building up your strength.'

'We could do it tomorrow night. Before she goes.'

'Sure,' Duggan said. 'I'll let you know if that's okay.'

They came back onto Bachelors Walk and Duggan pointed to the car. 'Want a lift?'

Gifford lowered his head and squinted at the car. 'You've got a passenger. And not one of the fairer sex.'

'My boss.'

'No thanks,' Gifford shivered. 'Two intelligence men together. That'd fry my brain.'

'Check the morgue,' Duggan said as he left him. He sat into the car and told McClure about Benny.

'Christ,' McClure muttered.

They remained silent until they passed the Four Courts. Ahead of them, the sky was lightening to the west, the first breaks appearing in the clouds.

'You should have some back-up when you meet Glenn,' McClure said.

'I don't think I need any,' Duggan said, as casually as possible. 'Especially now that we know that he's not anybody's agent. I mean, a real agent.'

'Still. We don't know that he won't be armed.'

'It's unlikely.'

'True. But there's no harm in being careful.'

'I'd rather do it alone,' Duggan said, concentrating on the road ahead and hoping that McClure was not going to insist on sending someone with him. 'I'd like to keep this operation as small as possible. Keep Gerda's involvement within the circle of people who already know about her. She's very nervous about people discovering her true identity.'

McClure said nothing until they stopped at the barrier to headquarters and waited for it to be raised. 'What about your Special Branch friend? Does he know about her?'

'No.'

'You trust him?'

'Yes,' Duggan let the clutch up.

'Does he know about this operation?'

'No.'

'Maybe he could back you up.'

In their office Sullivan was whistling some jaunty tune that Duggan thought he should know but couldn't name. 'You did it,' Duggan nodded to himself. 'Congratulations.'

'Thank you,' Sullivan bowed his head in formal acknowledgement.

'When's the wedding?'

'There's no hurry.'

'But she won't get the widow's pension if she's only a fiancée.'

'Ah, would you stop that,' Sullivan said. 'That joke's worn thin.'

What joke? Duggan wondered, refraining from pointing out that it was Sullivan himself who had ascribed that motive to Carmel. But things had clearly changed and he thought he knew why. He smiled at the thought, covering it with another question. 'When did you pop the question?'

'In the restaurant. It's overpriced if you ask me. But it worked out very well. The waiter noticed me doing it and next thing two glasses of champagne arrived on the house. They did it very discreetly. No fuss. Nobody said anything.'

'Carmel was impressed?'

'Yeah,' Sullivan laughed. 'Especially as she thought I'd arranged it all beforehand.' He paused. 'Listen, we're going out to celebrate at the weekend. You should come along. I'll get you another date with one of Carmel's or Breda's friends.'

'Thanks. But I might have a date myself.'

'Even better. Bring her along.'

'It might be a bit soon for that,' Duggan said. 'It might frighten her off to meet all you lot in one go.'

Sullivan narrowed his eyes. 'This is a real date? Not with your homo friend?'

'That joke's wearing thin too,' Duggan said. 'He's got his girlfriend staying with him for the weekend.'

Sullivan widened his eyes. 'How'd he manage that?'

'His charm, I suppose.'

'What about his parents?'

'He lives in a flat.'

'What about her?'

'What about her?'

'She's willing to stay with him for the weekend?'

Duggan nodded.

'How'd he manage that?'

Duggan shrugged and his phone rang. The orderly on the switchboard said in a flat voice, 'your batman'.

'Speak of the devil,' Duggan said to Sullivan as he waited for the call to be put through.

'No new stiffs in the morgue,' Gifford said on the phone.

'That's good.'

'Unless he's still floating down to sea.'

'Will you drag the Liffey from' – Duggan paused – 'I don't know, where does it start? From there down to the bay and back again.'

'I'll just go get my fishing net, general.'

'By the way,' Duggan said, looking at Sullivan. 'One of the staff officers here wants to know the secret of your success with women.'

'Well, finally,' Gifford snorted, 'military intelligence gets around to seeking answers to matters of real importance.'

'What'll I tell him?'

'Tell him to change uniform. Join the Garda Síochána, a body of men whose uniform stands for uprightness, helping old ladies and children across the street. Not like that mucky green thing worn by lowlifes who hide behind ditches and snipe at innocent people.'

Duggan replaced the receiver and said to Sullivan, 'He says join the guards. Women can't resist their uniform.'

Sullivan rolled his eyes.

Duggan reached over and lifted the receiver of the special phone and listened to its hum for a moment.

'Still working?'

Duggan nodded. 'But our man's gone missing.'

'Another great plan down the Swanee,' Sullivan said in a contented tone.

'We'll see.' Duggan pulled a newspaper over and the phone rang. 'A lady for you,' the switchboard operator said.

'Paul?' Gerda said, her voice hushed with excitement. 'He's called.'

'And?' Duggan prompted.

'He'll meet us at that place at eight o'clock.'

'Great. Did he say anything else?'

'No. It was very short.' She was still whispering.

'Okay. I'll call around to you after work.'

'I can't,' she said. 'I've agreed to go out to eat with the girls from the digs.'

'Can't you skip it?'

'They've been talking about this for a long time and I kept putting them off. They'll think I'm a right bitch if I don't come.'

'Okay,' he sighed. 'I'll pick you up at half-seven. Will it be over by then?'

'Oh, yes,' she said. 'Clerys restaurant.'

Duggan replaced the receiver and clapped his hands. 'Another plan is working,' he beamed at Sullivan.

'That didn't sound like work,' Sullivan smirked.

'It's work, all right. God never closes one door but he opens another.'

'You know we're on standby here tonight? In case the bombers come again.'

'I know,' Duggan said with a hint of impatience. 'But this is more important.'

Sullivan gave him a sceptical look.

Gifford was doing his impersonation of a corner boy again, standing with a sneer on his face at the corner of Bachelors Walk and O'Connell Street. He spotted Duggan's car behind the swarm of bicycles and the row of carts and horse-drawn cabs waiting at the junction and sauntered down and got in just as the line of traffic began to move.

'Anything?' Duggan asked.

'Not a thing. You'd think the place had been deserted since the dawn of time.'

'He's cleaned it out?' Duggan glanced at him.

'Don't know. I couldn't see in. We'll come back when it's dark. See if there's any light inside. Maybe find him hiding in the tea chest.'

Duggan turned his attention back to the traffic on Eden Quay, ready to speed up and change gear at the first chance to get past everything that was keeping them to a cycling pace. He saw his opportunity on Amiens Street and raced away with a roaring engine.

'Tut, tut,' Gifford murmured. 'Getting impatient are we?'

'Listen,' Duggan ignored him. 'I need your help tonight.'

Gifford listened in silence until Duggan had finished telling him the bare outline of the plan. 'Very fishy,' Gifford observed.

'What is?'

'That none of your lads are involved.'

'There's a reason why not many people know about it. And why it has to be kept that way.'

'You sure you're not off on another of your solo runs, are you?' Gifford gave him a squint-eyed look. 'That's going to get a poor innocent policeman into trouble?'

'No, nothing like that.'

'Nothing to do with your mad relatives?'

'Nothing,' Duggan laughed.

'And this woman who'll be with you? She's not your cousin?'

'Jesus, no.'

'She's the mysterious girlfriend? That some of your fellows want our fellows to follow?'

'Look,' Duggan said. 'I can't tell you at the moment. But I'll explain later.'

'Need-to-know, huh,' Gifford nodded to himself. 'So that I can't reveal anything when I'm caught and tortured.'

Duggan laughed. 'You've been going to too many pictures.'

'I'll get to meet her later? The girlfriend?'

'Maybe. But you'll meet her tomorrow night anyway. Is that still on with Sinead?'

'Yeah. She can't wait.'

They went by Fairview and under the railway bridge onto Clontarf Road and the sky brightened out over the bay.

'Very flattering, I suppose,' Gifford said in a discursive tone. 'That the security of the state rests on my ability to follow this guy through empty suburban streets all on my own without him seeing me.'

'He won't expect to be followed,' Duggan said, remembering how Glenn had hurried away from his last meeting with Gerda without a backward glance.

'Why not? In my vast experience people up to no good are always twitchy about their surroundings.'

'This guy isn't. He's just,' Duggan searched for the right word, 'an amateur. He's not a criminal. Not a spy. Just someone out of his depth.'

'Like yourself.'

'Ha, ha.' Duggan turned off the coast road.

'Out of his depth in what?'

'That's what we're trying to find out exactly.'

They fell silent as they turned into the road where Benny Reilly lived and Duggan slowed down. The road was wet, the children's ice slide now a sheen of water. The trees dripped onto patches of dirty snow on their sheltered sides. Benny's van was still parked in his driveway. There was no sign of life in the house, no smoke from the chimneys, but no telltale milk deliveries on the doorstep or letters hanging from the letter box either. It was difficult to tell through the shine off the ground floor window if the curtains were open or closed.

'So he hasn't taken off in the van,' Gifford said as they turned into the next road and came to a halt, the engine idling.

'What do we do now?' Duggan mused.

'Fucked if I know,' Gifford smiled. 'You're the boss. I'm only riding shotgun.'

'We could take a look at his barn.'

'I can't imagine Benny hiding out in the hay,' Gifford said. 'But if the horse is gone we'll know he's ridden off into the sunset. We might even hear Gene Autry singing a song.'

That's about it, Duggan thought. Benny had taken the opportunity he'd given him to make a run for it. No doubt, he'll turn up sooner or later and the guards will get him for black marketeering but that doesn't matter to me. As far as catching Goertz is concerned, he's just another dead end.

Duggan sat in the Prefect in the gloom of Sackville Place at the side door of Clerys department store, eager to get going. He looked at his watch: it was five minutes to half-seven, only three minutes since he'd last checked it. He'd had the whole afternoon to plan the meeting, go back over everything he knew about Glenn, and figure out what they wanted to know from him. Which wasn't a lot now that they knew the source of the letter from Churchill to Roosevelt and about Tyler Kent and the Right Club. It was good to be going into a rendezvous knowing most of the answers, only needing to fill in more details. And, with luck, get some more documents.

A group of women came out the door of Clerys, silhouetted against the dim light of O'Connell Street, handbags hanging from elbows. One broke away and Gerda came towards him, waving back over her shoulder as one of them called something after her. She sat in and asked, 'Am I late?'

'Dead on time,' he leaned over to kiss her but she held him back with a hand on his chest and then leaned forward to give him a peck on the cheek.

'They told me how to treat you,' she giggled. 'How to reel you in. Like a big fish.'

He caught sight of the others still watching and then turning away and leaving the laneway. 'Didn't you tell them you'd already done that?' he laughed at the image of himself flopping helplessly on a river bank.

She put an arm around his neck and pulled him to her and kissed him deeply. When they finished he held her face in his hands and rested his forehead against hers and looked into her deep eyes. 'Ready?'

She nodded and he started the car and stopped at O'Connell Street to let a bus go by, its blue-lit interior giving it a ghostly presence. There was no sign of Gerda's friends. 'They're going to the Adelphi,' she said in answer to his query. 'To the new Errol Flynn picture.'

He turned towards the bridge.

She leaned her head on his shoulder. 'I bought another blanket for us today,' she said. 'It was the last day of the sale.'

He squeezed her knee with his spare hand and then took it back to change gear as he accelerated down Pearse Street. They were silent as they went by Westland Row and the gasworks and over the hump of the bridge at Grand Canal harbour, its dark warehouses and chemical works hulking in the added blackness of their own shadows. After the bridge at Ringsend he passed close to the anti-aircraft battery in the park: there were no signs of activity there but he knew they were on full alert tonight, the first clear night since the last bombing.

He took the coast road, following the map he had memorised in the office the previous evening, and the night brightened with a half-moon blotting out the stars. Its reflection glittered on the distant sea, barely visible beyond the stretch of sand, like something half seen, half imagined. She raised her head from his shoulder to watch the flashes of the lighthouses: from Poolbeg, beyond to the Bailey, out to the distant Kish lightship, and around the sweep of the bay to Dun Laoghaire.

'You think they'll come back tonight?' she asked, still looking out to sea.

'I don't know,' he said. 'It's a perfect night for it if they want to.'

She kept her face to the sea and he counted off the roads running inland until he approached the right one and slowed down.

'You all right?' he asked.

She nodded but he didn't see her, looking the other way for the turn.

'You can wait in the car,' he took the turn. 'If you want to change your mind.'

'And how will you talk to him?'

'I'll speak English.' He drove slowly along a tree-lined road, following its slow bend to where the house should be.

'With a funny accent?'

He shrugged and let the car coast to the kerb just beyond where he thought the house was. There were no other cars on the narrow road and the houses were hidden behind hedges and walls. The street lights were off and no light came from any of the hidden houses. We could be in the middle of the country, Duggan thought, but for the regular gateways. He switched off the lights and the engine and turned to her.

'I'm all right,' she said.

'Sure?'

She nodded.

'I don't think there's any danger,' he said. 'He's not dangerous.'

'That's not what you said before.'

'We know a bit more about him now. He's not working for anyone important.'

'So his information's not important?' she asked, confused.

'Yes, it is. Very important. But he's not dangerous.'

She searched his eyes in the gloom.

'Okay?' he asked again.

She nodded.

They got out and closed the doors as quietly as they could, conscious of the silence. Duggan glanced around, wondering if Gifford was in position. You could deploy a whole platoon here and nobody'd see them, he thought. The shadows were so many and so deep.

Gerda led him back to the house and opened one side of the double gate with a rasping click that sounded like a shot in the silence. A gravel path led directly to a garage at the side of a modern bungalow with two bow windows flanking the entrance. Duggan guided her off the gravel and onto the grass of a lawn enclosed by thick shrubs with random patches of grey snow still lining their bases. She led him to the glass-panelled hall door and opened it with her key.

The bone-chilling cold of an unoccupied building seeped into them as soon as they entered. She closed the door behind them and they stood in the hall for a moment, breathing the damp air, listening to the silence, feeling like intruders. Then Duggan moved down the hall, looking into the rooms. They were empty of furniture, diminished by its absence. Lumps of soot had fallen into the fireplaces and bounced onto the wooden floor in the sitting room.

Gerda waited in the hall for him to finish and he led her towards the back of the house to a half-conservatory with one wall of glass looking out to the back garden.

He took the keys from her and opened a side door and went into the garden. It was surrounded by evergreens and divided in two by a wooden trellis which probably hid a vegetable patch and trailed flowers in summer. Beyond the trellis, he saw the outline of two stumpy apple trees. He turned around in a full circle – the garden was not overlooked by any buildings.

'We'll talk to him here,' he said when he came back in, locking the door behind him.

Gerda nodded. She stood in the middle of the floor, her arms folded tight under her breasts.

Duggan went to the door and flicked on the light switch, hoping the electricity was still connected. A weak bulb came on, its saucer-like shade casting the ceiling into darkness. He opened the door to the hall to let the light show through to the front door and looked at his watch. It was five minutes to eight.

He took a deep breath, feeling his excitement rise. This was going to be okay. He'd get the information he wanted. And get Gerda out of all this.

He went over to her and she unfolded her arms and he took hold of both her hands and she squeezed his with tension. 'Okay?' he looked into her eyes.

She took a deep breath and nodded.

'*Sehr gut*,' he smiled.

They held each other's hands and gazes and waited.

Nineteen

A tentative knock on the glass of the door came exactly on time. Duggan pulled Gerda closer for a moment and kissed her and then let her go.

Her heels clicked on the tile floor of the conservatory and then made a drumbeat on the wooden floor of the hall as she went. Duggan unbuttoned his overcoat and his jacket and checked his revolver was in position in the shoulder holster. He let the coats hang loose and stood at attention for a moment, listening to a murmur of voices. Then he joined his hands in front of him, altering the pose but not relaxing it.

The door opened and Gerda came in followed by Roddy Glenn. Up close, he was younger than Duggan expected, maybe eighteen or nineteen. His fair hair, light blue eyes, and creamy skin added to the impression, making him look younger than he probably was. Duggan wondered inconsequentially if he even needed to shave yet. Glenn's eyes flicked from Duggan, around the empty room, at their reflections in the dark window, and back to Duggan.

'*Guten Abend*,' Duggan gave him a curt nod. '*Sie haben noch mehr Dokumente für uns?*'

Glenn glanced at Gerda as she translated for him, 'Do you have more documents for us?' Duggan gave an inward sigh of relief: he didn't understand German.

'Not yet,' Glenn said to Duggan. 'I hope to have some more in the next week. Did you get the one I sent you?'

Duggan waited for Gerda to translate, keeping his eyes on Glenn who watched her as she did it. His accent was unplaceable, definitely English but not very strong.

'It was interesting but too late,' Duggan said in German. 'Roosevelt has been re-elected now.'

'You can still use it in America. To expose his lies. And stop them sending arms to England.'

'Why didn't you give us this document before the election?' Duggan demanded, playing out the dialogue in slow motion as Gerda translated back and forth.

'We tried,' Glenn said with an air of frustration. 'But England is a police state now. We couldn't get it to you.'

'We've been here all the time,' Duggan said.

'We sent information to the Italian embassy before they joined the war and then we tried some other embassies in London but they were no help.'

'You could have come to us here.'

'We tried but England's a police state. They wouldn't let us travel here. Even before they started their arrests. They've even put members of parliament in jail. Without trials or anything.'

'Why did they let you come?'

'Because they don't know about me. I wasn't a member of the group.'

'Because you are a British spy,' Duggan said, spitting the German word '*spion*'. '*Ein Provokateur.*'

Glenn was shaking his head, recognising the word even before Gerda translated. 'No, no,' he pleaded. 'Please believe me. My uncle is a member of the peace movement and he's been put in jail. He asked me to deliver this document to you.'

'What is this peace movement?'

'People who want peace. Important people who want to end this needless war.'

'The British Union of Fascists?'

'No. We are a separate organisation.'

'Does it have a name?'

'The Right Club.'

'Ah, an English club,' Duggan said with a hint of derision. 'I've never heard of it.'

'Because they've been suppressed by the warmongers. Locked up without trial. Harassed and intimidated.'

Duggan gave a dismissive shrug.

'They're good people,' Glenn blurted. 'They want to stop all the bombing. Of your cities and our cities. There's no need for it. England and Germany shouldn't be fighting each other. There's no reason for it.'

'You seem to forget that England declared war on us.'

Glenn nodded as Gerda translated. 'That was a mistake. Caused by the Jews and their conspirators setting natural friends at each other's throats. It should never have happened. And it's only got worse since the Zionist Churchill got in.'

Duggan glanced at Gerda and saw a flash of anger in her eyes but her tone remained neutral as she translated.

'Where do you get these documents?' Duggan changed the subject.

'From a patriotic American. Who was disgusted by Roosevelt's lies, telling the American people he wouldn't drag them into the war while conspiring with Churchill and other Jew-lovers to do just that.'

'Who's this patriotic American?'

'He's been put in jail by the English. With the help of Roosevelt.'

'So you have no more documents?'

'We hope to get more. There are more patriotic Americans who can see what is happening.'

'Where are they? Do you know them?'

'Our people are looking for them.'

'Your people?' Duggan sounded sceptical. 'I thought they were all in jail in the English police state.'

'We're rebuilding our organisation. There are a lot of patriots who believe as we do. Who see through the conspiracies that have caused this war.'

'Do you have many supporters here? In Ireland?'

Glenn looked confused by the question. 'No,' he said. 'We are not looking for supporters here. But there must be people here who want peace too.'

That's enough, Duggan thought. He's got nothing more of use to us. 'You will keep us informed of your progress?' he said in German.

Glenn nodded. 'And you will be able to use our information in America?'

'Yes. It is very useful.'

'It's the key to peace now,' Glenn said, sounding now like he wanted to talk more. 'If America doesn't help England then we will have to make peace with Germany. It's the only way to stop all the unnecessary bombing and killing now. England can't stand up by itself. It's been undermined by all the Jew bankers and so-called refugees we've let in over the centuries who've wormed their way into society in their usual way and destroyed it from within.'

Gerda cut him off by beginning to translate in an angry voice and then saying to Duggan in German, 'I'm not going to listen to this shit.' Duggan nodded to her.

Glenn mistook the anger in her tone for approval of what he was saying and went on: 'The Führer is right about the causes of the war. He sees through this conspiracy and we should be standing with him and not fighting each other like they want us to do. The main thing stopping us from doing that is the Jew lobby in America who want to keep it going, making their fortunes, and laughing while we kill each other.'

Gerda stepped in front of Duggan and gave him an angry look. '*Geduld*,' he said to her under his breath. Patience. He watched Glenn over her shoulder as his eyes brightened with zeal and his voice grew more strident.

'They're all around Roosevelt, all his advisers. And he's a secret Jew himself. Real name is Rosenfeld. Which explains everything. The American people will not allow him to help the warmonger Churchill once they know what his real aim is and why he's surrounded himself with Jew advisers.'

Gerda reached inside Duggan coats and pulled out his revolver and stepped away from him and turned to Glenn. She pulled back the heavy hammer with her left hand as Duggan said, 'Jesus Christ. Stop.' Glenn stopped in mid-sentence, a look of shock on his face at the gun, compounded by Duggan's sudden outburst in English. Duggan threw his arms around Gerda and reached for the gun. It went off with a deafening bang.

The heavy bullet threw Glenn back against the wall and he slipped down into a sitting position. His eyes blinked several times and his limbs twitched as they tried to hold onto life. Blood oozed from this chest, a spot steadily spreading and darkening his light tweed coat. His eyes went still and sightless.

Gerda dropped her gun hand and her body shuddered and tears flowed down her face. She turned and buried her face in Duggan's chest.

'Fuck, fuck, fuck,' he said, feeling the sobs wracking her body as he reached down and took the gun from her hand. He stepped back from her. 'What the fuck did you do that for?' he demanded.

'Nazi,' she said through her tears. 'He won't tell any more lies now.'

He stepped over to Glenn and looked down at him and slapped

the wall hard with the palm of his free hand, his mind racing. Fuck. What do I do now? Fuck.

'Jesus Christ,' he looked at her. She was standing where he had left her, her head down, her arms loose by her sides, looking shrunken. Self-defence, one part of his mind suggested, clicking through the problems and options. I can say he lunged at me, I had no choice.

He bent down beside Glenn, and felt the pockets of his overcoat. He ran his hands down Glenn's sides, moving one of his still warm hands out of the way, avoiding his sightless eyes and the dark blood. Nothing. No weapon. Fuck.

He straightened up and put his head back against the wall and closed his eyes. 'What'd you do that for?' he repeated.

'You heard what he said,' she didn't raise her head.

'He was just a stupid fucking messenger,' he looked at her. 'Talking shit.'

'He wanted the Nazis to win,' she looked up at him. 'To kill us all.'

'The British have locked up all this Right Club,' he said. 'They know who they all are.'

She looked up. 'You knew that?'

Oh, Christ, he groaned to himself.

A movement caught the corner of his eye and he turned as the door opened slowly with a creak, expecting to see Gifford, or, worse, Anderson. The man who entered slowly was neither. He was tall and blonde and had a pistol hanging from his right hand. Duggan raised his revolver, thumbing back the hammer in one move, thinking 'five rounds left' as he put the first pressure on the trigger.

'No, Paul,' Gerda shouted, 'Don't shoot.'

Thoughts raced through his mind. New Year's Eve. Dinner dance. Breda dancing. American cultural attaché. Max something. Spy.

The man at the door spread his hands, pointing the pistol away to the side, at the floor, and then relaxed his grip and took it into his palm. He glanced at Gerda and then at Duggan. Duggan lowered his Webley, easing the hammer down, his thoughts in turmoil. Max Linqivst dropped his pistol into his coat pocket and stepped into the room and bent down to put a finger on a vein in Glenn's neck.

He straightened up and said, 'I'm—'

'I know,' Duggan cut him short and turned back to Gerda, feeling sick, unconsciously raising the gun and pointing it at her. 'You've been working for them all along.'

'No, no, no,' she shook her head with each denial.

'So what the fuck's he doing here?'

'I can explain,' Linqvist said.

'This was your idea?' Duggan nodded down at Glenn.

'Christ, no,' Linqvist said in surprise. 'I presume you had to do it.'

'She did it,' Duggan spat back, swinging the revolver back towards Gerda. 'Not me.'

Linqvist took in a deep breath and puffed his cheeks and let them deflate slowly, trying to figure out what was going on. Gerda crossed her arms and closed her eyes and rocked herself back and forth on her heels.

'You should be proud of her,' Duggan added, the viciousness of his tone trying to overcome the sickness in his stomach. 'There's nothing she won't do for you.'

He stepped over to the window and looked out but only saw the scene behind him. He gulped in some air, finding it hard to breathe, and tried to think of what to do. A man shot with my gun. By a woman I thought I loved. Who was just using me all the time. Oh, fuck.

But he couldn't think straight.

All he could think of was how she had used him. His mind wouldn't go beyond that, wouldn't focus on what would happen next, on the inevitable inquiries, the probable court martial. A picture of them making love on the office floor came into his mind. He felt like throwing up and gulped some more air.

He saw her reflection move towards him and tensed as she came up behind him. '*Komm mit mir*,' she whispered. '*Bitte. Ich liebe dich.*'

He resisted an immediate urge to turn and push her away, torn between the sense of betrayal and the longing created by her closeness, and confused by her declaration of love.

She rested her head on his shoulder and put her arms around his chest. He wanted to shake her off but couldn't. He watched her hands clasp each other in the window and saw her forehead resting on his shoulder. She tightened her grip and then eased it again. 'I'm sorry,' she said.

They stood like that for a while. His breathing calmed but his thoughts were all over the place, bouncing from betrayal to love, from having to call the guards to finding another way out of this mess. He saw the door opening and a short man come in and Linqvist whisper something to him. How many American spies can there be here? he wondered. Or maybe this one was a Brit. Jesus, what a mess.

He went to turn around and she released him but remained close. 'How could you?' he asked in an anguished voice.

'I wasn't working for them,' she said in German, searching his eyes. 'I only told them about this meeting because you said his information was important for America too.'

'And they told you to shoot him?'

She shook her head. 'No, no. They said they'd follow him afterwards. Just wanted to know who he was. Same things you wanted to know.'

He shook his head in disbelief.

She lowered her eyes. 'I want to go to America.'

'You did a deal with them?'

She nodded.

'That's why you killed him?' Over her shoulder he could see Linqvist and the other man kneeling on either side of Glenn, going through his pockets.

'No, no,' she shook her head with emphasis. 'I couldn't listen to any more of that shit. I've heard too much of it.'

'That's all it was,' he protested. 'Shit. You can hear it every week on *Germany Calling.*'

She gave a deep sigh. 'You don't understand what these people are like. It's not just shit to them. They believe it. They want to kill us all. All the Jews. We'll never be safe here. And they will kill you too if you resist.'

He shook his head, about to remonstrate, but she cut him off. 'You're a good man and I know you believe you can stop them here but you can't. I hear people talking about how you beat the British and the Black and Tans and you're great at guerrilla war but you don't know these people. They'll put a stop to your guerrilla war very quickly. They will line up and execute twenty or fifty Irishmen every time one of your resistance fighters even shoots at a German. Every single time. How long will your guerrilla war last then? And they will do to us what they're doing to the Jews everywhere else.'

Yes, yes, Duggan thought, shaking his head with impatience. Now's not the time for a political debate about Nazism. Linqvist and the other man were standing up, looking at him. He had to make a decision. Call the guards. Face the music. Or? What?

'The guards called to my parents in Cork,' Gerda said in a flat voice. 'Wanting to know where my sister and I are.'

'Ah, Jesus,' Duggan breathed into her hair as he hugged her close. So that was it. That bastard Anderson.

Linqvist gave a polite cough which sounded so incongruous that it almost made Duggan laugh. 'What do you want to do here?' he inquired.

'You find anything?' Duggan asked back, playing for time as he let go of Gerda.

'Nothing much.' Linqvist held out a wallet and took a slip of paper from it. 'Using his own name by the looks of it. Receipt for another week in a guesthouse on Baggot Street. Place called the Inishfallen. He was planning to stay around for another while.'

Duggan hardly listened to what he was saying. He took a deep breath, committing himself, and said, 'You will take her to America?'

Linqvist nodded.

'Immediately?'

Linqvist nodded again.

Gerda grabbed his hand. '*Komm mit mir*,' she said and turned to Linqvist and added in English, 'He can come too?'

The other man gave a short laugh. 'That could be arranged,' Linqvist shrugged without any enthusiasm. 'We need more soldiers.'

'I thought you were neutral,' Duggan said.

'Sure,' Linqvist flashed a mirthless grin. 'We're all neutral against somebody. Listen,' he added, waving a hand behind him at Glenn's body. 'We can clean this up. If you want.'

'How?'

'You don't need to know that. It'll be like it never happened.'

'You'll get rid of the body?'

'It'll be like he just disappeared. Suits us. It'll stop any of his friends in England still on the loose from trying this route to the Nazis again. Suits you. Won't have to face the military police, lot of questions. All that.'

And get Gerda safely away, Duggan thought. There was no other good alternative for her. Even if I say I shot him, that he'd turned hostile, that I thought he was reaching for a weapon. She'll be dragged into it even if she's disappeared. Especially if she'd disappeared, he realised. Then the question would be, who was she working for? And Christ knows where it would all end up. With me out of G2 at the very least. They didn't want trigger-happy people there. Or people who could be so easily fooled.

'And come with me,' Gerda was saying.

'I can't,' he turned to her and paused, giving it a moment's thought. 'No. I can't desert. Not at a time like this.'

'Please,' she said.

He shook his head, thinking of how hurt his father would be if he were to become a deserter, flee the country he had fought to create. In its hour of need. His father had taken part in the War of Independence and had no illusions about this war or neutrality but he would take desertion as a personal hurt as well as seeing it as an abdication of duty. His mother would be unhappy, too, but probably relived that he was further removed from harm's way. 'I can't. Really, I can't. Not now. Maybe later.'

'You're a good man,' she searched his eyes. 'I'll write.'

'Who are you now?'

'Grace Matthews,' she gave him a wan smile. 'But you know who I really am.'

He gave her a quick kiss and stepped away and headed for the door.

'By the way,' Linqvist stopped him. 'Did he have anything interesting to say before the conversation was, ah, terminated?'

Duggan tried to think back for any useful information. 'His uncle's a member of the Right Club. Probably on the list you have.'

'Any more documents?'

Duggan shook his head. 'Just a lot of talk about your President Rosenfeld and so on.'

'Okay,' Linqvist nodded, understanding. 'Thanks.'

Duggan walked out without a backward glance, his body drained, his brain numb.

Gifford emerged from the bushes of the neighbouring house, his revolver hanging in his right hand, and fell into step beside Duggan as he reached the footpath. 'What the fuck was all that about?' he demanded, glancing back over his shoulder to check if anyone was following. 'Who are those guys?'

'Americans.' Duggan opened the car doors and started the engine and drove off without a pause.

Gifford turned to look back but there was no sign of anyone. 'They drove up a few minutes after you,' he said. 'Then the victim arrived and went in. And one of those guys went into the house after the shot.'

Duggan drove without knowing where he was going.

'I went round to the garden after the shot and saw everything,' Gifford went on. 'Were you trying to tell me something from the window?'

'What?' Duggan said, distracted. 'I couldn't see you. Didn't know you were there.'

'Hmm,' Gifford took one more look behind and settled into his seat. They went by one side of the small triangular park in the centre of Sandymount. 'Wasn't very satisfactory,' he mused, returning to his normal demeanour. 'Like being in a cinema where the sound has broken down. Had to figure out what was going on from everyone's expressions. You want me to tell you what I thought was going on?'

Duggan let the car coast to a halt near a pub, rested his head on the steering wheel for a moment and then began to tell Gifford the whole story.

'Jesus,' Gifford said when he had finished. 'That's even more twisted than my version. I thought you'd shot him and she was trying to console you.'

Duggan saw the bullet hit Glenn again and throw him back against the wall and the blood seeping out and his dying eyes. He took out a cigarette and lit it, noticing the slight tremor in his hand as if it was someone else's.

'Gimme one of those,' Gifford said.

'He didn't deserve to die like that,' Duggan said aloud to himself.

'He was playing a dangerous game.'

You didn't see it, Duggan told himself. The suddenness, the violence, the simplicity, the finality. He shuddered. Someone has just walked over my grave, he thought.

A man emerged from a nearby pub and stopped to light a cigarette with the exaggerated care of a drunk. He got it going with the third match, looked around, saw them, and wandered over with a rolling gait as if he was on board ship in a leisurely swell. He tapped on the driver's window and Duggan rolled it down.

'D'you know your engine's running?' the drunk said. 'You're wasting the petrol.'

'Fuck off,' Duggan sighed at him.

'No, I mean, there's rationing,' the drunk continued, determined to finish his thought. 'Don't you know there's an emergency?'

'You hear what I said?' Duggan pulled back his coat and jacket and the man's eyes fixed on the butt of the Webley. He seemed to be hypnotised for a moment by the ring on its base and then backed away muttering, 'Sorry, sir', and giving Duggan a half-salute with his cigarette fingers.

'Jesus,' Duggan sighed, watching him go. 'Now I'm trying to frighten drunks. Maybe he'll call the guards.'

'Naw,' Gifford said. 'He probably thinks we're the IRA. He won't tell anyone.'

'What do you think they'll do? With the body?'

'Another one for the Wicklow Mountains.' Gifford blew out smoke without inhaling it. 'He'll have a fair bit of company up there. From the old days.'

Don't tell me things I'll have to report, Duggan remembered McClure saying to him. But he certainly didn't mean shootings. A dead body. Murder. He did mean his relationship with Gerda. Which was what this was all about. Or was it? 'Should I have called it in?' he asked, as much of himself as of Gifford.

'In my vast experience,' Gifford rolled down his window and tossed out the half-smoked cigarette, 'what people don't know doesn't bother them.'

Or it causes big problems, Duggan thought. If only I'd told her what I knew about Glenn. If she'd told me about the Americans. If that fucker Anderson had minded his own business. If I hadn't deliberately provoked Glenn. If, if, if.

'What we need to do now,' Gifford continued, 'is get our story straight. You met this Glenn character. He told you whatever he told you. He left. I followed him all the way to Baggot Street, using my exceptional surveillance techniques, never spotted once. But he got a bit careful at the last minute and I had to hang back further. He appeared to go into the Inishfallen guesthouse and I went home to my well-earned rest and slept the unbroken sleep of the just. And he'll never be seen again. Presumed to have gone back to wherever it was he came from. Right?'

Duggan nodded and threw out his butt.

'And what you need to do now,' Gifford pointed a finger at him, 'is to forget all about this German woman and find a nice cuddly culchie girl before you accidentally involve the whole country in some war or other.'

'Austrian,' Duggan corrected him. 'She's Austrian.'

Gifford shrugged. 'Same difference.'

He parked outside the Red House and stepped out of the car and realised that he had another cigarette in his hand that he had no memory of lighting. He leaned on the roof of the car for a moment and breathed in a last drag, which tasted stronger and more satisfying in the sharpness of the night air. The point of no return, he thought. Though really I've already passed that. But now I've got to commit the lies to paper.

He ground out the butt with his toecap and went in. He was aware immediately of the extra buzz in the building. Something has happened, he thought. More German bombs. But I heard nothing. Mustn't have been in the city.

Captain Anderson emerged from a doorway and almost bumped into him. 'Good work,' Anderson muttered and kept going. Fucker, he thought, assuming he was being sarcastic. But he can't know what has happened.

His office was empty but Sullivan's end of their table was strewn with papers so he was around somewhere. He took off his overcoat and sat in his chair and lit another cigarette without either wanting it or thinking about it. He pulled over the heavy Royal typewriter and went through the motions of putting two carbon papers between sheets of flimsy paper like a man under water. He twisted them around the platen, released the lock on it to straighten them and then locked them in place.

Someone came in behind him and he felt a light clap on his shoulder. 'Well done,' Commandant McClure said.

Duggan swung around and looked at him in surprise.

'We got Goertz,' McClure smiled. 'Your man came through.'

'My man?' Duggan struggled to remember Benny Reilly. All that seemed an age ago, another lifetime.

'He called a couple of hours ago,' McClure nodded at the special phone line on the desk. 'Just after you went out, apparently. But Sullivan was here. And Benny told him where Goertz would be after eight o'clock.'

'Where?'

'Blackheath Park in Clontarf. Not far from Reilly's own house in fact.'

Duggan shook his head, trying to rid his brain of the mush which seemed to have overwhelmed it. This was great news, after all the months they'd spent trying to track down Goertz. But he couldn't feel any sense of achievement.

'They found him in a passageway between the house and the garage,' McClure was saying. 'He'd tried to hide there when the guards knocked on the door. He didn't put up any resistance and confirmed his identity immediately. The guards have him in the Bridewell. Sullivan's down there too.'

'That's great,' Duggan made an effort to sound enthusiastic.

'The colonel said to congratulate you. Job well done.'

'Thank you, sir,' Duggan said formally.

'By the way, how did your meeting go?'

'I was just about to type up the report,' Duggan turned back to his typewriter to avoid McClure's eye. 'Nothing very much. He's related to one of the members of the Right Club but doesn't seem to have any contacts here.'

'Okay,' McClure didn't sound very interested. He clapped him on the back again and repeated, 'Well done,' and left.

Duggan propped his elbows on either side of the typewriter and rubbed his temples hard and stared into the machine's half-bowl of metal levers topped with back-to-front letters. All he could see was Gerda's dreamy smile as she laid her head on his shoulder after they had made love, all he could feel was her skin against his.

Twenty

'I nearly fell of the chair when the phone rang,' Sullivan laughed, still in high good mood the next morning as he divided the copies of his report into three. 'First I thought it was that joker Gifford acting the bollocks as usual.'

'What did he say?' Duggan made an effort to smile through his exhaustion.

'He said, "Is that Robert?" And I said, "Robert isn't here, can I take a message?" And he said, "The man you want is at Blackheath Park right now but he'll be gone by tomorrow, early." That was it. The boss decided we shouldn't wait around, sent the guards in right away.'

Duggan lit another cigarette though he didn't want one: his mouth already felt like an ashtray. He rubbed his left eye as the smoke caught it.

'If he'd run out the back and gone over the garden wall he'd probably have got away,' Sullivan said. 'The guards didn't really believe he was there, just went to the front door. It was only when one of them flashed a light down between the house and the garage that they saw him standing there. He didn't try to run or deny who he was or anything. Said he was a German officer. The best friend Ireland ever had.'

Duggan grunted. Sullivan initialled each of the copies, stood up with the reports in his hand and dropped one copy in front of

Duggan as he headed for the door. 'It's all there,' he said. 'Read all about it since you're the hero of the hour.'

'I wasn't even there.'

'Don't I know,' Sullivan gave him a happy grin. 'My name's on it now.'

Duggan scanned the report, another of Goertz's comments catching his eye. He said he was acting in the role of German military attaché since the Irish wouldn't let the Germans have one although they allowed the British one. He remembered his uncle Timmy telling him that: so Timmy really had met Goertz, he thought. Not that he had doubted it, but with Timmy it was always good to have independent confirmation.

He sat back and watched his cigarette burn in the ashtray, propped up by its growing cylinder of ash, waiting for it to collapse. He stirred himself when it did and the butt dissolved into ash. He reached for the phone and asked the switch for a number.

A man's voice answered, 'Adelaide Agency.'

'Could I speak to Miss Maher, please?'

'She's not here today.'

'When will she be back?'

'I don't know,' the man's tone turned sharp. 'Are you a friend of hers?'

'Thank you,' Duggan said as he hung up.

What was the point of that? he asked himself. None. No point to it at all. What was the point of anything? He sat back again and put his hands in his trouser pockets and closed his eyes. His mind was empty and he wasn't sure whether he had dozed off or not when he heard Sullivan say, 'Boss wants to see you.'

Duggan detoured into the toilet on his way to splash some water on his face. McClure was hanging up his phone as he entered.

'Our friend in External Affairs,' he nodded at the receiver. 'Mr Ó

Murchú. Full of the joys of life today. Positively ebullient by his stan-
dards. Got a stick to beat Hempel with at last. He's looking forward
to giving Herr Hempel a severe talking-to about Goertz. And get his
own back for all the lectures he's had to listen to from the Germans in
the last year.'

Duggan gave a wan smile as he took the chair McClure indicated
with a wave.

'Got them by the short-and-curlies now,' McClure continued.
'Goertz is telling all and sundry that he's a representative of the
German High Command. And that's he's been in contact with the
IRA. Which is not a very friendly position for a supposedly friendly
country which supposedly respects our neutrality and wishes it to
continue. Won't look good for the Germans if Goertz is put on public trial.'

'He will be?' Duggan asked in surprise.

'I doubt it actually,' McClure said. 'But Ó Murchú is going to
dangle that possibility over Hempel's head. If they don't back off certain things. Like asserting their right to increase their legation numbers with military types and spies. You know the way these diplomats
carry on. There'll be no explicit linkage but . . .'

'What about the bombings? Has Goertz said anything about
them?'

'Says he knows nothing. But that's why we should allow a proper
military attaché in the German legation. To avoid misunderstandings.'

'So he knows about their demand for more diplomats.'

'Would seem so,' McClure nodded. 'His capture has come just at
the right moment. Foynes is open again this morning. The Minister's
flying out to Lisbon today. On his way to America.'

With Gerda? Duggan wondered. It was possible that she was on
the same plane as Aiken. The British and Americans controlled the
Pan American flights from Foynes: when they went, who was allowed

onto them, everything. There was a British security agent posted there to oversee it all with the full knowledge of the Irish government.

'When will Mr Aiken get to America?' he asked, really wondering when Gerda might get there. And when he would hear from her. If he ever did.

'Sometime next week,' McClure said. 'He's staying in Lisbon a couple of days. Don't know why. Maybe waiting for an available flight. Maybe a holiday.' He paused. 'You look like you need one too. A holiday.'

'Didn't sleep much last night.'

'Half the city was on tenterhooks last night,' McClure nodded, assuming that was the reason. 'Waiting for another German bomb or two. Have you had a day off since Christmas?'

'Not really,' Duggan scratched his head, not sure he wanted time off.

'Take a few days off. Go down the country and get some fresh air.'

'Thanks but I'd like to talk to Goertz.'

'He can wait,' McClure waved away his reservation. 'He's not going anywhere and he's keen to talk. Already offering to decipher some of his coded messages we found last year in that house he was hiding in. Says they were just notes for himself.'

'But they were the same cipher as the one that sailor took to Lisbon,' Duggan said.

'Exactly,' McClure smiled. 'But he doesn't know we've got a copy of that message.'

More independent confirmation, Duggan thought, getting back into work mode. We can see what he was saying secretly to his bosses and what he says to us. 'Shouldn't we strike while the iron's hot? Keep him talking while he's willing?'

'Yes,' McClure agreed. 'But one of the other lads can do it. We don't need to speak German to him. His English is very good.'

'I'd like to do it,' Duggan said. Anything to take my mind off of other things. 'Since I've been involved for so long.'

'Fair enough. You start it anyway. Then take a few days off next week.'

'Thanks.' Duggan stood up. 'That'd be good. Maybe the end of next week.' I could get a lift down home with Timmy, he thought. Let my irritation with him occupy my thoughts

'By the way,' McClure flicked through the top few documents on a pile of papers. 'Got a message from MI5 this morning, requesting that we keep an eye out for one Roderick Glenn, nephew of one of the leading lights in the Right Club.' McClure gave him a conspiratorial smile. 'They think he may be the person sending postcards with secret messages to Mrs Smith in Chelsea.'

Duggan tensed. They couldn't know already, could they? He had no doubt the Americans would tell them. If the guy with Max wasn't British. But this was probably a coincidence. The word had hardly gotten back to London so quickly that they'd send a message like this so soon. 'I thought they'd be more interested in Goertz,' he said.

'We haven't told them about him. The colonel has decided not to. To let them read about it in the papers if and when the news of his arrest is released publicly.'

'Why?' Duggan asked, surprised.

McClure shrugged. 'I presume he thinks they need to be reminded every now and then that we're an independent country.'

Duggan took a deep breath. 'There's one other thing about the Glenn case,' he said. 'Gerda Meier. She doesn't want to be involved anymore. Finds it upsetting, listening to the German internees talking about how well the war is going for them.'

McClure stared at him, as if waiting for him to explain more. Duggan waited, knowing this mannerism of his by now, confident that he knew nothing of what lay behind the request.

'I can understand that,' McClure nodded at last. 'Give her our thanks. We'll see if we can find someone else to keep an eye on them.'

'Is it worth it?' Duggan had no desire to deal with someone taking her place.

'Of course,' McClure gave him a look of surprise. 'Look at what it produced. A letter from Churchill to Roosevelt. Who'd have predicted that?'

Author's Note

This is a work of fiction set against a background of real events although some liberties have been taken with the timeline of those events, like the sequence of German bombings of Ireland during the first three days of 1941. All the documents and newspaper reports quoted are genuine but the main characters are all fictional and their knowledge of these are not necessarily representative of what anyone in Ireland knew at the time.

Once again, I'm indebted to a number of people for their advice about military matters and comments on the first draft, notably Maurice Byrne. I have also relied on the series of documents about Irish foreign policy during the Second World War published by the Royal Irish Academy to get a flavour of the political and diplomatic issues of the time.

Special thanks to my editor Dan Bolger for his support and insightful comments and to all at Liberties Press.